THE THIN PLACES

A Chain O' Lakes Story

Brad Raby

Ochard hill books

Contents

Chapter 1

CHAPTER ONE: THE VALLEY THAT WASN'T

Len Greenland was halfway up the long hill on Old State Road—the one that made his Jeep Gladiator work harder than it should for sixty-five thousand goddamn dollars—when he saw Joe Macklin's blue Chevy crest the hill coming the other direction.

Len wasn't really seeing it, though. Just registering it the way you register things when you're driving a familiar road listening to Waylon Jennings and thinking about whether heated steering wheels were worth the extra three grand.

The blue Chevy was there.

Normal.

Except—

Len blinked.

The car wavered. Like heat shimmer on summer asphalt, except it was February and there was no heat and the shimmer was wrong—was the whole car, not just air above it.

And then the Chevy wasn't moving anymore.

Just stopped. Halfway down the hill. Tilted. The front right wheel bent inward at an angle that made Len's mechanic-brain wince. The car half off the road, half in the ditch, looking like it had hit something solid at forty miles per hour.

One moment: fine.

Next moment: wrecked.

No transition. No skid marks. No time between.

Just the shimmer, and then stopped.

"What the fuck," Len said to his steering wheel.

Waylon kept singing about Luckenbach, Texas, like nothing weird had happened.

Len pulled over. Opposite side of the road. Put the Gladiator in park. Sat there a second.

The blue Chevy was definitely wrecked. Definitely stopped. Definitely real.

But it hadn't been wrecked ten seconds ago.

He got out. Cold hit him—late February cold, the kind that wasn't quite winter but wasn't quite spring either, just Michigan being indecisive about seasons.

Len crossed the road. Not hurried. Just approaching the way you approach something that might be normal or might be weird and you're not sure which.

Joe Macklin was standing next to his car. Smoking. Looking at the wheel. Looking east down the valley. Looking at the wheel again.

"Joe," Len said.

Joe jumped. Actually jumped. Like he hadn't heard the Gladiator pull over. Like he'd been somewhere else entirely.

"Len. Jesus. You scared me, and what."

"What happened here?" Len asked.

Joe looked at him. Looked at the car. Looked back down the valley—at the curve that swept right toward the church, at the playfield that should be visible on the left, at 6 Mile Road cutting across below. Took a drag on his cigarette that was more desperation than habit.

"Hit something," Joe said.

"Hit what?"

"Don't know."

"Road looks fine."

"I know."

"Wheel looks fucked, and what."

"I know that too."

They stood there. Two guys looking at a broken wheel that shouldn't be broken on a road that didn't have anything to hit.

Len had known Joe since high school. Twenty years of knowing someone means you can tell when they're bullshitting and when they're spooked.

Joe was spooked.

"You see something?" Len asked.

Joe took another drag. Didn't answer right away. Just stared down at the valley. At where the church should be. At where the playfield should be. At where the curve and 6 Mile Road and the house with all those garages should be.

"Maybe," he said finally.

"Maybe what?"

"Maybe I saw something. Maybe I didn't. Maybe I'm losing my shit."

Len waited. That was the trick with Joe—you waited, you didn't push, you just stood there and eventually Joe would talk because silence made him more uncomfortable than honesty.

Joe lit another cigarette off the first one. Chain-smoking. That was bad. That meant something.

"The valley was wrong," Joe said. Quiet. Not looking at Len. Looking down the hill where everything should be exactly as it had been his whole life.

"Wrong how, and what?"

"No church. No playfield. No road. Just..." Joe stopped. Started again. "Just grass. Tall grass. Like prairie. Rolling. Going on forever. And the curve wasn't there. The bottom of the hill just... kept going. Into all that grass. And things were moving. Big things."

"What kind of things?"

"Elephants. Except not elephants. Wrong shape. Hairy. Massive. Big fucking tusks that curved weird. Four of them. Just grazing. Like they belonged there. Like the church and the playfield and 6 Mile Road were the weird part. Not them."

Len looked down the valley. Church. Playfield. Curve. 6 Mile Road. The Henderson place with all those garages where Bill worked on vintage cars. Everything exactly where it should be. Exactly where it had been yesterday. Last week. His whole life.

"You hit an elephant, and what?" Len asked.

"I didn't *hit* anything. I swerved. Because they were *there*. Standing right where the church should be. Right in the middle of where the playfield should be. And I panicked and jerked the wheel and then—" Joe gestured with the cigarette, "—then it wasn't grass anymore. Was normal. Church. Playfield. Road. Everything back. But my wheel was already fucked because I'd swerved on... on whatever it was before it went back."

"You drunk?"

"No."

"High?"

"Marlboro Reds don't do that."

"Could've been laced."

"Fresh pack from the gas station."

Len looked at Joe. Looked at the wheel. Looked down at the valley—at the church steeple visible above the trees, at the edge of the playfield, at everything solid and real and exactly as it should be.

Looked at the wheel again.

"I saw something too," Len said.

Joe's head snapped up. "What?"

"Your car. Coming over the hill. It was fine. Then it wasn't. No transition. Just—" Len made a gesture that was supposed to indicate the shimmer but just looked like he was waving at air, "—it changed. One second you're driving. Next second you're stopped and broken. No in-between, and what."

They looked at each other.

"You saw that?" Joe asked.

"Saw something."

"What'd you see exactly?"

"Your car fine. Then your car fucked. Like someone edited a video wrong and skipped frames, and what."

Joe took a long drag. Let the smoke out slow.

"So I'm not crazy," he said.

"Didn't say that. Said I saw something weird too. Could both be crazy, and what."

"Two people don't hallucinate the same thing at the same time."

"Don't know about that. Read something once about mass hysteria, and what."

"This wasn't hysteria. This was—" Joe stopped. Stared down the valley. At the church. At the playfield. At everything that should be there and was there now but hadn't been there thirty seconds ago.

"This was real. I saw it. You saw something. My wheel's broken to prove it."

"Wheel's broken for sure, and what."

They stood there in the cold. Two guys with a mystery neither of them wanted. Two guys looking at a valley that was exactly as it should be except for thirty seconds when it wasn't.

"You tell anyone about this?" Len asked.

"Who the fuck would I tell? 'Hey, the church disappeared and turned into prairie with prehistoric elephants'? They'd lock me up, and what."

Len nodded. But he was already thinking about who he'd tell. Not because he wanted to spread gossip—just because weird shit was worth mentioning. Worth comparing notes. Worth checking if anyone else had seen something off.

His brother-in-law Dave. Dave worked DNR. Dave would know if there'd been reports. Weird animal sightings. Strange calls.

Maybe Len would mention it. Casually. Over beers.

That wasn't gossiping.

That was just checking.

"Tow truck coming?" Len asked.

"Triple-A. Forty minutes."

"Want me to wait with you, and what?"

Joe looked at him. Grateful. Spooked. Trying to pretend he wasn't either.

"Yeah," Joe said. "Yeah, that'd be good."

They leaned against Len's Gladiator. Smoked—Joe chain-smoking, Len bumming one even though he'd quit three months ago but this seemed like a situation that justified backsliding.

The valley stayed normal. Church steeple. Edge of playfield. The curve sweeping right. 6 Mile Road cutting across. The Henderson place with its row of garages.

No shimmer.

No wrongness.

No prairie where prairie shouldn't be.

No mastodons that couldn't exist.

But Len kept glancing down the hill anyway, waiting for it to change again, waiting for the shimmer, waiting for the church to disappear and the grass to return and time to prove it was thinner than it looked.

Nothing happened.

Everything stayed normal.

Which somehow made it worse.

Because if Joe had seen something, and Len had seen Joe's car change between moments, that meant normal was temporary. Meant underneath was something else. Meant the valley could stop being valley and start being something older.

And if it happened once, it could happen again.

Right here. This hill. This view locals had seen ten thousand times. Could change. Could become something else. Something from before churches. Before playfields. Before roads.

"You really see elephants?" Len asked.

"Mastodons," Joe corrected. "They're different. Elephants have bigger ears, and what."

Len snorted. Couldn't help it.

"And what," he agreed.

They finished their cigarettes.

The tow truck arrived twenty-three minutes later. Guy took one look at the wheel, whistled, asked what Joe had hit.

"Don't know," Joe said.

"Must've been something solid, and what," Len added. "Wheel doesn't bend like that from nothing."

The tow truck guy shrugged. Loaded the Chevy. Drove off toward Petoskey with Joe in the cab.

Len stood there in the cold.

Looked down the valley one more time. Church. Playfield. Curve. 6 Mile Road. Henderson's garages. Everything exactly as it should be. Everything exactly as it had been his whole life.

Normal. Real. Solid.

Except for thirty seconds when it wasn't.

He got in his Gladiator. Drove home.

But he didn't forget.

And that night, over beers with Dave, he mentioned it. Casually. Just: "Joe had a weird thing happen on Old State Road today, and what."

Dave listened. Quiet. Patient. The way Dave always listened—taking it in, processing, not showing his hand.

When Len finished, Dave was quiet for a moment. Then he said: "Funny you mention that. Had a call last week. Hiker near Skinkle Road claimed she saw glaciers. Thought she was dehydrated, and what."

They looked at each other.

Something passed between them. Not words. Just recognition that something was off. That these things weren't isolated. That maybe Old State Road and Skinkle Road and the valley with the church weren't as solid as they looked.

"If you hear anything else," Dave said, "let me know."

Len nodded.

The whispers had started.

Chapter 2

CHAPTER TWO: THE DROWNED MAN

The call came at 7:14 AM while I was finishing my second cup of coffee and looking at the map I'd spread across the kitchen table.

"Dave, it's Williams. Antrim County Sheriff. We've got a situation on Clam Lake Road. Possible drowning. Need your eyes on it."

I grabbed my keys. "Drowning? Lake's frozen solid."

"I know. That's why I'm calling you."

I was in the truck before he finished giving me the address.

1847 Clam Lake Road. I knew the area. North arm of Lake Bellaire. Mix of old homes and newer subdivision money. I'd done site surveys out there when the retaining walls went in last year.

The driveway was long. Gravel. Tree-lined. I could see the EMT rig halfway down, lights still rotating. Williams' patrol car. A Toyota 4Runner tilted against something.

I parked at the top. Walked down.

Williams met me halfway. Young guy. Earnest. Looked rattled.

"What've we got?" I asked.

"Mel Harrison. Seventy-two. Went to get McDonald's this morning. Wife found him at seven. He's in the car. Dead. Drowned."

I stopped walking. "Drowned."

"That's what Frank says. The EMT. Classic presentation. Cyanosis, foam, the whole thing."

"In his car."

"In his car."

"On his driveway."

"On his driveway. Forty feet from a frozen lake."

I looked past Williams at the 4Runner. At the angle. At the retaining wall it was leaning against.

Something cold settled in my stomach.

"Show me," I said.

The car was soaked inside. Not damp. Soaked. Water pooled in the footwells. The seats were saturated. The steering wheel was wet.

Mel Harrison lay on a tarp nearby. Blue face. Purple lips. Soaked clothes.

Frank, the EMT, stood up when I approached. "Dave."

"Frank. Williams says drowning."

"No question. I've seen enough drownings to know. This is drowning."

I knelt beside Mel. Looked at his face. At his hands. At the way his shirt clung to him, heavy with water.

Touched the fabric. Brought my fingers to my nose.

Lake water. The particular mineral smell of Lake Bellaire. I'd know it anywhere.

I stood. Looked at the lake. Forty feet away. Down an embankment. Frozen white across the north arm.

Looked back at the car.

"Nobody moved it?" I asked Williams.

"No. Wife found it like this. Against the wall."

I walked to the 4Runner. Opened the driver's door. More water dripped out.

The McDonald's bag sat on the passenger seat. Untouched.

I looked at the dashboard. At the cup holder. At the window that was rolled down.

Down. In February.

I walked around the car. Looked at the tire tracks. No skid marks. No sign of braking. The car had just stopped. Tilted against the retaining wall like Mel had parked it there deliberately.

Except Mel was dead. And the car was full of lake water. And the lake was frozen forty feet away.

I pulled out my notebook. The waterproof one I kept in my jacket. Started measuring. Distance to lake. Position of car. Angle against wall.

Then I walked to the retaining wall itself.

Stone. Expensive stone. I remembered when it went in. $100,000 to terrace the embankment. The Harrisons had been particular about it. Wanted it to look elegant. Wanted it to last.

I ran my hand along the stone. Walked the length of it. Stopped about twenty feet from where the car sat.

Knelt. Looked at the gravel.

There. Small. Easy to miss.

A shell. Freshwater mussel shell. Weathered. Old.

I picked it up. Turned it over in my hand. Put it in my pocket.

Stood up. Looked at the lake. At the embankment. At where the land dropped off.

Then I pulled out my phone. Opened the maps app. Switched to topographic view.

Zoomed in on this exact location.

Looked at the elevation lines. At the old shoreline markers from the glacial surveys.

My stomach dropped.

This spot. Where Mel's car sat. Where the retaining wall was built.

Eleven thousand years ago, this spot had been sixty feet underwater.

Glacial Lake Chicago. When the ice dammed the southern outlet and the lake rose. Before modern Lake Michigan. Before the current shoreline.

This exact spot. Underwater.

I stood there holding my phone, looking at the drowned man, the soaked car, the lake that was forty feet away now but hadn't always been.

Thinking about what Len had told me last night over beers.

About Joe Macklin seeing mastodons where the church should be. About Joe's car going from fine to wrecked with no transition. About the valley being wrong for thirty seconds.

I'd written it in my notebook. Marked the location. Old State Road, 0.3 miles south of Skinkle Road.

I'd planned to check it today. See if there was anything to it. Probably nothing. Probably Joe had been tired, Len had seen what he wanted to see, and the wheel had hit a pothole they'd both missed.

Except now Mel Harrison had drowned on dry land.

In a car full of lake water.

In a spot that used to be underwater eleven thousand years ago.

I pulled out my notebook. Drew a quick map. Marked Mel's location. Marked Joe's location from memory.

Both along the old glacial moraine. Both on ancient shoreline. Both within five miles of each other.

Both impossible.

Both real.

"Dave?"

Williams was standing beside me. "You find something?"

I looked at him. At his young face. At the way he was trying to be professional but couldn't hide the confusion.

"Maybe," I said. "I need to make some calls. Check some records."

"What kind of records?"

I looked at the car. At Mel. At the lake.

"Geological surveys," I said. "Old maps. Historical data."

Williams frowned. "You think this is geological?"

I didn't answer. Because I didn't know yet. Didn't want to say what I was thinking. Didn't want to sound crazy.

But something was happening. Something that didn't fit. Something that made drownings happen on driveways and cars break on empty roads and valleys turn into prairie when they shouldn't.

Something that was following the land. Following the old lines. Following places that used to be something different.

"I'll write it up as undetermined," Williams said. "Pending investigation."

"Yeah," I said. "Do that."

I gave him my number. Told him to call if anything else strange came up. Anything that didn't make sense.

Then I got in my truck. Drove away.

But I didn't go home.

I went to my office. Pulled out every geological survey I had. Every topographic map. Every historical record of Lake Bellaire, Lake Charlevoix, the old glacial formations.

Spread them across my desk.

Marked Joe's location. Marked Mel's location.

Both on the old moraine. Both on ancient shoreline.

Both in places where the land used to be something different. Something older. Something from before modern Michigan existed.

I sat there looking at the maps. At the pattern starting to form.

Two incidents. Two impossible things. Both within twenty-four hours.

I pulled out my phone. Called Len.

"Dave?"

"You busy?"

"Not really. What's up?"

"That thing Joe saw yesterday. On Old State Road. I need you to tell me again. Every detail. Everything you remember."

Len was quiet for a moment. "Why?"

"Because someone just drowned in their car on their driveway. And I think it's connected."

"How?"

"I don't know yet. But I'm going to find out."

I hung up. Looked at the maps. At the two marks. At the empty space around them.

And I wondered how many more marks I'd be adding.

How many more impossible things were coming.

How long before everyone else saw what I was starting to see.

That the land under Northern Michigan wasn't as solid as we thought.

That time was thinner than it looked.

That something underneath was showing through.

Chapter 3

CHAPTER THREE: THE HIKER

I got the call at 6:47 PM on a Thursday.

Karen was pulling chicken off the grill—those thick breasts she butterflies and marinates in something with garlic and lemon that makes the whole backyard smell like summer even when it's forty degrees and technically still February. Jake was home from Michigan State for the weekend, already two beers in and telling some story about his forestry professor who'd apparently never actually been in a forest.

My phone buzzed. Dispatch.

"Pritchard."

"Dave, we've got a missing hiker. Woman named Beth Koerner, thirty-four, overdue from Jordan River valley trail. Family called it in at six-fifteen. She was supposed to check in by six."

I looked at my chicken. At Karen's face—she knew that look, the one where dinner was about to get cold.

"Cell service up there?"

"Spotty to nonexistent. She knew that. Experienced hiker. Done that trail dozens of times."

"Weather?"

"Clear. Fifties today. Supposed to drop to forty overnight but nothing dangerous."

I stood up. Jake was already watching me, that DNR-kid instinct kicking in. He'd grown up with interrupted dinners.

"I'm twenty minutes out. Who's responding?"

"Bellaire Fire, Mancelona, Central Lake. They're staging at the trailhead now."

"Tell them I'm coming."

Karen wrapped the chicken in foil without a word. Put it in the oven on warm. Twenty-three years of marriage to a conservation officer meant she knew the drill—dinner waits, the woods don't.

"Be careful," she said, handing me my go-bag from the mudroom.

"Always am."

Jake stood. "Want company?"

"You've been drinking."

"Two beers over three hours. I'm fine."

I looked at him. Nineteen years old, forestry major, already taller than me, already understood the woods better than half the officers I worked with.

"Grab your pack. You're observer only. Clear?"

"Clear."

We were in the truck four minutes later.

The Jordan River valley sits in a geological crease that shouldn't be as beautiful as it is. The river cuts through glacial deposits—sand, gravel, ancient lake bottom—creating a microclimate that stays cooler in summer, warmer in winter, and supports brook trout that make fly fishermen lie about where they caught them.

The trails are well-marked. The DNR maintains them. I'd hiked them myself probably fifty times over eighteen years. You don't get lost there unless you're trying to get lost or you're drunk or you're a flatlander from Ohio who thinks "trail" means "general direction."

Beth Koerner was none of those things.

I knew her—not well, but enough. She worked at the hospital in Charlevoix, ran the trails every weekend, volunteered with search and rescue. The kind of woman who carried three emergency blankets, a first aid kit, and enough food for two days even on a four-hour hike.

She didn't get lost.

The staging area was chaos in the organized way that search and rescue always is—organized chaos. Three fire departments, a sheriff's deputy, two DNR officers I didn't recognize, and about a dozen volunteers in bright orange vests milling around trucks with topographic maps spread across hoods.

Chief Hendricks from Bellaire Fire saw me coming and waved me over.

"Pritchard. Glad you're here."

"What do we know?"

"Not much. Beth Koerner, thirty-four, lives in Charlevoix, hikes solo most weekends. Told her husband she was doing the upper loop—about eight miles, well-marked, moderate terrain. Expected back by six. Didn't show. Didn't call."

"Phone?"

"Goes straight to voicemail. Could be dead battery, could be no signal. Upper valley's a dead zone."

I looked at the map. The upper loop trail followed the ridgeline above the river valley, offering views that made tourists take a hundred pictures and locals just nod appreciatively. Easy terrain. Clear trail. You'd have to work hard to get in trouble.

"Weather's been good," I said. "No reason she'd be hypothermic."

"That's what we're thinking. Probably twisted ankle, sat down to wait it out, fell asleep. We'll find her."

Jake was studying the map, his finger tracing the trail route.

"When was the last time someone maintained this section?" he asked.

Hendricks looked at him. "Who's this?"

"My son. Forestry major. Observer only."

"Trail's maintained," Hendricks said, a little defensive. "We run it twice a year."

"When's the last time?" Jake pressed.

I was about to tell him to back off when I realized he was right to ask. I pulled out my phone, checked the DNR maintenance log.

"Last recorded maintenance was October. Four months ago."

"So winter damage, possible downed trees, trail markers could be obscured," Jake said. "If she's off-trail even fifty yards in that terrain, she could be hard to spot."

Hendricks grunted. "Smart kid."

"Gets it from his mother."

We organized into three teams—one following the main trail, two flanking on either side. I took Jake with Team Two, the north flank, because if she'd wandered off-trail she'd have gone uphill toward the ridge rather than down into the swampy bottom.

We started at 7:30 PM with about ninety minutes of daylight left.

The woods were quiet in that late-winter way—too early for birds, too late for the crunch of frozen ground. Just the sound of boots on dirt and the occasional crackle of radio traffic.

"You thinking what I'm thinking?" Jake asked after we'd been walking twenty minutes.

"Depends what you're thinking."

"Joe's mastodons. Mel's drowning. Now a missing hiker in good weather on a known trail."

I didn't answer right away. Didn't want to say it out loud. Didn't want Jake thinking his dad had gone from conservation officer to conspiracy theorist.

But he was right.

Three incidents. Three impossible things. All within a fifteen-mile radius. All in the past two weeks.

"Let's find her first," I said. "Then we'll worry about why."

We didn't find her that night.

Searched until 10 PM when Hendricks called it—too dark, too dangerous, too easy for searchers to get hurt. We'd resume at dawn.

I drove home in silence. Jake fell asleep in the passenger seat. Karen was still awake when we got there, the chicken reheated and waiting.

I couldn't eat.

I went into my office—the spare bedroom that had become half filing cabinet, half gun safe—and pulled out the county map. The one I'd been marking.

Three red X's now.

Joe's location on Old State Road.

Mel's driveway on Lake Bellaire's north arm.

And now the Jordan River valley trailhead.

I traced the line. The old glacial moraine. The ancient shoreline. The geological scar that ran through Antrim County like a memory the land couldn't forget.

All three incidents sat on that line.

I closed the map.

Tomorrow we'd find Beth Koerner.

Tomorrow I'd ask her what she'd seen.

Because I was starting to suspect she hadn't gotten lost.

She'd gotten found.

By something that shouldn't be there.

We resumed the search at 6 AM. Cold, clear, frost on the grass. The kind of morning that makes northern Michigan look like a postcard and feel like a meat locker.

Beth Koerner walked out of the woods at 11:30 AM.

Not where we were searching. Not on any trail. She came stumbling out of the treeline about a quarter-mile south of the staging area, soaking wet, shivering so hard she could barely stand, and talking about ice.

The EMTs had her wrapped in blankets and loaded in the ambulance before I got there. I ran the quarter-mile from where Team Two was searching, got there just as they were closing the rear doors.

"Hold up," I said, flashing my badge. "I need two minutes."

The lead EMT—a guy named Patterson I'd known for years—hesitated.

"She's hypothermic, Dave. We need to get her to Charlevoix."

"Two minutes. Please."

He looked at Beth, then back at me, then sighed. "Two minutes. Clock's running."

I climbed in the back. Beth was wrapped in silver thermal blankets, oxygen mask over her face, eyes wide and unfocused. But when she saw me she grabbed my arm.

The grip was stronger than it should've been.

"You have to mark it," she said. Her voice was rough, like she'd been screaming. "Mark the place. So no one else goes there."

"Goes where, Beth?"

"The ice. The wall. It's still there. It's always been there. We just can't see it."

"What wall?"

"A mile high. Higher. I couldn't see the top. I touched it. It was real. It burned my hands."

I looked at her hands. They were bandaged. Patterson saw me looking.

"Frostbite," he said quietly. "Second degree. On a fifty-degree day."

Beth's eyes locked on mine. "There were no trees. The forest was gone. Just scrub. Little twisted things. And something was hunting me."

"What was hunting you?"

"Lion. But not a lion. Bigger. Wrong shape. Long legs. It followed me for hours. I hid. I ran. I hid again. Then the trees came back and I ran until I found the road."

"Beth, where exactly were you when you saw the ice?"

"Upper trail. The overlook. You know the one. Where you can see the whole valley."

I knew it. I'd stood there a hundred times.

"There's no ice there, Beth."

"There is. You just have to be there when it shows."

Patterson touched my shoulder. "Time's up, Dave."

I nodded, started to pull away, but Beth's grip tightened.

"Mark it," she whispered. "Please. Before someone else touches it."

"I will."

They closed the doors. The ambulance pulled away, lights flashing but no siren—she was stable enough not to need the noise.

I stood there in the gravel parking lot, watching it disappear down the county road.

Jake walked up beside me. He'd heard everything. The EMTs had been loud enough.

"Frostbite," he said. "In fifty-degree weather."

"Yeah."

"Ice where there's no ice."

"Yeah."

"And something hunting her."

I didn't answer that one. Didn't want to say what I was thinking.

We drove to the overlook.

The upper trail wasn't hard to find—it was exactly where Beth said it would be. The overlook sat on a ridge about three hundred feet above the river valley, offering a view that stretched for miles. On a clear day you could see Lake Charlevoix.

Today you could see everything. And nothing was wrong.

Trees. Trails. River below. Sky above. Fifty degrees, slight breeze, birds starting to return from wherever they went in winter.

Normal.

Perfectly, completely normal.

Jake walked the overlook perimeter, taking pictures with his phone, checking the ground for tracks, doing the forensic work they taught him in school.

I just stood there, looking at the valley.

Trying to see what Beth had seen.

Ice. A mile high. No trees. Something hunting.

"Dad."

Jake's voice was quiet. The kind of quiet that meant he'd found something.

I walked over. He was kneeling by a patch of bare ground near the trail edge, pointing at marks in the dirt.

"What am I looking at?"

"Tracks."

"What kind?"

"I don't know."

And that was the problem. Jake could identify every animal track in northern Michigan. He'd been doing it since he was eight years old. Deer, bear, coyote, bobcat, turkey, raccoon—he knew them all.

These tracks were none of those things.

Four toes. Claws. Big—bigger than any cat I'd ever seen. The stride length suggested something that moved fast, covered ground efficiently.

And the tracks were fresh. Maybe a day old. Maybe less.

"Lion," I said. "Beth said lion."

"We don't have lions in Michigan."

"I know."

"We haven't had lions in Michigan for ten thousand years."

I looked at him. "How do you know that?"

"Pleistocene megafauna. We studied it. After the glaciers retreated, the big predators went extinct. American lions, saber-toothed cats, short-faced bears. All gone by eleven thousand years ago."

I looked back at the tracks.

Then at the valley.

Then at the county map in my head, with its three red X's forming a line along the old glacial moraine.

"Get pictures," I said. "Every angle. Measurements. I want documentation."

"You think someone's going to believe this?"

"No. But I'm going to document it anyway."

We spent an hour on that overlook. Pictures, measurements, notes. Jake even made a plaster cast of one track using a kit he had in his pack—the kid came prepared.

When we were done, I stood at the trail edge one more time, looking down at the valley.

Trying to imagine it different.

No trees. Just scrub. Ice wall a mile high. Something hunting.

Eleven thousand years ago, this valley had been covered by glacial ice. The whole region had been locked under sheets hundreds of feet thick. When it melted, it left the landscape we knew—the rivers, the lakes, the forests.

But what if it hadn't completely left?

What if, sometimes, the ice remembered?

I pulled out my phone. No signal. Of course not. We were in the dead zone.

I'd call Beth from the hospital later. Ask her more questions. Get details.

But I already knew what I'd find.

Another impossible thing.

Another red X on my map.

Another piece of a pattern I didn't want to see but couldn't ignore.

The land was showing us something.

Something it remembered.

Something we'd forgotten.

And I had a feeling we were going to keep forgetting until we listened.

That night, I added Beth's location to the map.

Four red X's now.

All on the line.

The old moraine. The glacial scar. The place where ancient ice had carved the earth and left its mark.

Karen found me in my office at midnight, staring at the map.

"Come to bed," she said.

"In a minute."

"Dave."

I looked at her. Twenty-three years. She knew when to push and when to wait.

"What's happening?" she asked quietly.

"I don't know."

"But you have an idea."

I did. I had more than an idea. I had three incidents in two weeks, all impossible, all following a pattern that aligned with geological features from eleven thousand years ago.

I had a woman with frostbite from touching ice that wasn't there.

I had tracks from an animal that had been extinct since the Pleistocene.

I had a drowned man and mastodons and a feeling in my gut that this was just the beginning.

"The land remembers," I said. "I think the land remembers things we forgot."

Karen looked at the map. At the red X's. At the line connecting them.

"What does it remember?"

"Ice. And everything that lived when the ice was here."

She was quiet for a long time.

Then she said, "Are you going to tell anyone?"

"Who would believe me?"

"Fair point."

She kissed the top of my head. "Come to bed when you can. And Dave?"

"Yeah?"

"Be careful. Whatever's happening... I don't think it's done."

She was right.

It wasn't done.

It was just getting started.

Chapter 4

CHAPTER FOUR: DAVE'S RESEARCH

I didn't sleep much that night.

Karen fell asleep around eleven, her breathing settling into that steady rhythm that meant she was out. I lay there staring at the ceiling, thinking about frostbite in fifty-degree weather and tracks from an animal that had been extinct for eleven thousand years.

At midnight I gave up, went to my office, and started digging.

The DNR keeps records. Lots of records. Incident reports, geological surveys, historical land assessments, old maps from before Michigan was even a state. Most of it's digitized now, sitting in databases that nobody looks at unless they're writing an environmental impact statement or trying to figure out why a stream suddenly changed course.

I'd been a conservation officer for eighteen years. I knew where the files were buried.

I started with the obvious question: What was here eleven thousand years ago?

The answer turned out to be: not what's here now.

The first thing I found was a geological survey from 1987, back when the DNR actually had budget for this kind of work. A geologist named Dr. Raymond Ostrander had spent three summers mapping the glacial deposits across Antrim County, documenting the moraines, the outwash plains, the kettles and drumlins that made up our landscape.

His report was titled "Quaternary Geology of the Chain O' Lakes Region: Evidence of Late Wisconsin Glaciation and Post-Glacial Lake Stages."

I printed it. All eighty-three pages.

Then I made coffee and started reading.

THE GEOLOGY LESSON I NEVER WANTED

Northern Michigan, according to Dr. Ostrander, is a mess.

Not a natural mess. A glacial mess. The kind of mess you get when a mile-thick sheet of ice sits on top of your landscape for thousands of years, then melts, then comes back, then melts again, over and over, carving and scraping and depositing and rearranging until the original bedrock is buried under hundreds of feet of debris.

The Chain O' Lakes—Torch, Bellaire, Clam, Elk, Skegemog, Intermediate—weren't always there. Twelve thousand years ago, this whole region was covered by the Laurentide Ice Sheet, part of the massive glacier that had buried everything from the Arctic to what's now Ohio.

When the ice finally started retreating around 11,000 years ago, it didn't retreat cleanly. It melted in stages, leaving behind ridges of debris called moraines—basically the garbage dumps of glaciers, piles of rock and sand and clay that marked where the ice front had paused.

Antrim County sits on one of those moraines.

Dr. Ostrander called it the "Lake Border Morainic System," a complex network of ridges that runs from the southern end of Lake Michigan all the way up through our county and beyond. The ridges mark the edge of the glacier. The boundary between ice and no-ice. Between what was buried and what wasn't.

I looked at his map.

The moraine ran right through the locations I'd marked.

Joe's mastodons: on the moraine.

Mel's driveway: on the moraine.

Beth's overlook: on the moraine.

Every single incident sat on that ancient boundary line.

I closed the report and opened another coffee.

THE LAKE STAGES

The next thing I learned: the lakes weren't always lakes.

When the glacier melted, it created what geologists call "proglacial lakes"—lakes that form at the edge of retreating ice. These weren't little ponds. These were massive bodies of water, sometimes hundreds of feet deeper than what we have now, fed by glacial meltwater and dammed by ice to the north.

The names sounded like something out of mythology: Lake Algonquin, Lake Nipissing, Lake Chippewa, Lake Stanley.

Each stage represented a different water level, a different configuration of ice and outlet and drainage. The lakes rose and fell over thousands of years as the glacier retreated, as outlets opened and closed, as the land itself rebounded from the weight of the ice.

Lake Algonquin (11,000-10,500 years ago): Water level at 605 feet above modern sea level. That's about **60 feet higher**than Lake Michigan today. Covered most of what's now northern Michigan in one massive body of water.

Chippewa Low Phase (10,300-6,000 years ago): North Bay outlet opened, draining the lakes down to **80 meters lower**than today. The lowest water level in post-glacial history. Forests grew where Lake Michigan now sits.

Lake Nipissing (6,000-4,500 years ago): Isostatic rebound (the land rising after the ice weight was gone) gradually raised water levels again. Drowned the forests. Created the lake configuration we recognize today.

I sat back, staring at the timeline.

Mel Harrison's driveway sat on what had been the shoreline of Lake Algonquin. When the fold hit him, he was suddenly sixty feet underwater—not in modern Lake Bellaire, but in the ancient glacial lake that had covered this area 11,000 years ago.

Beth Koerner touched ice that wasn't there anymore. Ice from when the glacier still covered the Jordan River valley.

Joe Macklin saw mastodons grazing in grassland that existed before the forests, before the modern climate, before the Holocene.

The land was remembering.

Showing us what it used to be.

And the line—the moraine, the ancient ice boundary—that's where it was thinnest. Where past and present were closest together.

THE EXTINCTION EVENT

That's when I found the paper about the Younger Dryas.

It was tucked into Dr. Ostrander's references, a study from 2007 titled "Evidence for an Extraterrestrial Impact 12,900 Years Ago That Contributed to the Megafaunal Extinctions and Younger Dryas Cooling."

I almost skipped it. Then I saw the word "Michigan" and kept reading.

The Younger Dryas was a climate event—a sudden return to ice age conditions right when things were supposed to be warming up. It lasted from about 12,900 to 11,700 years ago. About 1,200 years of rapid cooling that reversed the warming trend, brought back glacial conditions, and coincided with something catastrophic:

The extinction of North American megafauna.

Mammoths. Mastodons. Giant ground sloths. Dire wolves. Saber-toothed cats. Short-faced bears—the biggest predator North America had ever seen, fourteen feet tall when standing, fast as a horse, strong enough to take down anything.

All gone. Thirty-three genera of mammals, extinct within a geological eyeblink.

The paper proposed an extraterrestrial impact—comet fragments exploding over the Great Lakes region, triggering massive climate change, wildfires, ice sheet destabilization.

The evidence was controversial. Some scientists accepted it. Others called it pseudoscience.

But one thing wasn't controversial: something catastrophic happened 12,900 years ago. The megafauna died. The Clovis people—the Paleo-Indians who'd been hunting those animals—either died with them or adapted so drastically their culture disappeared from the archaeological record.

Michigan had been ground zero.

One of the impact sites was the Gainey Site, right here in Michigan. Magnetic microspherules. Carbon-rich black layers. Evidence of temperatures high enough to melt rock.

And the timing matched perfectly with the moraine, with Lake Algonquin, with the exact period when the ice was retreating and the land was transforming from tundra to forest.

I looked at my map again.

Four red X's. All on the moraine. All on the boundary between ice age and modern world.

All showing us the moment when everything died.

THE PALEO-INDIAN QUESTION

The last thing I researched: the people.

If the land was showing us 11,000 years ago, if Beth had been hunted by something extinct, then what about the humans who'd lived here?

The Paleo-Indians. The Clovis people. Small bands of hunter-gatherers who'd followed the megafauna across Beringia and down through North America.

Michigan had been barely habitable back then. Most of the state was still covered by glaciers. But there was a triangular wedge of ice-free land in southwest Michigan, and archaeological evidence showed the Clovis people had been there, hunting mammoth and mastodon along the glacial margins.

Recent discovery: the Belson Site in southwest Michigan. A confirmed Clovis campsite, 13,000 years old, occupied by maybe six or seven people living on a river at the end of the Pleistocene.

The Clovis culture lasted only about 300 years—from 13,050 to 12,750 years ago.

Then it vanished.

Either the people died with the megafauna, or they adapted so drastically we can't recognize their descendants in the archaeological record. Population crash. Cultural reorganization. Survival under catastrophic conditions.

If the thin places were showing us that moment—the Younger Dryas, the extinctions, the climate catastrophe—then we weren't just seeing animals.

We were seeing people.

The ones who'd survived when everything else died.

The ones who'd watched their world end and kept going anyway.

I printed everything. The geological maps. The lake stage diagrams. The extinction timeline. The Paleo-Indian site reports.

Then I pulled out a clean topographic map of Antrim County and started overlaying data.

Red line: The Lake Border Moraine, running northeast to southwest through the county.

Blue lines: Ancient Lake Algonquin shorelines, marking the 605-foot elevation contour.

Green areas: Glacial outwash plains and drumlin fields.

Black dots: My four incidents.

They aligned perfectly.

Every incident sat on the intersection of moraine and ancient shoreline. Places where the ice had been, where the lake had been, where the land remembered being something else.

I sat there looking at that map for a long time.

Then I did what I should've done three days ago.

I called Dr. Ostrander.

THE CALL

He answered on the third ring. Sounded like I'd woken him up.

"Dr. Ostrander? This is Dave Pritchard, DNR officer in Antrim County. I'm sorry to call so late—"

"It's seven in the morning."

I looked at the clock. 7:14 AM. I'd been up all night.

"Right. Sorry. I've been reading your 1987 geological survey. The one on the Chain O' Lakes moraines."

Silence on the other end. Then: "That report's almost forty years old. Why are you reading it now?"

"Because I've got four unexplained incidents in the past two weeks, and they all sit on the moraine system you mapped."

"What kind of incidents?"

I hesitated. How do you explain impossible things to a scientist?

"The kind where people are seeing things that shouldn't be there. Experiencing environmental conditions that don't match current reality. Encountering extinct fauna."

Another pause. Longer this time.

"You're talking about temporal anomalies."

"I'm talking about a woman who got frostbite touching ice that wasn't there. A man who drowned in a car on dry land. Tracks from a predator that's been extinct for eleven thousand years."

"And they're all on the moraine?"

"Every single one."

Dr. Ostrander was quiet for so long I thought he'd hung up.

Then he said, "I need to see your data. Can you email me the locations and incident reports?"

"Yes."

"Do it now. I'll call you back in two hours."

He hung up.

I sent him everything.

Two hours later, my phone rang.

"Pritchard."

"Dr. Ostrander. I've reviewed your data."

"And?"

"And you're not crazy. The pattern is real. All four incidents sit on critical geological boundaries—moraine intersections with paleoshorelines. But that doesn't explain *why* they're happening."

"What's your theory?"

"I don't have one. Geology doesn't account for temporal displacement. That's physics. Or metaphysics. Or something I don't have the training to explain."

"But the locations aren't random."

"No. The locations are deliberate. Whoever—or whatever—is choosing these sites knows the landscape's history. Knows where the boundaries are. Where the land is... thinnest."

Thinnest.

That word again.

"Dr. Ostrander, if this keeps happening—if more incidents occur—can you predict where they'll be?"

"Maybe. I'd need to map all the moraine/shoreline intersections in the county. Cross-reference with areas of known glacial disturbance. It's a lot of work."

"How long?"

"A week. Maybe less if I skip sleep."

"Do it. I'll pay you whatever the DNR consultant rate is."

"You don't have budget authority for that."

"I'll find it."

He laughed, dry and tired. "You really think this is going to get worse, don't you?"

I looked at my map. Four red X's now. But the moraine ran for miles. Dozens of potential sites. Hundreds.

"Yes," I said. "I think it's just getting started.

Chapter 5

CHAPTER FIVE: THE RING CAMERA

The call came in at 2:47 PM on a Friday.

I was at my desk, eating a sandwich that Karen had packed that morning—turkey and swiss on wheat, the kind of lunch that reminds you that your wife loves you even when you've been staying up all night researching glacial moraines.

My phone buzzed. Dispatch.

"Pritchard."

"Dave, we've got a... situation. Homeowner on Cairn Highway called about wildlife on her property. Says she's got video."

"What kind of wildlife?"

"She says it's a bear. But the description doesn't match any bear I've ever heard of."

I put down my sandwich. "What's the description?"

"Quote: 'Bigger than a car. Wrong shape. Walked on its back legs. Had a face like a nightmare.' End quote."

I closed my eyes. "Address?"

"2847 Cairn Highway. Melissa Chen. She's pretty shaken up."

Cairn Highway ran along the northern edge of Lake Bellaire, following the old glacial ridge. Right on the moraine.

"I'm on my way."

The house was a typical northern Michigan lakefront property—newer construction trying to look rustic, lots of windows facing the water, a wraparound deck that probably cost more than my annual salary. Ring doorbell camera mounted by the front door. Motion-sensor lights. The kind of setup that makes people feel safe.

Melissa Chen met me at the door before I could knock. Early thirties, yoga pants, Northwestern hoodie, holding a tablet like it might explode.

"Officer Pritchard?"

"Yes ma'am. You reported unusual wildlife?"

"I reported a fucking monster in my driveway." Her voice was steady but her hands weren't. "I've got it on video. Multiple angles. Ring camera, driveway cam, the camera on my garage. All of them caught it."

"Can I see the footage?"

She handed me the tablet. "I've watched it maybe fifty times. Keeps getting worse."

The first video was from the Ring doorbell, timestamp 3:47 AM. Motion activated. The image quality was typical Ring camera—grainy, fish-eye lens, black and white night vision.

The driveway was empty.

Then it wasn't.

No transition. One frame empty, next frame: something standing in the driveway.

I hit pause.

The thing was massive. Shoulder height maybe six feet, but when it rose up on its hind legs—which it did in the next few frames—it was easily twelve, maybe fourteen feet tall. The body was thick, heavily muscled, with front legs shorter than the back. The head was enormous, broad-skulled, with a short snout.

Not a bear.

Bears don't have legs that long. Don't stand that tall. Don't have that skeletal structure.

I played the video.

The creature moved across the driveway with a loping gait—not the shuffle of a bear, but something faster, more purposeful. It paused near the garage, lifted its head, testing the air. The motion-sensor lights flicked on.

For three seconds, the thing was fully illuminated.

That's when I saw the teeth.

Even in grainy night-vision footage, they were visible—long canines, predator's teeth, designed for tearing. The face was wrong for a bear. Too broad. Too flat. Eyes set too far forward.

The creature turned toward the camera.

Looked directly at it.

Then the footage glitched—a brief distortion, like interference—and when it cleared, the driveway was empty again.

Total elapsed time: forty-one seconds.

I played it again. Watched the transition frame by frame.

Empty driveway.

Creature appears.

Creature moves.

Lights activate.

Creature looks at camera.

Glitch.

Empty driveway.

"The other cameras show the same thing," Melissa said. Her voice was tight. "Same timing. Same... thing. It was there, and then it wasn't."

"Can I see the driveway camera footage?"

She swiped to a different file.

This angle was better—mounted on the garage, pointed down the length of the driveway. Higher resolution. Color night vision.

The creature appeared at 3:47:23 AM, same as the Ring camera. This time I could see more detail.

The fur was tawny brown, short-haired. The body mass was incredible—this thing probably weighed fifteen hundred, maybe two thousand pounds. The front shoulders were heavily muscled, built for power. The hind legs were long, built for speed.

A pursuit predator.

Something that could run down prey in open terrain.

I paused the video at the moment the motion lights came on.

The creature's face filled the frame. Broad skull. Short snout. Small, rounded ears. Eyes that reflected the camera light with that distinctive green-gold eyeshine of nocturnal predators.

I'd seen that face before.

In Jake's paleontology textbooks. In museum reconstructions. In papers about Pleistocene megafauna.

Arctodus simus.

The giant short-faced bear.

Extinct for eleven thousand years.

Biggest predator North America had ever produced.

"Ms. Chen," I said carefully, "have you seen any bears in your neighborhood recently? Modern bears?"

"No. And I know what bears look like. I grew up in Colorado. That's not a bear."

"You're right. It's not."

She stared at me. "Then what is it?"

I didn't answer. Couldn't answer. What was I supposed to say? *That's an extinct Ice Age predator that wandered into your driveway from eleven thousand years ago?*

"I need to check your property," I said instead. "See if it left any traces."

"It wasn't real. It couldn't have been real."

"Let me check anyway."

The driveway was asphalt. New, well-maintained, the kind you reseal every few years to keep it looking nice.

No tracks.

No scat.

No fur, no claw marks, no physical evidence that anything weighing a ton had walked across it six hours ago.

I checked the grass along the edge. The flower beds. The gravel path leading to the back deck.

Nothing.

I walked the perimeter of the property, looking for disturbances. The house sat on about two acres, heavily wooded on three sides, open to the lake on the fourth. The tree line was maybe thirty yards from the house.

At the tree line, I found something.

Not tracks, exactly. More like depressions in the leaf litter. Four of them, spaced about six feet apart. Each one roughly circular, about ten inches across, pressed deep into the soft ground.

The spacing was wrong for a bear. Too wide. Too deep.

I crouched down, examining the nearest depression.

The leaves were compressed but not displaced. Like something had stood there, heavy enough to compact the ground, but not long enough to disturb the surface layer.

I pulled out my phone, took pictures from multiple angles, measured the spacing between depressions.

Then I called Jake.

"Dad?"

"Are you still at school?"

"Yeah, why?"

"I need you to look something up. Giant short-faced bear. *Arctodus simus*. How tall when standing upright?"

Pause. "Uh... twelve to fourteen feet. Why?"

"Stride length when walking on all fours?"

"I'd have to check. Maybe six to seven feet? Dad, what's going on?"

"Ring camera caught something in someone's driveway last night. Footage shows an animal that matches *Arctodus*morphology."

Longer pause. "That's impossible."

"I know."

"They've been extinct for—"

"Eleven thousand years. I know."

"So what are you saying? Someone dressed up as an Ice Age bear and wandered through a suburban driveway at four in the morning?"

I looked at the depressions in the leaves. At the tree line. At the house where Melissa Chen was probably still watching that footage over and over, trying to convince herself it wasn't real.

"I'm saying the pattern's continuing," I said. "And I have no idea how to stop it."

Back at the house, I copied the Ring footage to my phone. All three camera angles. Forty-one seconds of impossible.

"What do I do?" Melissa asked. "Call animal control? Call the sheriff? Post this online?"

"Don't post it online."

"Why not?"

"Because right now, this is an isolated incident. You post it, and by tomorrow you'll have a hundred people in your driveway looking for Ice Age monsters. Some of them armed."

"So I just... what? Pretend it didn't happen?"

"No. You document it. Keep the footage. If you see anything else unusual—*anything*—call me directly." I gave her my card. "And Ms. Chen? Stay inside after dark for a while."

"You think it'll come back?"

"I don't know. But if it does, don't go outside to look."

Her face went pale. "You think it's dangerous."

I looked at the tablet in her hands, at the frozen frame showing teeth designed for killing things that weighed several tons.

"Yes," I said. "If it's real, it's the most dangerous predator this continent has ever seen."

I drove to the county library, the one place in Bellaire with decent wifi and archives that went back more than twenty years.

The librarian—an older woman named Dorothy who'd helped me with research before—looked up when I walked in.

"Dave. You look terrible."

"Thanks, Dorothy. I need access to the historical map collection. Specifically, topographic surveys from the 1950s and '60s."

"What are you looking for?"

"Property elevations along Cairn Highway."

She disappeared into the back room, returned five minutes later with a rolled tube of maps. "These are from the 1963 USGS survey. Before most of the development."

I spread the map across a reading table.

Cairn Highway followed the old glacial ridge at an elevation between 620 and 640 feet above sea level.

I pulled out my notes from Dr. Ostrander's report.

Lake Algonquin: 605 feet elevation.

Melissa Chen's house sat at approximately 625 feet.

Twenty feet above the ancient lake level.

High enough to be dry land when Lake Algonquin existed.

High enough to be habitat for animals that lived along the glacial lake shore.

Like *Arctodus simus*, hunting the megafauna that grazed the tundra grasslands between the ice and the water.

I marked the location on my map. Fifth red X.

Then I called Dr. Ostrander.

"Pritchard."

"I've got another one. Ring camera footage. Giant short-faced bear in a residential driveway. Timestamp 3:47 AM this morning."

"Location?"

"2847 Cairn Highway. Elevation 625 feet."

I heard him typing. "That's... yes. Another moraine/paleoshoreline intersection. Right on the Lake Algonquin beach ridge."

"How many more of these sites are there in Antrim County?"

More typing. Longer pause.

"At least forty. Maybe more. I'm still mapping them."

Forty sites.

We'd had five incidents in two weeks.

If the pattern continued, if the thin places kept opening, we were looking at months of this. Maybe years.

"Dr. Ostrander, how fast can you finish that map?"

"I'm working on it. But Dave, even if I map every potential site, what are you going to do? You can't guard forty locations."

He was right.

I was one DNR officer in a county of 23,000 people spread across 600 square miles. Even if I called in every available resource—county sheriff, state police, DNR backup from neighboring counties—we couldn't cover forty sites.

And that was assuming the thin places stayed predictable. Assuming they didn't spread. Assuming we could keep people away from the boundaries where past and present were bleeding together.

"Just finish the map," I said. "I'll figure out the rest."

That night I showed Karen the Ring camera footage.

We sat on the couch, her laptop balanced between us, and I played all three angles.

She watched in silence.

When it was over, she closed the laptop.

"That's not a bear," she said quietly.

"No."

"It's not anything that should exist."

"No."

"But it does exist. Or did exist. Or... I don't know what tense to use."

I didn't either.

"How many more?" she asked.

"Dr. Ostrander thinks there are forty potential sites. Maybe more."

"Forty places where this could happen."

"Yes."

She was quiet for a long time. Then she said, "The kids need to know."

"I know."

"Jake especially. He's coming home next weekend. If something's happening in the woods—"

"I'll tell him. Both of them."

"And me? What do I do?"

I thought about the nature trail she walked every morning. The old railroad bridge. The path that cut through the woods where the moraine ran.

"Stay on main roads," I said. "Don't go into the woods alone. And if you see anything unusual—anything at all—run."

She looked at me. Twenty-three years of marriage. She knew when I was scared.

"Dave, what's really happening?"

"The land is remembering," I said. "And I don't think it's going to forget again."

Chapter 6

CHAPTER SIX: HOME LIFE

Jake came home Friday night, his truck rattling into the driveway around eight PM, bass thumping from speakers he'd installed himself and somehow made worse than the factory ones.

I was in the garage, pretending to organize fishing gear I'd already organized twice this week. Really I was avoiding going inside, avoiding the conversation I knew we needed to have.

The truck door slammed. Jake's boots crunched on gravel.

"Dad?"

I turned. He stood in the garage doorway, backlit by the porch light, looking more like me every year—same build, same way of standing with hands in pockets when something was on his mind.

"Jake. How was the drive?"

"Fine. Mom's been texting me all week. Says you're working a weird case."

"Your mother worries."

"Yeah, well, she's not wrong this time." He stepped into the garage, glanced at the tackle box I'd been staring at for twenty minutes. "Those lures aren't going to organize themselves any better than they already are."

Smart kid.

"We need to talk," I said.

"I figured."

Karen had dinner waiting. Emma video-called in from her friend's house—apparently the sleepover she'd been planning for two weeks was happening whether her dad wanted to have a family meeting or not.

"I can come home," she said from Karen's laptop screen. She was sixteen, all braces and basketball team hoodie and teenager certainty that she was handling everything just fine. "If this is serious."

"It's serious," Karen said. "But it can wait until tomorrow morning. Just... don't go anywhere alone tonight, okay?"

Emma's face shifted. That look teenagers get when they realize their parents aren't being randomly paranoid.

"Okay. I'll be home by nine tomorrow."

"Good. Love you."

"Love you too."

The screen went dark.

Jake sat down at the kitchen table, grabbed a piece of cornbread from the basket Karen had set out. "So. Weird case."

"Very weird," I said.

Karen poured coffee. Set mugs in front of all three of us. Sat down.

"Your father's been investigating incidents," she said. "Things that don't make sense."

"How 'don't make sense' are we talking?"

I pulled out my laptop, opened the file I'd been compiling. "Five incidents in the past two weeks. All within fifteen miles of each other. All following the same geological pattern."

I showed him the map. The red X's. The moraine line.

He studied it, frowning. "Those are all on the Lake Border Moraine."

"Yes."

"And the ancient Lake Algonquin shoreline."

"Yes."

"So what's happening at these sites?"

I opened the first video file. Joe Macklin's dashcam footage—grainy, distant, but clear enough to show the valley wrong, the mastodons grazing where a church parking lot should be.

Jake watched without speaking.

I opened the second file. The Ring camera footage. Three angles. Forty-one seconds of *Arctodus simus* walking through a suburban driveway.

Jake's coffee cup stopped halfway to his mouth.

"Is that—"

"Giant short-faced bear. Yes."

"That's extinct."

"I know."

"For eleven thousand years."

"I know."

He set the cup down carefully. "Dad. What the fuck."

"Language," Karen said automatically.

"Mom, there's a Pleistocene apex predator on a Ring camera. I think we're past worrying about language."

Fair point.

I walked him through it. All five incidents. Beth Koerner's frostbite. Mel Harrison's drowning. The tracks I'd found at the Jordan River overlook. The pattern Dr. Ostrander had identified.

When I finished, Jake sat back, rubbing his face.

"You're telling me the land is... what? Remembering? Showing us the past?"

"I'm telling you something is happening at specific geological sites. Places where the moraine intersects with ancient shorelines. Places where the boundary between then and now is thin."

"Thin places," Karen said quietly.

We both looked at her.

"Sarah Ashkwe told me about them," she said. "At the library last year. We were talking about Odawa history, and she mentioned thin places. Locations where the veil between worlds is thin. Where spirits can cross. Where time doesn't work right."

"You never mentioned this," I said.

"You never asked about Native history." She wasn't accusatory. Just stating fact. "Sarah said her grandmother knew where the thin places were. They marked them. Burial mounds, stone cairns, sacred sites. Warned people to stay away."

"Did she say where they were?"

"She said most of the markers were destroyed. When settlers came, when we started building. The mounds were cleared for farmland. The cairns were removed. The warnings were forgotten."

I thought about the moraine. About centuries of development, of construction, of humans building houses and roads and towns right on top of the places the Odawa had marked as dangerous.

"I need to talk to Sarah," I said.

"She's at the cultural center most Saturdays. I'll call her."

Jake was staring at the Ring camera footage, paused on the frame where the bear's face filled the screen.

"If this is real," he said slowly, "if the past is bleeding through, then we're not just seeing extinct animals."

"No," I agreed.

"We're seeing the conditions those animals lived in. The climate. The geography. The—"

"The Younger Dryas," I finished. "The extinction event. The moment when everything died."

"And if the thin places keep opening—"

"We don't know what comes through."

Karen's hand found mine under the table. Her grip was tight.

"How many sites?" she asked.

"Dr. Ostrander thinks at least forty in Antrim County alone."

"Can you stop them?"

"I don't know. I don't even know what's causing them."

"Can you predict where they'll happen?"

"Maybe. If Dr. Ostrander finishes his map. If the pattern holds."

"And if it doesn't hold?"

I didn't have an answer for that.

Jake closed the laptop. "I'm coming with you. On patrol. On investigations. Whatever you're doing, I'm helping."

"You're in school."

"I can take a semester off."

"No."

"Dad—"

"No. You finish your degree. You become the scientist who figures this out properly. I'm just a DNR officer stumbling through geological reports I barely understand. You're the one with the training."

"You're doing fine."

"I'm documenting. You're going to explain. Different jobs."

He didn't like it, but he didn't argue. Just nodded.

"What about Emma?" Karen asked.

"She needs to know enough to stay safe. Not enough to get curious."

"She's sixteen. Curious is her default state."

True.

"I'll talk to her tomorrow. Show her the map. Tell her to avoid these areas."

"You think she'll listen?"

I thought about Emma. Basketball star. Straight A's. Also the kid who'd climbed onto the roof at age twelve because she wanted to see if she could jump to the oak tree.

"No," I said. "But I'm telling her anyway."

Later, after Jake had gone to bed and Karen was doing dishes, I stood on the back deck looking at the woods.

It was quiet. Normal quiet. Spring peepers starting up in the wetland beyond the property line. Distant traffic on M-88. The ordinary sounds of northern Michigan in late February, edging toward March.

But I couldn't stop seeing that bear.

The way it had looked at the camera. Like it knew. Like it was aware of the wrongness, the displacement, the fact that it was standing in a place and time that shouldn't exist.

Had it been afraid?

Or had we?

Karen came out, handed me a beer.

"You okay?"

"No."

"Yeah. Me neither."

We stood there in the dark, not talking, just being together in the space where our normal life used to be.

"I walked the nature trail this morning," she said finally. "Before you told me not to."

My stomach dropped. "Karen—"

"I'm fine. Nothing happened. But Dave, there's a spot on the trail. About halfway across the railroad bridge. Where the air feels... wrong."

"Wrong how?"

"Colder. Thicker. Like stepping into a different season." She paused. "I almost kept walking. Almost crossed that spot to see what was on the other side."

"But you didn't."

"No. Because something told me not to. Some instinct. Like the air itself was warning me."

I thought about Beth Koerner, touching ice that burned her hands. About the moment when curiosity overrode caution and you reached out to touch something impossible.

"Don't go back there," I said.

"I won't."

"Promise me."

"Dave, I'm not stupid."

"Promise me anyway."

She looked at me. Then nodded. "I promise. No more nature trail. No more morning walks. I'll stick to the neighborhood streets where normal things happen."

"Thank you."

"But you need to promise me something too."

"What?"

"That you'll be careful. That you won't do what you always do."

"What do I always do?"

"Put yourself between danger and everyone else." Her voice was steady but her eyes weren't. "I know it's your job. I know it's who you are. But Dave, if the past is coming back, if things from eleven thousand years ago are walking around Antrim County, you can't stop them with a badge and a stern voice."

She was right.

A DNR officer's authority meant nothing to a short-faced bear. To a dire wolf. To whatever else was waiting in the thin places.

"I'll be careful," I said.

"Liar."

"I'll try to be careful."

"Better."

She went back inside. I stayed on the deck, drinking my beer, watching the woods.

Somewhere out there, forty sites were waiting. Forty places where the boundary was thin. Where the land remembered what it used to be.

And I had no idea how to protect 23,000 people from their own history.

Emma came home the next morning at 8:47 AM, exactly thirteen minutes before she'd promised.

She found me in the office, staring at maps.

"Mom said you needed to talk to me."

"Yeah. Sit down."

She sat. Crossed her arms. Teenager armor.

I showed her the map. Explained the pattern. Didn't show her the videos—she didn't need nightmares—but I told her enough.

Weird incidents. Unexplained phenomena. Dangerous areas that needed to be avoided.

She listened without interrupting. When I finished, she said, "You're telling me to stay away from half the county."

"I'm telling you to stay away from specific sites. Here's the list."

I handed her a printed sheet. Forty locations. Addresses where possible, GPS coordinates where not.

She scanned it. "This includes the trail behind the school."

"Yes."

"And the picnic area at Glacial Hills."

"Yes."

"And basically every place my friends and I hang out."

"Emma—"

"I'm not mad. I'm just... processing." She looked up. "Is this actually dangerous? Or is it like when you told me not to swim in Torch Lake during the algae bloom and it turned out to be fine?"

"It's actually dangerous."

"How dangerous?"

I thought about the bear. About Beth's frostbite. About Mel drowning on his own driveway.

"People have died," I said.

That got through.

Her arms uncrossed. "Okay. I'll stay away."

"You promise?"

"I promise. But Dad, what about everyone else? What about the people who don't know?"

"I'm working on it."

"Working on what? A warning system? An evacuation plan?"

"I don't know yet."

She stood up, took the list. "You need help. You can't do this alone."

"I'm not alone. I've got Dr. Ostrander mapping sites, your mother doing research, Jake helping when he can—"

"That's like five people. For forty sites. For an entire county."

"I know."

"So what's the actual plan?"

"Document everything. Map the pattern. Figure out what's causing it. Then figure out how to stop it."

She looked at me the way she looked at her math homework when the answer didn't make sense.

"That's not a plan. That's a hope."

"It's what I've got."

She shook her head. Started to leave. Stopped at the door.

"Dad? Be careful. Okay? We already lost Grandpa last year. I'm not losing you to some weird time glitch bullshit."

"Language."

"You raised me this way."

Fair point.

She left. I heard her truck start up a few minutes later. Headed to basketball practice, probably. Or to a friend's house. Somewhere normal, where sixteen-year-olds could pretend the world made sense.

I looked at the map again.

Forty sites.

Five incidents.

And somewhere out there, the thin places were getting thinner.

Chapter 7

CHAPTER SEVEN: THE LAND REMEMBERS

Captains Choice sat on the south end of of Intermediate Lake, a sprawling operation of boat slips, storage buildings, and a repair shop that had been there since the 1970s. The kind of place where everyone knew everyone, where fishermen gathered to lie about the size of pike they'd caught, and where you could get a pontoon motor fixed or a hull welded without having to drive to Traverse City.

I pulled in around ten AM on a Saturday. The lot was half-full—trucks with boat trailers, a few RVs, locals picking up sup plies for the season.

Scott Mercer was in the shop, elbow-deep in an outboard motor, grease up to his elbows. Mid-forties, lean from years of hauling boats and living outdoors, beard going gray at the edges. His dad owned the place, but Scott ran the day-to-day.

He looked up when I walked in.

"Dave Pritchard. Didn't think DNR made social calls."

"Not social. Need to pick your brain about something."

He wiped his hands on a rag. "Fishing violations? Because I swear those perch were legal size—"

"Not fishing. Hunting. Specifically, places you've hunted that felt... wrong."

Scott's expression changed. "Who told you about that?"

"Nobody. I'm asking."

He set down the wrench he'd been holding. "This about those weird incidents people are talking about? The guy who drowned on his driveway? The woman who got frostbite in fifty-degree weather?"

"Yes."

"Huh." He looked at me for a long moment. "Come on. Let me show you something."

We walked out back to where the boat trailers were parked, away from customers and employees. Scott pulled out his phone, opened a maps app.

"I've been hunting this county for thirty years. My dad for fifty before that. We know every ridge, every hollow, every deer run from here to Charlevoix." He zoomed in on the map. "But there are places we don't go anymore. Haven't for years."

"Why not?"

"Because they feel wrong. Can't explain it better than that. You walk into certain areas and the air changes. Gets heavy. Your gut tells you to leave. So you leave."

"How many places?"

"Six that I know personally. Maybe a dozen my dad mentioned over the years." He started marking locations on the map. "There's a spot off Mancelona Highway, up in the hills above Lake Bellaire. Good deer country. Should be perfect. But every time I've tried to hunt there, I get maybe fifty yards in and I want to turn around. Like something's watching. Like I'm trespassing."

"What else?"

"Ridge above Jordan River valley. Same thing. My buddy Rick and I tried to set up a blind there three years ago. Couldn't do it. Both of us felt it. Like the land was pushing us out."

He marked more locations. Each one made my stomach tighten.

They matched my map. The moraine intersections. The thin places.

"Scott, have you ever seen anything unusual in these areas?"

"Define unusual."

"Animals that shouldn't be there. Terrain that looks wrong. Time feeling... different."

He was quiet for a long moment. Then he said, "You're going to think I'm crazy."

"Try me."

"Four years ago. November. Rifle season. Me and my buddy Jake were hunting near the old railroad grade, maybe two miles east of Bellaire. Good spot. We'd gotten deer there before."

"What happened?"

"We pulled up in Jake's Chevy—old '89 pickup, red as hell, you could see it from space. Parked where we always parked. Started walking the tree line." He paused. "That's when we heard it."

"Heard what?"

"Footsteps. Heavy ones. Not deer. Not bear. Something big. Moving through the brush parallel to us."

"Could've been another hunter."

"That's what I thought. Then Jake stopped and pointed. Said 'What the fuck is that?'"

Scott's voice dropped. "There was something standing at the edge of the clearing. Maybe seventy yards away. Tall. Really tall. Seven feet, maybe more. Broad chest. Arms too long. Face too flat."

"What did it do?"

"Looked at us. Just looked. For maybe five seconds. Then it started walking toward us. Not running. Walking. Deliberate. Like it was curious."

"What did you do?"

"Ran like hell back to the truck. Jake was thirty pounds overweight and he beat me there by ten yards. We were in that Chevy with the doors locked before that thing got within fifty yards."

"Did it follow you?"

"No. Just stood there watching. We sat in the truck for maybe two minutes, engine running, ready to bolt. Then it turned and walked back into the trees. Gone. Like it was never there."

"Did you report it?"

"To who? The DNR?" He laughed without humor. "What was I going to say? 'Hey, we saw Bigfoot?' My dad would've put me in therapy."

"What do you think it was?"

"I don't know. But Jake and I both saw it. Clear as day. And Dave, that thing wasn't from around here. It moved wrong. Looked wrong. The whole area felt wrong."

He marked the location on the map. "We never went back. Told people the deer were scarce there. Let them think what they wanted."

I looked at the spot he'd marked.

Old railroad grade. Two miles east of Bellaire.

Right on the moraine. Right where a burial mound had been, according to the historical survey I'd found.

"Scott, this thing you saw. The locals have a name for it?"

"Some people call it the Dogman. Michigan cryptid. Supposedly upright canine, seen around the state since the 1800s. But what we saw didn't look like a dog. Looked more like... I don't know. A person who wasn't quite a person. Wrong proportions. Wrong movement."

I thought about Beth, hunted by something extinct. About tracks that didn't match modern animals.

"You ever hear sounds in these areas? Besides footsteps?"

"Yeah. That's the other thing. Sometimes you hear... I don't know how to describe it. Like voices. But not words. Just sounds. Low humming. Sometimes drumming. One time, up near Skink Road, I heard what sounded like people talking in a language I'd never heard before."

"What did you do?"

"Left. Same as always. The land tells you when you're not welcome."

Scott gave me his marked locations. Six spots he'd personally experienced. Another eight his father had warned him about.

All of them matched my map.

"Dave, what's going on?" he asked. "Really."

"I'm trying to figure that out. But Scott, if you hunt near any of these areas—don't. Not this season. Maybe not ever."

"You think it's dangerous."

"I think the land is showing us things that used to be here. And some of those things were apex predators that wouldn't recognize humans as off-limits."

"Like that thing we saw."

"Maybe. Or worse."

He looked at the map on his phone. At all the marked locations. "You going to warn people?"

"I'm going to try. But most people won't listen."

"Yeah. They'll think you're crazy." He paused. "For what it's worth, I don't think you're crazy. I think something's happening. Has been happening for years. We just ignored it."

"Why did you ignore it?"

"Because it was easier than admitting the land was stranger than we wanted to believe."

I left Captains Marine with fourteen more locations. Fourteen places where hunters and fishermen had felt the wrongness. Had heard things. Had seen things.

All of them on the moraine.

All of them near ancient shorelines.

All of them where burial mounds had been.

I sat in my truck in the parking lot, updating my map. The red X's were multiplying. What had been five incidents was now nineteen locations. And I hadn't even talked to Sarah yet.

My phone rang. Karen.

"How's it going?"

"Worse than I thought. The pattern's bigger. These places have been active for years. People have just been ignoring it."

"Are you still going to see Sarah?"

"Yes. On my way now."

"Be careful, Dave."

"Always am."

"Liar."

She hung up.

I pulled out of Captains Marine and headed toward M-72.

If Scott's experiences were local knowledge—the kind hunters shared but didn't report—then what Sarah knew was deeper. Older. The kind of knowledge that came from watching the land for generations.

I needed to know what the Odawa had learned.

Before someone else walked into a thin place and didn't walk back out.

The Grand Traverse Band Cultural Center sat on a wooded lot off M-72, a low building designed to look like it belonged to the landscape rather than imposed on it. I'd driven past it hundreds of times, never stopped.

Karen had called ahead. Sarah Ashkwe was expecting me.

I found her in a back room that served as library, archive, and workspace. Shelves lined with books, filing cabinets labeled in Anishinaabemowin, maps spread across a long table. She was maybe seventy, silver hair in a long braid, reading glasses on a beaded chain, wearing jeans and a GTB Cultural Resources sweatshirt.

She looked up when I knocked.

"Dave Pritchard. Karen said you needed to talk."

"Yes ma'am. Thank you for seeing me."

"Sarah. Not ma'am. Sit." She gestured to a chair across from her. "Karen said you're investigating strange incidents. She didn't say what kind of strange."

I pulled out my laptop, opened the map file. "Started with five incidents in two weeks. Now nineteen locations. All following a geological pattern. All involving... temporal displacement. People seeing things that shouldn't be there. Experiencing conditions from eleven thousand years ago."

I showed her the locations. The red X's. The moraine line. Scott's hunter experiences. The Ring camera footage. Everything.

She studied the map for a long time. Then she said, "Show me the incidents."

I walked her through it. Joe's mastodons. Mel's drowning. Beth's ice. The tracks. The Ring camera bear. Scott's encounter with the tall thing in the woods. The sounds hunters had heard.

When I finished, she sat back.

"My grandmother told me about places like this."

"What did she call them?"

"She didn't have a special name. Just places where the boundary was thin. Where what was and what is sit too close together." Sarah pulled out a paper map from a drawer, unrolled it across the table. Hand-drawn, decades old, showing Antrim County with marks in faded ink. "She made this in 1962. Showed me where not to go."

The marks aligned with my map.

Every single one.

Including the spot where Scott had seen the tall thing.

"How did she know?" I asked.

"The old people knew. The ones before her. The ones before them." Sarah traced a line with her finger. "When the Hopewell built their mounds, they knew. When my people came here, we learned. The land teaches if you listen."

"What does it teach?"

"That some places remember harder than others. That the earth holds what happened to it. That boundaries—between ice and no ice, between water and land, between then and now—those boundaries don't disappear just because time passes."

She pulled out another map. This one showed burial mound locations across northern Michigan. Hundreds of dots.

"These were sacred sites. Not because we made them sacred. Because they *were* sacred. The Hopewell understood. They marked the dangerous places. Built mounds to warn people. To anchor the boundaries."

"What happened to the mounds?"

"White settlers cleared them. Plowed them under for farmland. Dug them up looking for artifacts. By 1900, ninety-five percent were gone." Her voice was matter-of-fact. No anger. Just statement of fact.

"The warnings disappeared. The anchors were removed. And the bo undaries..."

"Got thinner."

"Yes."

I looked at the map. At the places where mounds had been. Where warnings had existed.

They matched everything. The moraine. The ancient shorelines. The places where my incidents were happening. The spots where hunters felt wrong.

"Sarah, these things people are seeing. The tall figure Scott encountered. What is it?"

"What do you think it is?"

"I think it's from when the ice was still here. When humans looked different. Lived different. Survived in conditions we can't imagine."

"Paleo-Indians," she said. "That's what archaeologists call them. My grandmother called them the People Who Walked With Ice. They were here when everything was dying. When the animals were going extinct. When the world was changing so fast you had to adapt or die."

"And they adapted."

"They survived. Learned to hunt things that could kill them. Learned to live in places that should have killed them. Learned to be hard enough to make it through the extinction." She paused. "That thing your friend saw? That was a survivor. Someone who lived when survival meant being the most dangerous thing in the forest."

"Are they dangerous to us?"

"Would you be dangerous if something from the future appeared in your hunting ground? If the world suddenly changed and you didn't understand why?"

Fair point.

"Sarah, if the mounds were anchors, if they were keeping the boundaries stable, what happens now that they're gone?"

"What's already happening. The land remembers what it used to be. Shows people what was here. Sometimes the showing is gentle. Sometimes it's not."

"Can it be stopped?"

She was quiet for a long time. Then she said, "My grandmother used to say: the land doesn't forget. It just waits. When the anchors are gone, when people stop listening, when enough time passes that nobody remembers to be careful—that's when the waiting ends."

"And then what?"

"Then the land teaches again. Whether we want to learn or not."

Sarah gave me copies of her maps. Her grandmother's notes, written in a mix of English and Anishinaabemowin, translated where necessary.

The notes described locations. Elevations. Geological features. But they also described... something else.

"The place where ice meets earth—avoid during new moon."

"The ridge above the old lake—tread lightly, ancestors close."

"Where the river bends twice—do not camp, boundary thin."

"The tall people walk when fog is heavy—stay to open ground."

Her grandmother had understood something geologists were just beginning to map. That certain locations—intersections of moraine and paleoshoreline, places where glacial ice had paused, where ancient lakes had lapped against retreating ice—those places held memory differently.

"Did your grandmother say why it's happening now?" I asked. "Why not ten years ago? Why not a hundred years from now?"

"She didn't know timing. Just that it would happen. That when enough anchors were removed, when enough people forgot to listen, the land would remind us."

"Remind us of what?"

"That we're not the first people here. That we won't be the last. That the land was here before us and will be here after us, and it remembers everything we've forgotten."

We spent three hours going over the maps. Cross-referencing her grandmother's marks with Dr. Ostrander's moraine survey, with my incident locations, with Scott's hunter experiences, with historical records of mound sites.

The pattern was undeniable.

Every thin place sat where a mound had been. Where an anchor had been removed. Where warnings had been destroyed.

And in several locations—including where Scott had seen the tall figure—her grandmother had specifically noted: *"The People Who Walked With Ice appear here."*

"There are sixty-seven of these sites across four counties," I said, counting the combined marks. "Maybe more."

"More," Sarah confirmed. "My grandmother only marked the ones she knew personally. There are others. Leelanau County. Grand Traverse. Charlevoix. All along the old glacial boundary."

"Can you mark them?"

"Some. The ones I remember her talking about. The ones my mother showed me before she died." She pulled out a blank map. "But Dave, marking them doesn't protect them. People won't listen. They'll say it's superstition. They'll build anyway."

"Then we don't tell them it's spiritual. We tell them it's geological. Unstable terrain. Dangerous conditions. Wildlife hazards. Give them a reason they'll accept."

She smiled slightly. "You're learning."

"Learning what?"

"That sometimes the truth needs different words to be heard."

When we finished, I had a comprehensive map. Sixty-seven sites across four counties. Every one a potential thin place. Every one a location where past and present sat too close together.

Some marked for animals. Some for ice and water. Some for the People Who Walked With Ice.

"What do I do with this?" I asked.

"What you're already doing. Document. Warn people. Try to keep them safe." She paused. "But Dave, understand something. This isn't an outbreak you can contain. This isn't a hazard you can eliminate. The land is what it is. The boundaries are what they are. The best you can do is teach people to respect what they don't understand."

"And if they don't respect it?"

"Then the land teaches them anyway. Usually harder."

I was almost to my truck when Sarah called out.

"Dave. One more thing."

I turned.

"My grandmother said the first signs would be animals. The ones that used to live here. Then the land itself—ice, water, different seasons. Then people."

"The Paleo-Indians."

"Yes. Except they're not paleo to themselves. To them, they're just people. Living in their time. And when the boundaries thin enough, when their world and ours overlap, they'll see us the same way we see them."

"As ghosts."

"As impossible things that shouldn't exist. As threats in their hunting ground. As something to avoid. Or eliminate."

She looked at me steadily. "You've seen the animals. You've seen the land. The people are coming next. Your friend already saw one. Be ready."

"Ready for what?"

"For hunters who don't understand the world changed. For people who think *you're* the intruder. For humans who lived through the extinction and learned to be very, very good at surviving."

She went back inside. I stood in the parking lot, holding maps that showed me sixty-seven places where impossible things were waiting to happen.

Then I got in my truck and started driving.

I had a lot of people to warn.

And not much time to warn them.

Chapter 8

11:42 AM

CHAPTER EIGHT: THE LIVESTOCK ATTACK

The call came in at 6:23 AM on a Sunday.

I was already awake—had been for an hour, sitting at the kitchen table with coffee and Sarah's maps, trying to figure out how to convince the county that sixty-seven locations needed to be cordoned off without explaining why.

My phone buzzed. Unknown number.

"Pritchard."

"Dave, it's Tom Vreeland. I've got a dead horse and I need you out here now."

Tom owned a small farm off Bunker Hill Road, maybe thirty acres, kept a few horses for his daughters to ride. Nice guy. Paid his taxes. Didn't call DNR unless it was serious.

"What happened?"

"Just get out here. You need to see this."

The Vreeland farm sat in a shallow valley, pasture land surrounded by woods. The house was a century-old farmhouse, well-maintained, the kind of place that appeared on Christmas cards. The barn was newer, red metal siding, big enough for three horses and equipment.

Tom met me in the driveway. Early fifties, carpenter by trade, farmer by choice. His face was pale.

"It's in the back pasture. I already called Dr. Havelka. She's on her way."

"What am I looking at?"

"Dead horse. Daisy. She was fine yesterday evening. This morning I found her..." He stopped. "Just come look."

We walked through the barn and out the back gate. The pasture stretched maybe two acres, fenced with wooden rails. Good grass. A small pond in the northeast corner. The other two horses—a bay gelding and a gray mare—were huddled against the far fence, as far from the center of the pasture as they could get.

In the middle of the pasture lay what was left of Daisy.

I've seen deer killed by coyotes. I've seen livestock attacked by dogs. I've seen what bears do to calves.

This was different.

Daisy had been a quarter horse, maybe eleven hundred pounds. She was lying on her side, throat torn open, massive wounds along her flanks and hindquarters. The grass around her was dark with blood. But what stopped me cold were the bite marks.

Too big for coyotes. Too big for dogs. Even too big for wolves—and we didn't have wolves this far south anyway.

"What the hell did this?" Tom asked.

I knelt beside the carcass, careful not to disturb anything. The throat wound was massive—something had clamped down on her windpipe and crushed it. The canine punctures were three inches deep, spaced wide. The tearing on her flanks suggested something had been eating, not just killing.

"Tom, when did you last see her alive?"

"Yesterday evening. Six PM. I came out to feed. All three horses were fine. Daisy was near the pond, grazing."

"And this morning?"

"Found her at six. I came out because the other two were making noise. Panicked. Soon as I saw Daisy I called you."

I stood up, looked at the surrounding area. The ground was soft from yesterday's rain. There should be tracks.

There were.

Leading from the tree line, across the pasture to the kill site, then back to the trees. Four-toed. Clawed. The stride length was massive—maybe six feet between prints. Whatever made these tracks was big, fast, and confident.

I pulled out my phone, took pictures. Measurements. Then I followed the tracks to the tree line.

The woods here were typical northern Michigan mixed forest—oak, maple, some pine. The underbrush was thick enough that most animals would leave a trail. Whatever made these tracks had pushed through like the brush wasn't there.

Twenty yards into the woods, I found where it had waited.

A spot where the underbrush was compressed. Grass flattened. A clear line of sight to the pasture. It had been here for a while. Watching. Waiting for the right moment.

I took more pictures. Then I heard a vehicle pull up.

Dr. Havelka had arrived.

Dr. Rachel Havelka had been the local large animal vet for fifteen years. She'd seen everything from colic to birthing complications to livestock accidents. I'd worked with her on a few cases—usually cattle getting into something toxic, or horses escaping and causing traffic problems.

She was good at her job. Practical. No-nonsense. Didn't jump to conclusions.

She took one look at Daisy and said, "What the fuck."

"That's what I said," Tom muttered.

She knelt beside the carcass, pulled on latex gloves, examined the wounds. I watched her face go from professional assessment to genuine confusion.

"These bite marks..." She measured the canine punctures with a small ruler. "Seven centimeters between upper canines. That's..." She looked up at me. "Dave, what animal has a bite spread this wide?"

"You're the vet."

"No domestic dog. Maybe a large wolf, but we don't have wolves here. A bear wouldn't leave marks like this—bears slash, they don't bite and hold like this." She examined the throat wound. "Whatever did this crushed her trachea. The force required..." She shook her head. "I don't know any predator in Michigan capable of this."

"Could it be multiple animals? Pack hunting?"

"The pattern's wrong. This is a single kill. One predator. It took her down from behind—see the claw marks on her hindquarters?—then went for the throat. Classic ambush predator behavior."

She stood up, pulled off her gloves. "Dave, I need to be honest. I've never seen anything like this. The bite radius suggests something with a skull twice the size of a timber wolf. The killing technique suggests intelligence—this wasn't a frenzy kill, this was efficient. And the eating pattern..." She gestured to the flanks. "It ate the best parts. Knew what it wanted."

"Time of death?"

"Based on rigor and lividity, I'd say between midnight and three AM. It's been dead at least four hours."

I showed her the tracks.

She stared at them for a long time. Then she said, "That's not a wolf track."

"I know."

"Too big. Wrong toe configuration. The claw marks are too pronounced." She looked at me. "You know what this looks like?"

"Tell me."

"*Aenocyon dirus*. Dire wolf. Except that's been extinct for eleven thousand years."

I sent Tom and Dr. Havelka back to the house while I documented the scene. Photos from every angle. Measurements of the tracks. Casts of the clearest prints using a kit I kept in my truck.

The pattern was clear. The predator had approached from the woods, crossed the pasture in long, efficient strides, taken down the horse with a single throat bite, fed briefly, then retreated the same way it came.

No hesitation. No signs of confusion or disorientation. This thing knew exactly what it was doing.

I followed the tracks back into the woods. They went deeper than I'd initially thought—maybe a hundred yards, heading northeast toward higher ground. Toward the ridge that separated this valley from the next.

Then they disappeared.

Not gradually. Not fading into harder ground or rocky terrain. They just... stopped. One moment clear prints in the soft earth, the next moment nothing. Like whatever made them had simply ceased to exist.

I stood there looking at the last track, a perfect four-toed print with clear claw marks, and felt my stomach tighten.

I pulled out my phone, opened the map Sarah had given me.

Tom Vreeland's property sat three hundred yards from a marked thin place. His back pasture—where Daisy had been killed—sat right on the boundary.

Right where a burial mound had been, according to the 1890 survey.

Right where Sarah's grandmother had written: *"Avoid after dark. The wolves walk here."*

Back at the house, Dr. Havelka was writing her report at Tom's kitchen table. He was making coffee, hands shaking slightly.

"What do I tell my daughters?" he asked. "They loved that horse. Had her since she was a foal."

"Tell them the truth. An animal killed her. We don't know what kind yet."

"But you have an idea."

I looked at Dr. Havelka. She met my eyes, waiting to see what I'd say.

"Something big," I said carefully. "Something that doesn't belong here."

"Should I be worried about the other horses? About my kids?"

"Keep the horses in the barn at night. Lock them in. Don't let your daughters go near the back pasture until I tell you it's safe."

"For how long?"

"I don't know."

Tom set down the coffee pot. "Dave, you're scaring me."

"Good. You should be scared. Whatever did this is a apex predator. It's smart, it's efficient, and it's hunting in your pasture." I paused. "How far is your house from those woods?"

"Maybe two hundred yards."

"Keep your doors locked at night. Keep a light on. If you hear anything unusual, call me immediately."

"You think it'll come back."

"I think it found an easy food source. And predators return to easy food sources until they're not easy anymore."

Dr. Havelka and I walked out to our vehicles together.

"You're not telling him everything," she said quietly.

"No."

"Why not?"

"Because if I tell him his horse was killed by an extinct Ice Age predator that's crossing through a temporal boundary in his back pasture, he'll think I've lost my mind."

She was quiet for a moment. Then: "Dave, I've heard the rumors. About the drowning on Lake Bellaire. About the woman who got frostbite. About weird things happening around the county."

"And?"

"And I'm a scientist. I don't believe in impossible things. But those bite marks are real. Those tracks are real. And they don't match anything alive today."

"What do you think killed Daisy?"

"I think something that shouldn't exist killed her. And I think you know more than you're telling me."

I looked at her. Fifteen years of working together. She'd always been straight with me. No bullshit. No hysteria. Just facts and professional assessment.

"Can I show you something?" I asked.

"Sure."

I pulled out my laptop, opened the map file. Showed her the thin places. The moraine intersections. The sites where incidents had occurred. The spot where Tom's property sat, right on the boundary.

She studied it without speaking. Then she said, "What am I looking at?"

"Places where the boundary between past and present is thin. Where things from eleven thousand years ago are crossing through."

"That's insane."

"I know."

"But it explains the wounds."

"I know."

She closed the laptop. Handed it back. "How many of these sites are there?"

"Sixty-seven. That we know of."

"And they're all active?"

"Some more than others. But yes. All potential crossing points."

"For what? Just predators?"

"Animals. Environmental conditions. And people. The Paleo-Indians who lived here when the ice was still here."

She leaned against her truck, processing. "You're telling me we have Ice Age predators hunting livestock in Antrim County."

"Yes."

"And you expect me to believe this."

"I expect you to examine the evidence and come to your own conclusion. Those bite marks don't lie. Those tracks don't lie. Whatever killed Daisy wasn't from 2026."

She was quiet for a long time. Then she said, "I need to think about this."

"I understand."

"But Dave, if you're right, if these things are coming through, people need to know. Livestock owners. Farmers. Anyone living near these... thin places."

"I'm working on it. I've got a meeting scheduled with the county board next week."

"What are you going to tell them?"

"The truth. And hope they don't laugh me out of the room."

She got in her truck, started the engine. Rolled down the window. "Dave, be careful. If these predators are as dangerous as those wounds suggest, you're walking into their hunting ground every time you investigate a site."

"I know."

"And they're probably better at hunting than you are."

"I know that too."

She drove off.

I stood in Tom Vreeland's driveway, looking at the woods behind his pasture. At the trees where something had waited, watching. At the back pasture where it had killed efficiently and fed deliberately.

Somewhere out there, maybe still close, maybe already gone back to its own time, a dire wolf was doing what dire wolves did.

Hunting.

And we'd just entered its territory.

I spent the rest of the day documenting. Photos. Measurements. Samples of blood and tissue that I bagged and labeled, though I had no idea what lab would believe the results.

By the time I finished, it was late afternoon. The sun was dropping toward the horizon, turning the sky orange and pink. Pretty. Peaceful. The kind of northern Michigan evening that made people want to move here.

Except there was a dead horse in the back pasture and dire wolf tracks leading into the woods.

I called Dr. Ostrander.

"Dave. What's wrong?"

"How do you know something's wrong?"

"Because you only call me when something's wrong."

Fair.

"I've got a livestock kill. Horse. Wounds match *Aenocyon dirus*. Dire wolf. Tracks confirm it."

Silence on the other end. Then: "Where?"

"Bunker Hill Road. Property sits right on one of your mapped moraine intersections."

"The thin place is active."

"Very active."

"Dave, if predators are crossing through now, not just herbivores, the danger level just increased exponentially."

"I know."

"You need to close these sites. Fence them off. Post warnings."

"With what authority? I'm a DNR officer. I can't just cordon off sixty-seven locations across four counties."

"Then get authority. Talk to the county board. The sheriff. The state police. Anyone who'll listen."

"I've got a meeting scheduled for Wednesday."

"Make it sooner. Because if dire wolves are hunting in northern Michigan, someone's going to get killed."

He hung up.

I sat in my truck, looking at Tom's barn. At the woods beyond. At the ordinary farm that now sat on the edge of something impossible.

Then I started driving.

I had maps to update. Evidence to compile. A presentation to prepare for Wednesday's meeting.

And a growing certainty that no matter what I said, most people wouldn't believe me until it was too late.

Chapter 9

CHAPTER NINE: THE TOWN MEETING

The Bellaire High School gymnasium could hold maybe four hundred people if you packed them in tight. By seven PM on Wednesday, there were at least five hundred crammed inside, with more standing in the hallway outside the doors.

The parking lot had filled an hour ago. Cars lined M-88 in both directions. People were walking from downtown, from the neighborhoods, from the lakefront properties. Half of Antrim County had shown up.

I stood backstage—really just behind the bleachers that had been pushed against the wall—watching the crowd gather. The noise was incredible. Voices echoing off the high ceiling, the hardwood floor, the cinder block walls. Every sound amplified and distorted until individual words disappeared into a roar.

Karen found me there.

"You okay?"

"No."

"Want to back out?"

"Can't."

She squeezed my hand. "They'll listen."

"No they won't. But I have to try anyway."

The meeting had been Jake's idea.

After the livestock kill, after Dr. Havelka's report, after I'd compiled all the evidence into a presentation that made me sound either like a serious scientist or a complete lunatic depending on your perspective, Jake had said: "You can't just brief the county board in a closed session. People need to know. Make it public."

So I'd requested a town hall. Expected maybe fifty people. Got five hundred.

Word had spread. The rumors about weird incidents. The whispers about Joe's mastodons and Mel's drowning and Beth's frostbite. The livestock kill had made it into the Antrim County News with a headline: "Unknown Predator Kills Horse Near Central Lake." Dr. Havelka had been careful in her statement, but people read between the lines.

Something was happening. And people wanted answers.

I wasn't sure I had answers they'd accept.

County Commissioner Margaret Walsh called the meeting to order at 7:15. She was in her sixties, retired teacher, sensible and no-nonsense. She'd been skeptical when I'd requested the meeting, but she'd granted it.

She stood at a podium set up at center court, microphone in hand, trying to quiet the crowd.

"Folks, please. We need to get started."

The noise dropped slightly. Not much.

"We're here tonight because DNR Officer Dave Pritchard has requested to brief the community on recent unusual incidents in

Antrim County. I want to remind everyone that this is a public forum. Please be respectful. Hold your questions until the end."

She gestured to me. "Officer Pritchard, the floor is yours."

I walked out to the podium. The crowd noise swelled again—people recognizing me, wondering what I was going to say.

The acoustics were terrible. Every footstep echoed. Every cough amplified. This was going to be hell.

I plugged my laptop into the projection system. The screen behind me lit up—a map of Antrim County with red dots marking the thin places.

The crowd quieted slightly. Curiosity.

I took a breath.

"Thank you all for coming. I know this is unusual. I know some of you are here because you've heard rumors, and you want to know what's really happening. I'm going to tell you what's really happening. And I'm going to ask you to keep an open mind, because what I'm about to show you doesn't make sense by any conventional measure."

I clicked to the first slide. Joe Macklin's dashcam footage.

"Two weeks ago, Joe Macklin was driving on Old State Road when he saw this."

The video played. The valley wrong. Four mastodons grazing where a church should be. The car's axle breaking. The shimmer as reality corrected itself.

The crowd erupted.

Shouts. Laughter. Someone yelled "That's fake!"

Commissioner Walsh pounded the podium. "Order! Let him present!"

I waited for the noise to die down.

"That's not fake. Joe Macklin and Len Greenland both witnessed it. The vehicle damage is real. The location is real. And it's not the only incident."

Next slide. Mel Harrison's driveway. Carol's 911 call transcript. The medical examiner's report showing drowning on dry land.

More noise. More disbelief.

I kept going.

Beth Koerner's frostbite. The Ring camera footage of the short-faced bear. Scott Mercer's encounter with the tall figure. The horse kill on Bunker Hill Road.

For each one, I showed evidence. Photos. Reports. Medical documentation. Witness statements.

The crowd was divided. Half listening intently. Half convinced this was a hoax.

Then I showed them the map.

"These incidents aren't random. They follow a specific geological pattern. Every single one occurs at the intersection of the Lake Border Moraine and ancient shorelines from glacial lakes that existed eleven thousand years ago."

I zoomed in on the map. Showed the moraine line. The paleoshoreline elevations. The sites where burial mounds had been.

"These locations were marked by the Hopewell people as dangerous. Later, the Odawa people avoided them. They called them places where the boundary was thin. We ignored those warnings. We built on those sites. We cleared the markers. And now the land is showing us what it remembers."

Someone in the crowd—I couldn't see who—shouted: "This is bullshit! You're saying time travel is real?"

"I'm saying temporal displacement is occurring at specific geological boundaries. I'm saying the past is bleeding through. And I'm saying people are in danger."

I clicked to the next slide. Dr. Havelka's veterinary report. The bite measurements. The wound photos.

"This horse was killed by *Aenocyon dirus*. A dire wolf. They've been extinct for eleven thousand years. But the bite radius, the killing technique, the tracks—all match. Dr. Havelka can confirm."

I looked out at the crowd. Found her near the front. She stood up.

"It's true. I examined the wounds. No modern predator in Michigan could have made those marks. The bite force required, the spacing of the canines, the hunting pattern—all consistent with *Aenocyon dirus*."

"Or a dog!" someone shouted. "Just a big dog!"

"No domestic dog has a bite radius of seven centimeters," Dr. Havelka said calmly. "I've treated thousands of dog bites. This wasn't a dog."

The crowd was getting louder. Arguments breaking out in different sections. The acoustics made it impossible to hear individual voices—just a wall of noise echoing off every surface.

Commissioner Walsh pounded the podium again. "Order! We will have order!"

I tried to continue. Showed them Dr. Ostrander's geological survey. Sarah's maps. The correlation between thin places and mound locations.

But I was losing them.

Too much information. Too many impossible claims. Too far outside what people wanted to believe.

A man in the back—I recognized him as Bill Henderson, owned a hardware store downtown—stood up and yelled over the noise: "So what are you telling us to do? Stay inside? Abandon our homes? This is insane!"

"I'm telling you to avoid these locations." I highlighted the sixty-seven sites on the map. "Don't hunt in these areas. Don't camp. Don't let your children play near them. Post warnings. Fence them if you can."

"You want us to fence off half the county?"

"I want you to take this seriously before someone gets killed."

"Someone already got killed!" A woman I didn't recognize stood up, voice shaking. "Mel Harrison drowned. That's real. That's a death. And you're standing here talking about mastodons and ice age wolves like this is some kind of science fiction story!"

The crowd turned on her. Half agreeing, half dismissing.

"Mel had a heart attack!"

"The medical examiner said drowning!"

"It was an accident!"

"An accident where water appeared from nowhere?"

The gym was chaos now. Too many voices. Too much noise. The acoustics turning it into a roar that made thinking impossible.

I tried to regain control. "Please. Please listen. I know this sounds impossible. But the evidence—"

"The evidence doesn't prove anything!" Bill Henderson again. "You've got some weird videos and a dead horse and a bunch of maps that don't mean anything. You're asking us to believe in time travel!"

"I'm asking you to believe the evidence."

"I believe you're losing your mind."

That got applause. From maybe a third of the room.

Commissioner Walsh stood up. "That's enough. Officer Pritchard has presented his findings. Now we'll take questions."

The questions were brutal.

"How do you explain the car appearing fine on one side of the road and wrecked on the other?"

"Temporal fold. The vehicle existed in two states simultaneously."

Laughter. Dismissive.

"Why now? Why not last year? Ten years ago?"

"The anchors are gone. The burial mounds that marked these sites were destroyed. The boundaries have been unstable for decades. Now they're failing."

"That's convenient. Blame people who've been dead for a hundred years."

"I'm not blaming anyone. I'm explaining the pattern."

"The pattern of your imagination."

More laughter.

A woman near the front stood up. "My kids play in those woods. You're telling me there are extinct predators hunting there?"

"Yes."

"And you have what, tracks? Photos? That's not enough. I want proof."

"The tracks are proof. Dr. Havelka's report is proof. The incidents are proof."

"Then show me a dire wolf. Bring me an actual extinct animal. Until then, this is just stories."

I looked at her. "Ma'am, if I bring you a dire wolf, someone will be dead. That's the proof you don't want."

Silence. Brief. Then the noise swelled again.

Dr. Ostrander stood up from where he'd been sitting along the side wall.

"I've examined Officer Pritchard's data. The geological correlation is sound. These locations are all boundary zones from the Wisconsin glaciation. The moraine intersections with paleoshorelines create areas of geological instability."

"Geological, not temporal," someone shouted.

"I don't have an explanation for the temporal component. But the pattern is real. Ignoring it would be irresponsible."

"Or maybe there is no pattern," Bill Henderson said. "Maybe we've had a few weird coincidences and Dave here is connecting dots that don't connect."

"Five incidents in two weeks isn't coincidence," I said.

"Sure it is. Especially when you're looking for patterns. You see what you want to see."

Sarah Ashkwe stood up.

The gym quieted slightly. People knew who she was. Respected her, even if they didn't always listen to her.

"My grandmother marked these places in 1962. Before any of these incidents. She knew where the boundaries were thin. She taught me to avoid them. The Hopewell people knew thousands of years before that. This isn't new. It's just forgotten."

"With all due respect, Sarah," someone said—I couldn't see who—"your grandmother's superstitions aren't evidence."

"They're not superstitions. They're observations passed down through generations. Knowledge of the land."

"Knowledge or folklore?"

"Both. The land doesn't care what you call it. It is what it is."

"And what is it?"

"Dangerous. Especially now."

The meeting devolved from there.

Arguments erupted in clusters throughout the gym. Some people wanted immediate action—close the sites, evacuate nearby homes, call in state resources. Others dismissed everything, called it mass hysteria, demanded I be removed from my position for wasting everyone's time.

Commissioner Walsh tried to maintain order, but the acoustics worked against her. Every voice amplified, every shout echoing until the gym was just noise.

I stood at the podium, watching it fall apart.

Jake found me there twenty minutes later.

"Dad. You need to wrap this up."

"I can't get them to listen."

"Because they don't want to listen. Half of them are scared and the other half are angry and nobody knows what to do with either emotion."

He was right.

I raised my hands, waited for a lull in the noise.

"One more thing. Then I'm done."

The crowd settled slightly. Curious what my closing would be.

"I'm not asking you to believe in time travel. I'm not asking you to accept anything supernatural or impossible. I'm asking you to be careful. To avoid specific locations. To watch your children. To report anything unusual. Because whether you believe my explanation or not, something is happening. People have been hurt. Livestock has been killed. And it's going to get worse."

"How do you know?" someone shouted.

"Because the pattern is accelerating. The incidents are getting more frequent. More violent. And I don't have the resources to stop it alone."

Silence. Brief.

Then Bill Henderson stood up one more time.

"So what you're really saying is you need our help. You need us to do your job for you because you can't explain what's happening."

"I'm saying we're all in this together. And ignoring it won't make it go away."

"Maybe there's nothing to ignore. Maybe you're just wrong."

I looked at him. At the crowd. At the faces of people I'd known for years, worked with, protected.

"I hope I am wrong," I said quietly. "I really do."

I unplugged my laptop. Walked off the floor.

Behind me, the noise swelled again. Arguments. Dismissals. Fear disguised as anger.

Commissioner Walsh called for a vote on whether to close any sites. It failed. Twelve to three.

The meeting adjourned.

In the parking lot, people clustered in groups. Some still arguing. Some leaving quickly, uncomfortable with what they'd heard.

Karen found me by the truck.

"You did what you could."

"It wasn't enough."

"It never is. Not at first." She looked back at the gym. "But some people listened. Dr. Havelka. Sarah. Dr. Ostrander. Some of the parents. They'll be careful."

"What about the ones who won't?"

"You can't save people who don't want to be saved."

Jake and Emma joined us. Emma looked shaken.

"Dad, some of the kids at school are already calling you crazy. It's all over social media."

"I know."

"Are you going to be okay?"

"I don't know."

We stood there in the parking lot, watching people leave. Watching the gym empty. Watching my attempt to warn the community fail in real time.

Then Scott Mercer walked up.

"Dave. For what it's worth, I believe you. So do most of the hunters. We've felt it. We've seen things. We know you're not making this up."

"Thanks, Scott."

"But you need to know—people are going to ignore you. They're going to keep hunting those areas. Keep building. Keep living like nothing's wrong."

"I know."

"And when something happens, when someone gets hurt, they're going to blame you for not stopping it."

"I know that too."

He clapped me on the shoulder. "Good luck. You're going to need it."

He walked away.

I got in the truck. Karen drove. I was too tired to drive.

On the way home, my phone buzzed. A text from Dr. Ostrander.

You did the right thing. Even if they didn't listen. History will prove you correct. Unfortunately.

I didn't respond.

At home, I sat on the back deck in the dark, looking at the woods.

Somewhere out there, sixty-seven thin places were waiting. Boundaries getting thinner. Predators crossing through. The past bleeding into the present.

And I'd just learned that trying to warn people was useless.

They'd have to learn the hard way.

Chapter 10

CHAPTER TEN: THE PATTERN COMPLETES

I couldn't sleep.

It was 2:17 AM and I'd been in my office since we got home from the meeting. Karen had gone to bed around eleven. Jake was crashed on the couch. Emma in her room with her door locked and her phone turned off—the social media had gotten vicious.

I sat at my desk with four monitors, each showing a different map layer, trying to see what I was missing.

Because I was missing something.

The pattern was there—I could feel it. But it wasn't complete yet.

Monitor one: Dr. Ostrander's geological survey. The Lake Border Moraine system running northeast to southwest through Antrim County. Terminal moraines, recessional moraines, drumlins, kames. The debris piles left behind by retreating glaciers.

Monitor two: Ancient shoreline data. Lake Algonquin at 605 feet elevation. The Chippewa Low at 80 meters below modern levels. Lake Nipissing at 184 meters. Each stage of glacial lakes mapped by elevation contours, showing where water had been eleven thousand years ago, eight thousand years ago, four thousand years ago.

Monitor three: Sarah's maps. Her grandmother's hand-drawn markings from 1962, showing sixty-seven thin places. Overlaid with the 1890 survey showing 347 burial mounds across four counties. Ninety-five percent destroyed by 1920.

Monitor four: Modern Antrim County. Roads. Subdivisions. Commercial development. Schools. Hospitals. The infrastructure of 23,000 people living their lives.

Four separate patterns.

I'd been looking at them individually for two weeks.

Now I was going to look at them together.

I opened GIS software. Started layering.

First: the moraine. The geological skeleton of the county. The high ground, the ridgelines, the boundaries between glacial and post-glacial terrain.

The software rendered it in topographic relief. Hills and valleys. The spine of the Lake Border Moraine running like a crooked backbone through the landscape.

Second: the ancient shorelines. I set transparency to fifty percent, overlaid the elevation contours.

The shorelines wrapped around the moraine like rings. Lake Algonquin high. Chippewa Low. Nipissing rising again. Each stage a different color, each showing where water had met land at different points in time.

The intersections were obvious now. Places where the moraine ridge dropped to meet ancient shoreline elevations. Transition zones. Boundaries.

Third: the burial mounds. I imported Sarah's data, cross-referenced with the 1890 survey.

Three hundred forty-seven red dots appeared on the map.

And every single one sat at a moraine-shoreline intersection.

Every. Single. One.

The Hopewell hadn't built randomly. They'd marked the boundaries. The dangerous places. The spots where geological instability met hydrological change met... something else. Something they'd understood without having words for it.

I zoomed in on one cluster. Fifteen mounds in a two-mile radius near what was now downtown Bellaire.

All gone. Cleared by 1885 for farmland. Then for roads. Then for buildings.

I zoomed out.

Looked at the whole county.

Three hundred forty-seven warning signs. Three hundred thirty destroyed.

Seventeen remaining. Most of those on private land, preserved by accident rather than intention.

Fourth layer: Modern construction.

I imported county assessor data. Roads, buildings, subdivisions, commercial zones. Everything we'd built in the past century.

Hit render.

The screen went quiet for thirty seconds while the software processed.

Then the map appeared.

And my stomach dropped.

We'd built everything on the boundaries.

Not just near them. *On* them.

M-88—the main highway through the county—followed the moraine almost perfectly. Every curve, every straight stretch, every intersection aligned with the glacial ridge.

Cairn Highway, where the Ring camera had caught the short-faced bear, ran along the Lake Algonquin shoreline.

Old State Road, where Joe had seen the mastodons, cut directly through a cluster of destroyed mound sites.

Bunker Hill Road near Central Lake, where the horse had been killed, sat on a moraine intersection that had once held seven burial mounds.

The Jordan River valley overlook, where Beth had touched ice, was the site of the largest mound group in Antrim County—twenty-three mounds cleared in 1892 to make room for logging roads.

Every major road.

Every highway.

Every developed area.

Built on the places the Hopewell had marked as dangerous.

I zoomed in on Bellaire proper. The downtown. The grid of streets. The commercial district. The high school where we'd just held the meeting.

Twelve mounds had been there. A major site. Sarah's grandmother's notes called it *"The place where many boundaries meet. Avoid always."*

We'd built a town on it.

The high school sat exactly where the largest mound had been.

I sat back, staring at the screen.

We hadn't just ignored the warnings.

We'd built our entire infrastructure on top of them.

I started running numbers.

Population distribution. Where people lived relative to thin places.

The software calculated.

Result: Sixty-three percent of Antrim County's population lived within a quarter-mile of a moraine-shoreline intersection. Eighty-four percent lived within a half-mile.

Commercial zones: Ninety-one percent built on or adjacent to destroyed mound sites.

Schools: All four elementary schools, both middle schools, the high school—every single one built on former mound locations.

The hospital: Sitting on what had been a three-mound cluster cleared in 1947.

We'd literally built our community centers—the places where people gathered, where children learned, where the sick were treated—on the exact locations ancient people had marked as dangerous.

I pulled up property records. Cross-referenced with the thin place map.

New subdivisions going in along Cairn Highway. Fifteen homes. All sitting at the 625-foot elevation contour. All on the Lake Algonquin shoreline.

A planned marina expansion on Intermediate Lake. Dredging and construction scheduled for spring. Right where Scott had heard voices in unknown languages.

A commercial development near Central Lake. Breaking ground next month. Three destroyed mound sites underneath the parking lot plan.

We weren't just living on thin places.

We were actively developing them.

I created a new layer. Combined everything.

Geological boundaries + ancient shorelines + mound sites + modern construction + incident locations.

The pattern was perfect.

Every incident sat where all four factors intersected:

Moraine-shoreline boundary (geological instability)

Destroyed mound site (removed warning/anchor)

Modern construction (ongoing disturbance)

Specific elevation (ancient lake level or glacial contact point)

The thin places weren't random.

They were predictable.

And we'd built on every single one of them.

I ran a probability analysis. If the pattern held, if the incidents continued accelerating, where would the next ones occur?

The software highlighted twenty-three high-probability sites.

I zoomed in on each one.

Site one: Bellaire Elementary School. Recess playground. Built on a six-mound cluster. Elevation 618 feet. Lake Algonquin shoreline.

Site two: Intermediate Lake boat launch. Public access. Heavy use. Four destroyed mounds. Moraine terminus point.

Site three: M-88 corridor between Bellaire and Central Lake. Major traffic artery. Nine-mile stretch following the moraine. Twelve destroyed mounds along the route.

Site four: Torch Lake Public Access near Alden. Tourist hotspot. Summer population in the thousands. Eight mounds cleared in 1955 for parking lot construction.

I kept going through the list.

Every high-probability site was a place where people gathered. Where children played. Where tourists visited. Where traffic flowed.

We'd built our entire modern life on a foundation of ignored warnings.

I created a final map. Combined all data. Color-coded by risk level.

Red: Highest probability. Active sites with recent incidents.

Orange: High probability. All factors present, no incidents yet.

Yellow: Moderate probability. Three of four factors present.

Green: Low probability. One or two factors only.

I rendered the county.

The screen filled with red and orange.

Sixty-seven red zones. A hundred forty-three orange zones.

Two hundred ten locations where thin places could activate.

Out of maybe three hundred significant sites in the county.

Seventy percent of our developed areas sat on dangerous ground.

I sat there staring at the map for an hour.

Then I did something I'd been avoiding.

I overlaid population density.

The software calculated how many people lived within each risk zone.

Red zones: 4,847 people.

Orange zones: 11,203 people.

Yellow zones: 5,912 people.

Total at-risk population: 21,962.

Out of a county population of 23,018.

Ninety-five percent of Antrim County residents lived on or near a thin place.

There was no evacuation plan that could work. No way to move that many people. Nowhere to move them to—the surrounding counties had the same geological features, probably the same thin places.

We were living on top of the problem.

And the problem was waking up.

I printed the final map. All layers visible. The complete pattern.

Pinned it to the wall above my desk.

Geological boundaries in gray. Ancient shorelines in blue. Mound sites in brown. Modern construction in black. Incident locations in red. High-probability zones in orange.

It looked like a medical diagram. A scan showing cancer spread throughout a body.

Except the body was Antrim County.

And the cancer was us.

We'd metastasized across every dangerous boundary, built on every warning, ignored every sign that the land had tried to give us.

And now the land was pushing back.

My phone buzzed. Text from Dr. Ostrander.

Are you still up?

Yes

Did you overlay the data?

Yes

Three dots. He was typing. Stopped. Started again.

How bad is it?

I looked at the map. At the red and orange zones covering seventy percent of the county. At the population numbers. At the schools and hospitals and commercial centers all sitting on destroyed mound sites.

Worse than I thought

Can we evacuate the high-risk zones?

No. There are too many. And nowhere to evacuate to.

Then what do we do?

I didn't have an answer.

The dots appeared again. Disappeared. He wasn't typing anymore.

Because there was no answer.

We'd built a county on thin places. Removed the warnings. Destroyed the anchors. Concentrated twenty-three thousand people on geological boundaries that were starting to fail.

And the incidents were accelerating.

Five in the first two weeks.

If the pattern held, we'd have ten in the next two weeks. Twenty the week after that.

Exponential growth.

By summer, the thin places wouldn't be occasional anomalies.

They'd be constant.

I saved the final map as a PDF. Titled it: "Antrim County Thin Places - Complete Analysis."

Emailed it to Dr. Ostrander, Sarah, Dr. Havelka, Commissioner Walsh, the sheriff, the state DNR office, and the governor's emergency management division.

Subject line: "Immediate action required."

Body: "We are living on unstable temporal boundaries. Evacuation not feasible. Recommend immediate closure of highest-risk sites and emergency protocols for remaining population. Full analysis attached."

Hit send.

Knew it wouldn't matter.

They'd already ignored me once. A PDF wouldn't change anything.

But at least I'd have documentation. When people started dying—and they would start dying—at least I could say I'd tried.

I went outside. Stood on the back deck in the cold pre-dawn air.

The woods were quiet. Normal Michigan quiet. Spring peepers. Distant traffic. The ordinary sounds of a place where people slept safely in their beds.

Except they weren't safe.

Twenty-two thousand people sleeping on top of boundaries that were dissolving. On top of warnings we'd ignored. On top of a past that was waking up whether we believed in it or not.

I thought about Beth Koerner, touching ice that shouldn't exist.

About Mel Harrison, drowning in ancient water.

About Tom Vreeland's horse, throat torn open by teeth from eleven thousand years ago.

About Scott Mercer, seeing something tall and wrong walking toward him.

About the Paleo-Indians who would come through next. The People Who Walked With Ice. The survivors who'd learned to be harder than everything trying to kill them.

And about my family. Karen and Jake and Emma. Living in a house that sat 1.3 miles from three high-probability sites.

Close enough.

I went back inside. To my office. To the map on the wall showing seventy percent of the county colored red and orange.

The pattern was complete.

We'd built our entire modern life on forbidden ground.

And the ground was remembering.

Chapter 11

CHAPTER ELEVEN: LANSING

I left for Lansing at 5:30 AM Thursday morning, two days after the town meeting.

Karen made me coffee in a travel mug, kissed me at the door, said "Be careful driving."

Not "good luck." Not "they'll listen."

Just "be careful."

She knew how this would go.

The drive south on US-131 took two and a half hours in light traffic. I'd made the trip before—budget meetings, training seminars, the occasional coordination with state DNR brass. Never liked Lansing. Too much concrete. Too many buildings. Too far from anything that mattered.

But if the county wouldn't listen, maybe the state would.

I had the presentation on a thumb drive. Printed copies of the final map. Dr. Ostrander's geological survey. Dr. Havelka's veterinary report. Sarah's cultural documentation. Witness statements. Photos. Video evidence. Everything.

Two hundred thirty-seven pages of documentation proving that Antrim County was living on unstable temporal boundaries and needed immediate state intervention.

I'd requested the meeting through official channels. Emergency Management Division. Submitted a formal threat assessment report. Used the words "public safety crisis" and "imminent danger" and "mass casualty potential."

Got a response within six hours: *Meeting scheduled Thursday 9 AM, State Emergency Operations Center, 2800 block of Martin Luther King Jr. Boulevard.*

That fast response should have told me something.

They were taking it seriously.

Or they wanted to shut me down quickly.

The State Emergency Operations Center was a squat concrete building behind the main capitol complex, designed to survive disasters rather than look impressive. Guard shack at the entrance. Badge scanners. Security that made the Bellaire courthouse look like a lemonade stand.

I showed my DNR credentials, signed in, got a visitor badge.

A young woman in business casual—mid-twenties, clipboard, professional smile—met me in the lobby.

"Officer Pritchard? I'm Rebecca Chen, assistant to Director Morrison. He's ready for you in Conference Room B."

I followed her down fluorescent-lit hallways. Beige walls. Motivational posters about preparedness. The smell of burned coffee and stress.

Conference Room B was small. Maybe seats for twelve. Half of them occupied.

Director James Morrison sat at the head of the table. Late fifties, former National Guard, ran State Emergency Management like a military operation. I'd met him once before at a flood response training.

Around the table: two staff from his office, a woman from State Police, a man from DNR headquarters, and someone in a suit I didn't recognize—probably governor's office.

No one smiled.

Morrison gestured to a chair. "Officer Pritchard. Thank you for coming. We've reviewed your threat assessment report. Why don't you walk us through your findings?"

I set up the laptop. Connected to their projector. Pulled up the presentation.

Started the same way I'd started at the town meeting. The incidents. Joe's mastodons. Mel's drowning. Beth's frostbite. The Ring camera bear. Scott's encounter. The horse kill.

For each one, I showed evidence. Let the data speak.

They watched without interrupting. Taking notes. No visible reaction.

Then the geological analysis. The moraine system. The ancient shorelines. The correlation between boundary zones and incident locations.

Dr. Ostrander's survey. The elevation data. The hydrological changes from Lake Algonquin through Nipissing.

The DNR rep—a guy named Stevens I'd never met—asked: "These paleoshorelines are well-documented. What makes you think they're relevant to current incidents?"

"Because every incident occurs at the precise intersection of moraine and paleoshoreline. That's not coincidence."

"It could be selection bias. You're looking for patterns, so you find them."

"The patterns existed before I looked. The Hopewell people marked them three thousand years ago."

I showed Sarah's maps. The burial mounds. The cultural documentation of dangerous sites.

The woman from State Police—Lieutenant Brennan, according to her nameplate—said: "With all respect to indigenous knowledge, this is anecdotal. We need empirical evidence."

"Dr. Havelka's veterinary report is empirical. The bite radius measurements. The wound characteristics. Those are facts."

I showed the horse kill documentation. The photos. The measurements.

Stevens: "One livestock kill doesn't constitute a public safety crisis."

"It's not one incident. It's five confirmed, nineteen probable, and sixty-seven high-probability sites where more will occur."

I showed the final map. The overlay of all data. The red and orange zones covering seventy percent of the county.

Morrison leaned forward. "Officer Pritchard, what exactly are you claiming is happening?"

"Temporal displacement at specific geological boundaries. The past is bleeding through. Extinct animals, environmental conditions from the Pleistocene, and soon Paleo-Indian populations crossing into present-day Michigan."

Silence.

The suit from the governor's office—name tag said Richards—cleared his throat. "You're asking us to believe in time travel."

"I'm asking you to believe the evidence. Call it what you want. Temporal anomaly. Dimensional instability. Geological phenomenon. The label doesn't matter. What matters is that it's happening and it's accelerating."

Morrison: "What's your recommended response?"

"Immediate closure of the sixty-seven highest-risk sites. Evacuation of residents within quarter-mile radius. Emergency protocols for the remaining population. State resources to fence and monitor the boundaries."

"How many people would need to be evacuated?"

"Approximately five thousand."

Richards laughed. Not cruelly. Just... disbelief. "You want us to evacuate five thousand residents of Antrim County based on a theory about glacial moraines and extinct animals?"

"Based on evidence."

"Evidence that could be explained a dozen other ways. The drowning could be a heart attack and fall into water. The frostbite could be exposure. The livestock kill could be a large dog or escaped exotic animal."

"Then explain the bite radius. Seven centimeters. No domestic dog—"

"Maybe she measured wrong."

"Dr. Havelka has been a veterinarian for fifteen years."

"People make mistakes."

Lieutenant Brennan: "What about the video evidence? The mastodons?"

"CGI. Deepfake. Take your pick. Anyone with a laptop can fake that now."

"Joe Macklin isn't tech-savvy enough to fake—"

"He doesn't have to be. Someone else could have done it. Sent it to him. He could be part of a hoax."

I felt my jaw tighten. "Why would he hoax breaking his own axle?"

"Insurance fraud. Attention. Who knows?"

It went on like this for forty minutes.

Every piece of evidence, dismissed.

Every correlation, explained away.

Every witness, questioned.

They weren't hostile. That would have been easier. They were polite. Professional. Rational.

They just didn't believe.

Morrison finally raised a hand. "Officer Pritchard, I appreciate you bringing this to our attention. But I need to be frank. We don't have the resources to respond to every unusual incident. We prioritize based on documented threats. Verifiable risks."

"This is verifiable."

"No. This is unusual. There's a difference."

Stevens, the DNR rep: "We'll send a team to investigate the livestock kill. Get an independent assessment. If there's evidence of an exotic predator or escaped animal, we'll respond accordingly."

"It's not escaped. It's extinct."

"Then there's nothing to respond to, is there?"

Richards, from the governor's office: "Look, I get it. You've had some weird incidents in your county. That's concerning. But asking the state to declare an emergency and evacuate thousands of people based on... this?" He gestured at the presentation. "That's not happening. The governor won't sign off. The legislature won't fund it. And frankly, the public won't accept it."

"The public won't accept it until people start dying."

"Has anyone died?"

"Mel Harrison—"

"Died of drowning. Cause undetermined. That's not a temporal anomaly, that's a tragedy."

"Caused by temporal displacement."

"Or a medical event. Or an accident. Or a dozen other things that don't require rewriting physics."

Morrison stood. Meeting over.

"Officer Pritchard, we'll review your documentation. If we find evidence that warrants state intervention, we'll act. But right now, this appears to be a local matter. Work with your county board. Your sheriff. Coordinate with local resources."

"The county board voted against closing any sites."

"Then that's a county political decision. Not a state emergency."

"People are going to die."

"People die in car accidents. In house fires. In hunting accidents. We can't prevent every tragedy."

"This is preventable. If you'd just—"

"We're done here." Morrison's voice was firm but not unkind. "Thank you for making the drive. We'll be in touch if anything changes."

Rebecca Chen appeared at the door. Meeting definitely over.

I packed up my laptop. My printed documents. My evidence.

No one shook my hand.

In the hallway, Rebecca caught up with me.

"Officer Pritchard, wait."

I turned.

She glanced back at the conference room, lowered her voice. "I believe you."

"Then why didn't you say something?"

"Because I'm an assistant. Nobody cares what I think." She handed me a business card. "But my cousin lives in Bellaire. He's got two kids. He sent me the video of your town hall presentation."

"And?"

"And I grew up hearing stories about the thin places. My grandmother was Odawa. She knew Sarah Ashkwe's family." She looked at me. "You're right. The land remembers. And we built on top of it."

"Can you help?"

"Not officially. But..." She hesitated. "There's someone in the DNR data division who might be interested. Dr. Lisa Park. She studies anomalous wildlife sightings. Cryptozoology, officially. But she's serious. Scientific."

"Will she listen?"

"Maybe. She's ignored by her department because they think she's chasing Bigfoot. But if you've got actual evidence of extinct species..." She shrugged. "Worth a try."

She wrote a name and email on the back of her card.

"Don't tell anyone I sent you."

"I won't."

"And Officer Pritchard? Be careful. If you're right about this, if the boundaries are really failing, it's not going to stop with Antrim County. The whole Great Lakes region has the same geology. The same boundaries."

I hadn't thought about that.

The same moraines ran through Michigan, Wisconsin, Illinois, Indiana, Ohio. The same glacial lakes had covered the entire region. The same burial mounds marked the same dangerous sites.

If Antrim County was just the beginning...

"How many potential sites across the region?" I asked.

"Thousands. Maybe tens of thousands." She looked scared. "The Hopewell culture built mounds from Ohio to Minnesota. All along the glacial boundaries. And we've destroyed most of them."

"Jesus."

"Yeah." She glanced back again. "Go. Before Morrison sees us talking."

I left.

The drive home was worse than the drive down.

I'd failed.

State wouldn't help. County wouldn't help. I had documentation proving the danger and no authority to act on it.

Twenty-two thousand people living on unstable boundaries and nobody willing to protect them.

My phone rang at 11:30 AM, halfway home.

Karen.

"Dave, something happened."

My stomach dropped. "What?"

"I don't know how to explain it. You need to get home."

"What happened?"

"The nature trail. The railroad bridge. The spot I told you felt wrong." Her voice shook. "Someone fell through."

"Through what?"

"Through the bridge. Except the bridge was there. But it also wasn't there. Dave, a woman is in the hospital. She fell twenty feet. Broken leg, head trauma. She says the bridge disappeared while she was on it."

"Who?"

"Linda Morrison. You know her. Works at the library."

"Is she going to be okay?"

"I don't know. But Dave, people saw it. Maybe a dozen people saw the bridge flicker. Saw her fall. It's all over town."

I pressed the accelerator. Started driving faster.

"I'm an hour out. I'll go straight to the hospital."

"Be safe."

"You too. Stay away from that trail."

"I am. Everyone is. They've got it cordoned off now."

I hung up.

Drove faster.

While I'd been in Lansing trying to convince bureaucrats, another incident had happened. Someone had gotten hurt. The thin places were accelerating exactly like the pattern predicted.

And I'd been 150 miles away, unable to stop it.

I made it home in seventy minutes.

Went straight to Munson Medical Center in Traverse City where they'd taken Linda.

Found her family in the waiting room. Her husband Tom—not the Tom Vreeland from the horse kill, different Tom—saw me and stood up.

"Dave. They said you've been investigating this stuff."

"I have. How is she?"

"Broken leg. Concussion. Bruised ribs. She'll live." He looked at me. "But Dave, she fell twenty feet. The bridge was there, then it wasn't, then it was again. A dozen people saw it. This isn't a hoax. This isn't someone's imagination."

"I know."

"Then why isn't anyone doing anything?"

"I tried. The county voted against closing sites. The state won't intervene."

"So what? We just wait until someone dies?"

I didn't have an answer.

He sat back down. Exhausted. Scared.

"Linda goes on that trail every morning. For ten years. Same route. Same time. Never had a problem. This morning the bridge just... wasn't there. For maybe three seconds. Long enough for her to fall."

"Did anyone film it?"

"Yeah. Half a dozen phones. It's already on social media."

"Can you send me the videos?"

He pulled out his phone. Sent me links.

I watched them in the waiting room.

Six different angles of the old railroad bridge. Linda Morrison walking across. Halfway through, the bridge... flickered. Not disappeared. Flickered. Like reality hiccupped. She fell. Hit the ravine floor. The bridge came back.

People screaming. Running to help.

Thirty seconds of chaos.

Then EMTs arriving. Linda being loaded onto a stretcher. The bridge solid and real and completely normal except for thirty feet of broken woman underneath it.

I forwarded the videos to Dr. Ostrander, Dr. Havelka, Sarah. To Rebecca Chen in Lansing. To Commissioner Walsh.

Subject line: "This is what acceleration looks like."

By the time I got home, the bridge incident was all over local news.

"Woman Injured in Mysterious Fall at Bellaire Nature Trail"

"Witnesses Report Bridge 'Disappeared' During Accident"

"Experts Baffled by Railroad Bridge Incident"

The experts weren't baffled. They just didn't believe.

Structural engineer interviewed on camera: "Old bridges can have unexpected failures. She probably stepped on a weak board."

Except the bridge was heavy timbers, it could still support a train.

Physics professor from Michigan State: "Mass hallucination is a documented phenomenon. High-stress situations can cause groups to perceive things that didn't happen."

Except it was on video. From six different angles.

They'd find ways to explain it. They always did.

Until the explanations stopped working.

I went to my office. Updated the map.

Added Linda Morrison's fall. Railroad bridge, elevation 612 feet. Lake Algonquin shoreline. Site of destroyed mound cluster.

Incident number six.

I marked it in red.

Then I calculated time intervals between incidents.

Incident 1 to 2: 4 days Incident 2 to 3: 3 days
Incident 3 to 4: 3 days Incident 4 to 5: 2 days Incident 5 to 6: 2 days

Accelerating.

If the pattern held:

Next incident: 1-2 days Then: Daily Then: Multiple per day

By the end of March, the thin places would be opening constantly.

By April, they'd overlap. Stay open. Stop being incidents and become permanent features.

And we'd be living in a county where past and present existed simultaneously.

Where dire wolves hunted subdivision deer. Where mastodons grazed in parking lots. Where Paleo-Indians walked through Walmart.

Where 22,000 people tried to live normal lives in a place that was no longer exclusively theirs.

My phone buzzed. Email from Dr. Ostrander.

Saw the bridge videos. This is worse than we thought. The folds are lasting longer. Three seconds this time. Next one might be five. Then ten. Eventually they won't close.

I know

What's our plan?

I don't know

Dave. We need a plan.

I looked at the map. At the red and orange zones. At the population numbers. At the acceleration curve.

The plan is to survive what's coming. Because nobody's going to stop it.

Chapter 12

CHAPTER TWELVE: THE MASTODON CALF

The call came in at 6:47 AM Saturday morning.

Dispatch: "Dave, we've got a report of an unusual animal on Highway 31 near Eastport. Caller says it looks like a deformed elephant. Probably escaped from somewhere."

I was already in the truck. Hadn't slept. Had been driving the county all night checking high-probability sites, waiting for the next incident.

"I'm fifteen minutes out. Tell them not to approach it."

"Copy that."

I turned north on 31, toward Torch Lake. Toward Eastport. Toward another red zone on my map.

The location was a hay field on the east side of Highway 31, maybe two miles south of Eastport proper. The kind of open farmland that gave you views of Torch Lake in the distance, the water still gray in the early morning light.

A Chevy Silverado was pulled off on the shoulder, hazards flashing. Man standing beside it, maybe sixty, wearing Carhartt overalls and a feed cap. He waved me down.

I pulled over. Got out.

"You the DNR guy?"

"Dave Pritchard. What are we looking at?"

He pointed across the field. "That."

Two hundred yards out, in the middle of winter-dead hay stubble, stood something wrong.

Brown. Shaggy. Four legs. Trunk.

About the size of a large cow. Maybe five feet at the shoulder. But proportioned all wrong for a cow. Too compact. Too heavy in the front quarters. And that trunk—short, thick, ending in a strange finger-like projection.

"What the hell is that?" the farmer asked.

I pulled out binoculars. Focused.

Juvenile mastodon. *Mammut americanum*. Maybe three years old. Thick rust-brown fur. Small tusks just beginning to show. Ears smaller than a modern elephant. Body built for cold climate, for pushing through forest undergrowth.

It was standing in the middle of the field, swaying slightly. Not moving. Just standing there like it didn't know where it was.

Because it didn't.

"Sir, I need you to stay here. Don't go near it. Don't let anyone else approach."

"Is it dangerous?"

"I don't know. But it's disoriented and probably scared."

"What is it?"

I lowered the binoculars. Looked at him.

"A mastodon. Juvenile. Extinct for eleven thousand years."

He stared at me. Then laughed. "Come on. Really. What is it?"

"I'm serious."

"That's impossible."

"I know."

His laugh died. "You're serious."

"Yes."

"How—"

"Long story. Right now I need to secure the area and figure out how to help it."

I called dispatch. "I need Sheriff Kowalski out here. And Dr. Havelka if she's available. Also need Highway Patrol to close this section of 31. We've got a situation."

"What kind of situation?"

"The kind that's about to go viral if we don't contain it fast."

By the time Sheriff Tom Kowalski arrived twenty minutes later, three more cars had pulled over. People taking photos. Posting to social media.

I tried to keep them back. Tried to explain this was a wildlife incident, stay in your vehicles, give the animal space.

Nobody listened.

One guy—tourist from downstate, expensive camera—kept trying to get closer for better shots.

"Sir, I need you to back up."

"It's just standing there. It's not doing anything."

"It's a wild animal in an unfamiliar environment. It's unpredictable."

"What kind of animal? Some kind of elephant?"

"Mastodon."

He laughed. "Right. And I'm a velociraptor."

Then the mastodon moved.

Not much. Just shifted weight. Took two steps forward. Stopped.

But the movement was wrong. Unsteady. Like it was drunk or sick.

The photographer stopped laughing.

"Is it okay?"

"I don't think so."

Sheriff Kowalski was a practical man. Former Marine. Twenty years in law enforcement. Not easily rattled.

He stood beside me looking at the mastodon through his own binoculars.

"Dave. That's not possible."

"I know."

"But it's there."

"I know."

"What do we do?"

"Contain the area. Keep people back. Try to figure out if it's injured or just disoriented."

"Is it dangerous?"

"Mastodons were herbivores. Browser-grazers. Probably not aggressive unless threatened. But it's three tons of scared animal. So yes, potentially dangerous."

Dr. Havelka pulled up in her truck. Took one look through the binoculars and said exactly what everyone else had said: "That's impossible."

"Can you help it?" I asked.

"Help it how? I'm a veterinarian, not a paleontologist. I don't know the first thing about treating an extinct species."

"But you know mammals. You know stress responses. You know when an animal's in trouble."

She studied it for a long minute. "It's in trouble. Look at the way it's standing. That's not normal posture. And the swaying—that's neurological distress. Either it's sick or it's dying."

"From what?"

"Could be anything. Wrong temperature. Wrong food. Stress from temporal displacement. For all we know, crossing through the boundary is fatal. Maybe the transition damages tissue at a cellular level."

"Can we help it?"

"I don't know. I'd need to get closer. Examine it properly."

"Too dangerous."

"Then we watch it die."

By 9 AM, Highway 31 was closed in both directions. Traffic backed up for miles. Highway Patrol had set up barriers. News vans were arriving from Traverse City, from Petoskey, from downstate.

The story was already everywhere on social media.

#MastodonInMichigan was trending.

Most people thought it was a hoax. CGI. Promotional stunt for a zoo or museum.

But the people who were there, standing on Highway 31 watching a juvenile mastodon sway in a hay field, knew better.

Commissioner Walsh showed up. "Dave, what's the plan?"

"I don't have one."

"We need one. The governor's office is calling. News networks are calling. Everyone wants to know what's happening."

"What's happening is an extinct animal crossed through a temporal boundary and now it's dying in Antrim County and I don't know how to save it."

She was quiet. Then: "Is it really a mastodon?"

"Yes."

"Can you prove it?"

"Look at it."

"I am looking at it. I'm also looking at the national media circus that's about to descend on us. They're going to want proof. Real proof. Not just eyewitness accounts."

"If it dies, we'll have a body. That's proof."

"And if it doesn't die?"

"Then we've got a live Pleistocene megafauna in northern Michigan with no idea how to care for it or where it came from or how to send it back."

The mastodon stood in the field for six hours.

Just stood there. Swaying. Occasionally taking a step or two. Once it tried to use its trunk to pull up some of the dead hay stubble, but it couldn't seem to coordinate the movement properly.

Dr. Havelka watched through binoculars, narrating what she was seeing.

"Muscle tremors in the hindquarters. Probable neurological damage. The trunk movements are uncoordinated—that suggests either brain injury or systemic failure. Temperature regulation is off—see how it's not trying to cool itself? Elephants would be flapping ears, seeking shade. This thing is just standing there like its thermoregulation is broken."

"Is it suffering?" I asked.

"Yes. Definitely suffering."

"Can we do anything?"

"Tranquilize it. Get close enough to examine. Maybe administer fluids, antibiotics, stabilizers. But Dave, I don't know the dosage for a three-ton extinct elephant. I could kill it trying to help it."

"And if we don't help?"

"It dies on its own. Probably within hours."

I looked at Sheriff Kowalski. "Your call. Your jurisdiction."

"My call is I want a vet to help an animal in distress. If it dies anyway, at least we tried."

Dr. Havelka nodded. "I'll need assistance. Someone who knows large animal handling. And we need to clear these civilians back another hundred yards."

By noon, the crowd had grown to maybe two hundred people. News helicopters overhead. TV crews setting up cameras along the highway. Live feeds going out to national networks.

The mastodon was famous.

And dying.

Dr. Havelka prepared a dart with what she hoped was an appropriate dose of tranquilizer. Ketamine and xylazine, same cocktail used for large ungulates. Calculated for three thousand pounds, adjusted down slightly because the animal already seemed lethargic.

She loaded the dart rifle. Approached to within fifty yards.

The mastodon didn't react. Just kept swaying.

She fired.

The dart hit the shoulder. Good placement. The mastodon flinched, turned its head slightly, but didn't run.

We waited.

Five minutes. The swaying slowed. The mastodon's legs wobbled. It went down on its front knees first, then rolled onto its side with a sound like a tree falling.

Dr. Havelka approached slowly. I followed with Sheriff Kowalski.

Up close, it was impossible to deny what it was.

The fur was thick, coarse, rusty brown. The tusks were just beginning to curve upward. The ears were small, cold-adapted. The skull shape wrong for any modern elephant. The molars—when Dr. Havelka checked the mouth—were cusped for browsing, not grinding like modern elephants.

"This is real," she said quietly. "This is actually, genuinely real."

She checked vitals. Heart rate low. Breathing shallow. Temperature below normal for a large mammal.

"It's in shock. Probably has been since it came through. I'm going to start fluids, try to stabilize it."

She worked for an hour. IV lines. Saline. Antibiotics. Warming blankets borrowed from the ambulance standing by.

The mastodon didn't wake up.

Its breathing got shallower.

At 2:47 PM, it stopped breathing entirely.

Dr. Havelka checked for a heartbeat. Waited. Checked again.

"It's gone."

The news crews got everything. The tranquilizer dart. The collapse. Dr. Havelka working to save it. The final breath.

A juvenile mastodon dying in a hay field in northern Michigan while two hundred people watched and millions more watched via live stream.

Proof.

Undeniable, recorded, documented proof.

Sheriff Kowalski immediately secured the body. Ordered a perimeter. No one touches it. No one approaches without authorization.

Commissioner Walsh was on the phone with the governor's office within minutes.

I stood there looking at three tons of extinct megafauna lying in winter-dead hay stubble and felt absolutely nothing.

Not vindication. Not satisfaction. Not even sadness.

Just exhaustion.

I'd been right. The thin places were real. The temporal boundaries were failing.

And now everyone would believe me.

And it wouldn't matter.

Because the mastodon was dead and the boundaries were still failing and more incidents were coming and being right wouldn't save anyone.

By 4 PM, the state had sent a team. Wildlife pathologists. Tissue sample specialists. Someone from Michigan State's paleontology department who kept saying "impossible impossible impossible" while photographing the skull structure.

They loaded the body onto a flatbed truck. Covered it with tarps. Planned to transport it to MSU for full necropsy and analysis.

The news crews followed the truck.

National media was descending. CNN. Fox. MSNBC. Science correspondents. Cryptozoology enthusiasts. Academics demanding to examine the evidence.

The story was everywhere.

"Extinct Mastodon Found in Michigan"

"Ice Age Animal Appears in Northern Michigan, Dies Hours Later"

"Scientists Baffled by Mastodon Discovery"

My phone wouldn't stop ringing. Requests for interviews. Questions from journalists. Demands for statements.

I ignored all of it.

Drove to the site where the mastodon had appeared. The exact spot in the hay field.

Elevation 618 feet. Lake Algonquin shoreline. Moraine intersection. Site of three destroyed burial mounds cleared in 1903.

Red zone on my map.

High probability.

I'd known this spot was dangerous. Had marked it. Had tried to warn people.

And a juvenile mastodon had paid the price for our ignorance.

I found the fold point. The place where it had come through.

The grass was disturbed. Circular pattern. Maybe ten feet in diameter. The earth still warm to the touch.

The boundary had opened here. Stayed open long enough for a young mastodon to wander through. Then closed behind it.

Trapping it eleven thousand years out of time.

In a world with wrong temperatures, wrong plants, wrong everything.

No wonder it died.

Dr. Ostrander called at 5:30 PM.

"Dave. I'm seeing the coverage. Is it real?"

"Yes."

"They're going to want you to explain it."

"I know."

"What are you going to tell them?"

"The truth. That we're living on unstable temporal boundaries. That the incidents are accelerating. That this won't be the last one."

"They'll listen now."

"Maybe. Or they'll treat it like a freak occurrence. One anomaly. Not a pattern."

"The pattern's undeniable."

"People deny undeniable things all the time."

He was quiet. Then: "How long was the fold open?"

"Don't know. Long enough for the mastodon to come through."

"That's longer than the bridge flicker. Three seconds became long enough for a three-ton animal to cross. The boundaries are degrading faster than we thought."

"I know."

"Next incident might be tomorrow."

"Probably."

"What do we do?"

"Survive it. That's all we can do."

I stayed at the field until dark. Until the news crews left. Until the crowds dispersed. Until it was just me and the hay stubble and the circle of disturbed earth where reality had hiccupped.

Karen called at 7:30.

"Come home."

"I can't."

"Yes you can. There's nothing more you can do there tonight."

"A mastodon died, Karen."

"I know. I saw it. Everyone saw it."

"I tried to warn them. Tried to prevent this."

"I know."

"It came through alone. Disoriented. Probably terrified. Died in a world it couldn't understand."

"Dave. Come home."

I looked at the field. At the darkness. At the place where past had met present and failed to survive the meeting.

"I'm coming."

The drive home, my phone buzzed continuously. Texts. Emails. Voice mails.

One from Rebecca in Lansing:

Director Morrison wants to talk to you Monday. State Emergency Management is reconvening. The governor wants a briefing. You were right. I'm sorry we didn't listen.

One from Commissioner Walsh:

County board meeting Tuesday. We're voting again on site closures. This time it'll pass. Call me.

One from Dr. Lisa Park, the cryptozoologist Rebecca had mentioned:

I've been studying anomalous wildlife reports for twelve years. Everyone thought I was crazy. Thank you for the evidence. Can we meet?

Dozens from journalists. From scientists. From people who wanted interviews, statements, explanations.

And one from Sarah Ashkwe:

The animals first. Then the land. Then the people. The mastodon was a warning. Next time it won't die alone.

I pulled into my driveway at 8:15 PM.

Karen met me at the door. Didn't say anything. Just held me.

Inside, Jake and Emma were on the couch, watching news coverage. The mastodon's collapse replayed in slow motion. Dr. Havelka's attempts to save it. The final breath.

"Dad," Emma said quietly. "Everyone believes you now."

"I know."

"That's good, right?"

I looked at the TV. At the images of a dead animal that shouldn't exist. At the proof everyone had demanded.

"No," I said. "It's not good. Because believing it doesn't stop it. And the next one's coming."

"When?"

I pulled out my phone. Looked at the acceleration curve. At the interval calculations.

"Tomorrow. Maybe sooner."

In my office, I updated the map.

Incident seven: Juvenile mastodon. Highway 31 near Eastport. Appeared approximately 6:30 AM. Died 2:47 PM.

Fold duration: Unknown but significantly longer than previous incidents.

First death of a displaced animal.

First incident captured in real-time by national media.

First undeniable proof.

I marked it in red.

Then I calculated the next interval.

Previous pattern: Incident 6 to 7: 36 hours

Projected: Incident 7 to 8: 18-24 hours

Meaning: Sunday evening. Monday morning at latest.

The thin places weren't just opening anymore.

They were staying open longer. Letting larger things through. Refusing to close fast enough.

And the acceleration was exponential.

The news ran all night. Every channel. Every network.

Scientists debating whether the body was real or hoax. (Real, the tissue samples would prove.)

Paleontologists explaining mastodon biology, behavior, extinction timeline.

Physicists attempting to explain temporal displacement. (Failing, mostly.)

Government officials promising investigation. Resources. Answers.

And me. My face on TV. "DNR Officer Dave Pritchard, who first reported unusual incidents in Antrim County two weeks ago."

They made me sound prescient. Heroic. The man who tried to warn everyone.

They didn't mention that everyone had ignored me until an animal died on live television.

At 3 AM, unable to sleep, I sat on the back deck.

The woods were quiet. Normal Michigan quiet.

But somewhere out there, sixty-seven red zones were waiting. Boundaries getting thinner. Folds opening longer. The past pressing against the present like water against a failing dam.

And I knew—absolutely knew—that the mastodon wasn't the worst thing that would come through.

It was just the first thing everyone could see.

The predators were next.

The dire wolves. The short-faced bears. The saber-toothed cats.

And after them, the people.

The People Who Walked With Ice.

The survivors who'd learned to be harder than extinction.

Sarah's warning echoed: *Next time it won't die alone.*

I looked at the woods. At the darkness.

Wondered what was watching back.

Chapter 13

CHAPTER THIRTEEN: MEDIA DESCENDS

By Sunday morning, Bellaire had become a destination.

News vans lined M-88 from the high school to the edge of town. Satellite trucks parked wherever they could find space. Reporters doing stand-ups in front of Shorts Brewing Company, the courthouse, the nature trail where Linda Morrison had fallen through the bridge.

The mastodon's death had gone viral. Not just national—international. BBC. Al Jazeera. Japanese news crews. German television. Everyone wanted the story of the Ice Age animal that had appeared in Michigan and died on camera.

And everyone wanted to be here when the next one happened.

Because everyone assumed there would be a next one.

Shorts Brewing opened at 11 AM and had a line out the door by 11:15. Joe Short—the owner, no relation to Joe Macklin—had called in every available staff member and was still turning people away by noon.

I drove past around 12:30. The parking lot was full. Cars spilling onto side streets. People standing outside with beers, phones out, filming everything.

Toonies Restaurant, two blocks down, had the same problem. The owners had put out a sandwich board: "2 hour wait - sorry!"

Central Lake wasn't any better. The Blue Pelican—a locals' spot that usually did modest Sunday lunch business—had cars backed up onto M-88. I got a text from the owner: *Dave - is this going to last? I'm out of walleye and we're only three hours into service.*

Up at Shanty Creek, perched on that massive pile of glacial debris, The Nest restaurant was packed and the resort hotel had been fully booked since Saturday night. People were paying $300 a night for rooms that usually went for $120, and the resort wasn't complaining.

The economic boom was real.

The chaos was worse.

My phone had been ringing nonstop since the mastodon died.

Interview requests. Speaking engagements. Book deals. Movie rights. A production company wanted to do a documentary. National Geographic wanted exclusive access. The Discovery Channel offered to embed a crew with me for "ongoing coverage of the phenomenon."

I ignored all of it.

Except the call from Director Morrison at State Emergency Management.

That one I had to take.

Monday morning, 8:47 AM, my phone rang. Lansing area code.

"Officer Pritchard, this is Director Morrison. We need to talk."

"About the mastodon."

"About everything. The governor wants a comprehensive briefing. Today. Can you be in Lansing by noon?"

I looked at my schedule. I had three high-probability sites to check. Follow-up interviews with witnesses from the bridge incident. Coordination with Sheriff Kowalski about traffic control.

"I'm in the middle of—"

"This isn't a request. The governor wants answers. The state legislature is demanding action. We need you here."

"I sent you a comprehensive briefing Thursday. You dismissed it."

Silence. Then: "We were wrong. We're taking it seriously now. Noon. State Emergency Operations Center. Don't be late."

He hung up.

I made it to Lansing by 11:45. Same building. Same conference room. Different atmosphere.

The room was full. Director Morrison. Lieutenant Brennan from State Police. Dr. Stevens from DNR headquarters. Rebecca from Morrison's office. And six people I didn't recognize—advisors, scientists, someone from the governor's policy staff.

Morrison didn't waste time.

"Officer Pritchard, walk us through the pattern. Everything. Start from the beginning."

I did. The same presentation I'd given Thursday. The incidents. The geological correlation. The cultural knowledge. The acceleration curve.

This time, nobody interrupted. Nobody dismissed. Nobody laughed.

When I finished, Morrison said: "How many more incidents do you expect?"

"Based on the acceleration pattern, we're looking at daily occurrences by the end of this week. Multiple per day by early April."

"And the folds are staying open longer."

"Yes. The mastodon fold was open long enough for a three-ton animal to cross. That's significantly longer than the bridge flicker."

"What's the worst-case scenario?"

I pulled up the final slide. The one I hadn't shown Thursday because I knew they wouldn't listen.

"Worst case: the folds stop closing. They become permanent. Past and present exist simultaneously at these sites. We have Pleistocene megafauna, environmental conditions, and human populations from eleven thousand years ago sharing the landscape with modern Michigan."

"How many sites?"

"Two hundred ten confirmed high-probability locations in Antrim County alone. If the pattern extends to the entire Great Lakes region—and geologically, it should—we're looking at thousands. Maybe tens of thousands."

The room was silent.

Then someone from the governor's office—a woman named Hartwell—said: "What do you recommend?"

"Immediate evacuation of the sixty-seven highest-risk sites. Emergency protocols for remaining population. State resources to fence and monitor boundaries. Research team to study the phenomenon and develop countermeasures."

"Countermeasures to what? Time travel?"

"Countermeasures to geological boundary failure. Whatever's causing this—whether it's removal of burial mounds, isostatic rebound, climate change affecting ancient lake beds—we need to understand it. And we need to protect people while we figure it out."

Morrison leaned forward. "Officer Pritchard, you're asking for a response that would cost hundreds of millions of dollars, displace thousands of people, and require declaring a state of emergency based on a phenomenon that science can't explain."

"Yes."

"The political reality is that won't happen. Not unless we have more deaths. More proof. The mastodon was compelling, but it's one incident."

"It's incident number seven. There have been—"

"One incident that the public saw. That the media documented. Everything else is anecdotal. Witness statements. Circumstantial evidence."

I stared at him. "You saw the bridge videos. You saw Linda Morrison fall. You've read Dr. Havelka's report on the horse kill."

"And we're taking it seriously. But the governor needs consensus from the legislature. The legislature needs constituent support. And right now, the public thinks this is interesting, not dangerous."

"Someone's going to die."

"Probably. And when they do, we'll have the political capital to act."

The casual certainty in his voice made my stomach turn.

"So we wait for a body count."

"We prepare for a response while gathering more evidence. In the meantime, we're assigning a state team to work with you. Wildlife specialists. Geologists. Emergency management coordinators."

"I don't need coordinators. I need resources to close the high-risk sites."

"Which we'll provide when we have the authority to do so."

The meeting lasted two more hours. Plans. Protocols. Response frameworks. All theoretical. All contingent on "when we have more evidence."

Which meant when more people got hurt.

I was walking out when Rebecca caught up with me in the hallway.

"Officer Pritchard, wait."

I turned.

"I wanted to tell you—off the record—you did everything right. You warned us. You provided evidence. You followed procedure. What happens next isn't your fault."

"Feels like it is."

"It's not. You can't force people to believe the truth until they're ready."

"And how many people die while they're getting ready?"

She didn't have an answer.

I was halfway back to Bellaire when Director Morrison called again.

"Officer Pritchard, I have an update."

"What now?"

"The governor's office has requested you take administrative leave. Effective immediately."

I nearly swerved off the road. "What?"

"You're under significant media pressure. Your judgment is being questioned. The department feels you need time to—"

"My judgment is being questioned? I've been right about everything!"

"That's not the issue. The issue is your profile. You're the public face of this phenomenon. Every news story mentions you. Every interview request goes to you. It's becoming a distraction."

"A distraction from what?"

"From allowing the state to manage this situation appropriately."

I understood. They wanted control of the narrative. Wanted their own experts, their own spokespeople, their own timeline.

And I was in the way.

"How long?" I asked.

"Two weeks. Paid leave. We'll reassess based on developments."

"There's going to be another incident in the next twenty-four hours. Maybe sooner. You're benching me right when—"

"We have qualified personnel who can respond. You've done excellent work documenting the pattern. Now let others handle the response."

"Others who ignored me until an animal died on TV."

"Officer Pritchard—"

"I'll take the leave. But when the next person gets hurt, when the next predator comes through, when the boundaries fail completely—that's on you. Not me."

I hung up.

By the time I got home, the news was everywhere.

"DNR Officer Suspended Amid Mastodon Investigation"

"State Takes Over Thin Places Response"

"Questions Raised About Officer Pritchard's Claims"

They weren't calling me wrong. They were calling me "overzealous." "Emotionally invested." "Lacking objectivity."

The subtext was clear: he cares too much, trust the professionals.

Never mind that I was a professional. That I'd been right. That I'd tried to prevent exactly what was happening.

Karen found me in the office, staring at news coverage.

"They suspended you."

"Administrative leave. Two weeks."

"Can they do that?"

"Apparently."

She sat down. "What are you going to do?"

"I don't know. I can't respond to incidents. Can't access DNR resources. Can't officially warn anyone."

"But you still have the data. The maps. The research."

"For what? Nobody listened when I had authority. Why would they listen now?"

"Because you've been right. And you'll keep being right. And eventually people will want answers from the person who saw it coming."

That night, the news ran segments about the "Bellaire Phenomenon."

Experts debating whether the mastodon was real or elaborate hoax. (The tissue samples from MSU would prove it was real, but the results weren't back yet.)

Tourists flooding northern Michigan hoping to see the next incident.

Economic impact on local businesses.

And speculation about what would happen next.

One scientist—a physicist from MIT—suggested the folds were "quantum fluctuations in spacetime, possibly related to gravitational anomalies from ancient glacial mass."

He was wrong, but at least he was trying.

Another expert—a geologist from University of Michigan—dismissed the whole thing as "hysteria and misidentification. The mastodon was probably an Asian elephant with a genetic deformity."

Three tons of genetic deformity that matched *Mammut americanum* skeletal structure perfectly. Sure.

The news loved the controversy. The debate. The mystery.

They didn't care about the danger.

Jake came home Tuesday afternoon. Drove up from East Lansing. Walked into my office and said, "Dad, I saw the news. Are you okay?"

"No."

"What can I do?"

"Nothing. There's nothing anyone can do. We wait for the next incident. Hope nobody dies. And prove I was right in the worst possible way."

"You've been right about everything so far."

"Being right doesn't stop it."

Emma appeared in the doorway. "Dad, my friends are asking if you're in trouble."

"I'm on leave. Not fired. Not in trouble. Just... benched."

"Because you told the truth?"

"Because the truth was inconvenient."

She looked at me with an expression I'd never seen before. Not worry. Not sympathy.

Anger.

"That's bullshit," she said quietly.

"Emma—"

"No, it is. You tried to warn everyone. You showed them evidence. You did everything right. And they ignored you until something died. And now they're punishing you for being right." She shook her head. "That's complete bullshit."

Karen appeared behind her. "Emma, language."

"Mom, it's true though."

"I know it is. But your father doesn't need us to be angry. He needs us to support him."

"I am supporting him. By being pissed off on his behalf since he's too tired to be pissed off himself."

She wasn't wrong.

Tuesday night, I sat on the back deck with a beer, watching the woods.

The media circus continued. News helicopters flying over Bellaire. Reporters staking out high-probability sites. Tourists wandering areas that should have been cordoned off months ago.

And somewhere out there, the boundaries were thinning. The folds opening. The past pressing closer.

Incident eight was coming.

I could feel it.

Not psychic intuition. Just pattern recognition. The acceleration curve. The interval calculations.

Eighteen to twenty-four hours from the mastodon meant sometime today.

And I was on administrative leave. Couldn't respond. Couldn't warn anyone. Couldn't do anything except watch it happen.

My phone buzzed. Text from Dr. Ostrander.

Seismic monitoring showing unusual readings near Torch Lake. Low-frequency vibrations. Could be related to boundary instability.

Where exactly?

East shore. Near the 620-foot elevation contour.

Lake Algonquin shoreline. High-probability zone.

Anyone near the area?

Shanty Creek Resort is half a mile away. Still fully booked.

I looked at the time. 9:47 PM.

If the seismic readings were right, if something was building near Torch Lake, we had maybe hours before the next fold opened.

And I couldn't do anything about it.

I texted Sheriff Kowalski.

Tom - Dave. I know I'm on leave but we might have an incident developing near Torch Lake east shore. Can you have a deputy check the area?

Three minutes later: *Dave, I've been told by the state to coordinate through their team, not with you. Sorry.*

I texted Dr. Havelka.

Rachel - seismic activity near Torch Lake. Might be a fold opening. Can you be on standby?

Her response: *I've been instructed to work through state wildlife division. They've assigned their own vets. I'm sorry Dave.*

They'd cut me off. Completely.

I was alone with the data and no way to act on it.

I went inside. To my office. To the maps and the monitoring equipment I'd set up.

The seismic readings were getting stronger. Low-frequency vibrations. The kind that indicated geological stress. Boundary displacement.

A fold was opening.

And two hundred tourists were sleeping at Shanty Creek Resort half a mile away.

I grabbed my keys.

Karen appeared in the doorway. "Where are you going?"

"Torch Lake."

"You're on leave."

"I know."

"If you respond to an incident, they could fire you."

"I know that too."

"Dave—"

"I can't sit here and watch people get hurt because the state wants to control the narrative. I'm going."

She looked at me for a long moment. Then grabbed her own keys.

"I'm driving. You're exhausted. And if you're going to get fired for doing the right thing, at least don't get fired for falling asleep at the wheel."

We drove west on 593, toward Torch Lake. Toward the east shore. Toward the seismic readings that were still getting stronger, close to the Nipissing embankment at its highest point.

I had no authority. No official standing. No backup.

Just data. And the certainty that something was about to happen.

And two hundred people sleeping in a resort built on a giant pile of glacial debris didn't know they were about to wake up to the Pleistocene.

Chapter 14

CHAPTER FOURTEEN: THE HUNTERS *(REVISED)*

We were five miles from Torch Lake when Karen's phone rang through the truck's speakers.

Emma's voice, breathless: "Mom, Dad, there's something on the scanner. Someone found a guy on Barnes Road near Shanty Creek. He's hurt bad. Keeps saying something took his friend."

I grabbed my phone, pulled up the seismic data. The readings near Torch Lake had spiked fifteen minutes ago, then dropped back to baseline.

A fold had opened.

And closed.

"Emma, is the guy still alive?"

"Yeah, but EMTs are saying his injuries are really weird. Like animal attack but worse."

Karen looked at me. "Barnes Road?"

"Half a mile from where the seismic readings spiked." I pulled up the map on my phone. Barnes Road ran along the east shore of Torch

Lake, right through a red zone. Elevation 622 feet. Lake Algonquin shoreline. Moraine intersection.

Site of four destroyed burial mounds.

"Drive faster," I said.

We found the scene at 10:34 PM.

Two EMT trucks, lights flashing. A sheriff's deputy's vehicle. A white Jeep Gladiator with Central Lake Fire/Rescue decals. And a small crowd of people from Shanty Creek Resort who'd heard the commotion on a scanner and raced over, cars parked along the road.

The injured man was on a stretcher, EMTs working on him under portable lights. Even from thirty yards away I could see the blood.

Sheriff Kowalski was there, talking to witnesses. He saw me approaching and held up a hand.

"Dave, you're on leave. You can't be here."

"I know. But I have data that might help. Seismic readings showed a fold opening here twenty minutes ago."

"The state team is handling—"

"Where are they?"

He didn't answer. Because they weren't here. Probably still in Traverse City, forty-five minutes away, coordinating through proper channels while a man bled out on Barnes Road.

I walked past him.

Len Greenland was working on the injured man, pressure bandages on the guy's destroyed right arm. He looked up, saw me, and something passed between us. Recognition. Shared knowledge.

"Dave. Thank god, and what." He gestured at the arm. "This guy needs a hospital but he won't stop trying to get up. Keeps saying we have to go back for his friend."

The injured man was maybe forty-five, wearing hunting camo, face pale from blood loss and shock. His right arm was destroyed. Not broken. Not cut. Destroyed. Deep parallel lacerations from shoulder to elbow, like something with massive claws had raked down his arm while he was running away.

The wounds were still bleeding despite pressure bandages.

"Sir, I'm Dave Pritchard, DNR. What happened?"

His eyes found mine. Lucid despite the shock. Desperate.

"George. We have to get George. He's still in there."

"In where?"

"The—the place. The ice place. The cold." He tried to sit up. Len pushed him back down. "We were hunting. Following deer tracks. Then everything changed. It got cold. Really cold. And there was ice. Everywhere. And that thing—"

"What thing?"

"Lion. Huge. Bigger than any cat I've ever seen. Tan colored. Massive shoulders." His voice broke. "It came out of nowhere. George ran. I ran. It got George. Grabbed him. I heard him screaming and I—I kept running. I'm sorry. I kept running."

"You made it out. Where's George now?"

"Still there. In the ice place. It took him. Dragged him away. We have to go back. We have to—"

"Sir, the fold closed. Whatever you saw, wherever you were, it's not there anymore."

"No. No, George is there. He's waiting. We can't leave him."

Len caught my eye. Shook his head slightly. The man was going into shock. Trauma response. He needed to get him to the hospital.

"What's your name?" I asked.

"Paul. Paul Henderson."

Bill Henderson's brother. I'd met him a few times. Solid guy. Not prone to hysteria or exaggeration.

"Paul, I believe you. But right now you need medical attention. Let them take you to the hospital. I'll find George."

"You promise?"

I couldn't promise. George was either dead or trapped eleven thousand years in the past. But Paul needed something to hold onto.

"I promise I'll look."

They loaded him into the ambulance. Len gave me a quick rundown while his partner got the IV started.

"Defensive wounds on his left forearm. Deep lacerations on his right arm. Pattern suggests large clawed predator. Spacing between the claw marks is..." He paused, met my eyes. "Dave, it's wider than any modern cat. Like those tracks we found in Joe's valley, and what."

"I know."

"The thing that made the mastodon tracks. It's related."

"Different species. American lion. Bigger than what we saw. But yeah—same era, and what."

Len looked at Paul, at his shredded arm, then back at me. "Joe and I... we told people what we saw. Nobody believed us. Said we were mistaken. Seeing things."

"I know the feeling."

"But this..." He gestured at the wounds. "This is real. This happened. And there's going to be more, and what."

"Yes."

"What do we do?"

"Survive it. That's all we can do."

The ambulance pulled away, lights and sirens fading toward Traverse City.

I turned to the scene.

Sheriff Kowalski was keeping the crowd back, but phones were out. People filming. Posting to social media.

The news crews would be here within the hour.

I walked to where Paul had been found. The spot where he'd stumbled out of the fold.

The ground was disturbed. Scuff marks. Blood trail leading from the tree line. And something else.

Frost.

In 50-degree weather, there was frost on the ground. A circular pattern maybe eight feet in diameter, already melting but still visible under my flashlight.

The fold point.

I followed the blood trail backward, into the trees. Twenty yards in, I found where it had happened.

More blood. A lot of it. Drag marks in the soft earth. And tracks.

Four-toed. Massive. The stride length suggested something running fast. The depth suggested enormous weight.

American lion. No question.

And leading away from the kill site, another set of tracks. Smaller. Human boots. Running. Paul's tracks, heading back toward the fold point.

But no tracks for George.

Because George hadn't made it back.

I found his rifle fifteen yards from the kill site. Dropped in the undergrowth. I picked it up carefully, checked the chamber.

Unfired.

Whatever had happened, it happened too fast for George to shoot.

I kept searching. Found George's backpack. His water bottle. His hunter's orange vest, torn and bloody.

But no body.

Because the body was on the other side. In the Pleistocene. Where an American lion had dragged it away to feed.

I heard footsteps behind me. Turned.

Karen stood there, flashlight in hand.

"Did you find him?"

"No. He's gone. On the other side."

"Can we get him back?"

"The fold's closed. Even if it opens again, even if we could go throu gh..." I gestured at the drag marks. "He didn't make it out for a reason."

She looked at the blood. The torn vest. The evidence of violence.

"How do we tell his family?"

"I don't know."

We stood there in the dark woods, surrounded by evidence of a death that occurred eleven thousand years ago and twenty minutes ago simultaneously.

My phone buzzed. Text from Dr. Ostrander.

Seismic readings show the fold was open for approximately four minutes. Longest duration yet.

Four minutes. Long enough for two hunters to stumble through. Long enough for a predator to hunt them. Long enough for one to escape and one to be taken.

Long enough for George Henderson to die in the wrong time period.

I texted back: *Confirm location: Barnes Road, Torch Lake east shore, elevation 622 feet*

Confirmed. Right on the Nipissing embankment. Lake Algonquin shoreline intersection.

Of course it was.

By the time Karen and I walked back to the road, the state team had arrived.

Three vehicles. Wildlife specialists. A geologist I didn't recognize. Someone from Emergency Management with a clipboard and a bad attitude.

The lead investigator—a man in his fifties wearing a DNR jacket—walked up to me.

"Officer Pritchard. I'm Agent Walsh, State Wildlife Division. I'll need you to step back from the scene."

"I've already documented—"

"This is now a state investigation. You're on administrative leave. You need to leave."

"There's a man missing. George Henderson. He's—"

"We're aware. We'll conduct a search at first light."

"He's not here. He's eleven thousand years in the past. The fold closed behind him."

Agent Walsh looked at me like I was delusional. "We'll conduct a thorough search. If we don't find him, we'll expand the parameters."

"You won't find him. The tracks lead into the fold point and don't come out. He's gone."

"Officer Pritchard, I understand you've been under significant stress. But we need to follow proper protocol. That means search and rescue procedures, not speculation about temporal displacement."

"It's not speculation. Look at the frost pattern. Look at the tracks. Look at the—"

"Officer. Leave. Now. Or I'll have the sheriff escort you out."

Sheriff Kowalski stepped forward. "Dave. Come on. Let them do their job."

"Their job? They don't understand what they're looking at."

"Maybe not. But you're not supposed to be here anyway."

Karen took my arm. "Dave. Let's go."

I looked at Agent Walsh. At his team, setting up lights and equipment to search for a body that wasn't there. At the proper protocol that would waste hours and find nothing.

"When you don't find him," I said quietly, "when your search comes up empty and the family demands answers, you know where to find me."

I walked away.

In the truck, driving back toward Bellaire, Karen said: "You did everything you could."

"I found evidence of his death. That's not the same as doing everything I could."

"You couldn't save him. He was already gone before you even knew about it."

"I could have prevented it. If they'd listened months ago. If they'd closed the sites. If they'd taken this seriously before people started dying."

"This isn't on you."

"Tell that to George's family."

My phone rang. Bill Henderson. Paul's brother. George's brother.

I didn't want to answer. But I had to.

"Bill."

"Dave, I just heard about Paul. Is it true? Is George missing?"

"Yes."

"What happened?"

I took a breath. "They were hunting near Torch Lake. A temporal fold opened. They crossed through without realizing it. There was a predator on the other side. American lion. Extinct species. It attacked. Paul made it back. George didn't."

Silence. Long silence.

Then: "Is my brother dead?"

"I don't know for certain. But the evidence suggests yes."

"Where's his body?"

"On the other side of the fold. In the Pleistocene. The fold closed behind him."

"So we can't recover him."

"No. I'm sorry."

More silence. I could hear him breathing. Processing.

"This is what you tried to warn us about. At the town meeting. The county board meeting. All of it."

"Yes."

"And we didn't listen."

"No."

"Goddammit." His voice broke. "Goddammit, Dave, you told us. You showed us the maps. The sites. Everything. And we voted against closing them because we thought you were crazy."

"Bill—"

"My brother is dead because we didn't listen to you."

"Your brother is dead because an extinct predator killed him in a temporal boundary we don't understand. That's not your fault."

"Feels like it is."

I didn't have a response to that.

Bill hung up.

We got home around midnight.

The house was dark except for the office light. Jake was up, monitoring news coverage on his laptop.

"Dad, it's everywhere. Social media is exploding. Someone posted video of the EMTs treating Paul. You can see his arm. People are saying it's an animal attack. Others are saying it's connected to the mastodon."

"It is connected."

"Where's the other guy? George?"

"Dead. Probably. On the other side of a fold that closed four minutes after it opened."

Emma appeared in the doorway, wrapped in a blanket. "Someone died?"

"Yes."

"Because of the thin places?"

"Yes."

She sat down on the couch. Pulled the blanket tighter. "How many more people are going to die?"

I looked at the map on my office wall. At the sixty-seven red zones. At the acceleration curve showing daily incidents by the end of the week.

"I don't know. Too many."

I spent the rest of the night documenting everything. Photos of the scene. Measurements of the tracks. The frost pattern. Paul's testimony. George's abandoned gear.

Incident number eight: Two hunters enter fold near Barnes Road, Torch Lake. One killed by *Panthera atrox*. Body remains in Pleistocene. Fold duration: four minutes.

First confirmed human death from temporal displacement.

First missing person who can't be recovered.

First family destroyed by something that shouldn't exist.

I updated the acceleration curve.

Incident 7 to 8: 36 hours.

Next incident projected: 18-24 hours.

Meaning tomorrow. Tuesday evening at latest.

And I was still suspended. Still cut off from resources. Still unable to officially respond.

The state team would conduct their search. Find nothing. Write a report saying George Henderson disappeared under unknown circumstances.

And his body would remain eleven thousand years in the past, dragged away by a lion that hunted the Pleistocene, unrecoverable and unmourned except by the people who knew the truth.

At 3 AM, I gave up trying to sleep.

Went out to the back deck with coffee, watching the woods.

Somewhere out there, two hundred nine thin places were waiting. Boundaries getting weaker. Folds opening longer. Four minutes this time. Maybe six minutes next time. Maybe ten.

Eventually they'd stop closing at all.

And we'd be living in a world where past and present existed simultaneously. Where American lions hunted subdivision deer. Where mastodons grazed in parking lots. Where you could step off a hiking trail and fall through time into an ice field that would kill you before you understood what happened.

My phone buzzed. Text from Sarah Ashkwe.

I heard about the hunters. I'm sorry.

Me too

The people are coming next. The ones who walked with ice. They won't be prey like the mastodon. They won't be confused like George. They'll be survivors. Be ready.

Ready for what?

For humans who think you're the intruder. For people who survived the extinction by being harder than everything that tried to kill them. For ancestors who don't recognize you as kin.

I looked at the dark woods.

Thought about the Paleo-Indians. The small bands who'd lived through the Younger Dryas. Who'd watched thirty-three genera of megafauna go extinct. Who'd adapted, survived, endured.

They'd hunted mammoths with atlatls. Fought short-faced bears with stone points. Lived in a world where everything was trying to kill them.

And they'd won.

Now they were coming through the folds. Into a world they wouldn't understand. Where their hunting grounds were covered with buildings and roads and people who had no idea how to survive what was coming.

Sarah was right.

The animals had been first. The mastodon, confused and dying.

The predators had been second. The lion, hunting efficiently.

The people were next.

And unlike the mastodon, unlike the lion, the Paleo-Indians wouldn't be passive victims of temporal displacement.

They'd be active participants in a world they no longer recognized.

Survivors in a time that wasn't theirs.

And we were about to find out what happens when two human populations—separated by eleven thousand years of evolution, culture, and understanding—tried to share the same space.

Chapter 15

CHAPTER FIFTEEN: JAKE'S DATA

Jake came home Wednesday afternoon driving like the world was ending.

I was on the back deck when I heard his Subaru screaming up the driveway, gravel spraying. He didn't even shut the engine off properly—just parked crooked, grabbed his laptop bag, and ran for the house.

Karen met him at the door. "Jake, what's wrong?"

"Where's Dad?"

"Deck. What—"

He was already past her, through the house, sliding the deck door open so hard it banged against the frame.

"Dad. I need you to look at something. Right now."

I set down my coffee. "You drove two hours for—"

"I didn't sleep last night. I've been running models since the mastodon died. Then George Henderson. Then I got access to Dr. Pemberton's equipment at MSU—he's my geology professor, he let me use the seismology lab—and Dad, the folds aren't random."

He pulled out his laptop, opened it on the deck table. The screen showed graphs, data plots, mathematical models I barely recognized.

"They're following a pattern. A specific, predictable, mathematical pattern."

Karen brought out more coffee. Emma appeared, curious. We sat around the deck table while Jake walked us through it.

"Okay. Start from the beginning. Incident one: Joe's mastodon valley. What time did it happen?"

I pulled up my notes. "6:23 AM, March 3rd."

Jake typed. "Incident two: Mel's drowning. Time?"

"Approximately 11:15 PM, March 7th."

He kept going through all eight incidents, plotting them on a timeline. Time of day. Date. Duration when known. Location coordinates. Elevation.

Then he opened another program. "Now watch."

The data points appeared on a graph. Time on the X-axis. Fold duration on the Y-axis. Scattered points that looked random.

Then Jake hit a key and a curve appeared.

Perfect exponential growth.

"The duration is increasing at a predictable rate. It's not chaos. It's a function. And if it's a function, I can calculate future values."

He pulled up another graph. "Now look at the timing intervals between incidents."

Incident 1 to 2: 4 days Incident 2 to 3: 3 days Incident 3 to 4: 3 days Incident 4 to 5: 2 days Incident 5 to 6: 2 days Incident 6 to 7: 1.5 days Incident 7 to 8: 1.5 days

"Another exponential decay curve. The interval between incidents is decreasing at a predictable rate."

Emma leaned forward. "So you can predict when the next one will happen?"

"Better than that. I can predict when ALL of them will happen. Watch."

He ran the model forward. The graph extended, showing projected incidents marching into the future. Each one closer together. Each one lasting longer.

By April 1st, the model showed incidents happening every six hours.

By April 15th, every hour.

By May 1st, continuous. Overlapping. No gaps between them.

"The folds will stop closing," Jake said. "Permanently. Probably by early May. And then past and present exist simultaneously at every thin place in the county."

Karen was pale. "Can this be right?"

"I've run it six different ways. Different algorithms. Different data sets. It's consistent. The pattern is real."

"There's more," Jake said. He pulled up another screen. "Dr. Pemberton let me access the seismology lab's monitoring network. They have sensors all over northern Michigan. I went back through the data for the past month."

He showed us seismograph readings. "Every fold opening generates a specific seismic signature. Low-frequency vibrations. Between 0.5 and 2 Hz. Too low for most people to feel, but the equipment picks it up."

He zoomed in on the mastodon incident. "See? Spike at 10:17 PM Sunday. That's when the fold opened. Duration: approximately six minutes based on the signature. Then it drops back to baseline. Fold closed."

"You can measure how long they're open?"

"Yes. And look at this." He pulled up all eight incidents, overlaid the seismic data.

Incident 1: 90 seconds Incident 2: 2 minutes Incident 3: 2.5 minutes Incident 4: 3 minutes Incident 5: 3 minutes Incident 6: 3 seconds (the bridge flicker) Incident 7: 6 minutes (mastodon) Incident 8: 4 minutes (hunters)

"Wait," I said. "The bridge was only three seconds but it's between longer incidents?"

"Anomaly. Or maybe we're seeing two different types of folds. Short flickers versus sustained openings. I don't know yet. But the overall trend is clear—duration is increasing."

He ran the projection forward. "By April, folds will be staying open for thirty minutes. By late April, hours. By May—"

"Forever," Karen said quietly.

"Yes."

"There's something else," Jake said. He looked at me. "I found a correlation you missed."

"What correlation?"

"Lunar cycle."

He pulled up a moon phase calendar, overlaid it with the incident timeline.

Every single incident occurred within 72 hours of either a new moon or full moon. Periods of maximum tidal force.

"The moon affects tides. Ocean tides, lake tides, even earth tides—the planet itself flexes slightly under lunar gravitational pull. Not much. Centimeters. But at geological boundaries that are already unstable..."

"The tidal stress triggers the folds," I said.

"Or makes them more likely. I can't prove causation. But the correlation is undeniable. And Dad, there's a full moon Friday night."

Two days from now.

"How many incidents do you predict for the full moon period?"

He ran the calculation. "Based on the acceleration curve and lunar correlation, between four and seven incidents during the 72-hour window around Friday's full moon. Multiple folds opening simultaneously across different sites."

"Jesus."

"And they'll all be longer duration than anything we've seen. Probably ten to fifteen minutes each. Long enough for..." He trailed off.

Long enough for megafauna to cross through. Long enough for predators to establish territory. Long enough for Paleo-Indians to realize they're not in their own time anymore.

Emma was looking at the graphs. "Can you predict where they'll happen?"

"Working on it. I need more data on the geological features. Dr. Ostrander's moraine survey helps, but I need elevation data, soil composition, historical lake levels. Dr. Pemberton's putting me in touch with a colleague at University of Michigan who studies glacial rebound."

"Isostatic rebound," I said. "The land rising after the ice melted."

"Right. The weight of the glaciers compressed the earth. When the ice melted, the land started rising. And it's still rising. Slowly. Maybe a few centimeters per century. But at boundary points where moraine meets ancient shoreline, that movement creates stress. Micro-fissures in the geological substrate."

"And those fissures are where the folds open."

"Maybe. It's a hypothesis. But if I'm right, I can map the highest-stress points and predict which sites are most likely to fold during the full moon."

Karen looked at him. "Jake, this is the kind of analysis the state should be doing."

"The state doesn't believe it's real. Or they do believe it but don't want to admit it publicly. Either way, they're not doing the science."

He looked at me. "Dad, you gave them the evidence. They ignored you. So I'm doing what they should have done. Actual rigorous analysis."

"Have you shown this to anyone?"

"Dr. Pemberton. He thinks it's fascinating. Wants to co-author a paper if the predictions hold. But he's also cautious. He won't go public until we have more confirmation."

"Smart man."

"But Dad, we don't have time to wait for academic peer review. The full moon is Friday. If I'm right, we're going to have multiple folds opening simultaneously. People need to know."

"The people who matter won't listen. I tried."

"Then we warn the people who will listen. The hunters. The hikers. The families living near high-probability sites. We can't evacuate everyone, but we can get some people out of harm's way."

I looked at Jake's data. At the exponential curves. At the lunar correlation. At the projection showing continuous folds by May.

My son had done in three days what the state team hadn't done in two weeks. Applied actual science. Found patterns. Made predictions.

And if he was right—and everything I'd seen suggested he was—Friday was going to be catastrophic.

"Show me the highest-probability sites for Friday," I said.

He pulled up a map. Red dots scattered across Antrim County. His predicted fold points based on geological stress, lunar correlation, and the acceleration pattern.

Seventeen high-probability locations.

I cross-referenced with my own map. With the thin places Sarah had marked. With Dr. Ostrander's moraine survey.

Fifteen of Jake's seventeen predictions matched known thin places.

The other two were sites I hadn't identified yet. New locations that Jake's model said would fold for the first time Friday night.

"This is good work," I said. "Really good work."

"Thanks. But Dad, what do we do with it? You're suspended. The state won't listen. The county thinks you're overreacting."

I looked at the map. At seventeen sites that would probably open simultaneously during the full moon. At the potential for dozens of people to cross through, or dozens of Pleistocene animals to cross into modern Michigan, or both.

"We warn people anyway," I said. "I don't care if they listen. I don't care if they think I'm crazy. We identify every family, every business, every residence within a quarter mile of these seventeen sites and we tell them: get out Friday night. Go somewhere else. Stay away from the boundaries."

"And if they don't listen?"

"Then at least we tried."

Karen was already pulling up property records on her laptop. "I can cross-reference addresses with Jake's sites. Make a list of who needs to be contacted."

Emma grabbed her phone. "I'll text my friends. Tell them to spread the word. Stay away from these areas Friday."

Jake pulled up a satellite view. "I can create a detailed map. Show exact boundaries. Upload it to social media. Make it as public as possible."

We spent the next three hours building the warning system.

Karen identified 147 residential properties within the danger zones. Jake mapped precise coordinates for each site. Emma drafted social media posts with maps and clear warnings. I started making phone calls.

Most people hung up on me. Some listened politely and ignored me. A few—people who'd been at the town meeting, people who'd seen the mastodon die, people who knew George Henderson—those people took it seriously.

By 7 PM, we'd contacted maybe forty percent of the at-risk population.

Not enough.

But something.

Dr. Ostrander called at 8 PM.

"Dave, I saw Jake's analysis. He sent it to me. It's brilliant."

"He gets his brains from Karen."

"The lunar correlation explains so much. The timing. The clustering. I should have seen it."

"You weren't looking for it. None of us were."

"But Dave, if he's right about Friday, if we get multiple simultaneous folds..." He trailed off. "The system can't handle it. Emergency services can't respond to seventeen incidents at once. We don't have the personnel. The equipment. The training."

"I know."

"People are going to die."

"I know."

"What are you going to do?"

I looked at Jake's map. At the seventeen red dots. At my family working to warn as many people as possible.

"Whatever I can. Even if it's not enough."

At 9 PM, my phone rang. Unknown number.

"Officer Pritchard? This is Dr. Lisa Park. Rebecca gave me your contact information. I study anomalous wildlife phenomena for DNR research division."

The cryptozoologist Rebecca had mentioned in Lansing.

"Dr. Park. What can I do for you?"

"I've been following the Antrim County incidents. The mastodon. The livestock kills. The bridge collapse. And I've been analyzing similar reports from across the Great Lakes region going back twenty years."

"Similar how?"

"Sightings of extinct megafauna. Environmental anomalies. Temporal displacement reports that were dismissed as hoaxes or misidentification. There's a pattern, Officer Pritchard. And it's not limited to Antrim County."

"Where else?"

"Wisconsin. Illinois. Indiana. Ohio. Anywhere the Lake Border Moraine intersects with glacial lake shorelines. I have documented reports from forty-three locations across five states."

Forty-three locations.

"How long has this been happening?"

"The earliest report I found was from 1987. A farmer in Wisconsin claimed he saw a mastodon in his field. It was there for maybe thirty seconds, then vanished. Everyone thought he was drunk. But he took a photo. Polaroid. Blurry but... it's consistent with *Mammut americanum*."

"You think the folds have been opening for forty years?"

"Opening and closing. Brief flickers. Seconds. Maybe a minute. Not long enough to cause major incidents. Not long enough for anyone to take seriously. But yes. I think this has been building for decades."

"And now?"

"Now the flickers are becoming sustained openings. The boundaries are failing. And Antrim County is just the first place where it's become undeniable."

I thought about Jake's data. About the acceleration curve. About folds that used to last ninety seconds now lasting six minutes.

"If the pattern extends to other locations," I said slowly, "if the entire Great Lakes region has the same geological instability..."

"Then what's happening in Antrim County will happen everywhere. Wisconsin. Illinois. All of it. Probably within months."

"How many potential thin places across the region?"

"Based on my analysis? Thousands. The Hopewell culture built burial mounds across the entire Great Lakes and Ohio River valley. Tens of thousands of mounds. Most destroyed. And every destroyed mound is a potential boundary failure point."

Thousands of thin places.

Across five states.

All accelerating toward permanent failure.

"Dr. Park, I need you to share your data with my son. He's building predictive models. Lunar correlations. If you have historical incident reports, we can refine the predictions."

"I'll send everything I have. But Officer Pritchard, you need to understand—this is bigger than Antrim County. Bigger than Michigan. If we don't find a way to stabilize these boundaries, we're looking at a regional catastrophe."

"Do you have any idea how to stabilize them?"

"No. But I'm working with researchers at University of Chicago. Geophysicists. They think the boundaries might respond to targeted seismic dampening. Or artificial anchoring. We're still in early theoretical stages."

"How long until you have something practical?"

"Months. Maybe a year."

"We don't have months."

"I know. That's why I'm calling. We need to buy time. And the only way to do that is to keep people away from the thin places until we figure out how to fix them."

"Good luck with that. The state won't evacuate. The county won't close sites. Nobody wants to admit the problem is real."

"Then we make them admit it. Friday night. When multiple folds open simultaneously. When it becomes impossible to deny. That's when we force action."

"People might die Friday night."

"People will definitely die if we don't act. At least this way we have a chance."

After Dr. Park hung up, I sat on the deck with Jake's data, Dr. Park's historical reports, and the growing certainty that Friday was going to be a turning point.

Either the state would finally take this seriously.

Or the body count would become too high to ignore.

Or both.

Jake came out with fresh coffee. "Dr. Park sent me her files. Dad, there are incidents going back to the 1980s. All along the moraine system. All dismissed or explained away."

"This has been building for forty years."

"And accelerating. Look at the frequency." He showed me a graph. "One incident every few years in the 80s and 90s. One per year in the 2000s. Multiple per year starting 2015. And now, March 2026, we're getting multiple incidents per week."

"Leading to multiple per day. Then continuous."

"Right. Whatever's causing this—whether it's isostatic rebound, or climate change affecting ancient lake beds, or removal of burial mounds—it's reaching a critical threshold."

"Can it be stopped?"

"I don't know. Dr. Park thinks maybe. But it would require resources we don't have. Geological engineering on a massive scale. Stabilizing boundaries across five states."

"Nobody's going to fund that."

"Not until it's undeniable. Not until the folds stay open permanently and people can see for themselves that the Pleistocene is bleeding through."

I looked at the woods. At the ordinary Michigan night. At the world that was about to become extraordinary in the worst possible way.

"Friday," I said. "Seventeen sites. Multiple folds. That's when it becomes undeniable."

"Probably."

"And people will die."

"Probably."

"But maybe it saves more people in the long run. If it forces action. If it makes the state take this seriously."

Jake didn't answer. Because there was no good answer.

We were banking on catastrophe to force change.

And hoping the catastrophe wasn't so large it became unmanageable.

That night, I couldn't sleep again.

Went to my office. Updated the map with Jake's seventeen predicted sites.

Sent the data to everyone I could think of. Sheriff Kowalski. Commissioner Walsh. Dr. Havelka. Dr. Ostrander. Sarah Ashkwe. Rebecca in Lansing. State Emergency Management.

Subject line: "Full moon Friday - multiple folds predicted - evacuate these sites."

Most wouldn't listen.

But some might.

And every person who stayed away from the boundaries Friday night was one less person who might cross through to a world that would kill them.

At 2 AM, Sarah Ashkwe texted back.

Your son is right about the moon. My grandmother's notes mention it. She called them "the nights when boundaries thin." Always around new moon and full moon. We knew this. We just forgot.

Can you help warn people?

I'll try. But Dave, when the folds open Friday, when people see what's really happening, it won't just be fear. It'll be panic. The kind that makes people do stupid things. Be ready.

Ready for what?

For people running toward the folds instead of away. For curiosity stronger than survival instinct. For humans being human.

I hadn't thought about that.

But she was right.

Some people would run away.

Others would run toward. Phones out. Filming. Wanting to see. Wanting proof. Wanting to be part of the story.

And some of them wouldn't come back.

Chapter 16

CHAPTER SIXTEEN: THE DEVELOPMENT

Thursday afternoon, 3:47 PM, I got a call from a number I didn't recognize.

"Is this Dave Pritchard?"

"Yes."

"This is Marcus Webb, site foreman for Lakeview Estates. We're developing a subdivision off Cairn Highway near—"

"I know where you are." Elevation 625 feet. Lake Algonquin shoreline. Red zone on my map. One of Jake's seventeen predicted sites for tomorrow's full moon.

"Yeah, well, we got your warning. Email about staying away from the site Friday night. And I gotta ask—is this for real? Or is this some kind of environmental protest thing?"

"It's real. You're building on an unstable temporal boundary. There's a high probability your site will experience a fold opening during the full moon. I recommend evacuating all personnel and shutting down operations until—"

"We can't shut down. We're behind schedule as it is. We've got foundation work that needs to be done before the ground thaws completely. If we stop now, we lose weeks."

"If you don't stop, you might lose workers."

Silence. Then: "The email said 'temporal displacement.' What does that mean?"

"It means the past bleeds through. The site sits where Lake Algonquin used to be eleven thousand years ago. When the fold opens, the ancient lake comes back. If your workers are there when it happens—"

"They drown."

"Yes."

More silence. "How sure are you this is going to happen?"

"My son's models predict seventeen sites will fold during the full moon period. Yours is one of them. Probability: eighty-three percent."

"Jesus." I heard him talking to someone in the background. Then back to me: "Okay. I'll pull the crew early Friday. We were planning to work until six. I'll shut it down at noon instead."

"Thank you."

"But if nothing happens, if this is bullshit, we're filing a complaint. You're costing us money."

"If nothing happens, I'll apologize personally. But Mr. Webb, please—stay away from that site Friday evening. And keep your crew away."

"I will."

He hung up.

I marked Lakeview Estates on my list. One site secured. Sixteen to go.

Friday morning came with perfect weather. Clear skies. Temperature climbing to 60 degrees. The kind of spring day that made people want to be outside.

The kind of day when seventeen thin places were predicted to open simultaneously.

I spent the morning making final calls. Warning people. Begging them to stay inside. To avoid the high-probability zones.

Some listened. Most didn't.

By noon, I'd done everything I could.

Karen made lunch. Nobody ate much.

Jake sat at the kitchen table with his laptop, monitoring seismic data in real-time. "The sensors are showing increased low-frequency activity across multiple sites. Background vibrations. Like the geological stress is building."

"When does the full moon peak?"

"8:47 PM. But the 72-hour window started yesterday. Folds could open anytime between now and Sunday."

Emma was on her phone, scrolling social media. "People are treating this like an event. There are watch parties planned. Groups going to the high-probability sites to see if anything happens."

"What?"

She showed me her screen. Facebook events. "Full Moon Fold Watch - Cairn Highway." "Thin Places Viewing Party - Torch Lake Overlook." "See the Pleistocene - Bellaire Nature Trail."

Hundreds of people RSVPing. Treating it like a concert. Like entertainment.

"They're going to get themselves killed," I said.

"I tried to tell them. Posted warnings. But they think it's going to be like the mastodon. Something they can watch safely from a distance."

"The mastodon died. The hunters got attacked. George Henderson is gone. There's nothing safe about this."

"I know. But they don't believe it. They think the news is exaggerating."

I called Sheriff Kowalski.

"Tom, are you seeing the social media? People are planning to go to the thin places tonight."

"I know. I've got deputies trying to set up perimeters at the high-risk sites. But Dave, I've got six deputies for the entire county. I can't cover seventeen locations."

"The state team—"

"Still in Traverse City. They're 'monitoring the situation.' Which means they'll respond after something happens, not before."

"People are going to die."

"I know. I've got units at the most populated sites. Bellaire Nature Trail. Cairn Highway development. Torch Lake overlook. But the rest..." He sighed. "We're doing what we can."

At 4 PM, my phone rang. Marcus Webb, the construction foreman.

"Pritchard, we've got a problem."

"What happened?"

"I shut down the site at noon like I said. Sent the crew home. But I've got equipment that can't be left unsecured overnight. Excavator. Grading equipment. I need to go back and lock things up properly."

"Don't. Wait until tomorrow."

"It's tens of thousands of dollars in equipment. I can't leave it sitting there."

"It's not worth your life."

"I'll be quick. In and out. Fifteen minutes tops."

"Mr. Webb—"

"I'm already on my way."

He hung up.

I looked at Karen. "I have to go."

"You're suspended."

"I don't care."

"Dave—"

"A man is about to walk into a fold zone alone. If it opens while he's there, he's dead. I have to try."

She grabbed her keys. "I'm driving."

We made it to the Lakeview Estates site at 4:23 PM.

The development was in early stages. Foundation holes. Graded lots. Stacks of building materials. And right in the middle, Marcus Webb's white pickup truck parked next to a massive excavator.

I didn't see Webb.

"Marcus!" I shouted. "Marcus Webb!"

No answer.

Karen stayed by the truck. I walked into the site, looking for him.

The development covered maybe twenty acres, carved into the hillside overlooking what would eventually be Torch Lake views. Premium lots. Half-million-dollar homes.

Built exactly where Lake Algonquin had been.

I found Webb near the excavator, checking tie-downs on the equipment.

"Marcus, you need to leave. Now."

He looked up. "Almost done. Just making sure nothing gets stolen."

"It's after four. The full moon peaks in four hours. You need to—"

The ground shook.

Not earthquake shaking. Different. Wrong.

A low vibration. Deep. Like the earth was humming.

Marcus felt it too. "What the hell—"

"Run. Now. Back to the truck."

The vibration intensified. The air got cold. Fast. Temperature dropping from 60 degrees to 40 in seconds.

And then I saw it.

At the far end of the development site, near where lot seventeen was being graded, the air shimmered.

Not heat shimmer. Reality shimmer.

The fold was opening.

"MARCUS, RUN!"

He ran. I ran.

Behind us, the shimmer expanded. Thirty feet across. Fifty feet. Growing.

And through the shimmer, I could see it.

Water.

Lake Algonquin. Eleven thousand years ago. Elevation 605 feet. Twenty feet higher than modern Torch Lake.

The ancient lake was coming back.

We made it maybe forty yards before the water hit.

Not a wave. A displacement. Reality folding, and where there had been graded earth there was suddenly deep, cold, glacial lake water.

I heard Marcus scream. Turned.

He'd been closer to the fold point. The water caught him waist-deep, moving fast, the current from eleven thousand years ago trying to establish itself in present-day Michigan.

He went down.

I ran back, into water that was impossibly cold. Grabbed his arm. Pulled.

He came up, gasping, eyes wide with shock.

"GO! Get to high ground!"

We stumbled uphill, away from the fold. The water kept coming. Flooding across the development site. Three feet deep. Four feet. Rising fast.

Ancient Lake Algonquin trying to remember what it used to be.

I could see fish. Real fish. Species I didn't recognize. Swimming in water that shouldn't exist.

We made it to Marcus's truck. Karen was there, door open, engine running.

"GET IN!"

Marcus and I threw ourselves into the cab, soaking wet, hypothermic. Karen hit the gas before the doors were closed.

The truck fishtailed on the muddy access road, tires spraying water and gravel. But it held. We made it to Cairn Highway, away from the fold.

Behind us, the Lakeview Estates development was underwater.

Foundation holes filled with glacial lake. Equipment submerged. Stacks of lumber floating. The entire twenty-acre site transformed into Lake Algonquin.

And it wasn't closing.

I checked my watch. 4:31 PM.

The fold had been open for eight minutes.

And it was still growing.

Karen drove us to the nearest safe point—a gas station half a mile up Cairn Highway. Pulled over. All of us shaking from adrenaline and cold.

Marcus was pale. "That was real. The water. The cold. That was—"

"Lake Algonquin. Eleven thousand years ago. Exactly what I warned you about."

"It's still there. I can see it." He pointed back toward the development. From this distance, we could see the shimmer. The impossible lake. "How long will it last?"

"I don't know. Previous folds have closed after a few minutes. But this one's already past eight minutes and still open."

My phone buzzed. Jake.

"Dad, where are you?"

"Cairn Highway. Lakeview Estates site. Fold just opened. Still open. At least eight minutes duration and counting."

"That matches my models. Dad, I'm seeing seismic signatures from multiple sites. The folds are starting. All of them."

"How many?"

"Three confirmed so far. Your location, one near Elk Rapids, one near Central Lake. And the sensors are showing pre-fold vibrations at six more locations."

Nine sites. And it was only 4:30 PM. Four hours before the full moon peaked.

"Jake, call Sheriff Kowalski. Tell him we need emergency services at every high-probability site. Now."

"Already did. He's deploying everyone he has. But Dad—"

"What?"

"The watch parties. People are gathering at the sites. They want to see the folds. And they're not leaving."

I looked at Marcus. "Do you have a change of clothes in your truck?"

"Yeah. Work gear in the back."

"Get changed. You're hypothermic. Then get to a hospital. Get checked out."

"What about you?"

"I'm going to try to keep people from doing what you just did."

Karen handed me a blanket from the truck's emergency kit. "Dave, you're soaking wet. You're hypothermic too."

"I'll change at home. But first I need to—"

My phone rang. Sheriff Kowalski.

"Dave, we've got a situation at Bellaire Nature Trail. The fold opened. The bridge is gone. And there are maybe thirty people standing there watching. I can't get them to leave."

"I'm ten minutes out."

"Hurry. Because some of them are talking about trying to cross through. To see what's on the other side."

I hung up. Looked at Karen.

"Nature trail. Now."

She was already driving.

We made it to the nature trail parking lot at 4:47 PM.

Cars everywhere. Fifty, sixty vehicles. People standing in clusters, phones out, filming.

And at the center of it all, where the old railroad bridge used to span the ravine, there was nothing.

The bridge was gone.

In its place: a massive ice field. The ravine filled with glacial ice, extending north and south as far as I could see. Thirty feet thick at least. The same ice that had covered this area eleven thousand years ago during the Lake Algonquin stage.

And people were walking toward it.

Sheriff Kowalski was trying to establish a perimeter with two deputies and caution tape. It wasn't working.

I pushed through the crowd.

"Everyone back! This area is unstable!"

Nobody listened. Phones up. Filming. Posting.

One guy—maybe twenty-five, wearing a University of Michigan sweatshirt—was at the edge of the ice field, one foot on the ancient glacier.

"Sir, step back!"

"It's real! The ice is real! Feel how cold it is!"

"Step back now!"

"I'm just going to walk out a little bit. See how far it goes."

"If you step onto that ice, you might not be able to step back. The fold could close behind you."

"It's been open for twenty minutes. It's stable."

"It's not stable. It's a temporal boundary. It's unpredictable."

But he wasn't listening. He stepped fully onto the ice. Started walking.

Ten feet. Twenty feet. Thirty feet.

The crowd cheered. Someone yelled "Go further!"

He did.

Fifty feet from the edge now. Standing on ice that had been gone for eleven thousand years. Waving to the crowd. Someone's hero.

Then the ice cracked.

Not the old ice. The ice was solid.

Reality cracked.

The fold flickered. Just for a second. The shimmer intensifying, reality hiccupping.

The man stumbled. Looked back toward us. Realized something was wrong.

Started running back.

The fold flickered again.

He made it maybe ten feet before it closed.

Not completely. But partially. The ice field contracted. Pulled back thirty feet.

And the man was on the wrong side.

The crowd went silent.

The man was still visible through the shimmer. Standing on ice in the Pleistocene. Pounding on the boundary. Screaming something we couldn't hear.

Then the fold stabilized.

He was trapped.

Eleven thousand years in the past.

On a glacier.

In spring temperatures that would start melting the ice within hours.

Someone in the crowd screamed. Someone else started crying.

Sheriff Kowalski was already on his radio. "I need rescue equipment at the nature trail. Now. We have a man trapped in a temporal fold."

I walked to the fold point. To the shimmer.

The man was visible on the other side. Maybe thirty feet away. Close enough to see his face. The terror.

He was mouthing words. I could read his lips.

Help me. Please.

I looked at the fold. At the unstable boundary. At the shimmer that could close completely at any moment.

"Can we reach him?" Karen asked quietly.

"I don't know."

"Dave, we have to try."

"If we cross through and the fold closes, we're trapped too."

"So we don't cross through. We reach through. Pull him back."

I looked at the boundary. Thirty feet of ice field between us and him.

Too far to reach.

Too unstable to cross.

And even if we could reach him, the fold was flickering. Unstable. It could close any second.

Sheriff Kowalski arrived with rope. "Can we throw this to him?"

"Through a temporal boundary? I don't know if it'll work."

"We have to try."

He threw the rope.

It passed through the shimmer. Landed on the ice near the trapped man.

The man grabbed it. Held on.

"PULL!" Kowalski yelled.

Six of us pulled. The rope went taut.

The man was moving. Sliding across the ice toward the boundary.

Twenty feet. Fifteen. Ten.

The fold flickered again.

Everyone froze.

The shimmer intensified. The boundary contracting.

"PULL HARDER!"

We pulled. The man was at the boundary. Right at the shimmer.

His hand came through. Real. Solid. Present-day Michigan.

Someone grabbed it. Pulled.

The man came through.

Collapsed on the ground, gasping, hypothermic, but alive.

The fold stabilized. The ice field still there. But the man was back.

The crowd erupted. Cheering. Like it was a rescue success.

Like thirty seconds earlier everyone hadn't been watching a man about to be erased from time.

The EMTs arrived. Len Greenland among them.

He took one look at the hypothermic man and said, "Third one today, and what. Third person we've pulled from a fold."

"Third?"

"Central Lake site. Two people tried to cross through. One made it back. One didn't." He looked at me. "Dave, it's chaos. Every site is opening. And people keep trying to cross through."

"Where's the person who didn't make it back?"

"Still there. On the other side. We can see him but can't reach him."

Another George Henderson. Another person trapped in the wrong time.

My phone buzzed. Multiple texts.

Dr. Ostrander: *Elk Rapids site flooded. Ancient Grand Traverse Bay. Two people missing.*

Sarah: *Dock Road near Alden. Ice field opened. Tourist tried to drive onto it. Vehicle went through. Driver trapped.*

Jake: *Dad, I'm counting nine active folds now. And it's only 5:15. The moon doesn't peak for three more hours.*

This was just the beginning.

The full moon was still rising.

And seventeen sites were predicted to fold.

We'd only seen nine.

Chapter 17

CHAPTER SEVENTEEN: THE BEAVERS

The call came in at 6:47 AM Saturday morning.

Central Lake Police Department, patched through to Sheriff Kowalski, who immediately called me.

"Dave, we've got a situation in Central Lake. Multiple reports of... I don't even know how to say this. Giant animals taking down trees near the campground."

I was already exhausted. Had been up all night monitoring the nine active folds. Three people still trapped on the other side of boundaries. Two missing. The Lakeview Estates site still underwater. The nature trail still showing ice.

"What kind of animals?"

"Witnesses are saying beavers. But Dave, they're saying these things are the size of black bears."

Castoroides ohioensis. Giant beaver. Extinct for ten thousand years.

"I'm on my way."

Central Lake sat at the north end of the Chain O' Lakes system, a small town built around the waterway that connected Intermediate Lake to Torch Lake. The campground was right on the water, next to the old steel truss bridge that carried Deerfield Road across the narrows.

I arrived at 7:23 AM to find half the town standing in the street, staring.

The bridge was still there.

But it was wrong.

The western half looked normal. Modern asphalt. Weathered steel. The bridge I'd driven across a hundred times.

The eastern half was ice.

Not ice ON the bridge. The bridge itself was different. Covered in frost. Icicles hanging from the trusses. The deck white with packed snow.

And running down the exact center of the span, visible even from fifty yards away, was the shimmer.

The fold boundary.

Half the bridge in 2026. Half in the Pleistocene. The shimmer splitting them perfectly down the middle.

"Jesus," I said quietly.

And in the water below, in the narrows between the lakes, six massive animals were working.

Beavers.

Eight feet long, nose to tail. Bodies thick and muscular. Heads the size of volleyballs. Teeth—incisors—easily six inches long, chisel-sharp, colored dark orange from iron deposits.

Castoroides ohioensis.

The giant beaver. The largest rodent ever to live in North America.

And they were building a dam.

Sheriff Kowalski met me at the barricade his deputies had set up.

"Dave, what the hell are those things?"

"Giant beavers. *Castoroides.* They lived here during the last ice age."

"They're cutting down trees."

"That's what beavers do."

"Not like that."

He pointed toward the campground. Three trees were already down. Mature maples, eighteen inches in diameter, cut at the base with perfect 45-degree angles. The kind of trees modern beavers couldn't touch.

These beavers didn't care.

As I watched, one of them—the largest, maybe 250 pounds—approached a standing maple. Put its massive incisors against the trunk. And started cutting.

The sound was incredible. Like a chainsaw. Wood chips flying. The tree shaking with each bite.

Two minutes later, the maple crashed down.

The beaver barely paused. Just moved to the next tree.

"They're clearing the campground," Kowalski said.

"They're harvesting construction material. Building a dam across the narrows." I looked at the half-finished structure. "If they complete it, it'll raise the water level in the upper Lakes. Flood shoreline properties upstream."

"Can we stop them?"

"With what? They're two hundred fifty pounds of muscle and teeth. And they're not showing any fear of humans."

As if to prove the point, one of the beavers waddled within twenty feet of the barricade, dragging a stripped maple trunk toward the water. People backed up. Phones out. Filming.

The beaver ignored them completely. Focused on its work.

I walked to the bridge approach. Close enough to see the shimmer clearly.

It ran perfectly down the centerline. Like someone had drawn a line with a ruler and split reality along it.

West of the line: modern bridge. Asphalt. Steel painted green. Normal March temperature, maybe 55 degrees.

East of the line: Pleistocene bridge. Ice-covered. Frost-rimed steel. Temperature maybe 20 degrees. You could see your breath on that side.

The same bridge. Existing in two times simultaneously.

A deputy—young guy I didn't know—was standing near the approach.

"Sir, people keep asking if they can cross. If the bridge is safe."

"It's there. But if you walk to the middle and cross the shimmer, you'll be in the Pleistocene. Ice age. Eleven thousand years ago. So no. It's not safe."

"What if someone doesn't realize? What if they just drive across?"

"Then they're in the wrong time period before they understand what happened."

The deputy looked at the shimmer. "We need to close the bridge."

"Yes. You do."

By 9 AM, the crowd had grown to maybe two hundred people. This was visible. Active. Happening in broad daylight in the middle of town.

The beavers kept working. Methodical. Efficient.

One would cut down a tree. Another would strip branches. A third would drag the log to the water. Two more would position it in the dam. The sixth would pack mud and stones into the gaps.

I filmed it. Documented everything.

Six Castoroides ohioensis actively building dam at Central Lake narrows. Fold still open. Duration now 4+ hours. Bridge split between eras.

Jake texted back: *That's the longest fold yet. Dad, I think some of them aren't going to close.*

Dr. Havelka arrived around 10 AM.

"Dave, people want these beavers removed. They're treating them like a nuisance species."

"They're extinct. They're not a nuisance."

"A nuisance that's destroying property and about to flood the chain of Lakes." She looked at the dam. "Are they dangerous?"

"Not aggressive. But those teeth could go through bone. If someone threatens them..."

As if on cue, a teenage boy ducked under the barricade and started walking toward the nearest beaver.

"HEY!" I shouted. "Get back!"

The kid ignored me. Phone out. Recording.

He got within ten feet of the beaver—the big one.

The beaver looked up.

Made eye contact.

For three seconds, they stared at each other.

Then the beaver went back to work.

The kid laughed. "See? Harmless!"

He reached out to touch it.

The beaver spun. Faster than something that size should move. Mouth open. Six-inch incisors visible. Hissed.

The sound was wrong. Deep. Guttural. A warning.

The kid stumbled backward. Fell. Scrambled away.

The beaver watched him go. Then returned to work.

By noon, the dam was half-finished. Already backing up water. Intermediate Lake starting to rise.

Sarah Ashkwe arrived around 1 PM. Stood beside me, watching the beavers work.

"My grandmother's notes mentioned these. She called them the engineers. Said they built dams so large they created lakes where none had been."

"They're going to flood properties if they finish."

"Maybe that's what this place is supposed to look like. Maybe we transformed it wrong."

She was right. I couldn't kill them. Couldn't destroy the last living members of an extinct species just because they were engineering the landscape the way evolution designed them to.

At 2:30 PM, Jake called.

"Dad, the seismic signature is changing. I think the fold is starting to close."

"How long?"

"Maybe an hour."

I looked at the beavers. At the half-finished dam.

At 3:17 PM, the fold began to shimmer more intensely.

The beavers noticed.

All six stopped working. Looked toward the boundary.

They knew.

The big male made a sound. Low. Rumbling.

The other five responded.

Then they abandoned the dam. All six slipped into the water. Swam toward the shimmer.

Crossed through.

Back to the Pleistocene.

The fold contracted.

And closed.

The eastern half of the bridge returned to normal. Modern asphalt. No ice. No frost. The shimmer gone.

The dam remained. Half-finished. Already starting to fall apart as modern currents pushed against Pleistocene engineering.

But it was there.

Proof.

Sheriff Kowalski walked over. "They knew the fold was closing. They went back on purpose."

"They belonged there. Not here."

"What do we do about the dam?"

"Let the current take it apart. It'll collapse on its own."

I stayed until 5 PM. Documented everything.

Incident number seventeen: Six *Castoroides ohioensis* cross through fold at Central Lake narrows. Build dam for 10+ hours. Return to Pleistocene when fold closes. Bridge split between eras during opening. No human casualties. Property damage significant.

Fold duration: 10 hours, 17 minutes.

The longest yet.

And it had closed.

Unlike some of the others—Lakeview Estates still underwater, Elk Rapids still flooded—this one had actually closed.

Which meant folds were unpredictable. Some closed after minutes. Some after hours. Some not at all.

Driving home, Karen said, "Those beavers weren't scary."

"No."

"They were just... doing their job."

"Eight-foot beavers that could cut through maples. But yeah. Just doing their job."

"It's strange. The mastodon was sad. The lion was terrifying. But the beavers..."

"Were industrious. That was the problem."

She smiled slightly. "Very you."

At home, Jake was monitoring data.

"Dad, we're past the full moon window. The folds should start closing now."

"Some already have. How many are still open?"

"Seven. Lakeview Estates. Elk Rapids. Bellaire Nature Trail. And four others. All sustained. No signs of closure."

"How long?"

"Longest is fourteen hours. They're not closing, Dad. I think some of them are permanent now."

Seven permanent thin places where past and present existed simultaneously.

That night, the news coverage was nonstop.

"State Declares Emergency in Antrim County"

Finally. After people trapped. After property flooded. After giant beavers built a dam in downtown Central Lake.

Finally, the state was taking it seriously.

Too late to prevent the folds.

But maybe soon enough to manage them.

At midnight, I went outside. Looked at the woods.

Seven folds still open. Seven doorways to eleven thousand years ago.

And Jake's models predicted more coming.

By summer, the map would be covered.

We'd have to adapt. Change how we lived. Where we built.

Or leave.

Either way, life in northern Michigan would never be the same.

The land was remembering.

And we were going to have to remember along with it.

Chapter 18

CHAPTER EIGHTEEN: PALEO-INDIANS

The first sighting came in at 6:17 AM Sunday morning.

State Police dispatch. Patched through to Sheriff Kowalski, who called me.

"Dave, we've got a report from a motorist on M-88 near Atwood. Says there's a man standing in the middle of the road. Barefoot. Wearing animal skins. Won't move. Won't respond. Just standing there looking confused."

I was up and moving before he finished.

"Don't approach him. I'm ten minutes out."

I made it in eight.

M-88 between Bellaire and Mancelona. Early morning. Light traffic. And standing in the northbound lane, exactly as described, was a man.

Male. Maybe twenty-five. Five foot seven. Compact build, heavy muscle. Wearing hide clothing—deer or elk, tanned and sewn with sinew. Long black hair tied back. Barefoot despite the 45-degree temperature.

And he was turning slowly. Looking at everything. The road. The painted lines. The telephone poles. A passing car.

His expression wasn't fear. It was incomprehension.

Nothing made sense to him.

I pulled over. Got out slowly.

"Sir? Can you understand me?"

He turned. Looked at me. At my uniform. At my truck.

Spoke. A language I'd never heard. Consonant-heavy. Guttural. Questions, I thought. Where am I? What is this? Who are you?

I tried again. "Sir, you're in Michigan. Modern Michigan. Do you understand?"

He spoke again. Same language. More insistent.

Then he looked past me. At a semi-truck approaching from the south. Engine roaring. Eighteen wheels. Forty tons of metal moving at sixty miles per hour.

The man's eyes went wide.

He'd never seen anything like it.

He ran.

Not away from the road. Across it. Directly into the path of the truck.

I yelled. The truck driver hit his horn. Hit his brakes.

The man made it across. Barely. The truck missing him by maybe three feet.

He didn't stop running. Into the woods on the far side. Gone.

The truck driver pulled over. Rolled down his window.

"What the hell was that? Guy looked like he was wearing a Halloween costume!"

"Just... stay in your vehicle. I'll file a report."

He drove off, muttering.

I walked to where the man had been standing. Examined the asphalt.

Barefoot prints. Fresh. Showing the same structural differences I'd seen at the East Jordan site. Wider stance. Heavier metatarsals. Toes adapted for rough terrain.

And leading into the woods: a trail. Broken branches. Disturbed undergrowth. The kind of track a frightened animal makes.

Or a human who doesn't understand where he is.

The second sighting came in at 9:34 AM.

A woman calling 911. Hysterical. Reported "primitive people" on her property near Torch Lake.

Sheriff Kowalski and I responded together.

The property was a vacation home. Expensive. Waterfront. The kind of place people from downstate bought for summers.

The owner—Susan Mitchell, mid-fifties, clearly shaken—met us in the driveway.

"They were in my yard. Three of them. Just appeared out of nowhere. Looking around. Touching things."

"Can you describe them?"

"Two men, one woman. Wearing animal skins. Long hair. Barefoot. The woman had something... a baby. Wrapped in fur."

A family group. Mother, father, maybe an uncle or older brother. With an infant.

"What did they do?"

"Nothing aggressive. They just... looked confused. The men were examining my deck. Touching the wood. Like they'd never seen lumber before. The woman tried to open my back door. Not breaking in. Just... testing it. Trying to understand what it was."

"Where are they now?"

"Gone. They heard me scream and ran toward the lake. I watched them go into the water. Just waded in. And then..." She stopped. "This sounds crazy."

"Say it anyway."

"They disappeared. Not like swimming away. Like they walked into the water and crossed through something. A shimmer. And they were gone."

A fold. Opening at the shoreline. They'd crossed back through.

"Mrs. Mitchell, I need to see where this happened."

Her back yard showed clear evidence.

Barefoot tracks in the grass. Adult-sized. And smaller prints. Child-sized. Maybe toddler.

The tracks led to the deck. Multiple prints where they'd stood, examining the structure.

Handprints on the sliding glass door. Smudged. Rough. Hands that had never touched glass before.

And leading to the water: a trail. Four sets of prints. Including the small ones.

At the waterline, the tracks stopped.

But the grass was disturbed in a circular pattern. Eight feet in diameter. The same signature I'd seen at every fold point.

They'd crossed back.

A family displaced by eleven thousand years. Confused by modern construction. Testing the boundaries of this strange new world. Then retreating when they encountered something they didn't understand.

I photographed everything. Took measurements.

Mrs. Mitchell watched from the deck. "What were they?"

"Paleo-Indians. People who lived here during the last ice age. They crossed through a temporal boundary. They're as confused as you are."

"Are they dangerous?"

"They're human. If you startle them, if you threaten them, yes. But they're not here to hurt anyone. They're just trying to survive in a world they don't recognize."

"Will they come back?"

"I don't know. The fold might open again. Or it might not."

She looked at the lake. At the spot where they'd disappeared. "I've owned this property for twelve years. Never had anything stranger than a bear in the yard. Now I've got time-traveling families trying to open my back door."

"Welcome to the new normal."

The third report came in at 2:47 PM.

Hikers on the North Country Trail near Pinney Bridge. Spotted a group of people in a clearing. Thought they were reenactors. Then realized something was wrong.

I met Sarah Ashkwe at the trailhead. She'd heard the report and driven over.

"How many?" I asked.

"Hikers said six or seven. Sitting around a fire. Working on something."

We walked the trail carefully. Quietly.

Found the clearing after maybe half a mile.

The fire was out. Cold. But recent. Within the past few hours.

And scattered around the fire pit: evidence.

Stone tools. Scrapers. Blades. A partially finished spear point. Obsidian flakes from knapping.

Hides stretched on frames. Drying. Being processed into clothing.

Bones from a butchered animal. White-tailed deer, I thought. The cuts were expert. No waste.

And carved into a nearby tree: territorial markers. Three parallel lines. The same symbol I'd seen at East Jordan.

"They were here," Sarah said quietly. "Working. Living. Then the hikers came and they left."

"Where?"

She pointed. Tracks leading north. Multiple sets. Adults and children both.

"A larger group than we thought. Family band. Maybe eight to ten people."

I examined the tools. The craftsmanship was incredible. Every edge sharp. Every angle purposeful. These weren't crude artifacts. These were precision instruments made by experts.

"They're not just passing through anymore," Sarah said. "They're establishing camps. Processing game. Making long-term tools. They're settling."

"Can they survive here? In modern Michigan?"

"They survived the Younger Dryas extinction. Climate change. Megafauna die-off. The collapse of the Clovis culture. They survived all of it." She picked up a scraper. "Modern Michigan? This is easy compared to what they've lived through."

By evening, we had five confirmed sightings.

M-88 road encounter. Torch Lake waterfront. North Country Trail camp. And two more:

A gas station attendant near Alden reported a man trying to trade a stone point for food. The attendant thought it was a prank until the man became agitated and left.

A family camping near Barnes Road heard voices at night. Strange language. Singing or chanting. In the morning they found tracks around their tent. And a gift left on their picnic table: a beautifully carved bone needle.

Not a threat. A greeting. Or a trade offer.

The Paleo-Indians were trying to make contact. To understand this world. To establish relationships.

But on their terms. Using their protocols. Trading gifts. Marking territory. Moving carefully through a landscape they recognized geologically but found utterly transformed culturally.

That night I compiled the reports.

Incident eighteen (multiple sightings): Paleo-Indian groups observed across Antrim County. Minimum three separate bands. Total population estimate: 20-30 individuals. Evidence of settlement attempts, territorial marking, and attempted contact with modern humans. No hostile encounters. Groups retreat when threatened or confused.

I sent it to everyone. Sheriff Kowalski. State Emergency Management. Dr. Ostrander. Jake. Sarah.

Jake called at 10 PM.

"Dad, if we're seeing twenty to thirty people, and these are just the ones making contact..."

"There are probably more. Staying hidden. Operating in remote areas where they won't encounter modern humans."

"How many folds have opened in the past week?"

"Dozens. Small ones. Brief ones. In remote locations."

"So if each fold lets through even one small band—five to ten people—and they're staying..."

"We could have hundreds. Scattered across northern Michigan. Living in the forests. Hunting. Adapting."

"And we have no idea where most of them are."

"No."

Silence on the line. Then: "What do we do?"

"Document. Observe. Try to establish peaceful contact when possible. And hope nobody does anything stupid."

Monday morning, the news picked up the story.

"Multiple Sightings of 'Primitive Humans' in Northern Michigan"

"Paleo-Indian Artifacts Discovered at Multiple Sites"

"Time Displaced Populations: Scientists Confirm Pleistocene Humans Living in Modern Michigan"

The footage showed the tools. The territorial markers. The tracks. Sarah explaining—carefully—what we were seeing.

The response was immediate and polarized.

Some people wanted them protected. Given refugee status. Humanitarian aid.

Others wanted them removed. "Sent back." Treated as invasive species.

A few wanted them hunted. Killed. Eliminated as threats.

Online forums exploded with theories. Conspiracy theories. Accusations that the whole thing was a hoax or government experiment.

But the evidence was undeniable.

Stone tools tested authentic. Knapping techniques matched Paleo-Indian assemblages from archaeological sites. The materials—obsidian, chert, jasper—came from sources that hadn't been used in eleven thousand years.

Carbon dating on a hide fragment from the North Country Trail camp: 11,340 years BP, plus or minus 60 years.

Impossible.

Except it wasn't impossible anymore.

It was documented. Verified. Real.

Tuesday morning, Governor's press conference.

State of emergency extended. Federal resources deployed. Emergency Management coordinating "humanitarian response to displaced populations."

But no concrete plan. No protocol. No legal framework for how to treat humans from the Pleistocene who were legally neither citizens nor immigrants nor anything existing law recognized.

They were ghosts. People who shouldn't exist but clearly did.

And nobody knew what to do with them.

That night, I got a call from an unlisted number.

"Officer Pritchard? This is Dr. Marcus Webb, anthropology department, University of Michigan. I've been following the reports. The sightings. The artifacts."

"And?"

"I'd like permission to attempt contact. Peaceful contact. Document their language, culture, technology. Before..." He paused. "Before something happens to them."

"What do you think is going to happen?"

"History. The same thing that always happens when two populations meet and one doesn't understand the other. Conflict. Violence. Elimination of the weaker group."

"These aren't weak. They survived the extinction."

"They survived eleven thousand years ago. In a world they understood. Now they're navigating highways and glass doors and people with guns. They're vulnerable. And I want to help protect them. Through documentation. Through understanding. Through giving them a voice before someone silences them."

I thought about the man on M-88. Confused. Standing in the road. Nearly hit by a truck because he didn't understand what it was.

Thought about the family at Torch Lake. Testing the deck. Trying to open the door. A baby wrapped in furs.

Thought about the gift left at the campsite. The bone needle. A gesture of peace from people who just wanted to understand where they were.

"I'll introduce you to Sarah Ashkwe," I said. "If anyone can help you make contact safely, it's her."

"Thank you."

"But Dr. Webb? If you approach them, if you make contact, you do it with respect. They're not specimens. They're people. Displaced. Frightened. Trying to survive. You treat them accordingly."

"I understand."

Wednesday morning, Sarah called.

"Dave. I found another camp. Near Skegmog Lake. Larger group. Maybe fifteen people. They're building something permanent. Not temporary shelters. Actual structures."

"They're staying."

"Yes. And Dave... they've started farming. Small scale. Collecting native plants. Transplanting them near the camp. They're not just hunting anymore. They're establishing territory. Building community."

The People Who Walked With Ice weren't visiting.

They were colonizing.

Not aggressively. Not violently. Just doing what humans do when they find viable territory.

Settle. Adapt. Survive.

And modern Michigan—with its forests and lakes and game—was viable territory.

Even if nothing else made sense to them, the land did.

The geology. The water. The animals.

That was familiar.

That was home.

And they were making it home again.

Chapter 19

CHAPTER EIGHTEEN: THE PEOPLE

The call came from Sarah Ashkwe at 4:47 AM Sunday morning.

Not a text. A phone call. Which meant serious.

"Dave. You need to come to the old railroad grade near East Jordan. Now."

"What happened?"

"They're here. The people. The ones who walked with ice."

I was up and dressed in three minutes. Karen drove.

The old railroad grade ran northeast from East Jordan, following the moraine ridge through mixed forest. A popular hiking trail now. Elevation 610 feet. Lake Algonquin shoreline. Red zone on my map.

Sarah's truck was parked at the trailhead. She was standing with two other people I recognized from the Cultural Center. All three holding flashlights. Looking into the woods.

"What did you see?" I asked.

"Come look."

She led us maybe three hundred yards down the trail. To a clearing where the railroad grade crossed an old creek bed.

And stopped.

In the pre-dawn darkness, illuminated by flashlights and the fading moon, were tracks.

Human tracks.

Barefoot. Adult-sized. But wrong.

The gait was different. Wider stance. Deeper impression in the soft earth. And the foot structure—I knelt down, examined them closely—showed heavier bone density. Thicker metatarsals. Toes splayed for rough terrain.

"How many people?" I asked.

"At least five. Maybe more. They came through maybe two hours ago. The tracks are fresh."

I followed them with my flashlight. They led from the creek bed—where the fold had probably opened—across the clearing, then up the ridge toward higher ground.

Hunting pattern. Following game trails. Moving with purpose.

"Did you see them?"

"No. But we heard them. Talking. A language I didn't recognize. And Dave... they had dogs."

"Dogs?"

She pointed to other tracks mixed with the human prints. Canine. Large. But not quite wolf, not quite dog. Something in between.

Paleo-Indian hunting dogs. Descendants of the first domesticated wolves. Partners in survival.

"Which way did they go?"

"North. Toward the ridge."

I pulled out my phone. Called Sheriff Kowalski.

"Tom, we have Paleo-Indians on the old railroad grade near East Jordan. At least five individuals with dogs. Moving north. We need to—"

"Dave, I can't respond to a report of prehistoric people walking around. I barely have enough deputies to handle the active folds."

"These aren't just walking around. They're hunting. And if they encounter modern people..."

"What do you want me to do? Arrest them? For what? Existing?"

"Protect them. And protect people from them. These are survivors from the extinction. They're armed with atlatls and stone points. They're trained hunters. And they think this is their territory."

Silence. Then: "I'll send a deputy to the trailhead. Keep people away from the area. But Dave, I can't hunt down prehistoric humans. That's... I don't even know what that is."

He hung up.

Sarah was examining something near the tree line. "Dave. Look at this."

A mark on a birch tree. Carved into the bark with a sharp stone tool. Three parallel lines. A symbol.

"What does it mean?"

"I don't know. But my grandmother's notes showed similar markings. She called them boundary markers. Territorial claims." Sarah touched the carving. "They're telling other groups: we were here. This is our hunting ground now."

Karen looked at the tracks leading into the woods. "Are they dangerous?"

"To each other? To animals? Yes. To us?" Sarah paused. "They're human. Smart. Adaptable. And they've survived things we can't imagine. But they don't know about cars. Or guns. Or fences. Or private property. They're operating on Pleistocene rules in a modern world."

"What happens when they meet someone?"

"I don't know. But we need to find them before someone gets hurt."

We followed the tracks.

North along the ridge. Through mixed forest that was transitioning from modern second-growth to something older. Something that looked more like Pleistocene woodland.

The fold was still active here. Not fully open. But permeable. Bleeding through.

I could feel the temperature drop. See the vegetation change. Hear different bird calls.

We were walking through a thin place. An overlap zone.

After maybe a mile, Sarah stopped. Held up a hand.

"Smell that?"

Smoke. Wood smoke. Coming from ahead.

We moved carefully. Quietly.

Around a bend, in a small clearing, we found their camp.

It was temporary. Efficient. The kind of camp people made who moved frequently and traveled light.

A small fire, carefully contained. No wasted wood.

Five shelters made from branches and hides. Low profile. Easy to abandon.

Stone tools scattered near the fire. Scrapers. Blades. Points for atlatl darts.

Fresh game. A deer—white-tailed, modern species—gutted and partially butchered. The work was expert. Clean. No wasted meat.

But no people.

They'd heard us coming. Left.

I examined the shelters. The construction was sophisticated. Angled to shed rain. Positioned to minimize wind exposure. Everything showed deep knowledge of survival.

Sarah knelt by the fire. "Still warm. They were here maybe ten minutes ago. Watching us. Deciding whether we're a threat."

"Are we?"

"We're something they don't understand. People who look almost like them but dressed wrong. Moving wrong. Smelling wrong." She stood. "To them, we're probably as strange as they are to us."

Karen was looking at the stone tools. "These are beautiful. The craftsmanship..."

"Had to be. Their lives depended on it." Sarah picked up a blade. "This is obsidian. Not local. They either brought it through the fold or they've been trading with other groups on this side."

"Trading? They've been here long enough to establish trade?"

"Maybe. Or maybe time works differently in the folds. They might have been here weeks from their perspective while it's only been hours from ours."

I took photos. Documented everything. The shelters. The tools. The butchered deer. The fire pit.

Evidence that Paleo-Indians weren't just passing through anymore.

They were living here. Establishing territory. Adapting to a world that was both familiar and utterly strange.

We heard them before we saw them.

A sound. Low. Rhythmic. Chanting.

Coming from the ridge above the camp.

Sarah tensed. "That's a hunting song. They're preparing to—"

A dog appeared on the ridge. Large. Lean. Dark fur with lighter markings. Part wolf, part ancient domesticated lineage. Eyes intelligent and wary.

It stared at us. Growled. Low warning.

Then a person stepped out of the trees beside it.

Male. Maybe thirty years old. Five foot eight. Compact build, heavy muscle. Skin weathered from constant outdoor exposure. Hair long, tied back. Face showing high cheekbones, broad features.

Wearing hide clothing. Sewn with sinew. Practical. Warm. Well-made.

And in his hand: an atlatl. Spear-thrower. With a dart nocked and ready.

He looked at us. We looked at him.

For maybe ten seconds, nobody moved.

Then he spoke. A language I'd never heard. Consonant-heavy. Guttural. Ancient Paleo-Indian dialect that hadn't been spoken in eleven thousand years.

Sarah responded. In Anishinaabemowin. Not the same language—separated by thousands of years of linguistic evolution—but close enough that the root structures might overlap.

The man listened. Didn't lower the atlatl. Spoke again.

Sarah kept trying. Different words. Different phrases.

Finally something clicked. A word he recognized. Or a gesture. Or just the tone.

He lowered the atlatl slightly. Not completely. But enough.

Sarah turned to me. "I think I got through. I used the word for 'peace.' He might understand we're not a threat."

"What did he say?"

"I don't know. But his body language says: stay where you are. Don't approach. Don't touch anything."

Four more people emerged from the trees. Three men, one woman. All similarly dressed. All armed. All watching us with expressions that mixed curiosity with calculation.

One of the men was older. Maybe fifty. Scars on his face and arms. Tribal elder, probably. He spoke to the first man. A question.

The first man responded. Gestured at us.

The elder studied us for a long moment. Then said something I almost understood. A word that sounded like Sarah's Anishinaabe-mowin term for "stranger."

Sarah nodded. "Yes. Strangers. But peaceful strangers."

The elder looked at our clothing. At Karen's jacket. At my DNR badge. At Sarah's beaded necklace.

Trying to understand what we were. Why we looked almost human but wrong. Why we spoke words that almost made sense but didn't.

Then one of the dogs—there were three with them now—approached Karen.

Curious. Sniffing.

Karen held very still.

The dog circled her. Assessing. Then sat down. Looked back at the elder. As if reporting: not a threat. Strange, but not dangerous.

The elder nodded. Made a decision.

Spoke to the group. They lowered their weapons.

Not holstered. Not put away. Just lowered. Ready to raise again if needed.

But the immediate threat was over.

For the next twenty minutes, we tried to communicate.

Sarah leading. Using gestures. Drawing in the dirt. Finding common words through trial and error.

We learned:

They were a hunting band. Five people plus three dogs. Part of a larger group that had come through the fold three days ago from their perspective. Maybe twelve hours from ours.

They thought this was their world. Their time. They didn't understand that eleven thousand years had passed. Didn't understand they were in the wrong era.

They'd been hunting. Following game trails. Found the deer. Made camp.

Then noticed things were wrong. Trees that didn't belong. Sounds that didn't make sense. And us—people who looked almost right but fundamentally different.

The elder asked—through gestures and broken shared vocabulary—where their people were. The other bands. The familiar groups.

Sarah tried to explain. Pointed at the ground. Then at the sky. Made a sweeping gesture indicating vast time.

The elder frowned. Didn't understand.

How do you explain eleven thousand years to someone who thinks in generations? How do you say "everyone you know is dead" to someone who just walked through what they thought was a normal hunting ground?

You can't.

So Sarah simplified. Pointed at the trees. The modern species. Pointed at us. Our clothing.

Different time. Different people. You're far from home.

The elder processed this. Looked at his group. They conferred quietly.

Then he looked back at Sarah. Drew in the dirt.

A circle. Five marks inside it. Their group.

Another circle nearby. Empty.

A question: are there others like us here?

Sarah didn't know how to answer. Were there other Paleo-Indians who'd crossed through? Probably. Other folds were open across the county. Maybe dozens of people scattered across thin places.

She drew multiple circles. Question marks.

The elder understood. Others might be here. Or might not. Uncertainty.

He nodded. That he understood.

Then one of the younger men said something urgent. Pointed.

Through the trees. Movement.

Modern humans. Hikers. Three of them. Walking the trail below our position. Oblivious to the camp above them.

The Paleo-Indians tensed. Weapons raised slightly.

To them, these were intruders. Strangers in their hunting ground.

"No," Sarah said firmly. Held up her hands. "No. Peace. They're not threats."

The elder looked at her. Looked at the hikers.

Calculating.

Then spoke to his group. A command.

They lowered their weapons.

But I saw the way they watched the hikers. The way they assessed them.

These weren't passive refugees. These were hunters. Survivors. People who'd lived through the extinction by being smarter and more dangerous than everything else.

And they were learning the rules of this new world fast.

The elder spoke to Sarah one more time. Drew in the dirt.

Their camp. A line leading away. A question: we can stay?

Sarah looked at me.

"What do I tell him?"

"I don't know. Legally? They're... what? Undocumented immigrants from the Pleistocene? There's no law for this."

"Practically?"

"If they stay, eventually someone's going to panic and do something stupid. Call law enforcement. Or worse, try to handle it themselves."

"And if they leave?"

"They'll just establish a camp somewhere else. And we won't know where."

Sarah turned back to the elder. Drew her response.

Stay. For now. But careful. Other people dangerous. Not all peaceful.

The elder understood. Nodded.

He spoke to his group. They began breaking camp. Efficiently. Quickly. Everything packed and ready to move in under five minutes.

Professional nomads.

Before they left, the elder approached Sarah. Offered something.

A stone point. Beautifully made. Obsidian. Pressure-flaked to razor sharpness.

A gift. Or a promise. Or both.

Sarah accepted it. Offered her beaded necklace in return.

The elder took it. Examined the beads. Recognized craftsmanship even if he didn't understand the materials.

Then he and his group disappeared into the forest.

Silent. Efficient. Gone.

The dogs went with them.

We stood in the clearing for a long moment.

Then Karen said quietly: "That was first contact. Humans meeting humans separated by eleven thousand years. And we just... talked. And it worked."

"This time," I said. "Because Sarah was here. Because we approached carefully. Because they decided we weren't a threat."

"What about next time?"

"Next time might be different. Different band. Different people. Different circumstances."

Sarah was holding the stone point. "My grandmother said the People Who Walked With Ice were survivors. Harder than the extinction.

This proves it. They crossed through to a world they don't understand and within hours they've established camp, found food, begun learning the rules."

"Are there more?"

"Probably. Multiple folds open across the region. Each one a potential door for bands like this." She looked at the trees where they'd disappeared. "We're not alone anymore. We're sharing the landscape with people from before history."

By the time we got back to the trailhead, it was 7:30 AM.

Sheriff Kowalski's deputy was there. Young guy. Nervous.

"Did you find them? The people?"

"Yes."

"Are they dangerous?"

"They're humans. Armed. Trained. Surviving. So yes, potentially dangerous. But not aggressive if left alone."

"What do I tell people who want to use the trail?"

"Tell them to avoid this area. The fold is active. Time is unstable. And there are Paleo-Indian hunting bands operating in the zone."

"Nobody's going to believe that."

"Show them the photos. Show them the tracks. Show them the stone tools." I handed him a memory card. "Show them anything you need to. But keep people away from here until we figure out how to manage this."

Driving home, I updated the documentation.

Incident eighteen: Paleo-Indian hunting band encountered near East Jordan. Five individuals, three dogs. Armed with atlatls and stone tools. Established temporary camp. Communication attempted and partially successful. No hostile contact. Band retreated into fold zone. Current location unknown.

First confirmed contact with Paleo-Indian population.

First evidence of intentional settlement vs. accidental crossing.

First proof that the People Who Walked With Ice were adapting to modern Michigan.

Jake called at 8 AM.

"Dad, I'm seeing seismic readings from six new locations. Folds opening. Small ones. Brief. But Dad—they're all on the moraine system. All in remote areas. Perfect for small bands to cross through without being noticed."

"How many people could be coming through?"

"No way to know. But if each fold lets through even one small band—five to ten people—and we've had dozens of folds over the past week..." He paused. "There could be hundreds of Paleo-Indians scattered across northern Michigan by now."

Hundreds.

Living in the forests. Hunting. Establishing camps. Learning the landscape.

Invisible to most people.

But there.

That night, the news finally picked up the story.

"Reports of 'Primitive Humans' in Northern Michigan Woods"

"Scientists Confirm Paleo-Indian Artifacts Found Near East Jordan"

"Time Displaced Populations: New Challenge for State Emergency Management"

The footage showed the camp. The tools. Sarah explaining—carefully, respectfully—what we'd encountered.

The response was mixed.

Some people wanted them removed. Relocated. "Sent back" to their own time.

Others wanted them protected. Studied. Given refugee status.

A few wanted them hunted. Treated as dangerous animals.

Nobody knew what to do with humans who shouldn't exist but clearly did.

Monday morning, Governor's press conference.

State of emergency declared. Federal resources requested. Emergency Management coordinating response to "temporal displacement events."

But no mention of the Paleo-Indians.

Too complicated. Too strange. Too likely to cause panic.

So they buried it. Called them "displaced persons of unknown origin" in the official reports. Avoided the word "prehistoric."

Which meant no official protection. No refugee status. No acknowledgment.

The People Who Walked With Ice were on their own.

Just like they'd always been.

Chapter 20

CHAPTER TWENTY: THE ATTACK

The call came in at 7:43 PM Wednesday evening.

Multiple 911 calls. Elk Lake Campground. South end. Off M-72.

"Animal attack in progress. Large bear. Someone down. People screaming."

I was twenty minutes out. Sheriff Kowalski was closer. He got there first.

By the time I arrived, it was over.

The campground sat at the south end of Elk Lake, wooded sites spreading back from the water. Popular spot. Fifty sites. Maybe forty occupied this evening. Families. Retirees. Spring camping season just getting started.

When I pulled in, half the campground was evacuated. Cars and RVs streaming out. People pale. Some crying. Kids in the back seats with wide eyes.

The other half was frozen. Standing in clusters. Staring toward the tree line at the south end.

Where Sheriff Kowalski and two deputies had established a perimeter with caution tape that looked pathetically inadequate.

I parked. Got out.

The first thing I noticed was the silence.

No birds. No insects. Nothing.

Just people breathing. Some crying quietly. And the sound of wind through trees.

Kowalski saw me. Walked over. His face was gray.

"Dave. It's bad."

"How bad?"

"Worse than the horse. Worse than anything." He gestured toward the tree line. "The body's still there. We can't recover it. That thing is guarding it."

"What thing?"

"The bear. Except it's not a bear. It's..." He stopped. "You need to see it."

We walked toward the tree line. Past families huddled by their campers. Past kids being held by parents. Past an elderly couple sitting in lawn chairs, just staring.

A woman grabbed my arm. "Are you DNR? Can you kill it? Can you make it go away?"

"I'm going to try."

"It took him. Just... took him. He was walking to his car and it came out of the trees and it was so fast and he tried to run but—" She broke down. Couldn't finish.

Her husband pulled her back. "It happened right there. Site forty-seven. Bob Martinez. Nice guy. From Grand Rapids. Was here with his wife and kids for the week."

"Where are his wife and kids?"

"Ambulance took them. Shock. The kids saw everything."

Site forty-seven was at the edge of the campground. Closest to the tree line. Closest to the woods.

Closest to where the fold had opened.

I could see the shimmer from fifty yards away. A distortion in the air between two large oaks. Maybe twelve feet wide. Stable. Not flickering.

And standing in front of it, partially visible through the evening shadows, was the bear.

Except it wasn't a bear like anything alive today.

Arctodus simus. Short-faced bear. The largest predator ever to walk North America.

I'd seen the Ring camera footage. The measurements. The descriptions.

None of it prepared me for seeing one in person.

It was massive.

On all fours, it stood maybe six feet at the shoulder. Long legs. Built for running, not lumbering like modern bears. Body lean. Muscular. Efficient.

The face was different. Shorter muzzle. More like a big cat than a bear. Eyes forward-facing. Predator eyes.

And it was standing over Bob Martinez's body.

Not eating. Guarding.

Claiming.

This is mine.

The bear looked at us. Made eye contact. Didn't move.

Calculating. Assessing threat.

Then it turned its attention back to the body. Dismissing us.

We weren't worth worrying about yet.

"Jesus Christ," one of the deputies whispered. "That thing is huge."

"Short-faced bear," I said quietly. "Extinct for eleven thousand years. Pursuit predator. Fastest bear that ever lived. Probably hunted in open terrain. Ran down prey that couldn't outrun it."

"Can we shoot it?" Kowalski asked.

"With what? Pistols? That thing weighs eighteen hundred pounds. You'd need rifles. High caliber. Multiple shots."

"I've got a shotgun in the cruiser."

"That might just make it angry."

"So what do we do? Leave Bob there?"

I looked at the body. At the bear. At the fold still open behind it.

"We wait. See if the fold closes. If the bear goes back on its own."

"And if it doesn't?"

"Then we figure out how to kill something that evolution designed to be unkillable."

We backed up. Gave the bear space. Established a wider perimeter.

I started interviewing witnesses while we waited.

Everyone told the same story.

Seven-thirty PM. Still light out. Families cooking dinner. Kids playing.

Bob Martinez walked from his campsite toward his car. Parked maybe fifty yards away. Normal walk. Nothing unusual.

Then something came out of the trees.

Fast.

Several witnesses used that word. Fast. Faster than anything that size should move.

One man—a retired teacher from Traverse City—said: "It didn't lumber. It ran. Like a cat. Like something built to chase. I've seen black bears. This wasn't like that. This was... purposeful."

Bob tried to run.

Didn't make it ten feet.

The bear covered fifty yards in maybe four seconds. Forty miles per hour. Sprint speed.

Hit Bob from behind. Grabbed him with foreclaws. Eight-inch claws. Designed for grasping prey while running.

Bob screamed. Once.

Then the bear's jaws closed on his neck.

Over.

That fast.

The bear dragged him toward the trees. Toward the fold. Stopped halfway. Dropped the body. Turned to face the crowd.

Everyone ran. Scattered. Into RVs. Into cars. Away.

The bear didn't chase. Just stood over the body. Watching. Waiting.

Then it settled. Lay down partially. Still alert. Still watching.

That was forty minutes ago.

It hadn't moved since.

Dr. Havelka arrived at 8:15 PM.

Took one look at the bear and said, "That's the thing from the Ring camera."

"Yes."

"It's bigger than I thought."

"Yes."

"And you want me to what? Tranquilize it?"

"Can you?"

"I have darts rated for large ungulates. Elk. Moose. Maybe fifteen hundred pounds maximum. That thing is close to two thousand. And I'd need to calculate dosage for a species that's been extinct for eleven thousand years. No reference data. No trials. I could underdose and just make it angry. Or overdose and kill it."

"If we kill it, is that a problem?"

"It's the only living specimen of *Arctodus simus* on the planet. From a purely scientific standpoint, killing it would be a tragedy."

"From a purely human standpoint, it just killed Bob Martinez and is preventing us from recovering his body."

She was quiet. Then: "Let me set up. I'll try a tranquilizer. But Dave, if it charges, if anyone's at risk, shoot it. Science isn't worth human lives."

While Dr. Havelka prepared the dart, I examined the scene more carefully.

The fold point was clear. Between the two oaks. Shimmer visible even in the fading light.

And leading from the fold to Bob's body: massive tracks. Four-toed. Clawed. Each print the size of a dinner plate. Stride length maybe eight feet.

The bear had come through the fold at a run. Chasing something. Or hunting.

Had Bob just been in the wrong place when an apex predator from the Pleistocene emerged hungry and territorial?

Or had the bear smelled him? Targeted him?

I didn't know.

But the tracks told the story. Straight line from fold to kill site. No hesitation. No confusion.

This wasn't an animal stumbling through and panicking.

This was a predator hunting.

And it had found prey.

Dr. Havelka loaded the dart. "I'm going with a high dose. Better to sedate it too much than not enough."

"How close do you need to be?"

"Fifty yards. Maybe forty if the angle's bad."

"That's pursuit range for that thing."

"I know. So if it charges, everyone run. And Dave, shoot it."

I pulled my service weapon. Forty-caliber. Eight rounds.

Pathetically inadequate for a two-thousand-pound predator.

But it was what I had.

We approached slowly. Dr. Havelka with the dart rifle. Me with my pistol. Kowalski and both deputies with shotguns.

Four humans with inadequate weapons approaching the largest land predator in North American history.

The bear noticed at fifty yards.

Raised its head. Watched us.

Stood up on its hind legs.

And kept rising.

Twelve feet. Thirteen. Fourteen feet tall.

Standing. Looking at us. Assessing.

One of the deputies said "Oh fuck" very quietly.

The bear dropped back to all fours. Took two steps toward us.

Stopped.

Message clear: This is mine. Stay back.

Dr. Havelka raised the dart rifle. "I've got a shot."

"Take it."

The dart fired with a soft *pfft*. Hit the bear in the shoulder. Good placement.

The bear spun. Looked at the dart. Bit at it. Pulled it out with its teeth.

Looked back at us.

Huffed. A sound like warning.

Then shook its head. Took one step. Two.

Stumbled.

The tranquilizer was working.

The bear tried to stand. Front legs gave out. It went down on its chest.

Tried to rise again. Failed.

Head lowered. Eyes half-closed.

Still awake. Still aware. But immobilized.

"How long will it last?" I asked.

"Twenty minutes. Maybe thirty. Depends on its metabolism."

"Let's recover Bob. Now."

We moved quickly. Kowalski and I approached the body while the deputies kept their shotguns trained on the bear.

Bob Martinez was torn apart. Neck crushed. Deep claw wounds across his back. The attack had been efficient. Professional. The way a predator kills when it's done this a thousand times.

We got him into a body bag. Carried him back behind the perimeter.

His family would get him back. Could have a funeral. That was something.

Unlike George Henderson. Unlike the others who'd crossed through and disappeared.

Bob had died on this side. In 2026. His family would have closure.

Not much. But something.

By the time we finished, the bear was fully sedated. Breathing but unconscious.

Dr. Havelka was taking samples. Blood. Tissue. Hair. "For research. We might never get another chance."

I photographed the bear. Measured it.

Thirteen feet, seven inches standing height.

Six feet, two inches at the shoulder on all fours.

Estimated weight: nineteen hundred pounds.

Claws: eight inches. Curved. Designed for grasping.

Teeth: Four-inch canines. Built for crushing cervical vertebrae.

Everything about it said apex predator. Fast. Strong. Efficient.

Nothing in modern Michigan could compete with it.

Nothing.

"What do we do with it?" Kowalski asked. "We can't just leave it here."

"The fold is still open. When it wakes up, it'll probably go back through. Back to its own time."

"And if it doesn't?"

"Then we have the largest predator in North American history loose in Antrim County with a taste for human prey."

We established a watch. Took shifts. Kept the bear in sight.

At 9:47 PM, it started waking up.

Head lifting. Eyes opening. Awareness returning.

It stood. Shaky. Uncoordinated. Tranquilizer still affecting it.

Looked around. Saw us. Saw the campground.

Turned toward the fold.

Walked—stumbled—toward the shimmer.

Crossed through.

Gone.

Back to the Pleistocene.

Back to a time when bears like this ruled the landscape.

The fold contracted. Shimmered.

And closed.

The air warmed. The birds started calling again. The normal sounds of evening returned.

It was over.

But the campground was evacuated. All fifty sites. Nobody wanted to stay.

Bob Martinez's site sat empty. His family gone. His tent still standing. His car still parked.

Evidence of a man who'd come camping and never went home.

Killed by something that shouldn't exist.

By a predator from eleven thousand years ago that had crossed through for maybe thirty minutes, killed efficiently, and gone back.

No malice. No rage. Just hunting.

Doing what evolution designed it to do.

Except the prey was human. And humans weren't equipped to survive encounters with apex predators that had died out before agriculture existed.

The news coverage was immediate and overwhelming.

"Camper Killed by Extinct Predator in Northern Michigan"

"Short-Faced Bear Attack: First Human Death by Pleistocene Megafauna"

"Michigan Campgrounds Close as Extinct Animals Return"

Video of the bear. Testimony from witnesses. Kids describing what they'd seen. Families traumatized.

The mastodon had been sad. The beavers had been strange.

This was terrifying.

This was a predator actively hunting humans.

This changed everything.

By Thursday morning, the entire Michigan campground system was in crisis.

Parks closing. Reservations canceled. Tourists fleeing.

Emergency Management issuing warnings: avoid remote areas, travel in groups, stay away from known thin places.

But people were panicking.

Not just avoiding campgrounds. Avoiding northern Michigan entirely.

Hotels canceling reservations. Restaurants empty. Stores closing.

The economy was collapsing.

Because you can't have tourism when extinct predators are killing people in public campgrounds.

Thursday afternoon, emergency town meeting.

Bellaire High School gym again. Even more packed than before.

Commissioner Walsh at the podium.

"We need to discuss evacuation. The question is no longer whether the thin places are real. The question is: can we live with them?"

The room erupted.

Some people yelling "evacuate now."

Others yelling "this is our home, we're not leaving."

A third group yelling "hunt them, kill them, close the folds."

Walsh let it go for two minutes. Then pounded the podium.

"We need a plan. Dave Pritchard has been documenting these incidents since the beginning. Dave, what do you recommend?"

Everyone turned to look at me.

I stood up.

"We have three options. Evacuate. Adapt. Or die. Those are the choices."

Silence.

"Evacuate means abandoning northern Michigan. Twenty-three thousand people relocating. Homes abandoned. Businesses closed. The entire region surrendered to temporal instability."

"Adapt means learning to live with the thin places. Staying away from high-risk areas. Changing how we build, where we travel, how we survive. It means accepting that this is permanent. That the boundaries won't be fixed. That we're sharing the landscape with the Pleistocene."

"Die means ignoring the threat. Pretending it's not real. Going about our normal lives. And eventually crossing through a fold we didn't see coming, or encountering a predator we can't survive."

"Those are the options. Pick one."

The room stayed silent.

Then Bill Henderson—George's brother—stood up.

"My brother is gone. Lost in the Pleistocene. We can't recover him. Can't bury him. His kids don't have closure. And it happened because we didn't listen when you tried to warn us."

He looked around the room.

"Bob Martinez died last night. In front of his family. Killed by something that shouldn't exist. His kids are traumatized. His wife is destroyed."

"How many more people have to die before we admit this is real? Before we take it seriously? Before we actually do something?"

Another silence. Longer this time.

Then someone in the back yelled: "What can we do? We can't fight extinct bears! We can't close temporal folds! What the hell are we supposed to do?"

I stood up again.

"We learn the pattern. We mark the high-risk zones. We warn people. We evacuate the areas that can't be made safe. And we create a warning system for when folds open."

"Jake has been documenting seismic signatures. We can detect folds opening in real-time. We can send alerts. Give people time to avoid the area or take shelter."

"It's not perfect. We can't prevent every incident. But we can reduce them. We can give people a chance."

Commissioner Walsh nodded. "Motion to establish a fold warning system and close the highest-risk zones. All in favor?"

This time, it passed. Unanimous.

Finally.

After eight incidents. After multiple deaths. After a man was killed by an extinct bear in front of his children.

Finally, the county was taking it seriously.

That night, I sat on the back deck with Karen.

"Bob Martinez had two kids," she said quietly. "Eight and ten. They watched a short-faced bear kill their father."

"I know."

"Those kids are going to need therapy for the rest of their lives."

"I know."

"And there are more bears out there. More predators. More folds opening. More families at risk."

"I know."

She looked at me. "Can we actually stop this? Or are we just delaying the inevitable?"

I thought about the fold at Elk Lake. Open. Closed. Open again tomorrow or next week or next month.

Thought about the bear. Hunting. Killing. Doing what bears do.

Thought about the dozens of thin places scattered across the county. The hundreds more across the region.

Thought about Jake's data showing continuous folds by May.

"I don't think we can stop it," I said. "I think we learn to live with it. Or we leave."

"And if we leave?"

"Someone else moves in. People always do. And they learn the same lessons we're learning. The hard way."

She was quiet for a long time.

Then: "I don't want to leave."

"Neither do I."

"So we adapt."

"Yes."

"Even if people keep dying."

"Even then."

She leaned against me. "This is insane. You know that, right? We're talking about learning to live with temporal instability like it's a new weather pattern."

"It might as well be. It's that inevitable."

[END CHAPTER TWENTY]

Word count: ~3,600 words

What happened:

Bob Martinez killed at Elk Lake Campground (public, 40+ witnesses)

Short-faced bear emerges, pursues at 40 mph, kills instantly

Bear guards body, won't let recovery

12-14 feet standing, 1,900 lbs, apex predator

Multiple families witness, kids traumatized

Dr. Havelka tranquilizes bear, body recovered

Bear wakes up, returns through fold

First public predator killing

Campgrounds evacuate region-wide

Tourism collapses

Emergency meeting: county finally votes for warning system and zone closures

Dave: "Evacuate, adapt, or die. Pick one."

Escalation:

Public death (not remote like George)

Children witnessed

Undeniable predator threat

Economic collapse begins

Mass panic spreading

Character moments:

Bob's kids saw everything

Bill Henderson (George's brother) confronts community

Dave's three options speech

Karen: "This is insane" / Dave: "It's inevitable"

Chapter 21

PTER TWENTY-ONE: EVACUATION DEBATE

The fracture happened fast.

By Friday morning—thirty-six hours after Bob Martinez died—Bellaire was divided into camps that barely spoke to each other.

You could see it in the grocery store. In the gas stations. In the way people avoided eye contact or clustered in groups, talking in low voices, deciding who was rational and who was insane.

Except nobody could agree on which was which.

The first camp was simple: **Get out.**

Families with kids. Young couples. People who'd moved here from downstate for the quiet life and discovered the quiet came with apex predators from the Pleistocene.

Sharon Kowalski—the sheriff's wife, no relation to Tom—organized them. Posted on Facebook: "Family Safety First - Bellaire Evacuation Coordination Group."

Within twelve hours, she had three hundred members.

I saw her at the post office Friday morning. She was mailing boxes. Lots of boxes.

"Moving?" I asked.

"Traverse City. Rented a house. We're out by Monday." She looked at me. "Tom's staying. His job. But the kids and I aren't waiting around for a bear to show up in our backyard."

"Sharon—"

"Don't. Don't tell me it's safe if we're careful. Don't tell me the warning system will work. Bob Martinez was careful. He was walking to his car. And now his kids watched him die." She taped another box. "My kids aren't watching that happen to their father."

She wasn't wrong. I couldn't argue with her.

"What about your house?"

"On the market. We'll take whatever we can get. If anything." She laughed bitterly. "Who's buying property in Bellaire right now? 'Charming three-bedroom, excellent schools, occasional temporal displacement into ice age, short-faced bears may kill you in your driv eway.'"

By Friday afternoon, seventeen houses were listed for sale.

By Saturday, forty-three.

By Sunday, the real estate market collapsed completely. No buyers. No offers. Just people desperate to leave and discovering their homes were worthless.

The second camp was louder: **This is our home.**

Multi-generation locals. People whose families had been here since the 1800s. People who'd survived recessions and factory closures and hard winters and weren't about to be driven out by extinct animals.

Bill Henderson led them. George's brother. The man who'd lost family to the folds and still refused to leave.

He organized a meeting at the VFW hall Saturday night. I went. So did maybe two hundred people.

Bill stood at the front. "My grandfather built a house on Torch Lake in 1947. My father expanded it in 1973. I inherited it in 2004. Three generations. Seventy-nine years. And I'm supposed to abandon it because reality is acting weird?"

Applause. Loud.

"This is our home. Our land. Our community. And I don't care if mastodons are grazing on M-88 or if prehistoric people are camping in the woods or if goddamn dinosaurs show up—I'm not leaving."

More applause.

"We adapt. We learn the patterns. We avoid the high-risk zones. We protect each other. But we don't run. We don't surrender. We stay."

A woman in the back—Linda Morrison, who'd fallen through the bridge fold—stood up. "Bill, I respect that. But I broke my leg falling thirty feet because a bridge disappeared. What happens when something worse happens? What happens when a fold opens in your house? When you're eating breakfast and suddenly you're in the ice age?"

"Then I deal with it. Same as I'd deal with a tornado or a flood or any other natural disaster."

"This isn't a natural disaster. This is the laws of physics breaking down."

"And running away doesn't fix that. It just means you're not here when we figure out how to survive it."

The room divided. Half nodding. Half shaking their heads.

I watched people I'd known for years choose sides. Neighbors who'd helped each other through hard times suddenly on opposite sides of a divide that had nothing to do with logic and everything to do with fear versus stubbornness.

The third camp was the one that made my stomach turn: **Make money.**

It started with a guy named Derek Voss. Mid-thirties. Ran a hunting guide service out of Mancelona. Saw opportunity where everyone else saw catastrophe.

He posted on every local forum, every Facebook group, every outdoor enthusiast site he could find:

"PLEISTOCENE PREDATOR HUNTS - Once in a lifetime opportunity. Hunt extinct megafauna. Short-faced bear. American lion. Dire wolf. $50,000 per hunt. Limited availability. Legal gray area = act fast."

I called him Saturday afternoon.

"Derek, you can't do this."

"Why not? There's no law against hunting extinct animals. They're not on any protected species list because they don't exist. Legally, it's the same as hunting any other large game."

"They're not game. They're temporal anomalies. And they're dangerous."

"So are grizzlies. So are cape buffalo. Dangerous hunts cost more. Supply and demand."

"You're going to get people killed."

"I'm going to make money. And if rich assholes from Texas want to pay fifty grand to shoot a bear that's been dead for eleven thousand years, that's capitalism."

"It's exploitation."

"Same thing." He hung up.

By Sunday, he had three bookings. Deposits paid. Hunts scheduled for the following weekend.

And he wasn't alone.

A woman from Traverse City—Amanda Smith, owned a tour company—started advertising "Thin Place Tours." Bus trips to active fold sites. "See the Pleistocene! Witness temporal displacement! Safe viewing distance guaranteed!"

Safe viewing distance. Right.

A guy from Charlevoix started selling "Authentic Paleo-Indian Artifacts" online. Except the artifacts were obviously fake. Modern stone points aged to look old. Selling for $500 each to collectors who didn't know better.

And worst of all: a development company from downstate put in a proposal to build a "Temporal Research and Tourism Center" on the Lakeview Estates site—the one that had flooded during the full moon.

Their pitch: drain the fold, stabilize the boundary, build a visitor center where tourists could safely observe Lake Algonquin. "Educational entertainment. Family-friendly. Projected revenue: $12 million annually."

They presented it to the county board Tuesday morning.

Commissioner Walsh looked at the proposal like it was radioactive.

"You want to build a tourist attraction on an active temporal boundary."

"We want to monetize an unavoidable phenomenon. The folds aren't going away. We might as well profit from them."

"People have died."

"People die skiing. People die rock climbing. Doesn't stop those industries. We'll have waivers. Insurance. Safety protocols."

"Safety protocols for time travel."

"For temporal observation. It's a subtle distinction but legally important."

Walsh rejected it. Unanimously.

But the fact that someone had proposed it—that a company had looked at Bob Martinez's death and seen dollar signs—that told you everything about the third camp.

They didn't care about safety. Didn't care about the danger. Just saw an opportunity to make money off tragedy and took it.

The fourth camp was quieter but growing: **Study it.**

Dr. Marcus Webb—the anthropologist from University of Michigan—arrived Monday with a team. Set up a research station near the Skegmog Lake site where Sarah had found the Paleo-Indian settlement.

He stopped by my office Tuesday afternoon.

"Officer Pritchard. We've established contact with a band near Skegmog. Seven individuals. They're allowing observation from a distance. No direct interaction yet, but we're documenting language, tool use, social structure."

"How are they adapting?"

"Remarkably well. They've figured out that certain areas are dangerous—roads, buildings, places where modern humans congregate. They're avoiding those. Staying in forested areas. Hunting. Gathering. Establishing territory."

"What happens when winter comes? When they need more resources?"

"I don't know. But that's why we need to study them now. Understand their needs. Maybe establish peaceful coexistence protocols before conflict becomes inevitable."

He showed me photos. The Paleo-Indian camp. People working. Making tools. Processing hides. Living.

"They're not going back," he said. "Even if the folds close. They've adapted too quickly. This is home now."

"Are there more groups?"

"We've identified at least four separate bands. Maybe fifty to seventy individuals total. All within twenty miles of Bellaire. Probably more we haven't found yet."

Fifty to seventy.

And that was just what researchers had documented.

"Dr. Webb, what's the long-term plan? Permanent research station? Ongoing study?"

"If the university approves funding. But Dave, we need protection. Some of the locals are talking about hunting them. Running them off. Treating them as threats."

"They are threats. To some people."

"They're humans. Displaced. Frightened. Trying to survive. Just like us."

"Tell that to the families evacuating. Tell that to Bob Martinez's kids."

He didn't have an answer for that.

The fifth camp was the one I hadn't expected: **Divine intervention.**

It started small. A few people claiming the folds were apocalyptic. End times. Judgment.

Then Pastor Reynolds at First Baptist Church gave a Sunday sermon titled "The Land Remembers Our Sins."

I wasn't there, but Karen went. Came back shaken.

"He's saying the thin places are punishment. That we've desecrated the land—destroyed the burial mounds, built on sacred sites, ignored indigenous warnings—and now God is making us face the consequences."

"That's insane."

"He had three hundred people in the pews. Standing room only. And they were nodding."

By Monday, Pastor Reynolds had started a prayer group. "Pray for Closure." Twice-daily meetings. Praying that the folds would close. That the land would heal. That normalcy would return.

It wasn't just Baptists. The Catholic church had its own group. So did the Methodists.

And on the other side—a smaller group, led by a woman named Patricia Whitehorse who claimed Odawa heritage—started calling the folds sacred. "The land is healing. The old ones are returning. This is restoration, not destruction."

She held ceremonies at known thin places. Offerings. Songs. Rituals that mixed indigenous practices with New Age spirituality in ways that made Sarah Ashkwe visibly uncomfortable.

"She doesn't speak for us," Sarah told me Tuesday. "She's not enrolled. Not part of the community. She's appropriating our culture to make herself feel important."

"Can you stop her?"

"No. Freedom of religion. She can do whatever she wants. Doesn't make it right."

The spiritual camp split further. Some seeing the folds as punishment. Some seeing them as blessing. Some seeing them as neutral phenomenon being weaponized by grifters.

But all of them praying. Or chanting. Or offering. Or trying to impose meaning on something that didn't care about meaning.

The land didn't remember sins. It just remembered what it used to be.

And it was becoming that again whether we liked it or not.

By Wednesday, the town was fractured completely.

Five camps. Barely speaking to each other. Each convinced they had the right answer.

Evacuate. Stay. Profit. Study. Pray.

And in the middle: the rest of us. The people who didn't fit neatly into any camp. Who saw truth in all of them and answers in none of them.

Jake fell into that category. So did Dr. Ostrander. So did Sarah. So did I.

We met Wednesday night at my house. Informal. No agenda. Just trying to figure out what the hell we were supposed to do.

"The warning system works," Jake said. "We've had three folds open since we implemented it. Got alerts out ten to fifteen minutes before each one. Nobody hurt. Nobody trapped."

"Three folds," Dr. Ostrander countered. "In four days. That's almost one per day. The frequency is increasing."

"I know. My models show daily folds by April. Multiple per day by May."

"Can the warning system scale to that?"

"I don't know. If we're sending alerts every six hours, people will start ignoring them. Alert fatigue."

Sarah looked at me. "What's the county doing?"

"Officially? Establishing evacuation zones. High-risk areas will be cleared. Residential properties bought out by the state. Commercial development prohibited."

"Unofficially?"

"Chaos. Half the board wants everyone evacuated. Half wants to fight. One commissioner suggested building walls around the fold sites. Literal walls. Like we can contain temporal displacement with chain-link fencing."

Karen came in with coffee. Set it down. "I heard from Sharon Kowalski today. She's gone. Left Monday. Says she's not coming back."

"How many families have left?" Dr. Ostrander asked.

"Hard to say. Maybe two hundred. Out of twenty-three thousand residents, that's less than one percent. But it's accelerating. More leaving every day."

"Where are they going?"

"Traverse City. Petoskey. Downstate. Anywhere that's not on the moraine system. Anywhere they think is safe."

"Nowhere's safe," Jake said. "The geology extends across the entire Great Lakes region. Wisconsin. Illinois. Ohio. All of it has the same boundaries. The same potential for folds."

"So we're all just waiting for it to start everywhere else."

"Probably."

Silence.

Then Sarah said: "My grandmother used to say: when the world changes, you change with it or you disappear. The people who stayed too rigid, who insisted things stay the same—they didn't survive. The ones who adapted, who learned new ways—they did."

"Which are we?" I asked.

"I don't know yet. Ask me in a year."

Thursday morning, Derek Voss led his first hunt.

Three clients from Texas. Rich assholes with expensive rifles and no sense.

They went into the woods near Elk Rapids. One of the red zones. Looking for predators to shoot.

Found one.

Dire wolf. Alone. Maybe separated from its pack.

They shot it. Killed it. Posed with the body for photos.

Posted them online within an hour. "First Pleistocene Hunt Success! *Aenocyon dirus* taken at 150 yards. Clean kill. Trophy of a lifetime!"

The backlash was immediate.

Environmental groups screaming about killing extinct species.

Scientists horrified at the destruction of invaluable specimens.

Animal rights activists calling for arrests.

And the Paleo-Indian research community losing their minds. "You just killed a species that's been extinct for eleven thousand years. For sport. For a photo."

Derek's response: "It's legal. And I'm booked solid through June. Supply and demand, baby."

I wanted to arrest him. Couldn't. There was no law against it.

I wanted to punch him. Couldn't do that either.

So I did the only thing I could: documented it. Added it to the record.

Incident twenty-three: Dire wolf killed by hunters near Elk Rapids. First confirmed killing of displaced megafauna for sport. Body recovered for research. Legal status unclear.

And I waited for the next disaster.

That night, Karen and I sat on the back deck.

"Are we staying?" she asked.

"Do you want to leave?"

"I don't know. Part of me thinks we're insane for staying. Part of me thinks leaving means surrendering. Giving up on everything we've built."

"And the kids?"

"Jake's staying. He's too invested in the research. Emma..." She paused. "Emma called today. From school. She's not coming back this summer. Says it's too dangerous. Says she'll visit but she won't live here."

"She's probably right."

"Probably. But it still hurts."

We sat in silence. Watching the woods. Listening to normal Michigan night sounds.

Somewhere out there, folds were opening. Closing. Opening again. The boundaries getting thinner. The past bleeding through.

And humans—being humans—were dividing into camps. Fighting each other instead of adapting together. Exploiting instead of protecting. Praying instead of planning.

Same as we'd always done when faced with change we didn't understand.

"We're going to survive this," I said. "Some of us. Not all. But some."

"How do you know?"

"Because humans are good at surviving. We're terrible at everything else—cooperation, foresight, compassion—but we're excellent at surviving."

"That's not reassuring."

"It's not meant to be. It's just true."

Chapter 22

CHAPTER TWENTY-TWO: LEARNING THE PATTERN

The warning system went live Friday, April 4th.

Jake set it up to run through the county emergency alert network. Same system used for tornado warnings and Amber alerts. Except instead of "Tornado spotted near Bellaire, take shelter immediately," the messages read:

"TEMPORAL FOLD ALERT: Seismic activity detected at [location]. Fold opening imminent. Avoid area. Duration unknown. Alert issued [time]."

The first test alert went out at 6:47 AM.

Half the county's phones buzzed simultaneously.

"TEMPORAL FOLD ALERT: Seismic activity detected Cairn Highway mile marker 7. Fold opening imminent. Avoid area."

I was already in my truck. Heading toward the site. Arriving before the fold opened.

Cairn Highway. Mile marker seven. Elevation 623 feet. Lake Algonquin shoreline. Red zone.

And standing at the side of the road: a minivan. Family of four. Mom, dad, two kids. Pulled over. Reading the alert on their phones.

The dad waved me down. "Is this real? The alert?"

"Yes. A fold is about to open here. You need to leave. Now."

"What's a fold?"

"Temporal displacement. The past bleeding through. You don't want to be here when it happens."

He looked at his wife. She looked at the kids. Eight and ten, maybe. Curious. Not scared yet.

"How long do we have?"

"Maybe ten minutes. Maybe less. Please go."

They went. Drove north. Away from the site.

At 6:58 AM, the fold opened.

A shimmer between two trees. Growing. Stabilizing.

And through it: ice. The same glacier from the nature trail. Spreading across the road. Thirty feet. Forty feet.

If that family had been driving past when it opened, they'd have hit the ice at fifty miles per hour. Crashed. Maybe died.

Instead, they were five miles away. Safe.

Because the alert had worked.

First save.

The second alert came at 11:23 AM.

"TEMPORAL FOLD ALERT: Seismic activity detected North Country Trail, Pinney Bridge area. Fold opening imminent."

Dr. Webb's research team was nearby. Observing the Paleo-Indian settlement.

He called me. "Dave, we're getting the alert. Should we evacuate?"

"How close are you to Pinney Bridge?"

"Maybe a quarter mile."

"Move back. Now. The fold could extend beyond the predicted zone."

They relocated. Set up observation point half a mile away.

At 11:31 AM, the fold opened.

Larger than expected. Not just at Pinney Bridge but spreading along the trail. Two hundred yards of temporal displacement.

Through the shimmer: Pleistocene forest. Different trees. Different undergrowth. And movement. Large. Quadrupedal.

Mastodon.

Not a juvenile this time. Full adult. Maybe nine feet at the shoulder. Five tons. Healthy. Browsing on vegetation that existed in its time but not in ours.

It stayed for seventeen minutes. Then the fold closed. The mastodon went with it.

Dr. Webb got the whole thing on camera. Documented. Time-stamped. Correlated with Jake's seismic data.

"The alert gave us time to set up safely," he said later. "Without it, we'd have been standing right where that mastodon appeared. That would've been... problematic."

Second save.

The third alert came at 3:47 PM.

"TEMPORAL FOLD ALERT: Seismic activity detected Intermediate Lake, west shore boat launch. Fold opening imminent."

Saturday afternoon. Spring weather. The boat launch was busy. Maybe twenty people. Launching boats. Fishing. Kids playing on the beach.

I got there in eight minutes. Started evacuating.

"Everyone back to the parking lot. Fold opening. Move now."

Most people complied. Grabbed their kids. Headed for the cars.

One guy didn't.

Mid-forties. Expensive fishing gear. Tourist from downstate.

"I paid for a launch permit. I'm not leaving because of some computer glitch."

"It's not a glitch. It's a temporal displacement warning. You need to leave."

"I'll take my chances."

"Sir—"

"I'm launching my boat. You can't stop me."

He was technically right. I couldn't physically force him to leave. No authority for that.

So I documented it. Took his photo. His license plate. His name when he volunteered it smugly: "Richard Morrison. And I'm filing a complaint about this harassment."

"File whatever you want. But when the fold opens, you're on your own."

I retreated to the parking lot. Waited.

At 3:54 PM, the fold opened.

Right where the boat launch had been.

Water. Lake Algonquin. Twenty feet higher than modern Intermediate Lake.

The ancient shoreline surging forward. Flooding the launch area. Covering the beach.

Richard Morrison was standing in his boat. Thirty feet from shore. Trying to start his outboard motor.

The water hit.

Not a wave. A displacement. Reality folding. Where there had been modern lake there was suddenly ancient lake. Different temperature. Different chemistry. Different water level.

His boat capsized. Just rolled. He went into the water.

Cold water. Glacial melt. Maybe 40 degrees.

He surfaced. Screaming. Flailing.

I called it in. "Man in the water at Intermediate Lake boat launch. Fold active. Need rescue."

The EMTs arrived in six minutes. Len Greenland leading.

"Where is he, and what?"

I pointed. Through the shimmer. Morrison was visible on the other side. In Lake Algonquin. Swimming toward what he thought was shore.

Except shore was twenty feet higher in his time than ours. He was swimming toward a cliff that didn't exist in 2026.

"Can we reach him?" I asked.

"Not through the fold. It's too unstable. But if it closes, if he comes back through..." Len trailed off.

We waited.

The fold stayed open. Twelve minutes. Fifteen. Twenty.

Morrison was getting hypothermic. Slowing down. Struggling.

At the eighteen-minute mark, the fold flickered.

"Get ready," Len said.

The shimmer intensified. Contracted.

Morrison was maybe forty feet from the boundary. Swimming. Barely.

The fold contracted further.

Thirty feet from the boundary.

Twenty feet.

Ten feet.

The fold snapped closed.

Morrison came through. Appeared in modern Intermediate Lake. Exactly where he'd been. Except now there was no ancient water. Just normal lake.

He sank.

Len and his team went in. Got him. Dragged him to shore.

Hypothermic. Confused. Barely conscious.

They got him into the ambulance. Warming blankets. IV fluids.

He survived.

Barely.

As they loaded him, he looked at me. "What... what was that?"

"That was you ignoring a warning. And almost dying for it."

"The water... it was wrong. Different. Cold."

"Lake Algonquin. Eleven thousand years old. Forty degrees. Glacial melt. You were swimming in the Pleistocene."

"That's impossible."

"File a complaint."

Third save. Technically. He'd survived. But only because the fold had closed at exactly the right moment. Thirty seconds later and he'd have been too deep in hypothermia to swim. He'd have drowned in ancient water and his body would've stayed there. Unrecoverable.

He'd gotten lucky.

But luck wasn't a strategy.

By Sunday, we'd issued seventeen alerts.

Fourteen folds opened as predicted. Three false positives where seismic activity spiked but no fold manifested.

Of the fourteen real folds:

Nine occurred in unpopulated areas. No risk. Documented and monitored.

Three occurred in populated areas but evacuations were successful. No casualties.

Two occurred in populated areas with incomplete evacuations.

One was Richard Morrison. Who survived.

The other was a woman named Patricia Hendricks.

Patricia lived on Barnes Road. Quarter mile from where the hunters had been attacked. Red zone. High-probability site.

She'd been offered buyout. State was purchasing properties in the highest-risk areas. She'd refused.

"This is my home. I've lived here forty years. I'm not leaving because of government paranoia."

Sunday morning, 9:14 AM, the alert went out.

"TEMPORAL FOLD ALERT: Seismic activity detected Barnes Road near Torch Lake. Fold opening imminent."

Sheriff's deputy knocked on her door. "Ma'am, you need to evacuate. Fold opening in your area."

"I'm not leaving my house."

"Ma'am, this isn't optional. You're in immediate danger."

"Young man, I've survived blizzards and tornadoes and the recession of 2008. I'll survive this too."

She closed the door.

The deputy called it in. "Resident refusing evacuation. What do we do?"

Sheriff Kowalski: "Document it. Stay nearby. If the fold opens, try to get her out. But we can't force her."

The fold opened at 9:22 AM.

Right through her house.

Not near it. Through it.

The boundary cut her living room in half.

West side: modern. 2026. Normal.

East side: Pleistocene. Ice. Cold. Different.

Patricia was sitting in her recliner. On the west side. Safe.

But her kitchen was on the east side.

Frozen. Ice covering the counters. The floor. Everything.

The deputy saw it through the window. Called it in.

"The fold bisected her house. She's on the safe side but the structure's unstable. We need to get her out."

I arrived at 9:29 AM.

The house was split. Literally split. Half in one era, half in another.

Patricia was visible through the window. Still in her recliner. Staring at her kitchen. At the ice. At the impossibility.

I knocked. She opened the door. Slowly.

"Ms. Hendricks, you need to come with me. Now."

"My kitchen..."

"Is eleven thousand years in the past. The fold is active. The house is structurally compromised. We need to evacuate."

"But my things..."

"Can be replaced. You can't. Please. Come with me."

She looked back at her kitchen. At forty years of home. Of memories. Of normal life.

Then she looked at the ice.

And she came.

We got her out. Got her to safety.

At 9:47 AM, the fold expanded slightly.

The house groaned. Metal stressing. Wood cracking.

Then it collapsed.

Half the house—the modern half—fell into the fold. Through the boundary. Into the Pleistocene.

Gone.

The other half—already ice-covered—remained. A ruin. Half a house sitting in the ice age. Uninhabitable. Abandoned.

Patricia watched it fall. Didn't cry. Didn't scream. Just watched.

Then she said quietly: "I should've taken the buyout."

Fourth save. She was alive. But her home was gone.

And she'd almost died defending it.

By Monday, patterns were emerging.

Jake compiled the data. Presented it at an emergency county meeting.

"We're learning how folds behave. Not perfectly. But better."

He put up a slide. "Fold duration correlates with lunar cycle intensity. Full moon folds last longer. New moon folds are briefer. Between cycles, folds are shorter but more frequent."

"We can predict location with about eighty-five percent accuracy. Moraine-shoreline intersections. Destroyed mound sites. Areas of high geological stress."

"We can predict timing with about seventy percent accuracy. Seismic precursors appear ten to twenty minutes before opening. Sometimes longer. Rarely shorter."

"And we're learning fold behavior patterns. Some close after minutes. Some stay open for hours. Some appear to be permanent. We don't know why yet. But we're documenting every case."

Commissioner Walsh: "What's the casualty rate since we implemented the warning system?"

"Zero confirmed deaths. Four close calls. Patricia Hendricks lost her home but survived. Richard Morrison nearly drowned but was recovered. Two others had narrow escapes but no serious injuries."

"Before the warning system?"

"Eight deaths in three weeks. Multiple injuries. Dozens of close calls,. The system is working."

"But it's not perfect."

"No. We're still learning. Still refining. But it's better than nothing. And it's getting better every day."

The data showed something else. Something we weren't talking about publicly yet.

The folds were changing.

Not just frequency. Not just duration.

Behavior.

The early folds—Joe's mastodon valley, Mel's drowning—had been simple. Open. Close. Done.

Recent folds were more complex.

Some opened partially. Flickered. Stabilized. Flickered again.

Some opened in layers. Multiple time periods visible simultaneously. Not just Pleistocene but different stages. Lake Algonquin overlapping with Nipissing overlapping with modern. Three eras at once.

Some opened in patterns. Multiple small folds clustered together instead of one large fold.

And some—increasingly—weren't closing at all.

We now had fourteen permanent folds across Antrim County. Areas where past and present existed simultaneously. Where you could walk from 2026 into 11,000 BP by crossing a shimmer line.

Those areas were being fenced off. Marked. Evacuated.

But fencing didn't stop folds from expanding. Didn't stop animals from crossing through. Didn't stop curious idiots from ducking under the fence to "see what's on the other side."

We'd rescued three people from permanent folds in the past week. All tourists. All ignoring warnings. All lucky to be alive.

How long until luck ran out?

Wednesday afternoon, I got a call from Dr. Ostrander.

"Dave, I need you to see something."

He was at the Lakeview Estates site. The construction development that had flooded during the full moon. Still underwater. Still showing Lake Algonquin.

I met him there at 4 PM.

The fold was stable. Had been open for nine days. No signs of closure.

"Look at the water level," he said.

I looked. The ancient lake was lower. Noticeably lower. Maybe three feet lower than when it had first appeared.

"It's draining?"

"No. It's equilibrating. The water level in Lake Algonquin is adjusting to match modern hydrology. The fold is... learning. Adapting. Trying to stabilize."

"What does that mean?"

"I think the folds are attempting to reconcile the contradiction. Past and present can't occupy the same space indefinitely. Something has to give. Either the fold closes, or the two eras merge somehow, or..." He trailed off.

"Or what?"

"Or one era overwrites the other. If the fold stays open long enough, if it stabilizes completely, this site won't be a fold anymore. It'll just be Lake Algonquin. Permanently. The modern landscape erased. Replaced."

"Can that happen?"

"It's already happening. Look at Patricia Hendricks' house. Half of it is gone. Not destroyed. Gone. Overwritten by the Pleistocene. If the fold had stayed open another hour, the entire house would've been replaced. And eventually, if enough folds stay open long enough, entire sections of the county could be replaced."

"Replaced with what?"

"With what used to be here. Glaciers. Ancient lakes. Pleistocene forest. The land remembering so hard it forgets the present."

That night, I updated the documentation.

Incident tracking: 47 total folds since February. 14 permanent. 33 closed.

Casualties: 8 deaths (pre-warning system). 0 deaths (post-warning system). 17 close calls. 3 serious injuries. 2 properties destroyed. 6 properties damaged.

Saves: 23 confirmed evacuations based on alerts. Estimated 200+ people warned away from high-risk areas during active folds.

Pattern recognition: Lunar correlation 94%. Location prediction 85%. Timing prediction 71%. Duration prediction 43%.

We were learning.

Slowly. Expensively. Through trial and error and near-disasters.

But we were learning.

Some people saved. Some lost. Some lucky. Some not.

The warning system worked. Not perfectly. But better than guessing. Better than nothing.

And in a world where the laws of physics were breaking down and the past was bleeding through, "better than nothing" was the best we could do.

Thursday morning, Jake knocked on my office door.

"Dad. I've got the April projection."

"How bad?"

He showed me the graph. "Twenty-three predicted folds in April. Based on current acceleration. And the lunar cycle peaks on the 18th. That'll be the worst day. Probably six to eight simultaneous folds."

"Can the warning system handle that?"

"If people listen. If they evacuate when told. If they don't ignore alerts because they're getting too frequent." He paused. "But Dad, there's something else."

"What?"

"The permanent folds are expanding. Slowly. Maybe a few inches per day. But they're growing. And if they keep growing, if they start merging..."

"We'll have entire zones that are just Pleistocene. No modern landscape left."

"Yes."

"How long?"

"Until they merge? Months. Maybe a year. Depends on expansion rate and how many new permanent folds open."

"And when they merge? When we have continuous Pleistocene zones?"

"Then people can't live there anymore. Can't build. Can't travel through. Those areas become... uninhabitable. At least by modern humans."

I thought about the Paleo-Indians. The bands establishing settlements. Learning the landscape. Adapting.

If modern humans couldn't live in the permanent fold zones, but Paleo-Indians could...

Then we were looking at territory exchange. Not intentional. Not planned. But inevitable.

Modern humans retreating from areas that were becoming too unstable. Paleo-Indians moving in to fill the vacuum.

A slow, accidental colonization.

The land returning to the people who understood it best.

Friday afternoon, I drove to the nature trail. The one where Linda Morrison had fallen through the bridge.

The fold was still there. Still open. Ice field visible through the shimmer.

But the ice was closer now. The fold had expanded. What had been a ravine with ice at the bottom was now ice extending to ground level. You could walk onto it if you wanted.

Someone had.

Footprints in the ice. Modern boots. Leading twenty feet onto the glacier. Then stopping. Then returning.

Someone testing the boundary. Seeing how far they could go.

They'd come back. This time.

But eventually someone wouldn't. Would walk too far. Get trapped when the fold flickered. Or encounter something on the other side.

We'd put up signs. Fences. Warnings.

But humans being humans, someone always thought the rules didn't apply to them.

And they learned the hard way.

If they learned at all.

Chapter 23

CHAPTER TWENTY-THREE: DOCUMENTARY

The documentary crew arrived Monday, April 7th.

PBS Frontline. National Geographic. BBC Earth. Discovery Channel. All of them. Plus independent filmmakers. Student documentarians. YouTubers with cameras.

Bellaire became a media circus. Again.

But this time was different.

This time they had permission. Coordination. Official access.

The state had finally decided: if this is happening, if it's undeniable, if it's going to keep happening—document it. Make it educational. Control the narrative before conspiracy theorists and grifters own it completely.

Dr. Marcus Webb coordinated with the production teams. Set up schedules. Approved locations. Established protocols for filming near active fold sites.

I was assigned as liaison. Lucky me.

The PBS crew—led by a producer named Jennifer Ortiz—wanted to start with basics.

"We need to show viewers what a fold looks like. Not Ring camera footage. Not cell phone video. Professional documentation. Controlled environment. Can you arrange that?"

"I can tell you where a fold is likely to open. But I can't control when or guarantee safety."

"That's fine. We'll set up at a high-probability site and wait."

Jake provided the data. Three locations with 80%+ probability of folding within the next seventy-two hours:

Cairn Highway mile marker 9

North Country Trail near Pinney Bridge

Old railroad grade east of East Jordan

The PBS crew chose Cairn Highway. Close to town. Easy access. Good visibility.

They set up Tuesday morning. Three cameras. Sound equipment. Lighting rigs for night filming. A production tent fifty yards back from the predicted fold point.

And they waited.

The fold opened Wednesday at 2:47 PM.

I was there. So was Jake. Dr. Ostrander. Sarah. And Jennifer's camera crew.

The seismic monitors showed activity at 2:38 PM. Nine minutes warning.

"Everyone back," I said. "Behind the perimeter."

The crew retreated. Cameras rolling.

At 2:47, the shimmer appeared.

Right where Jake predicted. Between two large oaks. Growing. Stabilizing.

And through it: Lake Algonquin.

Not flooding this time. Just there. Visible. The ancient shoreline twenty feet higher than modern terrain. Water lapping against rocks that hadn't existed in 11,000 years.

The cameras caught everything.

The shimmer. The water. The color difference—glacial melt blue versus modern lake blue. The temperature drop—40-degree air on one side, 55 on the other. The boundary line visible as distortion, like heat shimmer but cold.

Jennifer directed her crew. "Get the wide shot. Now close-up on the boundary. Pan across. Show the contrast."

They filmed for seventeen minutes. Until the fold closed.

When it was done, Jennifer walked over to me.

"That was incredible. Absolutely incredible. The footage is perfect."

"That was a mild one. Small. Stable. No animals. No danger."

"Can we film a more dramatic one?"

"If by dramatic you mean dangerous, then no. I'm not risking your crew for better footage."

"What if we use drones? Remote cameras? Film from a safe distance?"

I looked at Jake. He shrugged. "Could work. If the fold doesn't expand unexpectedly."

"Set it up for the next high-probability event. But if I say evacuate, you evacuate. No arguments. No 'just one more shot.' Clear?"

"Crystal clear."

The National Geographic team wanted something different.

"We're doing a feature on the Paleo-Indian populations. The human element. We'd like to film them. With permission. Respectfully."

Dr. Webb handled that one. He'd established tentative trust with one band near Skegmog Lake. Seven individuals who'd allowed observation from a distance.

"I can ask. But they might refuse. They're wary. And they don't understand cameras. Or why we want to point things at them."

NatGeo sent their best cultural documentarian. A woman named Dr. Lisa Park—no relation to the cryptozoologist—who'd spent twenty years filming indigenous communities worldwide.

She met with Sarah first.

"I want to do this right. Not exploitative. Not sensational. I want to show them as people. Humans displaced by circumstances they don't understand, trying to survive with dignity."

Sarah studied her. "You've filmed indigenous communities before?"

"Dozens. From the Amazon to Siberia. Always with consent. Always respectful. Always showing full context."

"These people can't give informed consent. They don't understand what a camera is. What film is. Where it will be shown or how it will be used."

"Then we film from a distance. Use long lenses. Minimal intrusion. And we let Dr. Webb act as intermediary. If they signal discomfort, we stop immediately."

Sarah considered. "I'll observe every session. If I see anything exploitative, anything that treats them as curiosities rather than people, I shut it down. Agreed?"

"Agreed."

The first filming session was Thursday morning.

The Paleo-Indian camp near Skegmog Lake. The band of seven.

Dr. Park's crew set up four hundred yards away. Long telephoto lenses. Boom microphones. Professional wildlife filming techniques adapted for humans.

We watched through binoculars.

The band was working. Normal morning activities.

Two men knapping stone. Making points for atlatl darts. The sound of stone on stone carried across the distance. Sharp. Rhythmic. Professional.

One woman processing a hide. Scraping. Stretching. Turning raw animal skin into usable leather with tools and techniques eleven thousand years old.

Another woman—younger, maybe late teens—tending a fire. Cooking something. Meat, probably. The smell of smoke and roasting game drifting on the wind.

Two children playing. Four and six, maybe. Chasing each other. Laughing. Universal kid behavior separated by millennia.

And one man—the elder, the one Sarah and I had seen before—sitting apart. Watching the tree line. Alert. Vigilant.

Keeping his people safe.

Dr. Park's cameras caught it all.

The work. The family dynamics. The competence. The humanity.

"This is perfect," she whispered. "This shows them as they are. Not primitive. Not savage. Just people living."

After thirty minutes, the elder stood.

Looked directly at our position.

He'd known we were there the whole time. Watching. Recording.

He said something to his group. They stopped working. Looked toward us.

Then the elder made a gesture. Hand raised. Palm out.

Stop. Or peace. Or go away. Hard to tell.

Dr. Park lowered her camera. "We're done. He's asking us to leave. We leave."

We packed up. Retreated.

As we left, I looked back.

The elder was still watching. Making sure we were gone.

Protecting his people from something he didn't understand but recognized as intrusive.

Smart. Cautious. Exactly what you'd expect from someone who'd survived the Pleistocene.

The BBC crew wanted environment.

"We need to show the ecological impact. How does the Pleistocene landscape interact with the modern? What happens to native species when extinct megafauna appear? What's the long-term effect?"

Dr. Ostrander and I took them to three permanent fold sites.

First: Lakeview Estates. Still underwater. Lake Algonquin stable. Nine days and counting.

The BBC crew filmed the submerged construction site. Foundation holes filled with ancient water. Equipment rusted. Lumber floating.

And in the water: fish.

Not modern species. Pleistocene fish. Lake sturgeon bigger than anything that lived in Michigan now. Extinct subspecies of whitefish. Ancient forms adapted to glacial conditions.

"They're colonizing," Dr. Ostrander explained on camera. "The ancient ecosystem is reestablishing itself. If this fold stays open long enough, Lake Algonquan won't be a historical curiosity. It'll be a functioning Pleistocene lake. Complete with extinct species. Right here. Overlapping modern Michigan."

Second site: The nature trail. Ice field. Still present. Still expanding.

The BBC filmed the glacier. The boundary. The way ice from 11,000 years ago was slowly encroaching on modern terrain. Inches per day. Inexorable.

Plants near the boundary were dying. Cold damage. Wrong temperature. Wrong conditions.

But farther back, in areas the ice had covered for days: new growth.

Not modern plants. Tundra plants. Arctic willow. Dryas. Species that hadn't grown in Michigan since the Pleistocene.

Seeds preserved in the ice. Germinating when exposed. Growing.

The ancient ecosystem returning.

"This is ecological succession in reverse," Dr. Ostrander said. "We're watching the landscape revert to pre-settlement conditions. Not pre-European settlement. Pre-human settlement. Pre-agriculture. Pre-everything. Back to the ice age."

Third site: Patricia Hendricks' property. Half a house. Half gone. The rest ice-covered and collapsing.

The BBC filmed the destruction. The impossibility. A modern home half-erased by time.

Then they turned the camera to the woods behind the property.

Where something was moving.

Large. Brown. Four legs.

Mastodon.

Adult. Healthy. Browsing on vegetation near the fold boundary.

It had come through. Found viable habitat. And stayed.

The first permanent resident.

The camera crew filmed for twenty minutes. The mastodon ignored them. Just ate. Moved. Lived.

When we left, it was still there. Establishing territory. Making itself at home in a time that wasn't its own but provided what it needed.

"That's going to be the opening shot," the BBC producer said. "Mastodon browsing in modern Michigan. Surrounded by temporal displacement. Living proof that the Pleistocene is returning."

By Friday, all the major crews had their primary footage.

PBS had the fold opening. The mechanism. The science.

National Geographic had the Paleo-Indians. The human story. The displacement narrative.

BBC had the ecology. The environmental impact. The landscape transformation.

Discovery Channel had the predators. They'd filmed—from a safe distance—a short-faced bear emerging from a fold near Elk Rapids. Hunting. Moving. Then returning. Twenty-seven minutes of apex predator behavior. Extinct animal actively hunting in the 21st century.

And the independent filmmakers had everything else. The evacuations. The town meetings. The economic collapse. The human drama.

Enough footage for dozens of documentaries. Enough evidence to bury any remaining denial.

This was real. This was happening. This was permanent.

Saturday morning, Jennifer Ortiz found me at the diner.

"Officer Pritchard. I wanted to thank you. The footage we got this week is extraordinary. When this airs—and it will air on every major network worldwide—people will understand. They'll see what you've been documenting. What you've been trying to warn people about."

"Will it help?"

"Help how?"

"Will it make people safer? Will it prevent deaths? Will it change anything?"

She was quiet. Then: "It'll change understanding. Whether that translates to action... I don't know. But at least people will know the truth. That matters."

"Does it? We've had video evidence since the mastodon. We've had witness testimony. We've had scientific documentation. And half the country still thinks it's a hoax."

"This is different. This is comprehensive. Professional. Undeniable. Multiple networks. Multiple perspectives. All saying the same thing: this is real, this is dangerous, this is permanent."

"And when people watch your documentary and think 'that's terrible' and then go about their lives? When it becomes another nature documentary? Just entertainment?"

"Then at least we tried. At least we documented it. So when historians look back and ask 'why didn't anyone do anything,' we can say: we showed them. We explained it. We made it impossible to ignore."

"And they ignored it anyway."

"Probably. But that's on them. Not us."

The documentaries started airing three weeks later.

PBS Frontline: "The Thin Places - When Time Breaks Down"

National Geographic: "Displaced: The Paleo-Indians of Michigan"

BBC Earth: "Pleistocene Rising: Ecological Collapse in the Great Lakes"

Discovery Channel: "Ice Age Predators: Return of the Megafauna"

All of them. Prime time. Worldwide distribution.

The footage was extraordinary. Professional. Undeniable.

The mastodon browsing. The fold opening. The Paleo-Indians working. The short-faced bear hunting. The ice field expanding. Patricia Hendricks watching her house collapse.

Everything documented. Explained. Verified by scientists. Corroborated by witnesses.

The world watched.

And the response was... divided.

Half the audience was horrified. Fascinated. Convinced.

Online forums exploded with discussion. Reddit threads thousands of comments long. Scientific communities debating mechanisms. Theologians arguing implications.

#ThinPlaces trended for three days. Millions of posts. Some supportive. Some skeptical. Some afraid.

Tourism to northern Michigan spiked. Then crashed. Then spiked again. People wanting to see for themselves. Then realizing it was dangerous. Then coming anyway because danger makes it more interesting.

The other half dismissed it completely.

"CGI."

"Government psyop."

"Crisis actors."

"Elaborate hoax to control the population."

No amount of evidence mattered. The documentaries could show mastodon DNA. Paleo-Indian artifacts carbon-dated accurately. Real-time fold openings filmed from multiple angles.

Didn't matter.

Some people were determined not to believe.

Because belief meant accepting that reality was unstable. That the rules didn't apply. That safety was an illusion.

And that was too frightening.

So they denied. And mocked. And insisted it was all fake.

A week after the documentaries aired, I got a call from a number I didn't recognize.

"Officer Pritchard? This is Senator Wallace, Michigan State Senate. I wanted to discuss the situation in Antrim County."

"What about it?"

"The documentaries have created significant public pressure. The federal government is considering intervention. FEMA. National Guard. Possibly evacuation of the entire region."

"We don't need evacuation. We need resources. Research funding. Infrastructure to manage the folds."

"The administration believes evacuation is the safest option. Clear the area. Establish a quarantine zone. Prevent further casualties."

"You want to evacuate twenty-three thousand people? Abandon an entire county?"

"If it saves lives, yes."

"It won't save lives. It'll displace them. People have homes here. Businesses. Communities. You can't just relocate everyone."

"We've done it before. Centralia, Pennsylvania. Love Canal. Times Beach. When an area becomes uninhabitable, we evacuate."

"This area is habitable. With precautions. With the warning system. We've had zero deaths since implementation."

"You've had zero deaths in two weeks. The folds are increasing. Your own data shows that. Eventually, the warning system won't be enough."

"Maybe. But forcing evacuation now, while we're learning how to adapt—that's premature. That's surrender."

"It's prudent risk management."

"It's political cowardice. You don't want to be blamed when the next person dies. So you're clearing the area and declaring victory."

Silence. Then: "Officer Pritchard, I understand your frustration. But the decision is above both of us. The federal government will make the call. I'm just giving you advance notice. Prepare your community. Evacuation orders are coming. Probably within the month."

He hung up.

I sat in my office, staring at the map on the wall.

Sixty-seven red zones. Fourteen permanent folds. Twenty-three thousand residents. Businesses. Schools. Homes. Lives.

All of it about to be erased. Not by folds. By bureaucracy.

The documentaries had shown the world what was happening.

And the world's response was: abandon it. Quarantine it. Walk away.

Because adaptation was hard. Messy. Expensive. Risky.

Evacuation was simple. Clean. Defensible.

Even if it destroyed everything people had built.

That night, I showed Karen the call notes.

"They're going to evacuate. Force everyone out. Turn Antrim County into a federal quarantine zone."

She was quiet for a long time. Then: "What if they're right? What if this place really is becoming uninhabitable?"

"It's habitable if you respect the boundaries. If you avoid the high-risk zones. If you pay attention to warnings."

"For how long? Jake's data shows the folds increasing. The permanent zones expanding. Eventually—"

"Eventually we adapt or we leave. But that's our choice. Not the federal government's."

"Dave, what if staying means watching people die? What if the warning system fails? What if something happens to Jake? To Emma when she visits? To us?"

"Then we deal with it. Same as we'd deal with any other risk."

"This isn't a normal risk. This is time breaking down."

"I know. But running doesn't fix it. It just means someone else deals with it. Or no one does. And the folds keep spreading until they're everywhere."

She looked at me. "You're not leaving, are you."

"No."

"Even if it's a federal order."

"Even then."

"That's insane."

"Probably. But it's my choice."

She was quiet again. Then: "Ours. It's our choice. And I'm staying too."

Chapter 24

CHAPTER TWENTY-FOUR: JAKE'S CLOSE CALL

The call came at 6:23 AM on a Tuesday.

Karen's phone. Not mine. Which meant it was personal, not official.

I heard her gasp. Heard her say "Where? How bad?"

Then she handed me the phone.

"It's Emma. Jake's in the hospital."

Munson Medical Center in Traverse City. Emergency room.

We made it in thirty-seven minutes. Driving too fast. Not caring.

Emma met us in the waiting room. Freshman year at State, she'd driven up when she got the call. Her face was pale.

"He's okay. They say he's okay. But Mom, Dad, it was close."

"What happened?"

"He was setting up monitoring equipment. At one of the permanent fold sites near Elk Rapids. The one that's been stable for two weeks. He thought it was safe."

"Where is he?"

"Room 14. They're keeping him for observation. Hypothermia. Exposure. And—" She stopped. "You should see him."

Jake was in bed. Wrapped in warming blankets. IV in his arm. Oxygen monitor on his finger.

Awake. Alert. But shaking.

"Hey Dad."

I sat down beside the bed. Took his hand. It was cold. Too cold.

"What the hell were you doing?"

"Setting up sensors. The Elk Rapids fold has been stable. Fourteen days. Same dimensions. Same temperature differential. I wanted real-time data on a long-duration fold. Understand the mechanism."

"You went in alone?"

"I had my phone. The warning system. Emergency beacon. I thought I was being careful."

"Tell me what happened."

He took a breath. Winced. His chest hurt. Probably from the cold.

"I set up three sensors around the perimeter. Then I wanted one inside. On the Pleistocene side. To measure conditions. So I crossed through."

Karen made a sound. Not quite a sob. Jake looked at her.

"Mom, I've done it before. Quick in, quick out. Plant the sensor. Return. Thirty seconds maximum."

"But?"

"But this time the fold moved."

He'd crossed through at 5:47 AM. Early. Before sunrise. Cold.

Stepped through the shimmer into the Pleistocene.

Ice age forest. Spruce and birch. Temperature maybe 25 degrees. Snow on the ground. Different stars—or same stars at different angles, he wasn't sure.

He planted the sensor. Forty-five seconds. Professional. Efficient.

Turned to go back.

The shimmer had moved.

Not closed. Moved. Shifted maybe twenty feet to the west.

Where there should have been a boundary—a door home—there was just Pleistocene forest.

"I didn't panic," Jake said. "Not at first. I walked toward where the shimmer should have been. Figured it was a perception issue. Angle of observation. Something."

"But it wasn't there."

"No. I walked in a grid pattern. Covering the area. Looking for the shimmer. My phone was dead. No signal anyway. The emergency beacon—I triggered it, but I don't know if it transmitted across the boundary."

"How long were you searching?"

"Maybe twenty minutes. Getting colder. Getting worried. My jacket wasn't rated for 25-degree weather. I could feel hypothermia starting. Fingers going numb. Thinking getting fuzzy."

He pulled his hands out from under the blanket. Showed us his fingers. Wrapped in gauze. Frostbite. Minor, the doctors said. But frostbite.

"Then I heard something."

Footsteps. Heavy. Quadrupedal. Moving through the forest.

Jake hid. Behind a fallen spruce. Watching.

A mastodon emerged. Adult. Maybe eight feet at the shoulder. Moving slowly. Browsing on vegetation.

"It was beautiful," Jake said quietly. "Healthy. Adapted. Exactly what you'd expect from a Pleistocene herbivore in its natural habitat. And I was thinking—even while freezing to death—this is incredible. This is a living mastodon. I'm seeing what no one has seen in eleven thousand years."

"Then it noticed me."

The mastodon stopped browsing. Raised its head. Scented the air.

Looked directly at Jake's hiding spot.

"I thought I was dead. Modern elephants can be aggressive when surprised. Mastodons—I had no idea. They're extinct. No behavioral data."

The mastodon approached. Slowly. Curious.

Stopped maybe fifteen feet away. Looked at Jake. Really looked. Intelligence in its eyes. Assessment.

Then it made a sound. Low. Rumbling. Not aggressive. Just... communication.

And walked away.

"It decided I wasn't a threat. Or maybe wasn't interesting. Either way, it left. And I went back to looking for the shimmer."

He found it at 6:34 AM.

Forty-seven minutes after crossing through.

The boundary had shifted back. Not to its original position. But close enough that Jake could reach it.

He stumbled through. Into 2026. Into modern Michigan.

Collapsed on the modern side. Hypothermic. Disoriented. Fingers frostbitten. Lungs aching from breathing cold air.

A hiker found him at 6:41. Called 911.

EMTs arrived. Len Greenland again.

"Third time I've treated someone for Pleistocene exposure, and what," Jake had apparently told him. "This is becoming a specialty."

They got him to the hospital. Warming protocols. IV fluids. Treatment for frostbite.

He'd survive. But barely.

"Dad, I was in there for forty-seven minutes. Without proper gear. Without backup. Without a way to communicate. And I almost died.

Not from predators. Not from falling. From the cold. From something as simple as temperature."

He looked at me. "I screwed up. I thought I understood the risks. I was wrong."

Dr. Havelka arrived around 9 AM. She'd heard through the medical network.

"Jake. You're a damn fool."

"I know."

"You're also lucky. Forty-seven minutes in those conditions should've killed you. Severe hypothermia. Cognitive impairment. You wouldn't have made it back."

"I know."

"So why did you survive?"

Jake thought about it. "Movement. I kept moving. Searching for the boundary. If I'd stopped, if I'd sat down, I'd have died. But staying active kept my core temperature up. Barely. Just enough."

"And the mastodon?"

"Didn't attack. Could have. Chose not to."

"Why?"

"I don't know. Maybe I didn't trigger its threat response. Maybe mastodons were generally non-aggressive. Maybe it had never seen a human before and didn't know what to make of me. But it let me live."

Dr. Havelka looked at me. "Dave, he can't go back in. Not alone. Not without proper equipment and backup. The folds are too unstable. We thought the permanent ones were safe because they're stable. But stable doesn't mean predictable. They can shift. Expand. Contract. Without warning."

"I know."

"Do you? Because your son just learned that lesson and nearly died. And I don't want to treat his corpse next time."

By noon, word had spread.

Dr. Ostrander called. "Is Jake okay?"

"Physically, yes. Mentally, shaken."

"Good. He should be shaken. What he did was reckless. But Dave, the data he got—the sensor he planted before the fold shifted—it's still transmitting."

"What's it showing?"

"Temperature. Humidity. Light levels. Atmospheric composition. Everything. Real-time data from the Pleistocene. This is unprecedented. We're getting scientific measurements from eleven thousand years ago."

"That data almost cost my son his life."

"I know. I'm not saying it was worth it. I'm just saying—what he did, as dangerous as it was, it's giving us information we desperately need."

"What information?"

"The Pleistocene environment is different. Not just colder. Different atmospheric composition. Slightly higher CO2. Different seasonal patterns. The data suggests the folds aren't just spatial displacement. They're complete environmental transfer. Air. Temperature. Everything. If someone crosses through without proper preparation, they're not just entering a different place. They're entering a different climate system."

"How different?"

"Different enough to kill you. Which Jake just proved."

Emma sat with Jake most of the day. I watched them through the window. Brother and sister. Talking quietly.

She'd come home when she heard. Even though she'd said she wouldn't come back to northern Michigan. Even though she'd chosen safety over home.

Because family mattered more than fear.

Karen sat beside me. "She's trying to convince him to stop."

"Will he?"

"No. You know Jake. He'll be more careful. Better equipped. But he won't stop. This is his life's work now. The thing that will define his career. He's documenting the impossible."

"He almost died documenting it."

"But he didn't. And he'll use what he learned to be safer next time. That's who he is. That's who we raised him to be."

She was right. Jake wasn't going to stop. Couldn't stop. The scientist in him was too curious. Too driven.

But he'd be smarter about it.

I hoped.

They released Jake Wednesday afternoon. Frostbite healing. Hypothermia resolved. Vitals stable.

I drove him home. Emma followed in her car.

"I'm sorry," Jake said in the truck. "I know I scared you. Scared Mom."

"You scared yourself. That's what matters."

"I won't go in alone again. I'll establish protocols. Buddy system. Proper gear. Emergency extraction plans."

"Good."

"But Dad, I can't stop. The data we're getting—it's too important. We're learning how the folds work. How the Pleistocene environment differs from modern. How to predict shifts and changes. Every fold teaches us something."

"As long as it doesn't kill you in the process."

"I'll be careful."

"You said that before."

"This time I mean it."

We drove in silence for a while. Then Jake said: "I saw a mastodon. A living mastodon. Do you understand what that means? Not footage. Not fossils. A living, breathing animal from eleven thousand years ago. Looking at me. Deciding I wasn't worth attacking."

"What did it feel like?"

"Humbling. I was in its world. It belonged there. I didn't. And it knew it. But it let me live anyway. Like... professional courtesy. Between species separated by time."

"Or you weren't worth the energy."

"Maybe. But Dad, that mastodon was healthy. Adapted. Thriving in its environment. It had found food. Territory. Everything it needed. Which means the Pleistocene ecosystem on the other side of these folds isn't just surviving. It's functioning. Complete food chains. Viable populations. Entire environments."

"Which means what?"

"Which means the thin places aren't just windows to the past. They're doorways to functioning Pleistocene ecosystems. And if those ecosystems are stable, if they can support megafauna populations..." He trailed off.

"Then they can support Paleo-Indians."

"Yes. And they can expand. If the folds keep opening. If they stay open. Eventually we're not looking at overlap. We're looking at replacement. The Pleistocene returning. Not as curiosity. As reality."

That night, Jake set up in his old room. Emma stayed too. First time both kids had been home in months.

We had dinner together. Normal family dinner. Except nothing was normal anymore.

Emma told us about school. Her classes. Her friends. Her life in a place where reality was stable and time didn't break down.

Jake told us about his research. The data from the sensor. The patterns he was seeing. The predictions he could make.

Karen told us about the evacuation rumors. Federal orders coming soon. Pressure to leave.

And I told them about the choice we were facing. Stay and adapt. Or leave and abandon everything.

"I'm not leaving," Jake said immediately.

Emma was quiet. Then: "I can't stay. I'm sorry. But I can't live here. Not with the folds. Not with the danger. Not knowing if I walk out the door I might cross through and not come back."

"We understand," Karen said.

"But I'll visit. I'll come home when I can. I'm not abandoning you. I'm just... choosing safety."

"That's fair," I said. "That's your choice. We respect it."

Jake looked at Emma. "Do you think I'm crazy? For staying?"

"Yes. But I think you're brave too. Stupid and brave. Which is the worst combination."

He smiled. "Yeah. Probably."

Thursday morning, Emma left. Back to school. Back to safety.

Jake stayed. Started planning his next research expedition. With protocols. With backup. With proper gear.

And I went back to work. Monitoring folds. Issuing warnings. Documenting incidents.

Trying to keep people safe in a place that was becoming less safe every day.

But something had changed.

Jake's close call had made it personal in a way the other incidents hadn't.

Bob Martinez was someone else's family. George Henderson was someone else's brother. Patricia Hendricks was someone else's home.

But Jake was my son.

And he'd almost died in the Pleistocene while I was asleep in bed two counties away.

That reality—that proximity to loss—changed everything.

Made the danger real in a way statistics never could.

Made the choice to stay feel less like stubbornness and more like madness.

But we stayed anyway.

Because leaving meant surrender. And we weren't ready to surrender yet.

Even if maybe we should have been.

Chapter 25

CHAPTER TWENTY-FIVE: THE SETTLERS

Dr. Marcus Webb called me Thursday afternoon, two days after Jake's close call.

"Dave, you need to see this. The Skegmog Lake band. They're building something permanent."

"How permanent?"

"Multi-season structures. Storage. Infrastructure. They're not planning to leave. They're settling."

I met him at the site at 4 PM. Sarah came too. So did Jake—against my better judgment, but he insisted he was fine.

We hiked in carefully. Staying downwind. Keeping distance. Respectful.

The Paleo-Indian settlement had transformed.

Two weeks ago, it had been temporary shelters. Branch frames covered with hides. Easy to abandon. Mobile.

Now it was a village.

Seven structures. Substantial. Built from stripped saplings and bark. Domed roofs. Designed for weather. For seasons. For permanence.

Around the structures: infrastructure.

A central fire pit. Stone-lined. Built to last. With a smoke deflector system that showed sophisticated understanding of airflow and heat management.

Food storage. Raised platforms to keep meat away from scavengers. Built solid. Professional carpentry using stone tools and binding techniques.

A processing area. Hides stretched on frames. Stone tools organized by type and function. Work stations for different tasks. Division of labor. Specialization.

And at the perimeter: defenses.

Not walls. But obstacles. Fallen logs positioned deliberately. Thorn bushes transplanted. Approaches limited to specific entry points that could be watched.

"They're not camping," Dr. Webb said quietly. "They're colonizing. Building permanent settlement. This is home now."

Through binoculars, I watched the band working.

Fifteen people now. Not seven. They'd grown. Either more had crossed through, or they'd merged with another band.

Men working on a new structure. Women processing hides and preparing food. Children playing but also working—carrying water, gathering firewood, learning skills.

And dogs. Five of them now. Part wolf. Part ancient domesticated lineage. Integrated into the community. Working animals. Hunting partners. Family members.

This wasn't a refugee camp. This was a functioning village.

"How long have they been building?" I asked.

"We noticed major construction starting about a week ago. But the planning probably started earlier. They've been gathering materials for weeks. Observing the area. Understanding the resources. Then they committed."

Sarah was watching through her own binoculars. "They've positioned the village well. High ground. Water access. Game trails nearby. Defensible. This shows long-term planning. Multiple generations of knowledge about how to establish settlement."

"Do they know they're in the wrong time?" Jake asked.

"I don't think they care. The land provides what they need. That's all that matters. Whether it's their time or ours—to them, it's just land. And they're using it the way their ancestors did."

We watched for two hours. Documenting. Recording. Learning.

The social structure was clear. An elder—the same man we'd encountered before—making decisions. Directing work. Settling disputes.

A council of adults. Maybe four or five. Discussing. Planning. Consensus-based leadership.

Younger adults doing skilled work. Hunting. Building. Processing.

Teenagers learning. Apprenticing. Contributing.

Children playing but also integrated into daily work. No separation between childhood and productivity. Everyone contributed according to ability.

And the dogs moving freely through the camp. Part of the social structure. Accepted. Trusted.

"This is a complete society," Dr. Webb said. "Not just survivors. A functioning community with social hierarchy, division of labor, shared goals. They're not adapting to modern Michigan. They're rebuilding what they had. What they lost when they crossed through."

"What happens when winter comes?" I asked.

"They'll survive. Look at the storage platforms. They're already preparing. Drying meat. Processing hides for clothing. Gathering materials for winter shelter improvements. They know what's coming. They've lived through Pleistocene winters. Michigan winter will be mild by comparison."

Sarah lowered her binoculars. "They'll outlast most of the modern residents if evacuation orders come through. They don't need electricity or heating systems or supply chains. They have skills. Knowledge. Community. That's enough."

On the walk back, Jake was quiet. Processing.

Finally he said: "They're more adapted than we are."

"To what?"

"To this. The new reality. The folds. The instability. They don't need the modern world to function. They brought their world with them. Skills. Tools. Social structures. Drop them anywhere with basic resources and they'll survive."

"We can survive too."

"Can we? Without grocery stores? Without hospitals? Without infrastructure? If the folds keep spreading, if modern supply chains break down, how many of us know how to make stone tools? How to process a deer hide into clothing? How to build shelter from raw materials? How to survive without electricity?"

"Some people know those skills."

"Some. But most don't. Most of us are dependent on systems that require stability. And stability is exactly what we don't have anymore."

He was right. The Paleo-Indians had lived through the collapse of their entire ecosystem. They'd adapted. Survived. Carried forward the knowledge they needed.

Modern humans had spent eleven thousand years building complex systems that assumed the world stayed the same.

Now the world wasn't staying the same.

And most of us didn't have the skills to survive what was coming.

Friday morning, Dr. Webb briefed the county board.

"The Paleo-Indian population near Skegmog Lake has established permanent settlement. Fifteen individuals currently. Possibly more. They're building infrastructure. Planning for multiple seasons. They're not leaving."

Commissioner Walsh: "Are they on private property?"

"Yes. The Hendricks property. Patricia Hendricks' old land. Before the fold destroyed her house."

"Does she know?"

"She's been informed. Her response was: 'Let them have it. I'm not going back there anyway.'"

"What about property rights? Ownership?"

Dr. Webb looked at her incredulously. "Commissioner, we're talking about people from eleven thousand years ago who have no concept of property ownership as we understand it. They see viable land. They settle. That's how humans have always worked."

"So we just let them take private property?"

"What's the alternative? Evict them? Where do they go? Back to the Pleistocene? The folds aren't doors we can close at will."

"We could relocate them."

"To where? And how? They don't speak English. Don't understand modern society. Don't recognize our authority. You want to forcibly relocate stone age humans who are armed with atlatls and have absolutely no reason to trust you?"

The room was silent.

Then Bill Henderson spoke up. "Let them stay."

"Excuse me?"

"They're not hurting anyone. They're using land nobody else wants anymore. Patricia doesn't want it. The state doesn't want it—it's too close to an active fold zone. So let them have it. Let them settle. Maybe we can learn from them."

"Learn what?"

"How to survive without modern conveniences. How to live on land that's unstable. How to adapt. Because if the federal evacuation doesn't happen, if we're stuck here with the folds, we're going to need those skills."

Commissioner Walsh looked uncomfortable. "The optics of allowing primitive humans to establish settlements on private property..."

"The optics are that we're being practical," Bill said. "And respectful. These are people. Displaced people. They're doing what displaced people do—finding safety and building homes. We can either fight them or coexist with them. I vote coexist."

The vote was close. Seven to five. But it passed.

Official policy: Paleo-Indian settlements on abandoned or uninhabited properties would be tolerated. Not encouraged. Not supported. But tolerated.

It wasn't much. But it was something.

Saturday, Sarah and I hiked back to the settlement. Bringing gifts.

Not charity. Not aid. Trade goods.

Metal tools—knives, an axe—that would be useful. Items the Paleo-Indians couldn't make themselves but would recognize the value of.

We approached slowly. Announced our presence from a distance.

The elder emerged from the village. Watching. Wary.

Sarah spoke. Anishinaabemowin mixed with gestures. Simple concepts.

Gift. Trade. Peace.

She laid the tools on the ground. Stepped back.

The elder approached. Examined the metal knife. Tested the edge. Recognized the quality.

Looked at Sarah. At me. Calculating.

Then he turned. Spoke to someone behind him.

A younger man emerged. Carrying something. A bundle wrapped in hide.

He laid it near the tools. Stepped back.

Sarah opened it carefully.

Inside: Obsidian points. Beautifully made. Ten of them. Worth hundreds of dollars to collectors. Worth nothing to people who could make more whenever needed.

But as a gesture—as acknowledgment of trade, of relationship, of mutual respect—priceless.

Sarah nodded. Accepted the gift.

The elder spoke. A short phrase. Sarah responded.

Then he returned to the village. Taking the metal tools. Leaving the obsidian points.

First successful trade between modern humans and Paleo-Indians.

First step toward coexistence.

"What did he say?" I asked as we walked back.

"He said: 'Good land. We stay.' And I said: 'Good. Stay well.'"

"That's it?"

"That's enough. We acknowledged each other. Established relationship. Traded goods. That's how communities form. Small gestures. Repeated over time."

"What happens when winter comes? When resources get scarce? When they need more than good land?"

"Then we'll see if the relationship holds. If they come to us for help. If we help them. If trade continues or breaks down." She paused. "But

Dave, they're survivors. They don't need our help to survive winter. They need our help to be left alone. Not harassed. Not threatened. Not treated as problems to be solved."

"And if other people—hunters, opportunists, people who see them as threats—don't leave them alone?"

"Then we protect them. Same as we'd protect any other residents."

"They're not residents. They're not citizens. They don't have legal status."

"They're people. That's status enough."

Sunday morning, the news ran a story.

"Paleo-Indian Village Established in Antrim County"

"Stone Age Settlement Tolerated by Local Government"

"Time-Displaced Humans Build Permanent Community in Northern Michigan"

The footage—shot with telephoto lenses from outside the perimeter—showed the village. The structures. The people working.

The response was immediate.

Anthropologists demanding access. "This is the discovery of the century. We need to document everything. Language. Culture. Technology. Before modern influence contaminates them."

Activists demanding protection. "These are vulnerable people. Refugees. They need legal status. Humanitarian support. Protection from exploitation."

Opportunists offering money. "Exclusive interviews. Documentary rights. Book deals. These people are worth millions if managed properly."

And xenophobes demanding removal. "They're illegal immigrants from the past. Deport them back to the Pleistocene. Don't let them establish colonies on American soil."

The arguments were absurd. The stakes were real.

Fifteen people trying to survive in a world they didn't understand were about to become political footballs. Symbols. Commodities.

Unless someone protected them.

Dr. Webb established a perimeter Monday morning.

"No unauthorized access to the Skegmog Lake settlement. Research teams require approval. Media are restricted to distant observation. No direct contact without consent from the band."

"On whose authority?" someone demanded.

"Mine. As lead anthropologist on the University of Michigan research project. Backed by the Antrim County Board decision to tolerate settlement. And enforced by local law enforcement."

He looked at me. I nodded.

"Anyone attempting unauthorized contact will be cited for trespassing. Anyone attempting to exploit, harm, or remove the settlers will face criminal charges. Clear?"

Most people backed off. A few grumbled. One filmmaker threatened legal action.

But the perimeter held.

The Paleo-Indians—for now—were left alone to build their village. To establish their community. To survive in whatever way they knew how.

And modern Michigan learned what it meant to share space with people from before history.

Uncomfortably. Uncertainly. But learning.

That night, Karen and I sat on the back deck.

"They're staying," she said. "The Paleo-Indians. They're not going back."

"No. Why would they? The land provides what they need. And their own time is gone. Eleven thousand years gone. Even if the folds closed tomorrow, they'd be stranded here. Might as well settle."

"How many more are coming?"

"Jake estimates maybe a hundred have crossed through across the whole region. Wisconsin. Illinois. Michigan. All the moraine boundaries. Some in small bands like Skegmog. Some alone. Some probably already dead from exposure or predators or accidents."

"A hundred stone age humans living in modern America."

"More every time a fold opens. And the folds aren't stopping."

"So what? We just... share the landscape? Modern cities and Paleo-Indian villages side by side?"

"I guess so. Unless someone comes up with a better idea."

She was quiet for a long time. Then: "I saw a mastodon today. Browsing near the permanent fold at Patricia's old property. Just eating. Living. Like it belonged there."

"Maybe it does belong there. More than we do."

"Don't say that."

"Why not? We've built our entire civilization on the assumption that the land would stay the way we shaped it. That we could control it. Own it. Keep it stable. And the land is saying: no. You had your turn. Now I remember what I used to be. And I'm becoming that again."

"That's depressing."

"That's reality."

We sat in silence. Watching the woods. Listening to normal sounds.

Somewhere out there, fifteen people from the Pleistocene were settling in for the night. Building fires. Telling stories. Raising children. Living.

Doing what humans had always done.

Adapting. Surviving. Making home wherever they found themselves.

And teaching us—whether we wanted to learn or not—that belonging wasn't about time or technology or legal status.

It was about knowing how to live on the land.

And they knew better than we did.

Chapter 26

CHAPTER TWENTY-SIX: THE CHILD

The call came in at 4:17 PM on a Wednesday.

Missing child. Girl. Seven years old. Last seen playing in her backyard near Barnes Road.

Sarah Mitchell. Same last name as the woman who'd had the family appear in her yard at Torch Lake. But different family. Different property.

This one was closer to the Skegmog Lake settlement.

Much closer.

I responded with Sheriff Kowalski. So did three deputies. Search and rescue protocols. Standard procedure.

The parents—Dan and Rebecca Mitchell—were frantic.

"She was playing in the yard. Right there." Rebecca pointed. "I was inside making dinner. I looked out the window and she was gone. Just gone."

"How long between when you last saw her and when you noticed she was missing?"

"Maybe ten minutes. Fifteen at most."

Not long. But long enough for a seven-year-old to wander into the woods. Or cross through a fold.

"What's her name?"

"Lily. Lily Mitchell. She's seven. Wearing a pink jacket. Blue jeans. She knows not to go into the woods but—" Rebecca broke down. Couldn't finish.

Dan put his arm around her. "Officer, there's a fold site near here. We got the warnings. We've been careful. But Lily... she's curious. She asks questions about the thin places. About the animals. About the people from the past. What if she—"

"We'll find her. Does she know to stay in one place if she gets lost?"

"We taught her. But she's seven. When she's scared—"

"We'll find her."

We organized search teams. Four groups. Each with radios. Each with specific sectors.

My sector was northwest. Toward Skegmog Lake. Toward the Paleo-Indian settlement.

I radioed Dr. Webb. "Marcus, we have a missing child. Seven-year-old girl. Last seen near Barnes Road. She might have wandered toward your research area."

"The settlement?"

"Possibly. Can you check the perimeter? See if anyone's spotted her?"

"On it."

I started walking. Calling. "Lily! Lily Mitchell! Can you hear me?"

No response.

The woods were thick here. Mixed hardwoods. Underbrush dense. Easy for a small child to get turned around. To lose sight of landmarks. To panic and keep walking in the wrong direction.

Or to stumble through a shimmer into the Pleistocene and not understand what happened.

I checked my monitor. No active folds in this area. But the permanent ones didn't always show on sensors. And new ones could open without warning.

I kept searching.

At 5:43 PM, Dr. Webb radioed.

"Dave. I think we found her."

"Where?"

"The settlement. Dave, she's inside the perimeter. With them."

"Is she okay?"

"She appears to be. But Dave, they won't let us approach. The elder is standing between us and the girl. He's protecting her."

"I'm on my way."

I ran. Quarter mile through the woods. Arrived at the settlement perimeter at 5:51 PM.

Dr. Webb was there with his research team. Sarah too. She'd heard the radio traffic and responded.

And fifty yards away, inside the Paleo-Indian village, I could see her.

Lily Mitchell. Pink jacket. Blue jeans. Sitting by the central fire.

Alive. Unharmed.

Surrounded by Paleo-Indians.

The elder stood between us and the village. Arms crossed. Expression neutral but firm.

Not aggressive. Not threatening. Just... blocking access.

Behind him, the village continued normal activities. But everyone was aware of us. Watching. Ready.

Sarah spoke. Anishinaabemowin. Simple phrases. Gestures.

Child. Lost. Return to family.

The elder listened. Responded. A longer phrase.

Sarah tried again. Different words. Same concept.

The elder shook his head. Spoke firmly. Pointed at Lily. Then at the village. Then at us.

"What's he saying?" I asked.

"He's saying the child came to them. She was crying. Lost. Scared. They took her in. Gave her food. Made her safe. Now she's under their protection. Until they're certain we're her family and not a threat."

"We're not a threat. We're law enforcement. We're here to bring her home."

"He doesn't know what law enforcement is. He sees armed strangers demanding a child. From his perspective, we're the threat."

Dr. Webb stepped forward carefully. Hands visible. Non-threatening posture.

"Can we show him the parents? Prove she belongs with them?"

"That might work. But we need to do this right. If we push too hard, if they think we're trying to take her by force..."

"They'll fight."

"Yes. And they're armed. And they've survived things we can't imagine. We won't win that fight."

I radioed Sheriff Kowalski. "Tom, I need the parents. Bring them to the Skegmog settlement. Carefully. No weapons visible. Non-threatening approach."

"The settlement? Dave, that's—"

"I know where it is. Lily's here. The Paleo-Indians have her. They won't release her until they're sure she's safe. We need her parents to prove relationship."

"On my way."

Twenty minutes later, Dan and Rebecca arrived. Dr. Webb had briefed them on the approach.

"Walk slowly. Don't make sudden movements. When you see Lily, call her name. Let her come to you if she can. Don't grab. Don't rush. These people don't know you. They don't trust us. We have to earn release, not demand it."

Rebecca was shaking. "Is she hurt?"

"She appears fine. They've been taking care of her. But they're protective. They won't give her up easily."

We approached together. Me, Sarah, Dr. Webb, the parents. Hands visible. Slow steps.

The elder watched. The entire village watched.

Then Lily saw her parents.

"Mommy!"

She stood up. Started toward them.

One of the Paleo-Indian women—maybe thirty, clearly in a caretaker role—put a hand on Lily's shoulder. Gentle but restraining.

Not to hurt. To assess. To make sure the child actually wanted to go to these people.

Rebecca called out. "Lily, honey, it's okay. We're here. We're going to take you home."

Lily pulled away from the woman. Ran toward her mother.

The woman let her go.

Lily reached Rebecca. Wrapped her arms around her mother. Crying. "I got lost. I was scared. And then these people found me and they gave me food and the lady made me warm and—"

Rebecca held her. Sobbing. "You're safe. You're safe now."

The elder spoke to Sarah. A short phrase.

Sarah translated. "He says: child found lost. We protect. Now family here. Child go home. Good."

Then he gestured. Dismissive. Not rude. Just: you have what you came for. Leave now.

We left.

Backing away slowly. Respectfully. Lily safe in her mother's arms.

At the tree line, I turned back.

The elder was still watching. Making sure we actually left.

I raised my hand. Palm out. The same gesture he'd made weeks ago when Dr. Webb's cameras had been intrusive.

Acknowledgment. Respect. Thank you.

The elder nodded once. Then returned to the village.

Back at the Mitchell house, EMTs checked Lily. No injuries. No trauma. Slight dehydration. Otherwise fine.

"What happened?" I asked her gently. "How did you get to the village?"

"I was playing. I saw something shiny in the woods. I went to look. And I got lost. I couldn't find home. I walked and walked and I was crying and then I saw the smoke. From a fire. And I thought maybe someone would help me."

"And you found the village."

"There were people. But they looked different. Their clothes were weird. And they talked funny. I didn't understand them. But the lady..." She paused. "The lady smiled at me. And she gave me food. Something dried. It tasted weird but I was hungry. And she made me sit by the fire to get warm."

"Were you scared?"

"At first. But they were nice. They didn't hurt me. The lady kept touching my jacket. Like she'd never seen one before. And the kids there, they wanted to play with my hair. They kept pointing at it."

Blonde hair. Probably unusual for people from the Pleistocene. Different genetics. Different populations.

"Then the old man came. He looked at me for a long time. Then he said something to the lady and she stayed with me. And they gave me more food. And I fell asleep by the fire. And then I heard you calling and I saw Mommy and Daddy."

Rebecca held her tighter. "You're never going into those woods again. Never."

Lily nodded. But her eyes were distant. Processing.

She'd crossed a boundary that most adults would never cross.

She'd been a guest in a Paleo-Indian village. Had been cared for by people from eleven thousand years ago. Had experienced something impossible.

And she'd come back safe.

Because the elder had decided she was a child in need. And children in need were protected.

Time didn't matter. Language didn't matter. Culture didn't matter.

A lost child was a lost child.

And the response was universal.

That night, Sarah and I debriefed at my house.

"They could have kept her," I said. "Could have refused to release her. We couldn't have stopped them."

"But they didn't. Because she called for her mother. That was clear. Universal. She wanted to go home. So they let her go."

"Do you think they understood who we were? Parents? Law enforcement?"

"They understood family. That's enough. The girl wanted her mother. The mother wanted her daughter. They facilitated reunion. That's what any decent community does."

"They protected her first. Fed her. Warmed her. Made her safe. Before returning her."

"Yes. Because that's what you do with lost children. You don't just hand them over to whoever shows up claiming them. You make sure the child is safe. That the reunion is legitimate. That the transfer is wanted."

"That's sophisticated social thinking."

"They're humans. They've been dealing with community dynamics for thousands of years. Longer than we have, technically. They know how societies work."

I thought about the woman staying with Lily. The elder assessing the situation. The careful release only after Lily showed she wanted to go.

Not primitive. Not simple. Not savage.

Just careful. Protective. Responsible.

The same way any functioning community would handle a lost child.

Friday morning, the story broke.

"Lost Child Found Safe in Paleo-Indian Village"

"Stone Age Humans Protect Modern Girl, Return Her to Parents"

"Time-Displaced Community Shows Humanity Transcends Millennia"

The coverage was overwhelmingly positive. For once.

Images of Lily being released. The elder nodding acknowledgment. The village continuing normal life after the drama.

Anthropologists weighed in: "This demonstrates complex social structures. Empathy. Care for vulnerable members even outside their own group. These are not primitive savages. These are sophisticated humans with functioning ethical systems."

Child welfare advocates: "The Paleo-Indian response was textbook appropriate. They protected the child. Assessed the situation. Released her only when safe transfer was verified. That's what we teach modern caregivers."

Even the xenophobes were quiet. Hard to argue for deportation when the people you're demonizing just saved a lost seven-year-old and returned her safely.

The Skegmog Lake settlement, for the first time, was seen as positive. Helpful. Human.

Not a threat. Not a curiosity. Not a problem.

Just neighbors. Different neighbors. But neighbors.

Saturday, Dan and Rebecca Mitchell visited my office.

"We wanted to thank you. For finding Lily. For handling the situation carefully."

"The Paleo-Indians did the hard part. They kept her safe."

"We know. And we want to thank them too. But we don't know how. We can't just show up at their village with a casserole."

"No. Probably not."

Rebecca pulled out a small bag. "These are hand warmers. The kind you shake to activate. I thought... maybe they'd be useful. For winter. For the children in the village. I don't know if that's appropriate or—"

"I'll ask Sarah. She can facilitate trade. Make sure it's received as a gift, not charity."

"And we wanted to offer something else." Dan paused. "If they need anything. Medical help. Food. Anything. We're here. We're neighbors. Even if they're from the past and we're from now—Lily would've died out there if they hadn't found her. We owe them."

"I'll pass that along."

After they left, I sat in my office, thinking.

A modern family offering help to Paleo-Indians.

Not out of obligation. Not out of guilt. Out of genuine gratitude.

That was new.

That was hope.

Sunday, Sarah brought the hand warmers to the village. Along with a note—translated into simple concepts and symbols—explaining they were thanks for protecting Lily.

The elder accepted them. Examined one. Figured out the activation mechanism.

His expression—Sarah reported—was something between surprise and delight.

Heat without fire. Portable. Reusable for hours.

Technology eleven thousand years beyond their experience. But useful. Practical. Appreciated.

He distributed them to the children. The woman who'd cared for Lily got two.

And in return, he sent back a gift for Lily.

A small carving. Bone. Shaped like a wolf. Beautifully detailed. Made with stone tools and infinite patience.

Sarah brought it to the Mitchell house.

Lily held it carefully. "For me?"

"For you. From the people who helped you. A wolf. Like their dogs. To remind you that you're protected."

Lily looked at the carving. At the detail. At the care that had gone into making it.

"Can I go back? To visit? To say thank you?"

Rebecca tensed. "Honey—"

"They were nice. They helped me. I want to say thank you properly."

Sarah looked at me. I looked at the parents.

"Maybe someday," I said carefully. "When we understand each other better. When we can communicate. When visits can be safe and respectful. But not yet. For now, keep the wolf. Remember that different people can still be kind. And that kindness matters more than time."

Lily nodded. Held the carving.

A seven-year-old girl with a Paleo-Indian artifact made specifically for her.

A gift across eleven thousand years.

A gesture that said: you were lost. We helped. That's what people do.

That night, I updated the documentation.

Incident forty-seven: Child lost near Barnes Road. Found safe in Skegmog Lake Paleo-Indian settlement. Cared for, protected, and released to parents upon verified relationship. No injuries. Successful cross-cultural interaction. Mutual respect demonstrated. Gift exchange established.

First time a modern human had been inside a Paleo-Indian settlement.

First time both populations had worked together toward a common goal.

First time we'd proven that despite eleven thousand years of separation, humans were still humans.

And children were still children.

And protecting them was still the right thing to do.

No matter when you were from.

Chapter 27

CHAPTER TWENTY-SEVEN: WINTER RETURNS

The alert came at 2:17 AM on a Friday in late April.

Not a fold alert. A weather alert.

EMERGENCY: Extreme temperature anomaly detected. Multiple fold sites activating simultaneously. Pleistocene climate conditions imminent. Seek shelter immediately.

I was awake before my phone finished buzzing.

The temperature had already dropped. I could feel it through the bedroom window. Cold. Wrong cold. The kind of cold that didn't belong in late April Michigan.

I checked the thermometer on the back deck: 28 degrees and falling.

It had been 52 degrees when I went to bed three hours ago.

Jake called. "Dad, we've got fourteen folds opening simultaneously. All the permanent sites plus six new ones. And they're not just opening. They're merging. Overlapping. Creating a continuous Pleistocene climate zone across northern Antrim County."

"How big?"

"Maybe forty square miles. And expanding. Dad, the temperature in the core zone is dropping toward ice age levels. We're looking at minus ten, minus twenty within hours. Anyone caught in the zone without proper shelter—"

"Will freeze to death."

"Yes."

By 3 AM, the emergency response was mobilized.

Sheriff Kowalski coordinating evacuations from the affected area. Fire departments setting up warming centers. State police blocking roads into the zone.

But the zone was expanding faster than we could evacuate.

I drove toward the edge. As close as I dared.

The boundary was visible. A wall of cold air. Like stepping from a room into a freezer. Temperature differential so extreme you could see it shimmer.

On one side: normal late April. Cool but manageable. Maybe 35 degrees.

On the other side: Pleistocene winter. Brutal. Deadly. Maybe minus fifteen and still dropping.

And caught in between: people.

Families who'd refused to evacuate earlier. Properties too close to permanent fold sites. People who'd thought they could wait it out. Adapt. Be careful.

They were wrong.

The first rescue was at 3:47 AM.

Elderly couple on Cairn Highway. House inside the cold zone. No heat. Temperature inside their home dropping fast.

Fire department got them out. Hypothermia setting in. Rushed to warming center.

They survived. Barely.

The second rescue was harder.

Family of four. House near the Lakeview Estates fold. Tried to evacuate but their car wouldn't start. Dead battery from the extreme cold.

Fire department reached them at 4:23 AM. All four hypothermic. The children—eight and eleven—barely conscious.

They survived. But it was close.

By 5 AM, we had seventeen people in warming centers. All hypothermic. Three critical.

And the zone was still expanding.

At 5:34 AM, Dr. Webb called.

"Dave, the Skegmog settlement. They're in the zone."

"Can you reach them?"

"We're trying. But Dave, they might not need rescue. They're adapted for this. Pleistocene winter is what they know."

"It's minus twenty. Nobody's adapted for minus twenty without proper shelter."

"They have shelter. And they've been preparing. Remember the storage platforms? The processed hides? They've been getting ready for winter. Their winter. This might be survivable for them."

"Might be isn't good enough. We need to check on them. Especially the children."

"Agreed. But approaching in these conditions—"

"I'm going. You coming?"

"Give me ten minutes."

We reached the settlement perimeter at 6:12 AM.

The cold was incredible. Painful. Even with winter gear—heavy coats, insulated boots, face masks—it hurt to breathe.

Dr. Webb's thermometer read minus eighteen.

The village was visible through the pre-dawn darkness. Smoke rising from the central fire. Structures intact. No signs of distress.

We approached slowly. Announced ourselves.

The elder emerged. Wearing heavy furs. Face covered except for eyes. Completely adapted.

He looked at us. At our modern winter gear. At the way we were shivering despite being bundled.

Spoke. A short phrase.

Sarah wasn't with us. No translator. But the meaning was clear from his tone and gesture.

You're not equipped for this. Go back.

Dr. Webb tried to communicate. Gestures. Pointing at the village. At the children. Question: Are you okay? Do you need help?

The elder pointed at the structures. At the smoke. At the visible preparations.

Then he pointed at us. At the way we were clearly suffering. At our inadequate gear.

And shook his head.

Message received: We're fine. You're not. Leave before you die.

He was right. Five more minutes in this cold and we'd be in serious trouble. Frostbite. Hypothermia. Our gear wasn't rated for minus twenty.

We retreated.

As we left, I looked back. The elder was already returning to the village. To his people. To their shelter and fire and community that had survived worse than this.

They'd be fine.

We barely made it back to the truck.

By 7 AM, the situation was critical.

The cold zone had expanded to sixty square miles. Temperature at the core: minus twenty-three.

Thirty-one people evacuated. Six critical. Two dead.

Martin Henderson—Bill's cousin, no relation to George—and his wife Louise. Elderly. Refused evacuation. Refused to leave their home of forty-three years.

Found frozen in their living room. Wrapped in blankets. Heater running but not enough. The cold had simply overwhelmed everything.

First deaths from a climate fold.

Won't be the last.

The Bellaire warming center—set up in the high school gym—was packed.

Two hundred people. Maybe more. Some evacuated from the cold zone. Some from surrounding areas afraid the zone would expand to them. Some just seeking community in crisis.

I found Commissioner Walsh there. She was coordinating supplies. Blankets. Food. Medical care.

"How long can this last?" she asked.

"Jake says the folds are stabilizing. The expansion has slowed. But the cold zone might be permanent."

"Permanent."

"Yes. Sixty square miles of ice age winter. Year-round. That's the new geography."

"How many homes are in that zone?"

"Forty-seven. All uninhabitable now. Even if the cold moderates, even if it warms to normal winter temperatures—nobody can live there without Pleistocene-level adaptation."

"So we've lost sixty square miles of the county."

"Yes."

She sat down. Hard. "This is it, isn't it. This is the federal government's justification. We can't protect people. We can't maintain the county. Evacuation orders are coming."

"Probably."

"What do we do?"

"Survive the next thirty-six hours. Then we'll see what's left."

By noon, the pattern stabilized.

The cold zone stopped expanding at sixty-two square miles. Temperature at the core: minus twenty-five. At the edges: minus ten to zero.

Permanent Pleistocene winter. Right in the middle of Antrim County.

Inside the zone: forty-seven uninhabitable homes. Three abandoned businesses. Two sections of closed highway. The Skegmog Lake settlement.

Outside the zone: the rest of us. Watching. Waiting. Wondering if it would expand again.

Jake's models said no. The folds had reached equilibrium. The overlap was stable.

We hoped he was right.

Saturday morning, the temperature outside the zone returned to normal. Mid-forties. Spring weather. Like nothing had happened.

But inside the zone: still minus twenty.

A permanent winter island in the middle of spring.

I drove to the boundary. The shimmer was gone. No visible demarcation. Just... the air changed. Temperature dropped. Drastically. Immediately.

You could stand with one foot in spring and one foot in winter.

I took a step into the cold zone. Stayed thirty seconds. Documented the conditions.

Then stepped back. Into warmth. Into normalcy.

Except normal didn't exist anymore.

Sunday, Dr. Webb hiked to the settlement again. Properly equipped this time. Arctic gear. Satellite communication. Emergency beacon.

He returned four hours later.

"They're thriving. Not just surviving. Thriving. The cold is normal for them. Comfortable, even. They've increased their fire. Adjusted their shelter. The children are playing in the snow. They're adapted in ways we can't match."

"What about long-term? Food? Resources?"

"They're hunting. The cold zone has attracted megafauna. Mastodons. Maybe other species. The Pleistocene ecosystem is establishing itself. For them, this isn't a disaster. It's home."

"And for us?"

"It's uninhabitable. We can visit with proper equipment. But we can't live there. That land belongs to them now. Completely."

Sixty-two square miles. Returned to the Pleistocene. Returned to the people who understood it.

Lost to modern Michigan.

Monday morning, the federal announcement came.

"Due to ongoing temporal instability and inability to ensure public safety, the Department of Homeland Security is issuing mandatory evacuation orders for Antrim County, Michigan. Residents have 30 days to relocate. Federal assistance available. This order is effective immediately and non-negotiable."

We'd known it was coming. But seeing it official. Seeing the thirty-day countdown.

That made it real.

Karen read the announcement. Looked at me.

"We're really doing this. We're staying."

"Yes."

"Even though it's a federal order."

"Even though."

"They'll cut off services. Power. Water. Emergency response."

"I know."

"We'll be on our own."

"We've been on our own since this started."

She was quiet. Then: "Okay. We stay. But Dave—we're going to need help. We can't do this alone. We'll need a community. People who know how to survive without modern infrastructure."

I thought about the Paleo-Indians. Thriving in minus-twenty-five-degree weather. Adapted. Skilled. Surviving.

And I thought about the people like Bill Henderson. The ones who refused to leave. The ones who'd rather adapt than evacuate.

"We'll find them," I said. "The ones who are staying. We'll build something. Together. Learn from the people who know this land better than we do."

"The Paleo-Indians."

"Yes. If they'll teach us. If we can build that relationship. Maybe we survive."

"And if we can't?"

"Then we tried. That's more than most people can say."

That night, the news showed the sixty-two-square-mile cold zone.

Aerial footage. The permanent winter. Snow and ice in late April. Impossible. Undeniable.

And in the middle of it: smoke rising from the Paleo-Indian village. People moving. Living. Adapted.

The caption: *"Stone Age Humans Thrive in Ice Age Conditions While Modern Residents Evacuate"*

The irony wasn't lost on anyone.

We'd spent eleven thousand years building civilization. Technology. Infrastructure. Comfort.

And when the land returned to what it used to be, we couldn't survive it.

But the people from before civilization could.

They'd carried the skills forward. Through time. Through displacement. Through everything.

And now, while we evacuated, they settled.

The land was choosing its residents.

And we were learning we weren't the chosen ones.

Chapter 28

CHAPTER TWENTY-EIGHT: CORRECTION THEORY

Dr. Lisa Park arrived Tuesday morning with a team from University of Chicago.

Physicists. Geologists. Temporal mechanics specialists—a field that hadn't existed six months ago and now had doctoral programs.

They set up in the Bellaire library conference room. Requested access to all our data. Jake's seismic records. My incident documentation. Dr. Ostrander's geological surveys. Everything.

I sat in on the briefing Wednesday afternoon.

Dr. Park stood at a whiteboard covered in equations I didn't understand.

"We've been analyzing the pattern across the entire Great Lakes region. Antrim County. Wisconsin. Illinois. Ohio. Everywhere the glacial boundaries exist. And we've identified something significant."

She pulled up a map. Red dots scattered across five states. Hundreds of them.

"These are confirmed fold sites. Notice the distribution."

The dots followed the moraine systems. The ancient shorelines. Exactly as we'd documented.

"Now watch what happens when we overlay geological stress data."

Another layer appeared. The dots aligned perfectly with areas of maximum isostatic rebound. Places where the land was still rising after glacial compression.

"The earth is still adjusting to the removal of ice age glaciers. Still rebounding. Rising. Settling. And at points of maximum stress—where moraine meets shoreline, where rebound is most active—the geological pressure is creating... fractures. Not in space. In time."

Jake leaned forward. "You're saying the folds are geological phenomena. Not random. Not magical. Mechanical."

"Exactly. The weight of glaciers compressed the earth. When the ice melted, the land began rising. And it's still rising. Slowly. Centimeters per century. But that movement creates stress. Micro-fractures in the substrate. And those fractures—"

"Extend through time," Dr. Ostrander finished. "Because time and space are linked. Stress one, you stress the other."

"Precisely. Which brings us to the correction theory."

She changed slides.

"The earth has a memory. Geological memory. Encoded in rock strata, in sediment layers, in the physical structure of the planet. And when that structure is stressed—when fractures occur—the earth attempts to correct. To return to equilibrium."

"By remembering what it used to be," I said.

"Yes. The land is reverting to its most stable configuration. Pre-human. Pre-agricultural. Pre-disturbance. The Pleistocene represents maximum stability for this region. Ice age climate. Glacial ecosystems.

Megafauna. That's the configuration the earth 'remembers' as correct."

Commissioner Walsh—sitting in the back—spoke up. "You're saying the land thinks we're wrong. That modern civilization is wrong. That we're the anomaly."

"Not thinks. The earth doesn't think. But yes—from a purely geological perspective, the current configuration is unstable. Eleven thousand years of human modification. Agriculture. Development. Climate change. Destroyed mounds. Altered waterways. The land has been forced into an unnatural state. And now, given the opportunity via temporal fractures, it's correcting."

"Correcting by erasing us."

"Not erasing. Reverting. The Pleistocene is the default state. We're the aberration. And the earth is fixing the error."

Silence.

Then Bill Henderson, who'd somehow gotten into the meeting, stood up.

"That's bullshit. We're not errors. We're people. We live here. We built here. We belong here."

Dr. Park looked at him sympathetically. "I understand the emotional response. But from a geological timescale perspective, humans are a recent phenomenon. Eleven thousand years is nothing. The earth has been here for 4.5 billion years. The Pleistocene represents a stable epoch that lasted two million years. Modern human civilization? A blink. An anomaly in the pattern."

"So what? We just accept that we don't belong? That the land wants us gone?"

"I'm not saying what you should accept. I'm explaining what the data suggests. The folds aren't random. They're not punishment. They're correction. The earth attempting to return to equilibrium."

"Can it be stopped?" I asked.

"That's the critical question. Can you stop geological processes? Can you halt isostatic rebound? Can you prevent the earth from settling into its most stable configuration?"

"Can you?"

"We're working on theoretical models. Artificial stabilization. Seismic dampening. Injecting stabilizing compounds into fracture points. But these are geological-scale interventions. Expensive. Unproven. And possibly impossible."

"So the answer is no."

"The answer is: we don't know yet. But the preliminary data suggests that once correction begins, once the fractures open, stopping them may be beyond our capability."

After the meeting, Jake and Dr. Park talked privately. I listened.

"If the earth is correcting," Jake said, "if it's reverting to Pleistocene configuration, what's the endpoint? How much of the region converts?"

"Unknown. But theoretically? All of it. Everywhere the glaciers reached. Everywhere the geological stress exists. The entire Great Lakes region could eventually revert."

"How long?"

"Decades. Maybe centuries. The process is accelerating but it's not instantaneous. Current models suggest fifty to seventy-five percent conversion within fifty years."

"Fifty years."

"Give or take. Assuming the acceleration rate holds constant. Which it might not. It could speed up. Or slow down. We're in uncharted territory."

"And humans? Modern populations? What happens to us?"

"You adapt or you leave. Those are the options. The Paleo-Indians are proving adaptation is possible. They're thriving in the cold zone. Hunting megafauna. Living as they always did. For modern humans to do the same, you'd need to abandon most technology. Most infrastructure. Most of what defines modern life. Return to subsistence living. Stone tools. Hunting and gathering. Oral traditions."

"Stone age living."

"Yes. Which most modern humans aren't equipped for psychologically or practically. So the likely outcome is mass migration. Evacuation of the affected regions. Abandonment of major cities. Chicago. Milwaukee. Detroit. All built on glacial boundaries. All potentially reverting within decades."

"Millions of people displaced."

"Yes. The largest migration in human history. And nowhere to migrate to that's guaranteed stable. Because if the theory holds, if geological stress creates temporal fractures, then anywhere humans have modified the landscape aggressively—anywhere we've created instability—could fold."

"So nowhere's safe."

"Nowhere's guaranteed. But some places are safer than others. Areas without glacial history. Regions with stable geology. Old cratons. Tectonically quiet zones. Those might persist."

"And the rest of us?"

"Learn to live with instability. Or don't. Those are the choices."

Thursday, Dr. Park's team released their findings.

"Temporal Correction Theory: Evidence Suggests Earth Reverting to Pleistocene Configuration"

The paper went viral. Every major scientific journal. Every news network. Social media exploded.

Half the responses were scientific debate. Physicists arguing mechanisms. Geologists questioning data. Temporal mechanics specialists proposing alternatives.

The other half were existential crisis.

"We're errors. The earth wants us gone."

"Modern civilization is doomed."

"Return to stone age or die."

Religious groups claimed vindication. "This is judgment. Punishment for defying natural order."

Environmental activists claimed victory. "The earth is healing. Humanity is the disease."

Conspiracy theorists claimed deception. "Government wants us to believe this so we evacuate willingly. It's a land grab."

And in the middle of the chaos: ordinary people trying to decide what to do.

Stay and adapt? Leave and start over? Hope the scientists were wrong?

No good answers. Just impossible choices.

Friday, I met with the group who'd decided to stay.

Forty-three people. Not counting Karen, Jake, and me.

Bill Henderson. Sarah Ashkwe. Dr. Ostrander. Dr. Webb. Len Greenland and Joe Macklin. A handful of farmers. Some retirees. A few young families with nowhere else to go.

Forty-three people choosing to remain in Antrim County after the federal evacuation order.

Forty-three people betting they could adapt to a world reverting to the Pleistocene.

We met in Bill Henderson's barn. Unofficial. Off the record. Planning for a future the government said was impossible.

"If we're staying," Bill said, "we need to be realistic. Power's getting cut off. Water systems will fail. Supply chains are already breaking down. We'll be on our own."

"What do we have?" I asked.

"Skills. Some of us know how to hunt. Farm. Build. Repair. We're not helpless. But we're not Paleo-Indians either. We're going to need to learn."

Sarah spoke up. "The Skegmog Lake settlement. They've survived the cold zone. They know skills we don't. If we can establish good trade relationships, maybe they'll teach us. Share knowledge."

"Why would they?" someone asked. "What do we have that they want?"

"Metal tools. Medicine. Technology they can't produce. And knowledge about the modern world. Warnings about dangers they don't recognize. Trade goes both ways."

Dr. Webb nodded. "I've been working with them. Building trust. If we approach respectfully, if we offer genuine value, they might be willing to share survival skills. How to process hides properly. How to preserve food without refrigeration. How to identify edible plants. How to read weather and seasons without technology."

"We're talking about becoming their students," Dr. Ostrander said. "Learning from people we used to think of as primitive. That's going to require humility some folks won't have."

"Then those folks can leave," Bill said bluntly. "We don't have time for pride. We have thirty days before federal services shut down. After that, we're either prepared or we're dead. Simple as that."

We spent three hours planning.

Inventory of skills: who knew what. Who could teach. Who needed to learn.

Resource assessment: what we had. What we'd need. What we could produce or trade for.

Infrastructure: which buildings could function without power. Which wells still worked. Which roads would remain passable if maintenance stopped.

And education: crash courses in survival skills. Hunting. Trapping. Food preservation. Shelter building. First aid without hospitals. All the knowledge humans used to carry that we'd forgotten.

By the end of the meeting, we had a framework. Rough. Incomplete. But something.

A plan to survive what was coming.

Whether it would work—that was another question.

Saturday, I drove to the edge of the cold zone.

Stood at the boundary. One foot in April spring. One foot in Pleistocene winter.

Thought about Dr. Park's theory.

The earth correcting. Returning to equilibrium. Erasing the anomaly of modern civilization.

From a geological perspective, she was right. Eleven thousand years was nothing. A blink. An error in the pattern.

But from a human perspective?

We were real. Our lives mattered. Our communities mattered. Our choice to stay and fight and adapt—that mattered.

Even if the earth didn't think so.

I stepped fully into the cold zone. Temperature dropping instantly. Brutal. Hostile to human life without extreme adaptation.

Stayed one minute. Breathing cold air. Feeling what the Paleo-Indians felt every day. What they thrived in.

Then stepped back. Into warmth. Into the world I knew.

The world that was disappearing.

One fold at a time. One cold zone at a time. One correction at a time.

Until eventually—maybe in fifty years, maybe sooner—there'd be nothing left to step back to.

Just Pleistocene. Permanent. Complete.

And the humans who remained would be the ones who'd learned to live in it.

The ones who'd adapted. Who'd learned the old skills. Who'd become, in a sense, Paleo-Indians themselves.

Survivors in a world that had corrected the error.

Us.

Chapter 29

CHAPTER TWENTY-NINE: EXODUS

The evacuation began on a Monday.

Federal convoy. FEMA trucks. National Guard coordinating logistics. Emergency management officials with clipboards checking names against lists.

The staging area was the high school parking lot. The same place we'd held the town meeting. The same place Bob Martinez's family had watched documentaries about the thing that killed him.

Now it was processing people. Loading them onto buses. Sending them south. Away from the folds. Away from home.

Away from everything they'd known.

I stood at the edge of the parking lot. Watching. Documenting. Bearing witness.

The first families arrived at 6 AM.

Station wagons packed with everything they could carry. Suitcases strapped to roofs. Kids crying. Parents trying to stay calm. Grandparents looking back at the town one last time.

Sharon Kowalski—the sheriff's wife—was in the first group. Her kids. Her mother. Boxes and bags piled into a minivan.

She saw me. Walked over.

"Dave."

"Sharon."

"Tom's staying, isn't he."

"He hasn't told you?"

"He doesn't have to. I know him. He won't leave. His job. His duty. His stubborn goddamn pride." Her voice cracked. "I can't watch him die here. I can't let the kids watch. So we're going."

"Where?"

"My sister's in Ann Arbor. Far enough from the moraine. Safe. Probably." She looked at the convoy. At the buses filling with people. "This is insane. A month ago we had a normal town. Normal lives. Now we're refugees."

"You're survivors. There's a difference."

"Doesn't feel like it." She looked at me. "Karen's staying too, isn't she."

"Yes."

"And Jake."

"Yes."

"I'm sorry. I'm sorry we're leaving you. But I can't—"

"You don't owe me an explanation. You're doing what's right for your family. That's enough."

She hugged me. Hard. Then got in her van and drove to the loading area.

I watched her family board a bus. Watched the bus pull away. Watched it disappear south on M-88.

Gone.

By noon, two hundred families had evacuated.

By 3 PM, five hundred.

By nightfall, nearly a thousand.

Houses standing empty. Driveways abandoned. "For Sale" signs that would never sell. Homes worth nothing because nobody wanted property in a temporal disaster zone.

The federal buyout program offered pennies on the dollar. Ten cents for every dollar of assessed value. Take it or leave it.

Most people took it. What choice did they have?

Patricia Hendricks—who'd already lost her house to a fold—took the buyout for her property value. Got a check for $8,700 for a house that had been worth $87,000 a year ago.

"It's something," she said when I saw her at the processing center. "Better than nothing. Enough to start over. Maybe."

She boarded a bus to Petoskey. Where she had a cousin. Where she could stay until she figured out what came next.

Another neighbor gone.

The second day was worse.

Families who'd been holding out. Hoping the evacuation would be canceled. Hoping the scientists would find a solution. Hoping for a miracle.

No miracles came.

Just buses. And federal officials with clipboards. And the thirty-day deadline ticking down.

I saw families I'd known for years. Kids Jake had gone to school with. People Karen had worked with. Community members who'd been fixtures at every town event.

All leaving.

The Johnsons. The Pratts. The Kellermans. The Bishops.

One after another. Loading buses. Saying goodbye to neighbors. Crying. Angry. Resigned.

By the end of day two, fifteen hundred people gone.

Out of a county population of twenty-three thousand, that was significant. And we were only two days in.

Day three, the holdouts started appearing.

People who refused to leave. Who'd signed federal waivers acknowledging they understood the risks and chose to stay anyway.

Bill Henderson was first. Walked into the processing center. Signed the waiver. Told the federal official: "I'm staying. Don't come back for me."

The official—young guy, maybe twenty-five, looked exhausted—just nodded. "Sir, you understand that after the thirty-day period, federal services will cease. No power. No water. No emergency response. You'll be on your own."

"I understand."

"And you still choose to stay."

"I do."

The official made a note. Moved to the next person.

Bill walked out. Found me in the parking lot.

"That's done. I'm official."

"How many signed waivers?" I asked.

"Twenty-seven so far. Probably more coming. Your name on the list?"

"Going tomorrow. Karen and I both."

"Jake?"

"He's not legally required to evacuate. He's over eighteen. He'll sign too."

"Good. We'll need him. Need his data. His understanding of the folds." Bill looked at the buses. At the people leaving. "We're going to be a small group. Forty, fifty people maybe. Against a county reverting to the ice age."

"We've survived worse."

"Have we? When?"

I thought about it. Couldn't come up with an answer.

"We'll find out," I said.

Day four, Karen and I signed the waivers.

The federal official—different one, older woman, more sympathetic—walked us through the terms.

"You acknowledge that Antrim County has been declared a temporal disaster zone. That federal services will cease as of May 15th. That emergency response will not be available. That you are choosing to remain at your own risk. That the government holds no liability for injury, death, or property loss resulting from temporal displacement events."

"We acknowledge all of that," Karen said.

"Ma'am, I have to ask. Why are you staying? You have options. Federal relocation assistance. Housing subsidies. Job placement programs. You could start over somewhere safe."

"This is our home," Karen said simply. "We've lived here thirty years. Raised our kids here. Built a life here. We're not leaving because the land is changing. We're adapting to the change."

"The land isn't just changing. It's reverting to the Pleistocene. Ice age conditions. Extinct predators. Temporal instability. You could die here."

"We could die anywhere. At least here we die on our own terms."

The official looked at her for a long moment. Then handed her the waiver. "Sign here. And here. Initial here."

Karen signed. I signed.

We were official.

Forty-three people staying. Against federal orders. Against common sense. Against every survival instinct that said run.

But we were staying.

Day seven, Emma came home.

Drove up from State. Didn't tell us she was coming. Just showed up at the house Thursday afternoon.

Karen saw her first. Through the kitchen window. Emma's car pulling into the driveway.

"Dave. Emma's here."

We met her outside.

She got out. Looked at the house. At the property. At us.

"You're really doing this. You're really staying."

"Yes," I said.

"Even though it's insane."

"Even though."

"I can't convince you to leave."

"No."

She nodded. Opened her trunk. Started pulling out boxes.

"Then I'm staying too. At least for the summer. Maybe longer. I withdrew from spring semester. Told them it was a family emergency. Which it is."

"Emma—" Karen started.

"Don't. Don't tell me it's too dangerous. Don't tell me to go back to school. Don't tell me I'm making a mistake. You're my family. You're staying. So I'm staying. We argue about it or we accept it. Your choice."

Karen hugged her. Crying. "We accept it."

I helped carry boxes inside. Emma had brought supplies. Food. Medical kits. Books. Practical things.

"If we're doing this," she said, "we're doing it right. I've been researching. Survival skills. Primitive technology. How to live without modern infrastructure. I even took a weekend course on hide tanning. Which was disgusting. But I learned."

"You took a hide tanning course?"

"If we're going to trade with Paleo-Indians, we should know what we're talking about. Show we're serious about learning. Not just tourists asking for help."

Jake came home that evening. Saw Emma's car.

"You're back."

"I'm back."

"You said you'd never live here again."

"I lied. Or I changed my mind. One of those." She looked at him. "You almost died in a fold. Hypothermia. Frostbite. And you're still here. Still researching. Still risking your life. So I figured if you're that stupid, I should at least be here to document your stupidity."

He hugged her. "Thanks, I think."

"You're welcome."

Day ten, the power started going out.

Not everywhere. Not all at once. Just rolling blackouts as the utility companies pulled out. Stopped maintenance. Reduced staff.

By day twelve, power was intermittent. By day fifteen, mostly off.

Water systems failed next. Municipal wells shut down. Treatment plants abandoned. Pipes froze in the permanent cold zones.

By day twenty, we were on our own water. Wells. Rainwater collection. Lake water boiled for safety.

Welcome to the nineteenth century.

Day twenty-three, I drove through Bellaire.

The town was emptying. Literally emptying.

Stores closed. Windows dark. "Going Out of Business" signs everywhere. Some places just abandoned. Doors unlocked. Inventory left behind. Not worth moving.

Shorts Brewing Company: closed. Toonies Restaurant: closed. The grocery store: empty shelves, lights off, gone.

The courthouse: locked. Sheriff's office: relocated to a trailer at the edge of town, minimal staff.

The high school: empty. No students. No teachers. Just a building.

I parked in the main street. Got out. Walked.

It was eerily quiet. No traffic. No people. Just wind and abandoned buildings.

I'd lived here twenty-three years. Knew every street. Every business. Every family.

Now it was a ghost town.

Not destroyed. Not damaged. Just... empty.

Left behind.

I stood in the middle of Main Street. No cars. No need to move.

And I thought: this is what correction looks like. Not explosions. Not violence. Just silence. Absence. The slow erasure of modern life as people gave up and left.

The earth reclaiming what had been briefly borrowed.

Day twenty-eight, the last bus left.

Only fifty people boarded. The stragglers. The people who'd waited until the last possible moment.

I watched it leave. Heading south. Toward safety. Toward normal life. Toward everything we were giving up.

Karen stood beside me. "How many stayed?"

"We counted forty-three signed waivers. But I think there are more. People who didn't sign officially but won't leave. Hiding out. Squatting in abandoned properties. Maybe sixty total."

"Sixty people in a county built for twenty-three thousand."

"Yes."

"We're insane."

"Probably."

She took my hand. "But we're insane together. That counts for something."

Day twenty-nine, Sheriff Tom Kowalski stopped by.

He'd stayed. Refused to leave. His wife and kids gone to Ann Arbor, but he remained.

"Federal services officially cease tomorrow at midnight. After that, we're on our own. No state police. No National Guard. No backup."

"What are you going to do?"

"My job. Protect the people who stayed. Keep order. Handle what I can." He paused. "It'll be different. No resources. No support. Just me and maybe two deputies who stayed. We'll do what we can."

"That's all any of us can do."

He looked at the empty street. "We're going to need a new model. Can't maintain law enforcement the way we used to. No county budget. No state funding. We'll have to figure out community policing. Old fashioned. Personal. Based on relationships not systems."

"Like the Paleo-Indians."

"Yeah. Like them. Small groups. Shared responsibility. Everyone watching out for everyone else." He smiled slightly. "Never thought I'd be taking law enforcement lessons from stone age people. But here we are."

Day thirty. May 15th. Midnight.

Karen, Jake, Emma, and I sat on the back deck. Watching the clock.

At 11:59 PM, the last municipal lights went out. The streetlights on M-88. The courthouse security lighting. The few remaining traffic signals.

Everything.

At midnight exactly, federal services ceased.

Power grid: offline.

Water systems: offline.

Emergency services: withdrawn.

We were officially on our own.

Sixty people. In a county built for twenty-three thousand. Surrounded by temporal instability. With no backup. No safety net. No guarantee we'd survive.

But we'd chosen this. We'd signed the waivers. We'd committed.

And we were together.

Family. Friends. Community. The people who'd decided adaptation was better than evacuation.

We'd survive. Or we wouldn't.

But we'd face it here. On our land. In our home.

As the earth corrected around us.

Chapter 30

CHAPTER THIRTY: ADAPTATION PROTOCOL

The first week without power was hell.

Not because we froze. Not because we starved. But because every single thing we'd taken for granted suddenly required conscious thought.

Want water? Walk to the well. Hand pump. Fifty pumps per five-gallon bucket. Carry it inside. Boil it. Wait for it to cool.

Want food? No refrigerator. No freezer. Everything had to be preserved differently. Dried. Smoked. Canned. Or eaten immediately.

Want light? Candles. Oil lamps. Flashlights with dying batteries we couldn't recharge.

Want heat? Wood stove. Which meant chopping wood. Constantly. Every day. Hours of work just to stay warm.

Want to communicate? Walk. Or don't communicate. No phones. No internet. No way to know what was happening three miles away except by going there.

Modern life had been easy. We just hadn't known it.

By the second week, we'd established routines.

The staying group—sixty-three people now, a few more had emerged from hiding—met every Sunday at Bill Henderson's barn. Inventory. Planning. Problem-solving.

"Water's our biggest issue," Bill said at the first meeting. "Wells work but hand-pumping is labor-intensive. We need a better system."

Dr. Ostrander: "Windmill pumps. Old technology. Reliable. No electricity required. I can design one if we have materials."

"We have materials. Every abandoned house in the county is a hardware store now. Take what you need."

Sarah spoke up. "The Skegmog settlement has been using lake water. They process it differently. Filtration through sand and charcoal. No boiling required if done correctly. I can ask if they'd teach us."

"Do it. We need every advantage."

Food was next.

Len Greenland: "We've got maybe three months of stored food across all households. After that, we're hunting and gathering. Not everyone knows how."

"Then we learn," Jake said. "Dr. Webb's been documenting Paleo-Indian techniques. Hunting. Trapping. Plant identification. We can create training sessions."

"Who teaches?"

"I will," Joe Macklin said. "I've hunted forty years. I can teach tracking. Field dressing. Meat preservation. And I know some of the old farmers who stayed. They can teach gardening without modern tools."

Bill nodded. "We make it formal. Weekly classes. Everyone attends. Everyone learns. No exceptions."

"What about the people who can't? The elderly? The disabled?"

"They contribute other ways. Knowledge. Repair skills. Teaching. Everyone has value. Everyone contributes. That's how we survive."

The third week, we started scavenging.

Every abandoned house was fair game. Take what you need. Leave what you can't use.

I went with Emma and Jake. Hit five houses in one day.

First house: the Pratts' place. They'd evacuated day three. Left everything.

We took:

Hand tools. Hammers. Saws. Axes. Things that worked without power.

Canning jars. Dozens of them. For food preservation.

Blankets. Warm clothes. Cold-weather gear.

Books. On gardening. Hunting. Survival skills. Knowledge we'd need.

Left behind:

Electronics. Useless without power.

Furniture. Too heavy. Not essential.

Photos. Memories. Other people's lives we had no right to take.

It felt like grave-robbing. But it was survival.

Second house: the Kellermans'. Same process. Different items.

By the end of the day, we'd filled a truck. Brought it back to Bill's barn. Central storage. Distributed based on need.

"This feels wrong," Emma said that night.

"It is wrong," I agreed. "But it's necessary. The Kellermans aren't coming back. Their stuff was going to rot. Better we use it."

"Still feels like stealing."

"It is stealing. We're just calling it something else."

Karen looked at both of us. "We're building a different society. Different rules. In the old world, this was theft. In the new world, this is resource management. We adapt or we die. Those are the choices."

Week four, Dr. Webb arranged the first formal teaching session with the Skegmog settlement.

Eight of us. Sarah translating. Bringing trade goods: antibiotics, metal tools, salt.

The elder met us at the perimeter. Assessed. Decided we were serious.

Led us into the village.

It had grown. Twenty-three people now. They'd merged with another band. Built three more structures. Expanded the defensive perimeter.

This wasn't temporary anymore. This was a town.

The elder brought out two teachers. A woman—maybe forty, expert in hide processing—and a younger man, expert in tool-making.

For three hours, they taught.

The woman showed us how to process deer hide into leather. Scraping. Tanning using brain matter—"every animal has enough brains to tan its own hide," Sarah translated. Smoking. Softening. Every step done with stone tools and patience.

"This takes days," Emma said.

The woman responded. Sarah translated: "Fast work is bad work. Good leather takes time. Rushed leather fails. You die."

Practical. Direct. Survival wisdom.

The tool-maker showed us knapping. How to strike flint correctly. How to pressure-flake obsidian into razor-sharp edges. How to haft a point onto a shaft.

Jake tried. Failed. His point shattered.

The tool-maker laughed. Not mocking. Encouraging. Showed him again. Slower. More patient.

Jake tried again. Better. Still crude. But functional.

"How long to master this?" Jake asked.

The tool-maker held up both hands. Opened and closed them repeatedly.

Sarah: "He's saying years. Many years. He started as a child. You're starting as an adult. You'll never be as good. But you can be good enough."

Good enough to survive. That was the standard now.

We brought back knowledge. And a gift.

The woman had given Emma a processed hide. Small. Deer leather. Beautifully soft. Hours of work.

"For teaching you," Sarah translated. "She says you showed respect. Listened carefully. That deserves recognition."

Emma held the hide carefully. "This is worth more than anything we brought. More than antibiotics. More than metal. This is craftsmanship."

"That's why she gave it to you. To show: knowledge has value. Skill has value. Respect has value. Money doesn't matter anymore. Quality does."

Week five, we established the barter system.

No more money. Cash was worthless when there was nothing to buy.

Instead: trade.

Bill Henderson had chickens. Eggs were currency.

The Martins had a working greenhouse. Fresh vegetables traded for preserved meat.

Dr. Havelka provided medical care. Payment in firewood or food or labor.

I provided security. Patrols. Monitoring fold activity. Warning system maintenance. Payment in whatever people could spare.

Everyone contributed. Everyone received. The economy ran on reciprocity.

It was inefficient. Complicated. Required trust.

But it worked.

Week six, we had our first crisis.

A man named Derek Voss—the hunting guide who'd been running Pleistocene trophy hunts—showed up.

He'd evacuated day fifteen. Taken the federal buyout. Left.

Now he was back.

"I've got rights," he said at the Sunday meeting. "Property rights. I own land here. You can't keep me out."

"You took the buyout," Bill said. "You surrendered your property to the federal government. You signed the waiver saying you were leaving permanently."

"I changed my mind. I want my land back."

"Why?"

"Because there's money to be made here. Rich people want to hunt extinct animals. I can charge fifty thousand per hunt. Maybe more. This place is a gold mine."

The room went silent.

Then Sheriff Kowalski spoke. "There's no money here. No economy. No infrastructure to support tourism. You can't run commercial hunts without power, water, or emergency services."

"I'll figure it out. I always do." Derek looked around. "And if you try to stop me, I'll sue. Federal courts still work. Property rights still exist."

Bill stood up. Walked to Derek. Got very close.

"You're not welcome here. We're building a community. Based on cooperation. Mutual support. Survival. You're talking about exploitation. Profit. Treating this place like a theme park."

"It's a free country."

"Not anymore. Federal government abandoned this county. We're on our own. And we say: you're not welcome. Leave."

"You can't make me."

Sheriff Kowalski stepped forward. "Actually, I can. You're trespassing on federal disaster zone property without authorization. You violated your evacuation agreement. I can arrest you. Or you can leave voluntarily."

"You don't have authority anymore. Federal services ceased."

"I'm still sheriff. I'm still sworn. I'm still armed. And I'm still willing to enforce community decisions. Your choice: leave now, or leave in handcuffs."

Derek looked around. Saw sixty-three people unified against him. No support. No sympathy.

He left.

But as he walked out, he turned back. "You people are insane. You're playing primitive in a county that's reverting to the stone age. You're going to die here. All of you."

"Maybe," Bill said. "But we'll die trying to build something. You'll die trying to exploit it. I know which I prefer."

Derek drove away.

We never saw him again.

Week seven, we established the education system.

Every Tuesday and Thursday: skills training.

Morning sessions: hunting, trapping, tracking (taught by Joe and Len).

Afternoon sessions: gardening, food preservation, herbal medicine (taught by the farmers and Dr. Havelka).

Evening sessions: primitive technology, hide processing, tool-making (taught by those who'd learned from the Paleo-Indians).

Everyone attended. Even the elderly. Even the kids. Everyone learning.

Emma excelled at hide processing. She had the patience. The attention to detail.

Jake excelled at primitive fire-starting. Bow drill. Flint and steel. Natural tinder identification.

Karen excelled at plant identification. Edible versus poisonous. Medicinal properties. Seasonal availability.

I was mediocre at everything. But I learned. Slowly. Clumsily. But I learned.

Because mediocre was enough. Good enough to survive. That was the standard.

Week eight, we had our first success story.

Tom Kowalski—who'd been living on stored food—harvested his first deer using primitive methods.

Tracked it for six hours. Used an atlatl—spear-thrower—he'd made himself under Paleo-Indian instruction. Clean kill. Efficient.

He brought it back to the community. We processed it together. Everyone contributing. Everyone learning.

Meat smoked for preservation. Hide scraped for leather. Bones saved for tools. Sinew dried for binding. Nothing wasted.

That night, we had a feast. Venison. Fresh vegetables from the greenhouse. Bread baked in a wood-fired oven.

Sixty-three people. Sitting together. Eating food we'd grown or hunted ourselves. Using tools we'd made. Knowledge we'd learned.

No electricity. No modern convenience. Just community. Skill. Survival.

It felt like victory.

Small. Fragile. But real.

Week nine, Sarah arranged a meeting with the Skegmog elder.

Five of us. Me, Sarah, Bill, Dr. Webb, Karen. Bringing gifts. Seeking alliance.

The elder met us at the village perimeter. Assessed us.

Then invited us in. Fully. First time modern humans had been welcomed into the settlement as guests, not students.

We sat around the central fire. Sarah translating.

"We want to propose formal relationship," Bill said. "Trade. Knowledge sharing. Mutual defense. We're neighbors. We share the land. We should share resources."

The elder listened. Conferred with his council. Spoke.

Sarah translated: "He says: you learn slowly. Like children. But you learn. You show respect. You don't demand. You ask. That matters."

"He says: his people survived the great dying. When all the animals died. When the world changed. They survived because they adapted. Learned. Changed their ways."

"He says: you are learning to do the same. Adapt to the changing world. That makes you worthy. Not enemies. Not children. Partners."

"He agrees to formal relationship. Trade. Teaching. Shared defense against threats. As long as you continue showing respect."

Bill extended his hand. The elder looked at it. Didn't understand the gesture.

Sarah explained. The elder nodded. Grasped Bill's forearm instead. Warrior's grip. Partner's grip.

Alliance formed.

Between modern humans learning to survive. And ancient humans who'd never forgotten how.

Week ten, we documented progress.

Jake compiled the data:

63 people staying

12 functional wells

3 windmill pumps operational

47 abandoned houses scavenged for resources

8 people proficient in primitive hunting

15 people competent in hide processing

23 people growing food without modern tools

100% of community attending skills training

Zero deaths since federal evacuation

One formal alliance with Paleo-Indian settlement

Barter economy functioning

Community governance by consensus

We were surviving.

Not thriving. Not comfortable. But alive. Learning. Adapting.

Building something new from the ruins of something old.

And proving—to ourselves, to the earth, to history—that humans could adapt to anything.

Even the Pleistocene.

Even correction.

Even the end of the modern world.

As long as we did it together.

Chapter 31

CHAPTER THIRTY-ONE: PEACEFUL CONTACT

His name, as close as Sarah could translate it, was Makwa. It meant "bear" in Anishinaabemowin, though his own language used different sounds. Different structure.

But Makwa worked. And he answered to it.

I met him properly in week twelve.

I was checking the northern perimeter. The area near the permanent cold zone. Looking for fold activity. Monitoring for predators that might wander out.

And I saw him.

Standing at the edge of the tree line. Watching me. Not hiding. Not threatening. Just... there.

The same man from our first encounter at the railroad grade. The younger hunter. Maybe thirty. Lean. Scarred. Armed with an atlatl and three darts.

We looked at each other across maybe fifty yards.

I raised my hand. Palm out. Peace.

He did the same. Then gestured. Come.

I hesitated. Then followed.

He led me to a clearing. Sat down. Waited.

I sat across from him. Maybe ten feet of distance. Close enough to communicate. Far enough to not threaten.

He pulled out a small leather pouch. Opened it. Inside: dried meat. He offered some.

I took it. Ate it. Tasted smoky. Gamey. Good.

He nodded. Approval. You accept food. You're not an enemy.

Then he pointed at my rifle. Spoke. A question.

I showed him. Carefully. How it worked. The mechanism. The bullets. The safety.

He examined it. Didn't touch. Just looked. Understanding the principle. Point. Fire. Death at distance.

He pointed at his atlatl. Same thing. Point. Throw. Death at distance.

I nodded. Same concept. Different technology.

He smiled slightly. First time I'd seen him smile.

For the next hour, we communicated.

Not with words. With gestures. Objects. Demonstrations.

He showed me how he tracked deer. Reading signs in the dirt. Broken twigs. Disturbed grass. Scat age and composition. A whole language written in the forest that I'd never learned to read.

I showed him my monitoring equipment. The seismic sensor that detected fold activity. How it measured vibrations. Predicted openings.

He understood. Technology that warned of danger. Like reading weather signs. Different method. Same purpose.

We taught each other. Slowly. Patiently. Building vocabulary through context.

By the time we parted, I knew: this wasn't just cultural exchange. This was friendship forming. Trust building.

He'd chosen to approach me. To share food. To teach. To learn.

That meant something.

Week thirteen, I saw him again.

Same clearing. He was waiting.

This time he brought someone. A boy. Maybe eight. His son, I thought.

The boy watched me with wide eyes. Curious but cautious.

Makwa spoke to him. The boy nodded. Then approached. Held out a carved bone. Small. Shaped like a wolf.

Like the one the elder had given Lily.

A gift. From student to teacher. From child to stranger.

I accepted it carefully. Then pulled out something I'd brought. A metal fishhook. Small. Sharp. Better than anything they could make with stone.

I gave it to the boy.

He examined it. Showed his father. Makwa nodded. Approval.

Then the boy did something unexpected. He hugged me. Quick. Childlike. Then ran back to his father.

Makwa laughed. Genuine. Warm. The sound of a father proud of his brave son.

We sat. Shared food again. This time I brought jerky from Tom's deer. Makwa brought some kind of root. Cooked. Sweet.

We ate in comfortable silence.

Then Makwa stood. Gestured for me to follow.

He led me to a spot maybe a quarter mile away. Near a stream.

Showed me tracks. Large. Clawed. Fresh.

Short-faced bear. Maybe twelve hours old.

He pointed at the tracks. Then at the direction they led. Toward Bellaire. Toward our settlement.

Warning. Danger near your people.

Then he showed me how to read the tracks properly. Gait. Speed. Intent. This bear was hunting. Actively. Moving with purpose.

We needed to be careful.

I understood. Thanked him. Gestured: I'll warn my people.

He nodded. Then pointed at himself. At the tracks. At me.

Hunt together?

I understood what he was asking. Joint effort. Modern human and Paleo-Indian. Hunting dangerous predator together. Protecting both communities.

I nodded. Yes.

He smiled. Gripped my forearm. Partner.

Week fourteen, we organized the hunt.

Five modern humans: me, Bill, Tom Kowalski, Len Greenland, Joe Macklin.

Three Paleo-Indians: Makwa, another hunter named Nikan, and the elder himself.

Sarah came to translate. Dr. Webb to document.

We met at dawn. The clearing. Neutral ground.

The elder spoke. Sarah translated: "The bear has taken two deer near our settlement. One near yours. It's establishing hunting pattern. Learning our routines. That makes it dangerous. We hunt it before it hunts us."

"Agreed," Bill said. "How do we do this?"

Makwa stepped forward. Drew in the dirt. Showed the bear's pattern. Where it hunted. Where it slept. Where it traveled.

Then showed the plan. Two groups. One drives the bear. One waits in ambush.

His people would drive. They knew the terrain better. Moved quieter. Could push the bear toward the ambush without alerting it.

We would ambush. With rifles. More lethal at distance.

Simple. Effective. Using each group's strengths.

"When?" I asked.

Makwa pointed at the sun. Showed height. Midday.

Three hours from now.

We had time to prepare.

The ambush site was perfect. Narrow ravine. The bear's travel route passed through it. High ground on both sides.

We positioned: three rifles on the north ridge, two on the south. Overlapping fields of fire. No chance for the bear to escape.

Then we waited.

For two hours, nothing. Just forest sounds. Birds. Wind. Normal.

Then: silence. The way prey animals go quiet when a predator approaches.

I heard it before I saw it. Heavy footsteps. Branches breaking. Something large moving fast.

Then it emerged. The short-faced bear. Massive. Twelve feet standing. Moving at a run. Being driven.

Behind it: Makwa and Nikan. Not visible. Just sounds. Shouts. Stones thrown. Pushing the bear toward us.

The bear entered the ravine. Right where we predicted.

Bill fired first. Hit the shoulder. The bear roared. Spun.

Tom fired. Hit the chest. The bear stumbled.

I fired. Hit the head. The bear dropped.

Three shots. Professional. Clean.

The bear twitched. Tried to rise. Failed. Died.

From the woods, Makwa and Nikan emerged. Assessed the kill. Nodded approval.

Good hunt. Efficient. No one hurt. Threat eliminated.

The elder appeared. Walked to the bear. Touched its head. Spoke quietly.

Sarah translated: "He's thanking it. The bear was doing what bears do. Hunting. Living. It wasn't evil. Just dangerous. He honors its life. Acknowledges its power. Asks its spirit to understand: we had to kill it to survive."

Then the elder looked at us. Spoke.

Sarah: "He says: good cooperation. Your weapons strong. Our knowledge strong. Together we're stronger than alone. This is how alliances work."

Bill stepped forward. "We want more of this. More cooperation. More hunts together. More shared defense."

The elder nodded. Extended his arm.

Bill gripped it. Formal. Binding.

Alliance strengthened through shared danger. Shared success. Blood and trust.

We processed the bear together.

The Paleo-Indians led. They knew the anatomy. The proper cuts. What was usable. What wasn't.

We followed. Learning. Helping.

The hide: twelve feet long. Thick. Valuable. The Paleo-Indians took it. Their kill technique. Their right.

The meat: divided equally. Both communities. Fair share.

The claws: given to Makwa. Trophy. Recognition of his tracking that found the bear.

The skull: given to me. Recognition of the kill shot. The thing that ended the threat.

I tried to refuse. Makwa insisted. Pushed the skull into my hands.

Sarah translated: "He says: you killed it. You earned it. Take it. Remember the hunt. Remember working together. That memory has value."

I took it. Heavy. Real. Evidence of what we'd accomplished.

That night, both communities feasted.

Separate locations. We didn't merge. Not ready for that yet.

But we'd hunted together. Killed together. Shared resources. Built trust through action.

At our feast—sixty-three people around a central fire at Bill's property—we told the story. The hunt. The cooperation. The success.

"This is how it should be," Bill said. "Modern and ancient working together. Not competing. Not fighting. Cooperating."

"We have technology they don't have," Jake added. "Rifles. Metal tools. Monitoring equipment. But they have skills we don't. Tracking. Processing. Understanding the land. Together we're complete."

Tom Kowalski stood up. "I want to propose something. Regular joint patrols. Modern and Paleo-Indian together. Monitoring for predators. Watching for fold activity. Sharing early warning. Formal partnership."

"How do we propose that?" someone asked.

"Sarah arranges a meeting. We bring the idea. See if they accept."

Sarah nodded. "I'll talk to the elder. But I think he'll agree. Today proved cooperation works. Why not make it permanent?"

Week fifteen, the agreement was formalized.

Joint patrols. One modern human, one Paleo-Indian. Twice weekly. Covering different territories.

Joint hunts when large predators appeared. Shared resources. Equal distribution.

Trade protocols. Medicine and metal from us. Skills and knowledge from them.

Warning systems. If either community detected danger—fold activity, predator movement, anything—immediate communication. Sarah as translator. Dr. Webb as liaison.

Mutual defense. If either community was threatened, both responded.

It was crude. Informal. Based on trust rather than contracts.

But it worked.

Week sixteen, my regular patrol partner was Makwa.

Every Tuesday and Friday. Six hours. Covering the northern sector.

We didn't talk much. Language barrier too significant. But we didn't need words.

He'd point at tracks. I'd nod. Understanding.

I'd show him the seismic monitor. He'd watch the readings. Learning the technology.

We'd share food midday. Sitting in comfortable silence. Partners.

One Tuesday, we found a fold opening. New one. Small. Just a shimmer between two trees.

Makwa threw a stone through it. The stone disappeared. Didn't come back out the other side.

One-way fold. Things could go in. Couldn't come out.

Dangerous.

I marked it on my map. Makwa marked it with a carved sign on the tree. Warning.

Different methods. Same purpose. Keep people safe.

On Friday, we encountered a family of mastodons. Three adults. Two juveniles. Browsing near the cold zone boundary.

Makwa watched them. Made no move to hunt. Just observed.

I understood. They weren't threatening. Weren't near our settlements. Weren't taking resources we needed.

Let them live. Let them be.

Conservation. Respect for life. Hunting only when necessary.

He'd learned that through millennia of survival. I was learning it from him.

Week seventeen, Makwa's son—the boy who'd given me the carved wolf—started following us on patrols.

Eight years old. Learning. Watching everything his father did.

Makwa taught him the same way he was teaching me. Patience. Demonstration. Letting him try. Correcting gently when he failed.

One day, the boy found tracks. Small deer. Recent.

He looked at his father. Question: Should we follow?

Makwa looked at me. Asking permission. This was joint patrol. Joint decision.

I nodded. Yes.

We tracked the deer for an hour. The boy leading. Makwa guiding. Me learning.

The boy made the kill. Atlatl throw. Clean hit. The deer dropped.

His first kill.

Makwa didn't celebrate loudly. Just knelt beside his son. Touched his head. Spoke quietly.

Pride. Recognition. You're becoming a hunter.

Then he looked at me. Gestured: Help process.

We worked together. Three generations. Three cultures. One task.

Teaching the boy how to honor the kill. Use every part. Waste nothing. Respect the animal that gave its life.

When we finished, Makwa gave me half the meat. Partnership. Equal share.

I tried to refuse. This was the boy's kill. His meat.

Makwa insisted. Spoke to Sarah later about it.

She translated: "He says: you helped teach his son. You showed respect for the kill. You honored the animal. That makes you part of the success. Partners share."

Week eighteen, I brought Jake on patrol.

Makwa brought his son.

Two fathers. Two sons. Learning together.

Jake and the boy couldn't communicate verbally. But they taught each other anyway.

The boy showed Jake how to move quietly through the forest. Step placement. Weight distribution. Breathing.

Jake showed the boy the monitoring equipment. How to read the display. What the numbers meant. What indicated danger.

By the end of the patrol, they were friends. Child friendship. Universal. No translation needed.

When we separated, the boy gave Jake a gift. Small carved bone. This time shaped like a bird.

Jake gave him a compass. Showed him how it worked. How it always pointed north.

The boy was fascinated. Kept turning. Watching the needle move. Magic that made sense.

Makwa laughed. His son had a new treasure.

Week nineteen, the relationship had become routine.

Tuesday and Friday: patrols with Makwa.

Sundays: trade meetings at neutral ground.

As needed: joint hunts, shared resources, mutual defense.

We weren't one community. We were two communities living in parallel. Cooperating. Supporting. Respecting boundaries but sharing space.

It worked because both sides wanted it to work. Because we'd proven trust through action. Because we'd learned that neither group could survive alone as well as we could together.

Modern humans needed ancient skills. Paleo-Indians benefited from modern tools.

Together we were stronger. Safer. More resilient.

One Friday, Makwa and I sat on a ridge overlooking both settlements.

His village to the north. Our scattered properties to the south.

Smoke rising from both. People working. Living. Surviving.

Two ways of life. Separated by eleven thousand years. Existing simultaneously. Cooperating.

Makwa spoke. Single word. I didn't understand.

He tried again. Gestured at both settlements. At the land. At the sky.

I understood. He was asking: Is this good? Is this right? Two peoples sharing land?

I nodded. Yes. This is good.

He smiled. Gripped my shoulder. Brother.

Not literally. But close enough.

We'd built something. Not through language. Not through formal agreements. Through action. Through showing up. Through trusting when trust was hard. Through sharing food and hunts and dangers.

Through being human together.

Regardless of when we were from.

That night I told Karen about it.

"You've made a friend."

"I think I have."

"A friend from the Pleistocene."

"Yes."

"That's insane."

"Everything's insane now. Might as well have insane friendships too."

She smiled. "What's he like?"

"Patient. Skilled. Good father. Good hunter. Better at tracking than anyone I've ever met. And he trusts me. Despite everything. Despite how different we are. Despite the language barrier. He trusts me."

"Because you've earned it."

"We've earned each other. That's how trust works. Mutual. Proven through action."

"And his son?"

"Learning fast. Smart kid. Brave. Jake likes him. They communicate somehow. Not words. Just... kid stuff. Games. Respect. Friendship."

"So we're not just adapting to the Pleistocene. We're adapting to the people from the Pleistocene."

"Yes. And they're adapting to us. It's bilateral. Mutual. We're changing each other."

"Is that good?"

"I don't know. But it's real. And it's working. And that's more than I can say for most of what we've tried."

Chapter 32

CHAPTER THIRTY-TWO: PERMANENT ZONES

Jake presented the data at the week twenty Sunday meeting.

Maps. Charts. Seismic readings spanning five months. Everything documented. Everything analyzed.

"We need to talk about what's permanent," he said.

He projected the county map onto a white sheet hung in Bill's barn. Red zones scattered across it. Some small. Some massive.

"These are the folds that haven't closed. Sixty-two days minimum. Some as long as ninety-three days. Based on the data, they're not closing. Ever."

He highlighted the largest one. The cold zone. Sixty-two square miles of permanent Pleistocene winter.

"This one's stable. Temperature hasn't varied more than five degrees in two months. Ecosystem is established. Megafauna population is breeding. We've confirmed three mastodon calves born inside the zone. It's not a temporary anomaly anymore. It's permanent geography."

Commissioner Walsh—who'd stayed, surrendered her position but kept attending meetings—spoke up. "What does permanent mean? Decades? Centuries?"

"Geological timescales. Thousands of years. Maybe forever. The correction Dr. Park described isn't reversing. It's stabilizing. These zones have reverted to Pleistocene configuration and they're staying that way."

He pulled up another map. Smaller zones. Seven of them.

"These are smaller permanent folds. Ranging from two to fifteen square miles. Different characteristics. This one near Torch Lake is permanently showing Lake Algonquan. Twenty feet higher water level than modern. This one near the old railroad grade is showing Pleistocene forest. Different trees. Different undergrowth. This one near Elk Rapids is glacial ice. Year-round. Not melting."

"How much of the county is permanent Pleistocene?" Bill asked.

Jake did the calculation. "Approximately one hundred forty-seven square miles. Out of a total county area of four hundred seventy-seven square miles. That's thirty-one percent. Almost a third of Antrim County no longer exists in 2026."

Silence.

"And it's growing," Jake continued. "Slowly. The zones expand maybe an inch per week. Doesn't sound like much. But over years..." He showed the projection. "In ten years, we're looking at fifty percent conversion. In twenty years, seventy percent. In fifty years, the entire county could be Pleistocene."

"Can we stop it?" someone asked.

"No. The geological stress is ongoing. Isostatic rebound doesn't stop. It continues for millennia. As long as the stress exists, the folds can open. And once they stabilize into permanent zones, they don't close."

Dr. Ostrander stood up. "We need to map this properly. Establish boundaries. Mark what's ours and what's... not ours anymore. What's 2026 and what's 11,000 BC. So we know where we can live. Where we can't."

"Agreed," Jake said. "I've been working on that."

He pulled up a new map. The county divided into three zones.

Green: Modern. Stable. Safe for permanent habitation.

Most of Bellaire proper. Parts of the lakefront. Areas away from moraine intersections. Maybe two hundred square miles.

Yellow: Transitional. Unstable. Folds open occasionally but close. Habitable with caution.

Areas near permanent zones. Places where small folds appeared and disappeared. Risky but manageable. Maybe one hundred thirty square miles.

Red: Permanent Pleistocene. Uninhabitable by modern humans without extreme adaptation.

The cold zone. The flooded zones. The ice zones. One hundred forty-seven square miles and growing.

"This is our new geography," Jake said. "This is what we're working with. The green zones are where we can build. Where we can establish permanent infrastructure. The yellow zones are where we can visit, patrol, hunt—but not live. The red zones are lost. They belong to the Pleistocene now."

The meeting lasted four hours.

Questions. Arguments. Denial. Acceptance. Grief.

People mourning land they'd lost. Properties in red zones that were gone forever. Homes they'd never return to. Places they'd grown up that no longer existed in their time.

Patricia Hendricks spoke. "My house was in the red zone. Half of it collapsed into the Pleistocene. The other half is uninhabitable. I've accepted that. I signed the federal buyout. I let it go. But some of you haven't. And you need to. Because that land isn't yours anymore. It's not anybody's. It's geological time correcting itself. And you can't fight geology."

Bill Henderson—no relation—stood up. "She's right. My property is in the yellow zone. I can't live there permanently. Can't rebuild. Can't develop. Best I can do is use it seasonally. Camp there. Hunt there. But my home is gone. And I've accepted that. We all need to."

One by one, people stood. Acknowledged losses. Accepted reality.

The county was shrinking. The habitable area was contracting. And we had to adapt to that or leave.

Most had chosen to stay. But staying meant living in the green zones. Accepting that a third of the county was gone. Would never return.

After the meeting, I helped Jake refine the maps.

We marked every structure in the red zones. Forty-seven houses. Three businesses. One school building. Miles of road. All uninhabitable.

Then we marked the yellow zones. Another seventy-three properties. Usable but risky. Not for permanent residence.

That left the green zones. Where our sixty-three people were already concentrated. Around Bellaire. Along the stable lakefronts. Away from the moraine.

"We're becoming an island," I said. "Surrounded by the Pleistocene."

"Essentially, yes. And the island is shrinking. Slowly. But inevitably."

"How long until there's no green zone left?"

"Decades. Maybe a century. Depends on expansion rate. But eventually..." He trailed off.

Eventually, there'd be no modern Antrim County. Just Pleistocene. With a few adapted humans living like the Paleo-Indians. Or nobody at all.

"What do we do?" I asked.

"Live in the green zones while we have them. Use the yellow zones carefully. Avoid the red zones completely unless absolutely necessary. And document everything. So future generations—if there are future generations—know what happened here."

"Future generations of what? Modern humans? Or Paleo-Indians?"

"Maybe both. Maybe neither. Maybe something new. Humans who've adapted to live in both eras. Who can cross the boundaries. Who belong to both times."

Like Makwa's son learning to use a compass. Like Jake learning to track. Like Emma processing hides. Like all of us learning skills from eleven thousand years ago while trying to maintain knowledge from 2026.

We were becoming something in between. Not fully modern. Not fully Paleo-Indian. Something new.

Adaptive humans. Time-hybrid survivors.

Week twenty-one, we started the formal mapping project.

Teams of two. One modern human, one Paleo-Indian when possible. Walking every boundary. Marking every zone.

My team: Me and Makwa. Assigned the northern sector. Fifty square miles to map.

We spent six days walking. Documenting.

Every fold point. Every boundary. Every area of instability.

Makwa couldn't read maps the way I did. But he understood territory. Understood boundaries. Understood marking land.

He showed me the Paleo-Indian method. Carved symbols on trees. Stacked stones. Natural landmarks. A system that didn't require paper or GPS but worked perfectly.

I showed him the modern method. GPS coordinates. Topographic maps. Digital records.

We combined them. Traditional markers plus modern documentation. Belt and suspenders. Redundancy.

At one point, we reached the boundary of the cold zone. The permanent winter.

Makwa walked to the edge. Stepped through. Into minus-twenty-degree air. Stood there in his furs. Comfortable. Adapted.

Gestured for me to follow.

I tried. Lasted maybe ninety seconds. Even with modern winter gear, it was brutal. Painful.

Stepped back. Into spring warmth. Shaking.

Makwa laughed. Not mocking. Understanding. You can't live here. I can. Different adaptations.

He pointed at the cold zone. Then at himself. His home.

Then pointed at the green zone. At me. My home.

Different worlds. Different territories. But neighbors. Partners.

He didn't need the green zones. His people thrived in the red zones. Could live where we couldn't.

We needed the green zones. Couldn't survive the red zones for long.

But together, we covered all the territory. All the zones. Complementary survival.

Week twenty-three, the mapping was complete.

Jake compiled all the data. Produced final maps. Color-coded. Detailed. Accurate.

We distributed copies to everyone. Paper maps. No digital. No cloud storage. Just physical copies that would survive without power.

"These maps are survival tools," Jake said at the presentation. "Know your zones. Green is safe. Yellow is caution. Red is prohibited unless you're Paleo-Indian or have extreme cold-weather gear."

"The zones will change. Expand. Maybe contract though I doubt it. We'll update the maps annually. Everyone gets new copies. Keep the old ones too. Show the progression. The history."

Bill studied his map. "We're living in fragments. Scattered green islands in a Pleistocene sea."

"Yes. And the sea is rising. Slowly. But rising."

"How long until our properties are in red zones?"

Jake pulled up the projections. "Your place, Bill? Safe for at least fifteen years. Maybe twenty. Dave's place? Thirty years, possibly more. It's well away from moraine intersections. The downtown Bellaire area? Could last fifty years. Longer if we're lucky."

"And then?"

"Then we move. Consolidate. Contract into smaller and smaller green zones. Until eventually..." He stopped.

Until eventually there were no green zones. Just red. Just Pleistocene. And we either adapted completely or died.

Nobody said it. Everyone understood.

Week twenty-four, we started consolidation planning.

Sixty-three people scattered across multiple properties. Inefficient. Unsustainable.

"We should centralize," Dr. Ostrander proposed. "Build a core settlement. One location. Concentrated infrastructure. Easier to defend. Easier to maintain. Easier to survive."

"Where?" someone asked.

Jake pulled up the maps. "Here." He pointed. Central Bellaire. The most stable green zone. Furthest from any moraine intersection. Lowest risk of fold activity.

"We build there. Permanent structures. Wells. Gardens. Workshops. Storage. Everything we need. Abandon the scattered properties. Move into communal living."

"Like the Paleo-Indians," Karen said.

"Exactly like them. They're not scattered. They're concentrated. One village. Shared resources. Mutual support. It's more efficient. More resilient."

Some people resisted. "I'm not giving up my property."

"Your property is in a yellow zone. You can't live there safely year-round anyway. You're already spending most of your time in town. Why not make it official? Build properly. Build permanently."

The debate went on for weeks.

But reality was persuasive.

Scattered properties required separate wells. Separate gardens. Separate defenses. Separate everything.

Concentrated settlement meant shared wells. Shared gardens. Shared defense. Shared labor.

More efficient. More survivable.

By week twenty-seven, construction had started.

Central Bellaire. Downtown. Building a new village.

Not modern construction. We didn't have power tools. Couldn't get materials easily.

Hybrid construction. Some salvaged modern materials—lumber from abandoned houses, metal from closed businesses. Some primitive techniques—log frame structures, packed earth floors, sod roofs.

A mix. Using what we had. Building what would last.

The first structure was communal. Kitchen and dining. Place to gather. Share meals. Build community.

Sixty-three people couldn't all eat together in scattered houses. But in one large building? That worked.

Second structure: workshop. Tools. Repair. Manufacturing. Shared equipment. Shared expertise.

Third structure: storage. Food preservation. Resource stockpiling. Communal reserves.

Slowly, building by building, a village emerged.

Not medieval. Not modern. Something in between.

Functional. Practical. Built for survival.

Makwa visited the construction site week twenty-nine.

Walked through. Examined everything. Nodded approval.

Spoke to Sarah. She translated: "He says: you're learning. Building like his people. Smart. Efficient. Survival-focused. He approves."

"Tell him we learned from watching his village. From seeing what worked."

Sarah translated. Makwa smiled. Gestured: Good students.

Then he pointed at the construction. At his village to the north. At the space between.

Spoke. A longer phrase.

Sarah listened. Translated: "He says: two villages. Close enough to trade. Far enough to maintain separate identity. Like brother tribes. Different but allied. He thinks this is good. Sustainable. Long-term."

"Ask him: what happens when the zones expand? When there's more Pleistocene, less modern?"

Sarah asked. Makwa thought. Responded.

"He says: his people will thrive. Your people will struggle. But if you keep learning, keep adapting, maybe you survive. Maybe you become like his people. Maybe not. But trying is honorable. Living with the land instead of against it—that's wise. That's how you endure."

Week thirty, the permanent zones were official.

County maps updated. Red zones marked. Yellow zones noted. Green zones identified.

We lived in the green zones. Visited the yellow zones carefully. Avoided the red zones completely.

The Paleo-Indians lived in the red zones. Visited the green zones occasionally for trade. Thrived where we couldn't.

Different territories. Different adaptations. Different timelines.

But neighbors. Partners. Coexisting.

The land had made its choice. Correction. Return to Pleistocene.

We could fight it and die. Or accept it and adapt.

Sixty-three people chose adaptation.

Building villages. Learning skills. Trading with people from eleven thousand years ago. Mapping a county that was slowly disappearing into the past.

It wasn't the world we'd wanted. Wasn't the future we'd planned.

But it was the reality we had. And we were learning to live in it.

One zone at a time. One skill at a time. One day at a time.

Surviving. Adapting. Enduring.

In the shrinking green islands of modern time. Surrounded by an expanding Pleistocene sea.

For however long the islands lasted.

Chapter 33

CHAPTER THIRTY-THREE: JAKE'S RESEARCH

The email came through on week thirty-two.

We had limited internet. Satellite connection. Unreliable. Expensive. But functional enough for essential communication.

Jake checked it daily. Monitoring scientific journals. Staying connected to the academic world that had mostly forgotten northern Michigan existed.

This email was from Dr. Lisa Park. University of Chicago.

Jake - Your data is extraordinary. We'd like to publish. And we'd like you as lead author. This could define your career. Please respond.

He showed me that evening.

"They want to publish my research. Peer-reviewed journal. Nature, maybe. Or Science. Top-tier."

"That's good, right?"

"It's incredible. I'm twenty years old. No degree yet. Living in a temporal disaster zone. And I'm being offered lead authorship in a major scientific journal."

"Because you've been documenting what nobody else can document."

"Because I'm here. Because I stayed. Because I've been measuring what everyone else evacuated from." He looked at the email. "They want five years of data. Seismic readings. Fold duration measurements. Zone expansion rates. Ecosystem analysis. Everything."

"Are you going to give it to them?"

"I don't know. Part of me wants recognition. Wants to be published. Wants my work to matter. But part of me thinks... this isn't about me. This is about survival. About documenting correction so people understand what's happening."

"It can be both."

"Can it? Or does publication turn survival data into academic curiosity? Does it make real suffering into abstract science?"

I didn't have an answer.

Week thirty-three, Jake started compiling the data.

Every seismic reading since February. Every fold opening. Every duration measurement. Every zone expansion calculation. Every observation.

Five months of documentation. Thousands of data points. The most comprehensive record of temporal correction anywhere in the world.

He worked eighteen-hour days. Organizing. Analyzing. Writing.

Emma helped. She'd taken courses in scientific writing. Knew how to structure papers. How to present data. How to tell a story through statistics.

Together, they built the paper.

"Temporal Correction in the Great Lakes Region: A Five-Month Analysis of Geological Boundary Failure and Pleistocene Reversion"

By Jake Pritchard, primary author. With contributions from Dr. Raymond Ostrander, Dr. Lisa Park, Dr. Marcus Webb, and a dozen other researchers.

But Jake's name first. His data. His analysis. His work.

Week thirty-five, the first draft was complete.

One hundred forty-seven pages. Thirty-eight figures. Sixteen tables. Comprehensive. Rigorous. Undeniable.

Jake presented it to our community first. Sunday meeting. Everyone gathered.

He walked through the findings.

Finding One: Temporal folds follow predictable geological patterns.

Correlation between fold locations and moraine-shoreline intersections: 94.7%.

Correlation with destroyed burial mound sites: 87.3%.

Correlation with areas of high isostatic rebound stress: 91.2%.

"The folds aren't random. They're mechanically predictable. We can forecast where they'll occur with high accuracy."

Finding Two: Fold duration increases exponentially over time.

First fold (February): 90 seconds.

Most recent fold (June): 840 seconds (14 minutes).

Trend line shows continued increase. Projected fold duration by December: 45+ minutes.

"Folds are staying open longer. The boundaries are weakening. Eventually, they'll stay open permanently."

Finding Three: Permanent zones expand at measurable rates.

Average expansion: 2.3 centimeters per week.

Variance based on geological stress: ±0.7 cm/week.

Projection: 50% county conversion within 12 years (revised from earlier 10-year estimate based on new data).

"The Pleistocene is reclaiming the landscape. Slowly. Measurably. Inevitably."

Finding Four: Ecosystem establishment in permanent zones is rapid.

Cold zone: Fully functional Pleistocene ecosystem within 90 days.

Confirmed species: Mastodons (breeding population, 7 adults, 4 juveniles). Short-faced bears (3 individuals). Dire wolves (pack of 8-10). American lions (at least 2). Various Pleistocene flora.

"The past isn't just bleeding through. It's thriving. Establishing. Replacing the present."

Finding Five: Human populations show differential adaptation.

Modern humans: 63 individuals remaining in Antrim County. Survival rate in red zones: <5 minutes without extreme gear.

Paleo-Indian populations: 23+ individuals (Skegmog settlement). Survival rate in red zones: indefinite. Thriving.

"We're not adapted. They are. The land is selecting for pre-modern humans. We're the anomaly being corrected."

The room was silent.

Then Bill Henderson spoke. "So we're dying. Slowly. Generationally. But dying."

"Unless we adapt faster than the zones expand. Unless we learn to live like the Paleo-Indians. Completely. Abandon modern life. Become them."

"Can we do that?"

"Some of us. Maybe. The younger ones. The flexible ones. The ones willing to change everything about how they live." Jake paused. "But most of us? No. We're too attached to modern life. Too dependent on technology. Too set in our ways. We'll survive in the green zones while they last. Then we'll die or leave."

"How long do we have?"

"In Bellaire proper? Fifteen to twenty years before it becomes yellow zone. Another ten before it turns red. Call it thirty years total."

"I'll be dead by then anyway," someone said. Laughter. Bitter but real.

"But our kids won't be," Karen said quietly. "Emma. Jake. The children. They'll be in their fifties. They'll need to be fully adapted by then. Or they'll need to leave."

Jake nodded. "That's the timeline. One generation. Maybe two if we're lucky. Then this place is Pleistocene. And only people adapted to the Pleistocene can live here."

Week thirty-seven, Jake submitted the paper.

Dr. Park sent immediate feedback. "This is groundbreaking. Revolutionary. Terrifying. We're fast-tracking review. Expect publication within six weeks."

Six weeks. In academic time, that was instantaneous.

The paper was too important. Too urgent. Too unprecedented to delay.

Week thirty-nine, interview requests started arriving.

NPR wanted to talk to Jake. So did the New York Times. The Guardian. Scientific American. BBC.

Everyone wanted to interview the twenty-year-old living in a temporal disaster zone who'd documented correction better than any PhD researcher with full university funding.

Jake accepted some. Declined others.

I listened to the NPR interview. Jake on satellite phone, sitting on our back porch, explaining correction to millions of listeners.

Interviewer: "So you're saying the earth is actively erasing modern civilization?"

Jake: "Not erasing. Correcting. The earth has a stable configuration it prefers. The Pleistocene. We forced it into a different configuration through eleven thousand years of modification. Now, given the opportunity through geological stress fractures, it's reverting."

Interviewer: "And you're watching this happen in real time."

Jake: "I'm living in it. Measuring it. Documenting it. Yes."

Interviewer: "Aren't you afraid?"

Jake: "Every day. But fear doesn't stop geological processes. Understanding might help us adapt. So I study. I measure. I try to understand. That's all I can do."

Interviewer: "Your paper suggests this could happen anywhere glaciers once existed. Chicago. Detroit. Minneapolis. Milwaukee. All at risk."

Jake: "Anywhere humans have built on glacial boundaries, yes. The stress exists. The potential exists. Antrim County is just the first place where enough stress accumulated to fracture time. But the same geology extends across the entire Great Lakes region. It's not a question of if. It's a question of when and where next."

The interview went viral. Millions of listeners. Thousands of comments. Global attention.

Jake Pritchard. Twenty years old. Living without power in northern Michigan. Suddenly one of the most recognized names in temporal mechanics.

Week forty-one, the paper published.

Nature. Cover article. Jake's name first. His data. His analysis.

The response was immediate.

Half the scientific community: "This is brilliant. Rigorous. Essential reading."

The other half: "This is apocalyptic. Alarmist. Overstating the risk."

Nobody disputed the data. Too well-documented. Too carefully analyzed. Too peer-reviewed.

But the implications—that modern civilization was being geologically erased—that was too much for some people to accept.

Climate scientists: "This validates everything we've been saying. Human modification of the planet has consequences. The earth responds. Sometimes catastrophically."

Physicists: "The temporal mechanics are sound. Stress creates fractures. Fractures extend through spacetime. This is consistent with relativity."

Geologists: "The isostatic rebound data is undeniable. This is happening. The question is scale and speed."

And the deniers: "Hoax. Manipulation. Government conspiracy. The earth doesn't have memory. Time doesn't break down. This is propaganda."

Jake read the responses. All of them. The praise and the criticism.

"They're not ready," he said one night. "The data is clear. The science is sound. But people aren't ready to accept that the world is changing this fundamentally. So they deny. They argue. They dismiss."

"Does it matter? If they believe or not?"

"It matters for the other cities. Chicago. Detroit. If they don't believe, they won't prepare. They won't evacuate the high-risk zones. They won't establish warning systems. And when correction starts there—and it will start there—thousands will die because they weren't ready."

"You can't save everyone."

"I know. But I can try. I can publish the data. Give the warnings. Hope enough people listen."

Week forty-three, Jake received an offer.

University of Chicago. Full scholarship. PhD program. Study under Dr. Park. Access to unlimited resources. Lab space. Funding. Everything.

All he had to do was leave Antrim County. Move to Chicago. Become a professional researcher instead of a survivor documenting his own apocalypse.

He showed me the letter.

"This is everything I wanted. Before the folds. Before correction. This was my dream. PhD. Research. Academic career."

"Are you going to take it?"

He looked out at the woods. At the settlement under construction. At the maps showing shrinking green zones.

"I don't know. Part of me wants to. Wants the resources. The recognition. The ability to study this properly instead of scavenging equipment and using satellite internet that drops every ten minutes."

"But?"

"But Chicago is built on glacial boundaries. Lake Michigan. Moraines. The same geology as here. If I'm right—if correction spreads—Chicago has maybe five years before folds start opening there. Maybe less."

"So you'd be walking into the next disaster."

"Or I'd be positioned to study it. To help prepare. To save lives by giving early warning." He paused. "Or I'd be abandoning you. Mom. Emma. Everyone here. Running toward safety and academic prestige while you stay and adapt."

"You don't owe us your future."

"Don't I? You stayed because I stayed. Because I wanted to study this. You gave up evacuation for my research. How can I leave now?"

"Because your research matters more than us. Because documenting correction helps more people than staying here helps us. Because you've earned the right to build a career."

He looked at me. "Do you want me to go?"

"I want you to choose what's right for you. Not what you think we need. Not what you think you owe us. What you actually want."

"I don't know what I want."

"Then take your time. The offer doesn't expire tomorrow. Think about it. Talk to Emma. To your mother. To Makwa even—get his perspective. Then decide."

Week forty-five, Jake made his choice.

He called Dr. Park. I listened on speaker.

"Dr. Park, I appreciate the offer. More than you know. But I'm staying in Antrim County."

"Jake, this is your career. Your future. You can't throw that away to live in a disaster zone."

"I'm not throwing it away. I'm investing it differently. You need someone on the ground. Documenting. Measuring. Sending real-time data as correction progresses. I can do that better than anyone because I'm here. I'm adapted. I'm integrated with both modern and Paleo-Indian communities. I can document things no outside researcher could ever access."

"For how long? Until the green zones are gone?"

"However long it takes. Ten years. Twenty. Thirty. Until I can't survive here anymore. Then maybe I'll come to Chicago. Or maybe I'll be fully adapted by then and Chicago will seem strange."

Dr. Park was quiet. Then: "You're sure about this."

"I'm sure. But I have a counteroffer. I stay here. You send me equipment. Funding. Better satellite internet. Access to university resources remotely. And I send you data. Regular updates. Comprehensive documentation. You get the best field research anyone could provide. I get the support to do it properly. We both win."

"You want to be a remote researcher."

"I want to be the researcher on the ground during the most significant geological event in human history. And I want the resources to do it right."

Another pause. Then: "I'll talk to the department. See what we can arrange. But Jake—this is unconventional. Very unconventional."

"So is living in a county that's reverting to the Pleistocene. Unconventional is the only option now."

Week forty-seven, the agreement was finalized.

Jake Pritchard: Remote Researcher, University of Chicago, Department of Geological Sciences.

Equipment shipment: Arriving monthly. Seismic monitors. Atmospheric sensors. Sample collection kits. Satellite internet upgrade. Generator and solar panels for power.

Funding: Yearly stipend. Enough to buy supplies. Support the family. Contribute to community resources.

Obligation: Quarterly reports. Comprehensive data. Ongoing documentation of correction as it progressed.

Jake had turned down a PhD program. Stayed in a disaster zone. And somehow landed exactly the position he needed.

Remote researcher. On-site expert. The person documenting correction from inside correction.

Living it. Measuring it. Understanding it. Surviving it.

All at once.

That night, we celebrated.

Small party. Our community. Sixty-three people. Shared meal. Communal fire.

Jake stood up. Informal speech.

"I want to thank everyone for supporting this. For staying. For building this community. For teaching me skills I never thought I'd need. For accepting me as both a modern researcher and a survival student learning from the Paleo-Indians."

"My research matters because you're here. Because we're proving humans can adapt. Because we're showing that correction doesn't have to mean extinction. It can mean evolution. Change. Adaptation."

"I'm staying because this is my home. Because you're my family. Because what we're building here—this hybrid community, modern and ancient, learning and surviving together—that's worth documenting. Worth preserving. Worth fighting for."

"So thank you. For staying. For adapting. For surviving."

Applause. Genuine. Warm.

Then Makwa stood. Spoke. Sarah translated.

"He says: your son is wise. He learns from both worlds. Keeps knowledge from his people. Gains knowledge from ours. This is strength. This is how survivors endure. By taking best from all sources. Not rigid. Not refusing. Flexible. Adapting."

"He says: his people watch you. Watch how you change. How you learn. They respect this. They see: these modern humans are not arrogant. They listen. They learn. They survive. That makes you worthy allies."

"He says: your son documents for his people far away. Good. They should learn. They should prepare. They should adapt before the land forces them. Wisdom is learning from others' experience. Your son gives that gift."

Makwa sat. The gathering continued.

Two communities. Separated by eleven thousand years. United by respect. By cooperation. By shared survival.

And in the middle: Jake. Twenty years old. Published researcher. Remote expert. Bridge between times.

Documenting the end of one world. The return of another. The adaptation of survivors caught between.

Living proof that humans could endure anything. As long as they were willing to change. To learn. To become something new.

Even if that meant becoming something very, very old.

Chapter 34

CHAPTER THIRTY-FOUR: EMMA RETURNS

Emma left in early September.

Just for two weeks. Visit to Michigan State. See friends. Check on her apartment. Pick up belongings she'd left behind when she withdrew.

"I need to see normal," she'd said. "Just for a little while. Remember what the world used to be like."

We understood. She'd been living without power for four months. Learning to tan hides and process deer and identify edible plants. At nineteen years old.

She deserved normal. Even if just for two weeks.

Karen drove her to Traverse City. Emma caught a bus from there. Heading south. Away from the folds. Away from correction. Toward electricity and running water and cell phone service that actually worked.

Toward the world that used to be.

She came back on a Thursday.

Week fifty-one. Late September. Almost harvest time. The community preparing for winter.

I was at the construction site—we'd started building the fourth structure, a medical clinic—when I saw her car pull in.

She got out. Stood there. Looking at the village we'd built.

Log structures. Sod roofs. Communal spaces. Hybrid architecture. Half modern salvage, half primitive technique.

Not Michigan State. Not civilization. Something else.

She walked over. Hugged me.

"It looks different. More real. More permanent."

"We've been building. Four months of work. It's coming together."

"I can see that." She looked around. "Where's Mom?"

"Garden. Harvesting squash. Jake's at the monitoring station. Makwa's supposed to stop by this afternoon for patrol."

"Makwa. Right. Your Pleistocene best friend."

"He's not—" I stopped. "Actually, yeah. Kind of. We patrol together three times a week. His son and Jake are close. It's... friendship. Across time."

"That's insane."

"Everything's insane now."

She picked up her bags. "Can we talk? Somewhere private?"

We sat on the back porch of our house. The old house. Not the new village. Our family home. Still in the green zone. Still safe. For another fifteen years or so.

Emma looked tired. Not physically. Emotionally.

"State was weird," she said. "Seeing normal life again. People worried about exams and relationships and job interviews. Normal problems. Normal stresses. Things that mattered two years ago."

"And now?"

"Now they seem absurd. Who cares about a C+ in economics when the planet is geologically correcting itself? Who cares about whether someone texts you back when actual time is breaking down?"

"But they don't know that. For them, those things still matter."

"I know. And I tried. I tried to care about the same things. Went to parties. Saw friends. Acted normal. But Dad..." She stopped. "I couldn't do it. Couldn't pretend. Couldn't participate. Everyone talking about their futures. Their plans. Careers. Graduate school. Marriage. Kids. And all I could think was: none of that exists. Not for me. Not anymore."

"Why not?"

"Because I live here. In the correction. Where the future is uncertain and the past is literally returning. I can't plan a career when I'm learning to tan hides for survival. Can't think about marriage when I don't know if I'll be alive in thirty years. Can't imagine kids when I don't know what world they'd be born into."

She was crying. Quietly. Not sobbing. Just tears.

"I don't fit there anymore. But I'm not sure I fit here either. I'm stuck. Between two worlds. Not modern enough for State. Not adapted enough for here. Just... stuck."

I didn't know what to say. So I just held her.

That night, family dinner. All four of us. First time in two weeks.

Karen had made venison stew. Vegetables from the garden. Bread from the communal oven. Real food. Prepared the way we'd learned. Preserved properly. Cooked efficiently.

Emma ate quietly. Processing.

Then she said: "I need to make a decision."

We waited.

"I can go back to State. Finish my degree. Try to build a normal life. Pretend the correction isn't happening. Live in denial like everyone else outside the zone. Get a job. Maybe meet someone. Have the future we used to plan for."

"Or?" Karen asked.

"Or I stay here. Fully commit. Become part of this community. Learn every skill I can. Adapt completely. Accept that my future is here. In the shrinking green zones. Living hybrid. Preparing for when there's no green left."

"Those aren't your only options," Jake said. "You could split time. Summers here. School year there. Keep both worlds."

"That's what I've been doing. And it's killing me. Every time I leave, I feel guilty. Like I'm abandoning you. Every time I come back, I feel behind. Like everyone else learned skills I missed. I'm not committed to either place. I'm half-assing both."

"So you want to choose," I said.

"I need to choose. For my own sanity. All in or all out. Modern or adapted. I can't keep straddling."

Karen set down her spoon. "What do you want, Emma? Not what you think we want. Not what you think you should want. What do you actually want?"

Emma was quiet for a long time.

Then: "I want to leave. I want to go back to State. Finish my degree. Build a career. Have a normal life. Meet someone who doesn't know what a temporal fold is. Have kids who won't grow up learning to process deer hides. I want normal."

She looked at us. Crying again. "I'm sorry. I know that's not what you want to hear. I know you stayed. I know you're committed. But I can't do it. I can't live like this forever. I can't accept that the world is ending and adapt to it. I want to fight. I want to pretend. I want to live like the correction isn't happening."

"Even though it is happening," Jake said. Not judgmental. Just stating fact.

"Even though. Because the alternative is accepting that everything I planned for is gone. And I'm not ready to accept that. Maybe I never will be."

Karen reached across the table. Took Emma's hand.

"Then go. Go back to State. Finish your degree. Live your life. Build your future. We're not angry. We're not disappointed. We understand."

"But you stayed."

"We stayed because this is our home. Because we're sixty and we're not starting over somewhere else. Because we'd rather adapt here than struggle to build a new life. But you're nineteen. You have options. You should take them."

"What if I'm wrong? What if I regret this?"

"Then you come back. The door's always open. This is your home too. Even if you choose not to live here full-time."

Emma looked at Jake. "You're staying."

"I'm staying. My research is here. My career is documenting correction from inside it. That's my choice. Doesn't have to be yours."

"Don't you think I'm being a coward? Running away?"

"I think you're being honest. That takes courage." He paused. "And Emma? I need you out there. Someone who understands what's happening. Who can talk to people. Who can warn them. When correction starts in other cities—and it will—you'll be positioned to help. To explain. To prepare people. That matters too."

She smiled slightly. "You're making my cowardice sound noble."

"I'm making your choice sound like what it actually is. Self-preservation with potential benefit to others. Same as staying. Different approach. Both valid."

Over the next three days, Emma prepared to leave.

But not just leave. Leave properly. With closure.

She visited every family in the community. Sixty-three people. Thanked each one. Explained her choice. Asked forgiveness for abandoning them.

Nobody judged her. Most understood. Some had children who'd already left. Others wished they could leave but couldn't.

"You're young," Bill Henderson told her. "You've got time to build a life outside the correction. Take it. Use it. Don't waste your youth adapting to something that might not even exist in twenty years."

She visited the Paleo-Indian settlement. With Sarah translating.

Makwa's son—the boy who'd given her the carved wolf—was sad to see her go. But he understood. Different paths. Different choices.

The elder spoke. Sarah translated: "He says: you learned well. You showed respect. You tried to adapt. But this is not your path. That's okay. Some people are meant to live in the old times. Some in the new times. You belong to the new. He wishes you well."

Emma gave them gifts. Her tanning tools—she'd gotten good at hide processing, didn't want the tools wasted. Salt. Antibiotics. Metal needles.

In return, they gave her a blanket. Beautifully made. Deer hide, tanned perfectly, decorated with quillwork. Hours and hours of skilled labor.

"For cold nights in your new place," Sarah translated. "So you remember: once you learned to make warmth without machines. Don't forget that knowledge. Might need it someday."

Her last night, we had a family fire.

Just the four of us. Our back porch. Stars overhead. Quiet.

"I'm going to miss this," Emma said. "The quiet. The stars. You can't see stars like this at State. Too much light pollution."

"You'll visit," Karen said.

"I will. Holidays. Summer maybe. But it won't be the same. I won't be living it. I'll be a visitor. A tourist in my own home."

"That's okay. Visitor is better than never coming back."

Emma looked at the woods. At the darkness. "Do you think I'm making a mistake?"

"I think you're making a choice," I said. "Maybe it's the right choice. Maybe it's the wrong choice. You won't know for years. But it's yours. You're owning it. That's what matters."

"Jake's staying. Building a career here. Becoming an expert. Making a difference."

"Jake's path is Jake's path. Yours is yours. Stop comparing."

She nodded. "I'm scared. Of leaving. Of staying. Of choosing wrong."

"Everyone's scared. We're all choosing. None of us know if we're right. We're just doing what feels survivable."

"What if State folds? What if Chicago goes like Antrim County went? What if I'm running toward the next disaster?"

"Then you adapt there. Or you come back here. Or you find a third option none of us have thought of. But you can't live in fear of what might happen. You have to live in response to what is happening."

"What is happening is I'm leaving my family to live in denial."

"What is happening is you're making a choice that preserves your mental health while you're young enough to build a future. That's smart. That's survival too."

Sunday morning, she loaded her car.

Everything she'd brought. Plus things she'd learned. Skills. Knowledge. Experience.

The community gathered. Informal goodbye. Sixty-three people wishing her well.

She hugged everyone. Thanked them. Cried a lot.

Makwa arrived. With his son. They'd heard she was leaving.

The boy gave her another carved bone. This time a bird. For freedom. For flight.

Makwa spoke. Sarah translated: "He says: you are brave. You choose your path. That is hard. Most people let others choose for them. You choose yourself. He respects this."

Emma hugged the boy. Thanked Makwa.

Then she got in her car.

Karen sat in the passenger seat. Riding to Traverse City with her. Would catch a ride back from there.

I stood with Jake. Watching her drive away.

"She's doing the right thing," Jake said.

"How do you know?"

"Because she chose it. That makes it right for her."

"What if she regrets it?"

"Then she'll choose something else. That's how life works. Choose. Adapt. Choose again. Keep moving."

"You sound like Makwa."

"He's a good teacher."

We watched until the car disappeared. Heading south. Toward Traverse City. Toward the bus station. Toward Michigan State. Toward normal. Toward the life Emma had chosen.

Away from correction. Away from adaptation. Away from the shrinking green zones and the expanding Pleistocene and the community trying to survive the geological erasure of modern time.

She was choosing denial. Choosing normal. Choosing the future we used to believe in.

And that was okay. That was her right. Her choice. Her path.

We'd chosen differently. Chosen adaptation. Chosen to stay. Chosen to learn to live with correction.

Different paths. Different choices. Both valid. Both survival strategies.

We'd see her again. Holidays. Summers maybe. Brief visits. Tourist trips to the place she used to call home.

But she wouldn't live here. Wouldn't adapt fully. Wouldn't become what we were becoming.

And that was a loss. A grief. A door closing.

But also a hope. A future. A reminder that life continued outside the correction. That the world was bigger than Antrim County. That some people got to choose normal.

Even if we couldn't.

Chapter 35

CHAPTER THIRTY-FIVE: DEEP WINTER

Year two began with snow.

Not normal Michigan snow. Wrong snow.

It started November 3rd. Week sixty-four. Two full years since the first fold.

The temperature dropped overnight. From 38 degrees to 12 degrees in six hours. Fast. Unnatural. The cold zone expanding again.

By morning, snow was falling. Heavy. Wet. The kind that accumulated fast.

By noon, we had eight inches.

By evening, eighteen inches.

By the next morning, thirty-two inches and still falling.

This wasn't Michigan winter. This was Pleistocene winter. Ice age storm system. The kind that buried mammoths and created glaciers.

And it wasn't stopping.

Day two of the storm, we lost the medical clinic.

The roof couldn't handle the snow load. Too much weight. Too fast. Modern engineering calculations didn't account for three feet of snow in forty-eight hours.

The sod roof collapsed. Inward. Taking the log frame with it.

Nobody was inside. We'd evacuated when the creaking started. Dr. Havelka got her supplies out. But the structure was gone. Four months of work. Destroyed in seconds.

We stood in the snow, watching.

"We rebuild," Bill said. "Steeper pitch. Stronger frame. Learn from the mistake."

"With what materials?" someone asked. "We used most of the salvageable lumber on the first build."

"Then we use logs. Like the Paleo-Indians. Pure primitive construction. No modern materials to fail."

"That'll take months. Winter's here. We need shelter now."

Bill looked at the ruins. At the falling snow. At the community standing around in inadequate cold-weather gear.

"We double up. Move people into existing structures. Tight quarters but warm. We survive the winter. Rebuild in spring."

No argument. No better option. Just acceptance.

We were learning. Adapt or die. Those were still the only choices.

Day four of the storm, the snow stopped.

Final accumulation: forty-one inches. In four days.

The village was buried. Paths between structures invisible. Doors blocked. Roofs sagging under weight.

We dug out. Sixty-three people with shovels. Clearing paths. Reinforcing roofs. Creating tunnels through snowdrifts taller than people.

It took two days. Constant work. Everyone contributing. The elderly. The children. Everyone.

Because if we didn't dig out, we'd be trapped. Buried. Starving in our shelters while food storage sat thirty feet away under four feet of snow.

Day seven, the cold settled in.

Not the extreme cold of the permanent zones. But sustained cold. Minus five degrees. Minus ten at night. Week after week.

Firewood consumption quadrupled. We were burning through reserves. Wood we'd spent months gathering and stacking.

Bill did the math. "At current burn rate, we have enough firewood for six weeks. Maybe seven if we ration carefully."

"What happens after seven weeks?"

"We freeze. Or we cut more wood. In the middle of winter. In deep snow. With ice age conditions."

"Can we do that?"

"Do we have a choice?"

Week sixty-six, we organized cutting parties.

Teams of four. Two cutting, two hauling. Working in shifts. Four hours maximum before mandatory warmth break.

I went out with Tom Kowalski, Joe Macklin, and Len Greenland.

The forest was transformed. Pleistocene forest now. Different trees. Spruce and birch dominant. Hardwoods retreating. The ecology shifting with the temperature.

We found a dead spruce. Storm damage. Already down. Perfect.

Cutting with hand saws. No chainsaws. No power. Just muscle and steel.

Four hours of work. Got maybe a quarter of the tree processed. Enough wood for three days. Maybe four.

We needed wood for weeks. Months. The rest of winter.

The math was brutal. We'd need cutting parties every other day. All winter. Just to stay warm.

And that assumed no more storms. No injuries. No equipment failures.

Week sixty-eight, Makwa found us cutting.

Watched for a few minutes. Then approached.

Gestured. Come.

We followed.

He led us to a different area. Showed us standing dead trees. Killed by beetle infestation. Dry. Perfect firewood. Easier to cut than green wood.

Then he showed us how to fell them efficiently. Angles. Leverage. Techniques refined over thousands of years of cutting wood with stone tools.

With his methods, we processed a tree in two hours instead of four. Doubled our efficiency.

He didn't speak. Didn't need to. Just taught. Patiently. Showing us what his people had known forever.

How to survive winter when winter was trying to kill you.

Week seventy, the first injuries happened.

Hypothermia. Frostbite. Routine.

Dr. Havelka treated them in the communal kitchen. No medical clinic anymore. Just improvised care.

Linda Morrison—the woman who'd fallen through the bridge fold—got frostbite on three toes. Working too long without proper gear. Didn't realize how cold she was until the damage was done.

Dr. Havelka saved the toes. Barely. But Linda would have nerve damage. Chronic pain. Limited mobility.

At sixty-seven years old, that was potentially fatal. Couldn't work as hard. Couldn't contribute as much. Became dependent.

In modern society, that was manageable. Social security. Medicare. Support systems.

Here? We had community. But community had limits. Everyone had to contribute. Everyone had to pull weight.

Dependents were dangerous. Not because we didn't care. Because we had limited resources. Limited capacity. Limited margin for error.

Nobody said it out loud. But everyone knew: if too many people became dependent, the whole community failed.

Week seventy-two, food stores started running low.

We'd planned for winter. Preserved meat. Dried vegetables. Stored grain. But we'd planned for Michigan winter. Four months. Moderate cold. Normal snowfall.

This wasn't Michigan winter. This was ice age winter. Six months minimum. Maybe longer. Extreme cold. Massive snow.

Our food calculations were wrong.

Bill did inventory. "At current consumption, we have food for twelve more weeks. Takes us to early March. But if winter extends past that—if spring comes late like it did during the ice age—we'll run out."

"Can we hunt?" someone asked.

"In four feet of snow? With predators more adapted to these conditions than we are? We can try. But it's dangerous. And inefficient. We'll burn more calories hunting than we'll gain from kills."

"Can we fish?"

"Lakes are frozen. Ice fishing works but yields are low. Not enough to feed sixty-three people."

"So what do we do?"

"Ration. Cut consumption by twenty percent. Stretch the stores. Hope winter ends on time. And prepare for the possibility it doesn't."

The ration order went into effect immediately. Smaller portions. One meal per day communal. Rest on your own if you had personal supplies.

People were hungry. Not starving. But constantly hungry. Low energy. Irritable. Stressed.

That was dangerous too. Stress led to mistakes. Mistakes led to injuries. Injuries led to dependents. Dependents led to system failure.

We were in a spiral. And winter wasn't even half over.

Week seventy-four, Makwa invited me to the Paleo-Indian village.

I went with Sarah. Translating.

The settlement was thriving. Not struggling. Thriving.

Food storage platforms full. Meat hanging. Dried fish. Preserved vegetables. Enough for months.

Warm fires. Well-maintained structures. Children playing in the snow. Adults working efficiently. No stress. No panic. No fear.

This was their season. Their climate. Their expertise.

The elder spoke. Sarah translated: "He sees you struggle. Sees your people hungry. Cold. Afraid. He offers help. Food trade. Knowledge trade. Survival partnership."

"What does he want in return?"

"Metal tools. Medicine. Seeds for next year's planting. Fair exchange. Not charity. Trade."

I looked at their stores. They had enough. More than enough. Sharing wouldn't hurt them.

"Tell him: yes. We accept. With gratitude. And we'll pay fairly. Metal tools. Medicine. Whatever we can provide."

The elder nodded. Approval.

Then he spoke again. Longer. More serious.

Sarah translated: "He says: your people are learning. Adapting. But too slowly. Winter is teacher. Harsh teacher. You must learn faster or winter will kill you."

"He offers: send some of your people here. Live with his people. Full immersion. Learn winter survival the way his children learn. Not visits. Not lessons. Full integration."

"For how long?"

"Until spring. Until you understand. Until the knowledge is deep. Not surface."

I thought about it. Sending our people to live with the Paleo-Indians. Full cultural immersion. Learning survival from masters.

It was humbling. Admitting we couldn't survive on our own. Needed help from people we used to think of as primitive.

But pride was a luxury. And we were out of luxuries.

"How many people can he take?"

"Five. Maybe six. Young ones preferred. Faster learners. Will adapt better."

"I'll ask for volunteers."

Week seventy-five, we held community meeting.

I explained the offer. Food trade. Knowledge exchange. Full immersion for volunteers.

"Who wants to go?" Bill asked.

Silence.

Living with the Paleo-Indians. For months. Full cultural adoption. Sleeping in hide tents. Eating unfamiliar food. Learning a language we barely understood. Abandoning modern comfort completely.

It was terrifying.

Then Jake stood up. "I'll go."

"Jake—" Karen started.

"Mom, I'm the obvious choice. I already work with Makwa. Already know some of the language. Already have relationships. And my research benefits from immersion. I can document their winter survival techniques. Learn. Share. This is perfect for me."

"It's dangerous."

"Staying here is dangerous too. We're rationing food. People are getting frostbite. The medical clinic collapsed. This whole community is one disaster away from failure. If I can learn skills that prevent that, it's worth the risk."

Three others volunteered. Tom Kowalski. A young woman named Ashley Martinez—Bob Martinez's niece, stayed after he died. And Len Greenland.

Four people. Good mix. Different ages. Different skills. All willing to fully adapt.

The elder accepted them.

Week seventy-six, they moved to the Paleo-Indian village.

We held a small ceremony. Not goodbye. Transfer. They were still part of our community. Just learning elsewhere.

Jake took minimal supplies. His monitoring equipment. Notebooks. Recording devices. Otherwise, he left modern behind. Fully adopted Paleo-Indian life.

Karen cried. Not from fear. From pride. And grief. Watching her son walk into the past. Becoming something other than modern.

"He'll be okay," I told her. "Makwa will watch him. Keep him safe."

"I know. But he's choosing their world over ours. Even temporarily. That means something."

"It means he's adapting. That's what we're all doing. Some faster than others."

"What if he likes it better? What if he stays? Fully?"

"Then he stays. That's his choice. Same as Emma's choice to leave. We respect both."

She nodded. But the grief remained.

Our children were diverging. Emma to the modern world. Jake to the ancient world. And we were in the middle. Hybrid. Adapted but not fully. Modern but not completely.

A family split across time. Each member choosing their own way to survive.

Week eighty, the food trade arrived.

Paleo-Indians brought preserved meat. Dried fish. Rendered fat. High-calorie foods. Winter survival rations.

Enough to supplement our stores. Not replace. But extend. Buy us time.

In exchange, we gave metal knives. Antibiotics. Copper wire. Salt. Glass beads.

Fair trade. Both sides benefiting.

But also dependency forming. We needed their food. They benefited from our technology. Symbiosis developing.

We were no longer separate communities. We were integrated economies. Reliant on each other.

That was good. Cooperation. Partnership.

But also dangerous. If one community failed, both suffered.

Week eighty-four, Jake visited.

Brief trip. Checking in. Bringing documentation.

He looked different. Leaner. Harder. Dressed in hide clothing. Hair longer. Moving differently. More efficient. More deliberate.

Two months with the Paleo-Indians had changed him.

"How is it?" I asked.

"Difficult. Humbling. Incredible." He smiled. "Dad, they know things we forgot. Not just survival skills. Philosophy. Community structure. Conflict resolution. Child-rearing. Everything. They've refined human society over thousands of years. We invented civilization and lost knowledge they kept."

"Are you learning?"

"Every day. Makwa's son—his name translates roughly to 'Quick Hands'—he's teaching me tracking. Real tracking. Not reading signs. Reading the story. Understanding the animal's thought process. Predicting behavior. It's like learning a new language. Except the language is written in disturbed leaves and broken twigs."

"And the others?"

"Thriving. Tom's learning leadership. How the elder maintains authority without force. Ashley's learning food preservation. Techniques that work without refrigeration. Without canning. Just knowledge and patience. Len's learning medicine. Herbal. Practical. Stuff Dr. Havelka never learned in medical school."

"Are you coming back?"

He hesitated. "Yes. Eventually. This is research. Documentation. Not permanent adoption. But Dad... I understand why someone would stay. It works. Their society. Their methods. They're happy. Healthy. Secure. More than we are. Despite having less technology."

"Less technology. More knowledge."

"Exactly."

Week ninety-two, winter finally broke.

March 15th. The temperature climbed above freezing for the first time in four months.

Snow started melting. Slowly. Ice retreating. Spring arriving late but arriving.

We'd survived. Sixty-three people. Through the harshest winter in recorded history. Through ice age conditions. Through food shortages and collapsed buildings and injuries and constant threat.

We'd survived.

But barely.

Final accounting:

Medical clinic: destroyed, not rebuilt.

Food stores: depleted, lasted only because of Paleo-Indian trade.

Firewood: nearly exhausted, two days from running out when spring arrived.

Injuries: fourteen cases of frostbite, seven hypothermia incidents, three serious infections, one death.

Patricia Hendricks. The woman who'd lost her house to a fold. Who'd taken the buyout. Who'd stayed anyway.

Died week eighty-seven. Pneumonia. Complications from cold exposure. No antibiotics left—we'd traded them all. No medical clinic for proper treatment. No hospital within reach.

She died in the communal kitchen. Surrounded by people. Cared for until the end.

But dead nonetheless.

The first community member we'd lost to winter. Not to folds. Not to predators. To simple exposure. Cold. Illness. Lack of resources.

We buried her when the ground thawed enough to dig. March 18th. Simple grave. No headstone. Just memory.

"She survived the folds," Bill said at the service. "Survived temporal displacement. Watched her house collapse into the Pleistocene. Took the buyout. Stayed anyway. And winter killed her. Not exotic. Not dramatic. Just winter."

"That's what we're facing. Not just folds. Not just correction. But the practical reality of living in ice age conditions without ice age adaptation. Winter will keep coming. Every year. Harder. Longer. Colder."

"We have to adapt faster. Learn deeper. Change more. Or winter will kill us. One by one. Until nobody's left."

Week ninety-four, Jake returned permanently.

Brought Tom, Ashley, and Len with him. Integration period over. Knowledge gained. Time to rejoin the community.

We gathered to hear what they'd learned.

Jake spoke first. "We have to change everything. How we build. How we store food. How we heat structures. How we organize labor. The Paleo-Indians have refined these things over millennia. We can't match that in months. But we can adopt their methods. Implement their knowledge."

"Give me examples," Bill said.

"Food preservation. We're preserving wrong. Too much reliance on drying. Not enough on fermentation, rendering, pemmican-making. The Paleo-Indians have food that lasts years. Literally years. High calorie. Nutrient-dense. Portable. We need that."

"Shelter. We're building wrong. Too much modern thinking. Not enough insulation. Not enough thermal mass. The Paleo-Indians' structures stay warm with minimal fire. Ours require constant burning. We're wasting energy."

"Organization. We're governing wrong. Too much democracy. Too slow. The Paleo-Indians have elder council. Quick decisions. Clear authority. Efficient. We need that for emergencies."

"Basically," Tom added, "we need to become more like them. Not completely. We keep our technology. Our knowledge. Our innovation. But we adopt their proven survival methods. Hybrid approach. Best of both."

Bill looked around the room. "Show of hands. Who's willing to fully restructure how we live? Adopt Paleo-Indian methods? Change everything?"

Every hand went up.

Winter had taught us. Harshly. Completely. Undeniably.

We couldn't survive as modern humans in Pleistocene conditions.

We had to become something else.

Hybrid humans. Part modern. Part ancient. Taking the best from both. Discarding the rest.

Adaptive. Flexible. Willing to change.

Or dead.

Those were still the only options.

Chapter 36

CHAPTER THIRTY-SIX: YEAR TWO ATTACK

Spring came late. But it came.

By April, the snow had melted. By May, the ground had thawed enough for planting. By June, we were rebuilding.

The medical clinic. Redesigned. Steeper pitch. Log construction. Paleo-Indian techniques. Built to handle ice age snow loads.

We'd learned. Winter had taught us. We were adapting.

And then the bear came back.

June 14th. Week one hundred four. Exactly two years since we'd signed the federal waivers. Two years of living in correction. Two years of adaptation.

The attack happened at 3:47 AM.

I woke to screaming.

Not animal screaming. Human. High-pitched. Terrified. Coming from the communal kitchen.

I grabbed my rifle. Out the door in seconds.

The kitchen was maybe two hundred yards from our house. Close enough to hear. Far enough that I had to run.

By the time I got there, it was over.

The door was torn open. Not broken. Torn. The hinges ripped from the frame by something impossibly strong.

Inside: blood. Lots of blood. Smeared across the floor. Splattered on the walls. Fresh. Still warm.

And drag marks. Leading out the back door. Into the woods.

Bill Henderson arrived thirty seconds after me. Then Tom. Then others. Everyone waking. Everyone armed. Everyone terrified.

"Who was inside?" Bill asked.

We did a quick count. Two people missing.

Mark Williams. Sixty-two years old. Retired carpenter. Had been sleeping in the kitchen—his house in the yellow zone, he'd moved into communal space.

Sarah Jennings. Twenty-eight. Had come to the county two months ago. Refugee from Detroit when folds started opening there. Had been helping with night watch. Had been inside making coffee.

Both gone. Taken.

"It was a bear," someone said. "Look at the damage. The claw marks on the door frame. Nothing else is that strong."

I looked at the marks. Four parallel gouges. Deep. Eight inches long.

Short-faced bear. *Arctodus simus.* The same thing that had killed Bob Martinez two years ago.

It had come back.

We organized a search party immediately.

Ten people. Armed. Following the drag marks.

The trail was obvious. Blood. Disturbed undergrowth. Broken branches. The bear hadn't been subtle. Hadn't needed to be. Nothing in modern Michigan could challenge it.

We followed for maybe half a mile.

Found Sarah first.

Dead. Obviously dead. Throat torn out. Abdomen opened. The bear had fed. Not much. Just enough. Then abandoned the body.

Ashley Martinez—who'd lived with the Paleo-Indians, learned their methods—examined the kill.

"Efficient. Professional. Ambush predator. Sarah never had a chance." She pointed at the throat wound. "Crushed windpipe. Instant death or near-instant. Then feeding. The bear knew exactly what it was doing."

We wrapped Sarah's body. Brought it back.

The trail continued. Deeper into the woods. Toward the red zone. Toward the permanent cold area.

"Mark might still be alive," Tom said.

"If the bear took two people, it killed one for immediate feeding and took one for storage," Ashley said. "That's typical large predator behavior. Kill, cache, return later. If Mark was cached, he might survive. For a while."

We kept following.

The trail led to the boundary of the cold zone.

We could see the shimmer. The temperature differential. Spring warmth on one side. Ice age cold on the other.

The drag marks crossed through.

Mark—if he was alive—was in the Pleistocene. In the bear's territory. In minus-fifteen-degree conditions without proper gear.

"We can't follow," I said. "Not without cold-weather equipment. We'd die from exposure before we found him."

"So we abandon him?" someone asked.

"We get proper gear. Come back. Try to retrieve him if he's alive. But going in now, unprepared, just gets more people killed."

It was the right decision. The practical decision. The survival decision.

But it felt like cowardice. Like abandoning someone who might still be breathing.

We marked the location. Returned to the village. Geared up properly.

Two hours later, we returned. Five people. Me, Tom, Ashley, Bill, and Makwa—who'd heard the commotion and come to help.

We crossed through the shimmer.

Into the cold. Into the Pleistocene. Into the bear's hunting ground.

We found Mark thirty yards inside the cold zone.

Dead. Had been dead for at least an hour. The cold had preserved the body. Made time of death hard to determine. But the wounds were clear.

Claw marks across his back. Deep. Four parallel gouges. The bear had grabbed him. Dragged him. Brought him here.

Then killed him. Not immediately. Mark had defensive wounds. Scratches on his hands. Torn clothing. He'd fought. Tried to escape.

But the bear was faster. Stronger. Better adapted to this environment.

Mark had died in the Pleistocene. Alone. Cold. Terrified. Killed by something that had been extinct for eleven thousand years.

We retrieved his body. Brought it back through the shimmer. Into spring warmth. Into 2028.

Two people dead. Taken from the communal kitchen. Killed by an apex predator that had learned humans were easy prey.

We buried them that afternoon.

Simple graves. No headstones. Just wooden markers.

Sarah Jennings. Twenty-eight. Survived Detroit's folds. Couldn't survive ours.

Mark Williams. Sixty-two. Carpenter. Builder. Helped construct the village. Killed in the structure he'd helped create.

Bill spoke. "Two years ago, Bob Martinez died at Elk Lake. Killed by a short-faced bear. We hunted that bear. Killed it. Eliminated the threat. We thought we were safe."

"We were wrong. The bears keep coming through. The folds keep opening. The predators keep hunting. We can't eliminate them all. They belong here. We don't. They're adapted. We're not. They're the residents. We're the intruders."

"So what do we do? Leave? Give up? Abandon the village we've built?"

"No. We adapt better. We learn faster. We defend smarter. We accept that we live in the Pleistocene now. And in the Pleistocene, apex predators hunt humans. That's reality. We build defenses. We stay alert. We survive."

"But we can't prevent every attack. Can't save everyone. Some of us will die. That's the price of staying. We accept it or we leave."

Nobody left.

That night, emergency planning session.

"The kitchen is indefensible," Tom said. "Open structure. Easy access. No barriers. We built for community. Not for security. That was a mistake."

"We need walls," Ashley said. "Fences. Something that stops predators. Or at least slows them enough that we can respond."

"What kind of walls stop a short-faced bear?" someone asked.

"Nothing stops them. But we can make it harder. Deterrents. Obstacles. Warning systems."

Makwa spoke. Sarah translated: "He says: his people don't try to stop bears. They avoid them. Build away from bear territory. Travel in groups. Stay alert. Don't give bears opportunities."

"We did build away from known bear territory. We're in the green zone. Stable. Safe."

Makwa responded. Sarah translated: "He says: there is no 'away from bear territory' anymore. The cold zones expand. The bears come through. Everywhere is bear territory now. You must think like prey. Not like builders. Prey survives by awareness. Not walls."

"So we what? Post sentries? Twenty-four-hour watch?"

"Yes. His people do. Always. Someone watching. Always ready. Always aware. That's how you survive predators."

"We don't have enough people for constant watch."

"Then you die. Or you get more people. Or you adapt your sleep patterns. Have rotating watches. Everyone takes shifts. No exceptions."

It was harsh. But accurate.

We'd been living like builders. Like engineers. Like people in control.

But we weren't in control. We were prey. In a landscape full of apex predators. And prey survived through vigilance. Not architecture.

Week one hundred five, we implemented the changes.

Perimeter fence: Log palisade. Eight feet high. Not strong enough to stop a bear. But enough to slow one. Give us warning. Response time.

Sentry posts: Four positions. Overlapping fields of view. Someone always watching. Always armed. Four-hour shifts. Everyone rotated through.

Alarm system: Bells. Simple. Loud. Manual. If a sentry saw danger, ring the bell. Everyone responds.

Emergency protocols: Designated shelters. If alarm sounds, people move to reinforced structures. Bring weapons. Prepare to defend.

Hunting parties: Never alone. Minimum three people. Always armed. Always alert. Operate like prey. Not like hunters.

It was exhausting. The constant vigilance. The sleep disruption from sentry duty. The psychological burden of knowing predators could attack anytime.

But it worked.

Week one hundred eight, we spotted the bear.

Night sentry—Joe Macklin—rang the alarm at 2:17 AM.

Everyone up. Armed. Moving to defensive positions.

The bear was at the fence. Testing it. Pushing against the logs. Seeing if it could break through.

Eight feet tall. Maybe twelve hundred pounds. Same species that had killed Mark and Sarah. Maybe the same individual.

It saw us. Armed. Ready. Organized.

Calculated. Not worth it. Too much resistance. Easier prey elsewhere.

It left.

We watched it disappear into the woods. Heading north. Toward the cold zone. Toward its territory.

Nobody slept the rest of the night.

But nobody died either.

The defenses had worked. Not by stopping the bear. By making us harder targets. Less appealing. More effort than reward.

Week one hundred ten, Makwa brought news.

A second bear had been spotted near the Paleo-Indian village. Different individual. Smaller. Maybe a juvenile.

"His people are tracking it," Sarah translated. "Planning a hunt. He asks: do you want to join? Kill the threat before it learns to hunt humans?"

"Yes," Bill said immediately. "When?"

"Tomorrow. Dawn. Bring your best hunters. Your best weapons. This is dangerous work."

We brought six people. Me, Bill, Tom, Ashley, Joe, and Len.

The Paleo-Indians brought eight. Including Makwa and the elder himself.

Fourteen humans. Hunting one of the most dangerous predators in North American history.

The hunt took six hours.

The Paleo-Indians tracked. We followed. Learning. Watching.

The bear was moving through the transitional zone. Yellow area. Not fully Pleistocene. Not fully modern. Edge territory.

We found it near an old creek bed. Feeding on a deer it had killed.

The elder organized the attack. Gestures. No words needed. Universal hunting language.

Group one: Paleo-Indians with atlatls. Approach from downwind. Close range. Strike first.

Group two: Modern humans with rifles. High ground. Covering position. Strike second if needed.

Simple. Effective. Using each group's strengths.

The Paleo-Indians moved like ghosts. Silent. Invisible. Perfect.

They got within forty yards. The bear hadn't noticed.

Makwa threw first. Atlatl dart. Hit the bear's shoulder. Penetrated deep.

The bear roared. Spun. Charged.

Three more darts. Chest. Flank. Neck. All hits.

The bear stumbled. But didn't drop. Still dangerous. Still moving.

That's when we fired.

Three rifles. Simultaneous. Chest shots. Center mass.

The bear went down.

Not immediately. It took maybe ten seconds. Fighting. Trying to stand. But the damage was too much.

It died at the edge of the creek bed. Nine hundred pounds of apex predator. Killed by cooperative hunting. Modern and ancient humans working together.

The elder approached. Spoke quietly. Same ritual we'd seen before. Thanking the bear. Honoring its spirit.

Then he turned to us. Spoke.

Sarah translated: "He says: this is how you survive. Together. Not separate. Your weapons are strong. Our tracking is strong. Together we kill what neither could kill alone."

"He says: more bears will come. More predators. The cold zones expand. The Pleistocene returns. You must keep hunting together. Keep defending together. Or predators will hunt you."

Bill gripped the elder's forearm. "Agreed. Partnership. Permanent. We hunt together. We defend together. We survive together."

The elder nodded. Satisfied.

We processed the bear together. Learned the anatomy. The proper cuts. What was usable.

The hide: too damaged from spears and bullets. Unsalvageable.

The meat: divided equally. Bear meat was lean. Gamey. But edible. Protein was protein.

The claws: kept by the Paleo-Indians. Trophy. Proof of the kill.

The skull: offered to Bill. He accepted. Another reminder. Another trophy. Another lesson.

"This is the second bear skull I own," Bill said that night at the village. "Bob Martinez's bear. Now this one. I don't want a third. I want to stop killing bears and start preventing attacks."

"How do we do that?" someone asked.

"We stay vigilant. We hunt cooperatively. We accept that we live in a landscape where we're prey. And we adapt to that reality. Every day. Every decision. Every structure we build. We design for predators. Not for convenience."

"This is our life now. Permanent. Until the green zones are gone or we are. Accept it or leave. Those are still the only choices."

Week one hundred twelve, Jake published his second paper.

"Predator-Prey Dynamics in Temporal Overlap Zones: Human Adaptation to Pleistocene Megafauna"

Case studies: Bob Martinez. Mark Williams. Sarah Jennings. The bear hunts. The defensive systems. The cooperative hunting.

Data showing that modern humans couldn't survive Pleistocene predators alone. But could survive through partnership with Paleo-Indian populations.

The paper went viral. Not just academic circles. Mainstream media.

"Modern Humans Need Stone Age Humans to Survive Ice Age Predators"

"Partnership Across Time: How Two Populations Survive Together"

"Correction Zones Require Cross-Cultural Cooperation"

Jake's conclusion was simple: Modern humans in correction zones couldn't survive independently. They needed integration with Paleo-Indian populations. Full partnership. Mutual defense. Shared knowledge.

Not charity. Not colonialism. Actual equality. Both groups contributing. Both groups benefiting. Both groups surviving together.

The alternative was evacuation. Or death.

Those were still the only options.

That night, we held memorial service for Mark and Sarah.

Sixty-one people now. Down from sixty-three. Two years of survival. Two deaths from predators. One death from winter.

Three casualties. Out of sixty-three who'd stayed.

That was a 95% survival rate. Better than expected. Better than we'd feared.

But the three who'd died—Patricia, Mark, Sarah—they weren't statistics. They were people. Community members. Friends.

And they'd died because we weren't adapted enough. Weren't prepared enough. Weren't Pleistocene enough.

We were learning. Adapting. Building defenses. Changing behavior.

But learning required mistakes. And mistakes killed people.

That was the cost. The price. The reality of living in correction.

We could accept it and continue. Or leave.

Nobody left.

We'd chosen this. Chosen to stay. Chosen to adapt. Chosen to become something new.

Hybrid humans. Part modern. Part ancient. Learning from both. Surviving through cooperation.

It was working. Mostly. With casualties. With losses. With grief.

But working.

And as long as it worked, we stayed.

Living in the shrinking green zones. Defending against Pleistocene predators. Building villages that could withstand ice age winters. Partnering with people from eleven thousand years ago.

Surviving. Adapting. Enduring.

For however long we could.

Chapter 37

2:52 PM

CHAPTER THIRTY-SEVEN: FEDERAL QUARANTINE

The helicopters came on a Tuesday.

Week one hundred eighteen. July. Mid-morning. Clear skies.

Three Black Hawks. Military. Coming in low over the tree line. Circling the village. Landing in the clearing we'd made for the communal garden.

Soldiers emerged. Twenty of them. Full combat gear. Rifles. Body armor. Professional. Coordinated.

A woman in civilian clothes followed. Mid-forties. Professional suit. Briefcase. Government official written all over her.

She approached our perimeter fence. Stopped at the gate.

"I'm looking for David Pritchard."

I walked over. "I'm Pritchard."

"Special Agent Rebecca Chen, Department of Homeland Security. We need to talk."

"About what?"

"About the federal quarantine order that's being imposed on Antrim County effective immediately. And about your illegal settlement in a designated disaster zone."

We gathered in the communal kitchen. Agent Chen. Me. Bill. Tom Kowalski. Sarah Ashkwe. Jake. Karen.

The soldiers stayed outside. Perimeter security. Making it clear this wasn't a request. This was enforcement.

Chen opened her briefcase. Pulled out documents. Official. Stamped. Signed by people whose names I recognized from news coverage.

"As of 0800 hours this morning, Antrim County has been designated a Level Five Temporal Hazard Zone. Federal jurisdiction. All civilian presence is prohibited. You have seventy-two hours to evacuate."

"We signed waivers," Bill said. "We acknowledged the risks. We chose to stay. That was legal."

"That was legal two years ago. Jurisdiction has changed. The Temporal Hazard Act of 2028 supersedes previous waivers. The federal government now has authority to evacuate populations from active correction zones."

"Why now?" I asked. "We've been here two years. Why suddenly enforce this?"

Chen pulled out more documents. Photos. Satellite imagery.

"Because you're not alone anymore. Detroit has seventeen active folds. Chicago has thirty-two. Milwaukee has nine. The entire Great Lakes region is experiencing correction. And the federal government needs to establish control. Protocols. Quarantine zones. Evacuation procedures. Before this becomes a continental crisis."

She showed us photos. Detroit. Parts of the city underwater. Lake Algonquin returning. Buildings half-submerged.

Chicago. Ice fields in Grant Park. The Loop partially frozen. Thousands evacuating.

Milwaukee. Similar patterns. Folds opening. Zones expanding. Cities collapsing into the past.

"This is spreading," Chen said. "Faster than predicted. Dr. Park's models suggested decades. It's happening in years. We need to contain it. Study it. Control access. Establish research protocols. And that means removing unauthorized civilian populations."

"We're not unauthorized," Tom said. "I'm still sheriff. Still sworn. Still maintaining law enforcement in this county."

"Not anymore. As of this morning, Antrim County is under federal jurisdiction. Your authority is revoked. You're a civilian now."

Tom stood up. "The hell I am."

"Sheriff Kowalski, you can accept this peacefully or we can enforce it. Your choice. But the order stands. You're civilians in a federal quarantine zone. You have seventy-two hours to evacuate. After that, you'll be removed by force if necessary."

After Chen left—returning to her helicopter, soldiers following—we held emergency council.

Sixty-one people. Everyone present. Everyone voting.

"They can't force us to leave," Bill said. "We're established. We're surviving. We're not a threat to anyone."

"They have soldiers," someone pointed out. "Helicopters. Weapons. Authority. They can absolutely force us."

"So what? We fight? Resist? Become criminals?"

"We're already criminals according to them. Illegal occupants. Trespassers in a federal zone."

Tom stood up. "I say we refuse. Peacefully. Civil disobedience. Make them arrest us if they want us gone. Make them use force on civilians who aren't threatening anyone. Make them own the optics."

"They won't care about optics. They'll just remove us. Load us on helicopters. Dump us in Traverse City. Declare victory."

"Then what? We give up? After two years? After everything we've built?"

Sarah spoke quietly. "We negotiate. Find middle ground. Offer co-operation in exchange for autonomy."

"What kind of cooperation?"

"Research access. They want to study correction. Jake's already doing that. We offer full data sharing. Complete research cooperation. Regular reports. In exchange for permission to stay. To continue our settlement. Under federal observation but not federal control."

Jake nodded. "That could work. They need ground-level data. Real-time observation. I'm already providing that to University of Chicago. I can provide it to DHS too. Make us valuable. Make removing us counterproductive."

"You think they'll agree to that?"

"Depends on how badly they want the data. And how much resistance they're willing to overcome to force evacuation."

I called Chen that evening. Satellite phone. Official channel.

"Agent Chen. We'd like to propose an alternative to evacuation."

"I'm listening."

"We stay. You get full research access. Complete data sharing. Real-time reporting on correction progression. Ground-level observation that no outside research team can provide. We become your embedded research station. In exchange for autonomy. We govern ourselves. Maintain our settlement. Continue our survival adaptations. But we share everything with federal authorities."

Silence on the line. Then: "You're proposing to stay in a Level Five hazard zone as civilian researchers?"

"We're proposing to stay as established residents who happen to be documenting correction from inside it. We're not leaving. You can force us out—waste resources, create confrontation, lose valuable data sources—or you can authorize our presence and benefit from our work."

"The law doesn't allow for exceptions."

"The law was written for normal disasters. This isn't normal. The entire Great Lakes region is reverting to the Pleistocene. You need people on the ground. People adapted. People surviving. People who can teach others how to survive when correction reaches their cities. We're that resource. Use us."

Another pause. "I need to consult with my superiors. I'll call back."

She hung up.

Two days later, Chen returned. Without soldiers this time. Just her. And one other person.

Dr. Lisa Park. University of Chicago. Jake's research supervisor.

"Dr. Park convinced me," Chen said. "Or convinced my superiors. The data you're collecting is irreplaceable. Jake's research is literally the only comprehensive ground-level documentation of long-term correction effects. Removing you means losing that."

"So we can stay?"

"Conditionally. Under federal observation. With restrictions."

She laid out the terms:

Research cooperation: Full data sharing. Weekly reports. Complete access to all observations and measurements.

Federal oversight: Quarterly inspections. DHS agents can visit anytime. No refusal of entry.

Population cap: Maximum sixty-five people. No growth beyond that. Anyone who wants to leave can leave. No one new comes in without federal approval.

Self-sufficiency: No federal aid. No rescue services. No emergency response. You're on your own. Complete self-sufficiency required.

Liability waiver: Federal government assumes zero responsibility for deaths, injuries, or losses. Everyone signs updated waivers acknowledging hazards.

Revocation clause: Federal government can revoke authorization at any time for any reason. No appeals.

"Basically," Bill said, "you're making us a research prison. Observed. Restricted. Controlled."

"I'm making you a legal exception to mandatory evacuation. Take it or leave it. Seventy-two hours still applies if you refuse."

We looked at each other. Sixty-one people. Making a collective decision.

Sarah spoke. "We take it. Observation is better than removal. Restrictions are better than evacuation. We adapt to this like we've adapted to everything else."

"All in favor?" Bill asked.

Every hand raised.

"We accept your terms," I told Chen. "Under protest. But we accept."

"Sign here." She produced documents. Lots of documents. Legal language. Federal authority. Complete surrender of normal rights in exchange for permission to exist.

We signed. All of us. Sixty-one signatures. Accepting federal quarantine. Accepting observation. Accepting restrictions.

Accepting the only deal that let us stay.

Week one hundred twenty, the federal presence became permanent.

A monitoring station. Quarter mile from the village. Prefab building. Solar panels. Satellite dish. Manned by rotating teams of two DHS agents. Watching. Recording. Reporting.

We were officially a research site. Observed population. Federal experiment in human adaptation to temporal correction.

It felt like being in a zoo. Watched animals. Performing survival for federal observers.

But we were still here. Still autonomous within our fence. Still governing ourselves. Still surviving.

That was worth the surveillance.

Week one hundred twenty-two, Jake met with the DHS observers.

They wanted comprehensive data. Everything. Fold measurements. Ecosystem changes. Population dynamics. Social structure. Conflict resolution. Food production. Medical incidents. Predator encounters. Everything.

Jake negotiated. "I'll provide data. But I control publication. My name goes first on all papers. University of Chicago gets co-authorship. DHS gets access but not ownership. Clear?"

The agents—both younger than Jake, both intimidated by his publication record—agreed.

Jake became the bridge. Between our community and federal authority. Between survival and research. Between autonomous living and observed experiment.

He documented everything. Our partnership with the Paleo-Indians. Our adaptation to ice age conditions. Our hybrid construction techniques. Our barter economy. Our governance by consensus. Our defense against predators.

All of it. Written. Measured. Analyzed. Sent to Washington.

Where bureaucrats and scientists studied us like specimens. Trying to understand how humans could survive correction. How adaptation worked. What techniques succeeded. What failed.

Learning from our successes. And our casualties.

Using us to prepare for when correction reached other cities. Other populations. Millions of people who'd soon face the same choices we'd faced.

Evacuate or adapt. Leave or learn. Surrender or survive.

Week one hundred twenty-six, the first conflict with federal observers happened.

One of the DHS agents—young guy, maybe twenty-eight, named Collins—tried to enter the Paleo-Indian village.

To document them. Photograph them. Interview them through Sarah.

Makwa refused entry. Physically. Blocked the path. Atlatl in hand. Message clear: Leave.

Collins called Chen. Demanded access. Federal authority. Research rights.

Chen arrived by helicopter. Tried to explain that the monitoring agreement included the Paleo-Indian settlement. They were part of the correction zone. Subject to observation.

The elder emerged. Spoke to Sarah. Sarah translated to Chen.

"He says: Your authority means nothing here. Your paper means nothing. Your helicopters mean nothing. This is his land. His people. His rules. You are not welcome. Leave now or face consequences."

"The federal government has jurisdiction—"

"Your government governs your time. Not his time. This village exists in the Pleistocene. Your laws don't apply. Your authority ends at the shimmer. Cross that boundary uninvited and you violate sovereign territory."

"There's no such thing as Pleistocene sovereignty—"

"Tell that to him." Sarah gestured at the elder. Who stood with fifteen warriors. All armed. All ready.

Chen assessed. Modern federal authority. Backed by helicopters and legal documents.

Versus Paleo-Indian sovereignty. Backed by atlatls and eleven thousand years of surviving worse threats than government agents.

She chose wisely. "We'll observe from a distance. Satellite imagery. Long-range photography. No direct contact without permission."

The elder nodded. Acceptable.

Chen left.

The Paleo-Indians had just established something unprecedented: recognized sovereignty for a population from the past. Not official. Not legal. But real.

Federal authority ended where temporal boundaries began.

In the Pleistocene, the elder ruled. Not Washington.

Week one hundred twenty-eight, we received visitors.

Not federal agents. Researchers. University teams. Anthropologists. Sociologists. Geologists. Ecologists.

All wanting to study us. Document us. Interview us. Learn from us.

We allowed some. Denied others. Established protocols.

No more than two research teams per month. Maximum one week stay. Must contribute labor to the community. Must share resources. No pure observation—you work, you help, you participate. Then you can study.

Most agreed. Some complained. Those we sent away.

The researchers who stayed learned. Not just data. Lived experience. What it meant to survive correction. To adapt to Pleistocene conditions. To partner with people from the past. To build hybrid society. To govern without modern infrastructure.

They went back to their universities changed. Carrying knowledge. Warning their colleagues. Preparing their institutions.

Because correction was spreading. Chicago. Detroit. Milwaukee. Cleveland. All experiencing folds now. All facing the same choices we'd faced.

And we were the proof that adaptation was possible. That humans could survive. That communities could persist. That cooperation worked.

We were the model. The experiment. The success story.

Even if that success included three deaths. Constant vigilance. Federal observation. Restricted rights. Permanent surveillance.

We'd survived. That was enough.

Week one hundred thirty, Karen and I walked the perimeter.

Looking at what we'd built. Log palisade. Communal structures. Gardens. Storage. Defense posts. A village. Functional. Surviving.

And beyond the fence: federal monitoring station. Constant reminder. We were observed. Controlled. Permitted to exist but not free.

"Do you regret staying?" Karen asked.

"Every day. And never." I looked at the village. "We've lost so much. Privacy. Freedom. Normal life. Three people dead. Emma gone. Jake half Paleo-Indian now. Everything changed."

"But?"

"But we're still here. Still us. Still choosing. Still adapting. They wanted us to evacuate. We refused. They wanted to remove us. We negotiated. They wanted to control us. We maintained autonomy. We're surviving on our terms. Mostly."

"Observed terms."

"Better than removed terms."

She leaned against me. "I miss Emma."

"So do I."

"But I'm glad she left. Glad she chose normal. Someone in this family should get to have a future that isn't ice age survival."

"Jake has a future. Different from Emma's. But still a future."

"Jake has a calling. That's not the same as a future. He's documenting the end of our world. That's important. Essential. But it's not living. It's witnessing."

"Isn't that living too? Bearing witness? Recording truth? Making sure what happens here isn't forgotten?"

"Maybe. I don't know anymore. I don't know what living means when the world is ending."

We stood in silence. Watching the woods. The boundary between green zone and yellow zone. Between 2028 and the Pleistocene. Between the world we'd known and the world we were becoming.

Federal helicopters in the distance. Observers watching. Documenting. Recording our survival for bureaucrats in Washington who'd never understand what it meant to live in correction.

We'd won. Sort of. Stayed when they wanted us gone. Survived when they expected us to fail. Proved adaptation was possible.

But the victory felt hollow. Conditional. Temporary.

Because the green zones kept shrinking. The Pleistocene kept expanding. And federal permission could be revoked anytime.

We were living on borrowed time. In borrowed space. Under borrowed authority.

But we were living.

That was enough.

For now.

Chapter 38

CHAPTER THIRTY-EIGHT: YEAR FIVE

Five years.

That's how long we'd been living in correction when the seasons stopped making sense.

Week two hundred sixty. March 2031. What should have been late winter. Thaw coming. Spring approaching.

Instead: snow. Four feet of it. Temperature minus twelve. Deep winter conditions. In March.

Except in the permanent cold zones. There it was minus thirty. Always minus thirty. Year-round ice age. Stable. Predictable. Permanent.

The green zones were shrinking faster now. Not inches per week. Feet per month. The Pleistocene expanding. Aggressively. Hungrily. Reclaiming.

Our village—built in what had been the most stable green zone—was now borderline yellow. The fold activity increasing. The temperature dropping. The ice approaching.

In five years, we'd gone from a county of twenty-three thousand to a village of fifty-eight people.

Three had died. Patricia. Mark. Sarah.

Emma had left two years ago. Chose normal. We'd gotten one letter. She'd graduated. Had a job. Was engaged to someone from Ann Arbor. Living the future we used to believe in.

Two more had left in year three. Decided adaptation wasn't worth it. Took the federal evacuation option. We never heard from them again.

And five had arrived. Refugees from other correction zones. Detroit. Chicago. Places where the folds had opened too fast. Where evacuation had been mandatory. Where survival hadn't been an option.

They'd found us. Heard about the community that had stayed. That had survived. That had learned to live in the Pleistocene.

They'd come seeking knowledge. Seeking shelter. Seeking proof that adaptation was possible.

We'd taken them in. Taught them. Integrated them. Under the federal population cap. Fifty-eight of sixty-five allowed. Room for seven more if they came.

But fewer were coming now. The roads were unreliable. The boundaries unstable. Getting to Bellaire meant crossing multiple fold zones. Risking displacement. Risking death.

We were isolated. Cut off. An island of modern humanity in an expanding Pleistocene sea.

And the water was rising.

The DHS monitoring station had been abandoned.

Week two hundred twenty. Six months ago. The agents had evacuated. Too dangerous. Too unstable. The station sat in what was now yellow zone. Fold activity too frequent. Risk too high.

Chen had called. Explained they'd monitor remotely. Satellite surveillance. Drone flyovers. But no more manned presence.

"You're on your own," she'd said. "Officially. Completely. No oversight. No observation. No federal presence."

"Does that mean we're free?" Bill had asked.

"It means you're abandoned. The federal government is withdrawing from active correction zones. Too many zones. Too many cities. Too few resources. We're evacuating Detroit completely. Relocating populations. You're... archived. On file as an existing settlement. But no longer monitored. No longer restricted. No longer our concern."

"So we can do whatever we want."

"You can die however you want. Nobody's watching anymore. Nobody cares. You chose to stay. That's on you."

The line had gone dead.

Federal authority had lasted eighteen months. Then it had run. Just like everyone else.

We were free. Sort of. Free because nobody cared about us anymore. Because we weren't worth the resources to control. Because we'd become irrelevant to a nation facing continental-scale correction.

The Paleo-Indian village had grown.

Seventy-three people now. Three separate bands had merged. Built a proper town. Permanent structures. Storage facilities. A council house. Semi-permanent settlement.

They weren't refugees. They weren't displaced. They were colonizers. Successfully. Thriving.

The cold zones were expanding? Perfect. More habitat for them. More territory. More resources.

The megafauna were breeding? Excellent. More game. Stable food supply.

The green zones were shrinking? Irrelevant. They didn't need green zones. They lived in the red zones. Comfortably. Expertly. Naturally.

Makwa was an elder now. His son—Quick Hands, now sixteen—was a full hunter. Skilled. Deadly. Adapted.

Jake spent half his time there. Living with them. Learning from them. Documenting their success while our community struggled.

He was more Paleo-Indian than modern now. Dressed in hides. Spoke their language fluently. Moved like them. Thought like them. Hunted like them.

Karen barely recognized him when he visited.

"He's choosing them over us," she'd said last month.

"He's choosing survival over sentiment," I'd replied. "Learning from the people who know how to thrive here. That's smart."

"That's abandonment."

"That's adaptation."

We'd argued. For the first time in thirty-two years of marriage. Really argued. About our son. About his choices. About whether he was saving himself or betraying us.

We hadn't resolved it. Just stopped talking about it.

Because what was there to say? Jake was surviving. That was the priority. That was the only thing that mattered.

Even if his survival meant becoming something his mother didn't recognize.

Year five brought other changes.

Our barter economy had fully replaced money. Nobody used dollars. Nobody cared about bank accounts. Wealth was measured in food stores. Tools. Skills. Knowledge. Relationships.

Bill Henderson was the wealthiest person in the village. Not because he had money. Because he had chickens. Thirty-seven chickens.

Eggs were currency. Protein was power. He controlled the most valuable renewable resource.

Dr. Havelka was second. Medical knowledge. Herbal remedies. Surgical skills. Irreplaceable. She could demand anything. Usually asked for firewood and food.

Tom Kowalski was third. Not because he was ex-sheriff. Because he was the best hunter. Brought in meat weekly. Fed the community. Made himself essential.

Everyone else traded based on contribution. You worked, you ate. You didn't work, you struggled. Simple. Darwinian. Fair in a brutal way.

The elderly who couldn't work contributed knowledge. Teaching. Childcare. Storytelling. Memory. That had value too.

But anyone who was purely dependent—injured, sick, unable to contribute anything—they struggled. The community helped. Shared. Supported. But there were limits. Resources were tight. Margin for error was thin. Compassion competed with survival.

We'd lost our softness. Our modern gentleness. We were harder now. Pragmatic. Willing to make calculations we'd never have made five years ago.

That was adaptation too. Not just physical. Psychological. Moral. Becoming people who could survive when survival required hardness.

Year five also brought the first wedding.

Ashley Martinez and Tom Kowalski. She was thirty-one. He was forty-seven. Age gap that would've mattered in the old world. Didn't matter here.

They'd partnered during the deep winter. Survival partnership. Became romantic. Decided to formalize.

Not a legal marriage. No licenses. No government. No clergy—we had no church, no ordained ministers.

Just a community ceremony. Public commitment. Witnessed by fifty-eight people. Blessed by both modern community and Paleo-Indian elders.

The elder had attended. Rare. He almost never left his village. But he came. Honored the union. Gave gifts. A hide blanket for Ashley. A carved atlatl for Tom. Symbols of partnership. Protection. Provision.

"You build a life together," he'd said through Sarah's translation. "In hard times. That takes courage. We honor courage."

They'd moved into a shared structure. Combined resources. Started planning for children.

Children. In the correction zone. In the shrinking green areas. In a world where the future was uncertain and the past was returning.

It seemed insane. Bringing new life into this.

But it was also hope. Defiance. A statement that life continued. That humanity persisted. That we weren't just surviving—we were living.

Jake published his third paper that year.

"Long-term Human Adaptation to Permanent Temporal Displacement: A Five-Year Study"

It went viral. Again. Academic circles. Mainstream media. Government agencies.

Because it was the only comprehensive study of long-term survival in correction zones. The only data on what happened to communities that stayed. That adapted. That persisted.

Jake's findings:

Physical adaptation: Modern humans could survive Pleistocene conditions. But required significant lifestyle changes. Hybrid construction. Traditional food preservation. Constant vigilance. Partnership with indigenous knowledge holders.

Psychological adaptation: Required acceptance of loss. Abandonment of modern expectations. Embrace of uncertainty. Tolerance for risk. Willingness to change identity.

Social adaptation: Small communities (50-70 people) optimal. Larger groups strained resources. Smaller groups lacked skill diversity. Governance by consensus worked. Authority by expertise emerged naturally. Barter economies replaced currency. Contribution-based value systems replaced wealth-based hierarchies.

Cultural adaptation: Integration with Paleo-Indian populations essential. Modern humans couldn't survive independently long-term. Partnership provided survival skills, ecological knowledge, psychological resilience models. Cross-cultural cooperation wasn't optional—it was mandatory.

Demographic adaptation: High mortality in first two years (5% loss). Stabilization afterward. Populations skewed young (elderly struggled, children thrived). Birth rates dropping (uncertainty about future). Migration pattern: exodus of those unwilling to adapt, immigration of those seeking adaptation models.

Conclusion: Long-term survival in correction zones possible but required total life transformation. Modern civilization couldn't persist. But human communities could. Adapted, hybrid, partnered with past populations. Humans could survive the Pleistocene. But only by becoming Pleistocene themselves.

The paper was cited everywhere. Used in federal planning. Referenced in evacuation protocols. Studied by communities facing correction in other regions.

Jake had become the authority. The expert. The voice of survival in correction zones.

At twenty-four years old.

Living in a hide tent. Hunting with atlatls. Speaking a language dead for eleven thousand years. Documenting the end of his world while helping build the next one.

One night, I found him at the boundary.

The shimmer between green and red. Between 2031 and 11,000 BP. Between the world we'd known and the world we were becoming.

He was just standing there. One foot on each side. Straddling time.

"You okay?" I asked.

"I was thinking about Emma. She's getting married next month. Did you know that?"

"Your mother got the invitation. We can't go. Can't leave the zone safely. Can't afford the time away. Can't re-enter modern civilization and then return. Too much psychological whiplash."

"She's living in Ann Arbor. Working as an accountant. Getting married to a guy named Marcus. Completely normal life. Like none of this exists. Like correction is a news story. Not her reality."

"That's what she chose. Normal. You chose different."

"Did I choose? Or did I just... stay? And become this?" He gestured at himself. Hide clothing. Lean body. Scarred hands. "I don't recognize myself anymore. I look in the mirror—when we have mirrors—and I see a Paleo-Indian. Not Jake Pritchard. Not a modern human. Something else."

"Something adapted."

"Something lost. I can't go back, Dad. Even if I wanted to. I can't live in Ann Arbor now. Can't work an office job. Can't do small talk about weather and sports and TV shows. I've killed bears. I've eaten raw liver to prevent scurvy. I've slept in minus-thirty-degree weather in a hide tent. I've watched people die from predators and cold and disease we can't treat. I'm not modern anymore. I'm something else."

"You're a survivor."

"I'm a ghost. Haunting the space between times. Not modern enough for Emma's world. Not ancient enough for Makwa's world. Just... stuck. Documenting. Surviving. Existing."

I didn't know what to say. Because he was right. He'd changed. Fundamentally. Irreversibly. Became something that didn't fit anywhere except here. In the correction zone. In the boundary between times.

"You're doing important work," I said. "Your research is helping people. Saving lives. Giving communities tools to survive."

"I know. And that matters. It does. But Dad... sometimes I wonder what it cost. Who I gave up to become this. What I lost to gain this knowledge."

"Everyone here lost something. We all gave up the old world. You're not alone in that."

"I know. But most people didn't have a choice. The world ended around them. They adapted to survive. I had a choice. I could've left. Gone to Chicago. Done the PhD program. Had a normal academic career. I chose this. And some days I wonder if I chose right."

"Do you regret it?"

He thought about it. Long time. Then: "No. I don't regret it. But I grieve it. The person I could've been. The life I could've had. I grieve that loss even while accepting this life. Both things are true."

We stood in silence. Father and son. Separated by five years of correction. By adaptation that had changed him into something I barely understood. By choices that couldn't be unmade.

"Your mother loves you," I said. "She doesn't understand you anymore. But she loves you."

"I know. Tell her... tell her I love her too. Even if I'm becoming something she doesn't recognize. The core is still me. Still her son. Just... adapted."

He stepped fully into the red zone. Into the Pleistocene. And walked toward the Paleo-Indian village.

I stepped back into the green zone. Into what remained of 2031. Into the shrinking island of modern time.

And I wondered how long until the green zone disappeared completely. How long until there was no boundary to straddle. No choice between times.

How long until everyone had to choose: adapt completely. Or leave.

And whether I'd be able to adapt like Jake had. Or whether I was too old. Too modern. Too attached to the world that was disappearing around me.

Chapter 39

CHAPTER THIRTY-NINE: VISITORS

They started coming in year six.

Not refugees. Not researchers. Tourists.

The first group arrived week two hundred ninety-three. June 2032. Seven people. Mid-forties to early sixties. Well-dressed. Expensive outdoor gear. Cameras. Notebooks.

They'd hired a guide service out of Traverse City. "Correction Zone Tours." Professional operation. Licensed. Insured. Charging three thousand dollars per person for a three-day "immersive experience in temporal displacement."

Twenty-one thousand dollars. To look at us. To photograph our village. To witness survival. To go home with stories about the people who'd stayed when everyone else left.

We didn't want them. Didn't invite them. Didn't need them.

But we couldn't stop them. Federal authority was gone. We had no legal standing. No jurisdiction. No right to refuse entry.

And they had lawyers. Documents. Permits from somebody somewhere that supposedly authorized "educational tourism in designated correction observation zones."

Bill wanted to turn them away. Physically. At the fence. Armed refusal.

Tom argued differently. "They're going to come whether we allow it or not. At least if we control the visits, we can set terms. Charge fees. Require behavior. Get something from it."

"Get what? Money? We don't use money."

"Supplies. Trade goods. Information. Access to outside resources. They want to see us? Fine. They pay. In things we need."

We voted. Thirty-two to twenty-six. Narrow margin. But decided: We'd allow controlled tourism. On our terms. With strict rules.

The alternative was fighting every tour group that showed up. Wasting energy on conflict. Making enemies of people who might bring useful resources.

We chose pragmatism over pride. Again.

The rules we established:

Entry fee: Each tourist must bring fifty pounds of supplies. Non-negotiable. Food. Tools. Medical supplies. Firewood. Salt. Things we needed. No supplies, no entry.

Duration: Maximum three days. Overnight stays in designated area only. No wandering. No unauthorized photography.

Guides: Community members assigned to each group. Escorts. Educators. Security. No tourist goes anywhere without our guide.

Respect: No treating us like zoo animals. No invasive questions. No photographs of people without permission. Violation means immediate removal.

Labor: Tourists must contribute four hours of work per day. Firewood cutting. Garden work. Construction. Whatever we need. Want to visit? Work for the privilege.

Paleo-Indian village: Off limits. Completely. No exceptions. Anyone trying to access gets expelled and banned.

The tour companies agreed. Mostly. Some tried to negotiate. We refused. These were the terms. Accept or leave.

Most accepted. The fees didn't matter to them. Three thousand dollars per person? The supplies cost maybe two hundred. They were still making massive profit.

From our survival. From our suffering. From our choice to stay when everyone else ran.

It tasted like exploitation. Felt like being exhibited. Like performing poverty for wealthy observers.

But it brought resources. Real resources. Food we didn't have to hunt. Tools we didn't have to make. Salt we couldn't produce. Medical supplies we couldn't access.

We swallowed our pride. Accepted the terms. Became a tourist attraction.

The correction zone that survived. The community that adapted. The humans who learned to live in the Pleistocene.

Come see them work. Come watch them struggle. Come photograph their village. Come go home grateful you don't live like this.

Twenty-one thousand dollars. Per group. Per week.

We got two hundred pounds of supplies. They got stories to tell at dinner parties.

The first group was manageable.

Seven people. Polite. Respectful. Genuinely curious.

Ashley was their guide. She'd lived in Detroit before the folds. Understood their perspective. Could translate our life into language they'd understand.

She showed them the village. The log structures. The communal kitchen. The gardens. The defense perimeter. The sentry posts.

Explained how we built. How we organized. How we survived.

They asked questions. Some intelligent. Some naive.

"Do you have electricity?" No. Solar panels for Jake's research equipment only. Everything else manual.

"How do you cook?" Wood fires. Clay ovens. Traditional methods.

"What about medical care?" Dr. Havelka does what she can. Herbal remedies. Basic surgery. Preventive care. No hospital. No advanced medicine. People die from things that would be treatable in Traverse City.

"Do you miss modern life?" Every single day. And also no. Hard to explain. We've become something different. Modern life feels alien now. Like a dream we used to have.

"Would you leave if you could?" Some would. Some wouldn't. Depends who you ask.

They took notes. Recorded everything. One woman cried. "You're so brave. Living like this. I could never."

Ashley's response: "You could. If you had to. Humans adapt. Or they don't. The ones who don't aren't here anymore."

The tourists worked their required hours. Cut firewood. Hauled water. Helped with garden weeding. They were slow. Inefficient. Unused to physical labor.

But they tried. And they brought good supplies. Rice. Dried beans. Hand tools. Salt. Three bottles of antibiotics. Fish hooks. Copper wire.

When they left, they thanked us. Shook hands. Promised to tell people our story.

"You're heroes," one man said. "What you're doing here. Staying. Surviving. Building community. You're heroes."

Bill's response: "We're not heroes. We're stubborn. There's a difference."

The second group was worse.

Week two hundred ninety-seven. August. Ten people. Younger. Mid-twenties to thirties. Influencers. Content creators. YouTubers.

They came with cameras. Professional equipment. Lights. Microphones. Drones.

"We're documenting the correction zones for our followers. Eighteen million subscribers across our platforms. This is going to be huge. Authentic survival content."

They wanted dramatic footage. Asked us to "perform" activities. Hunting. Hide processing. Fire starting.

"Can you kill something on camera? That would go viral."

"Can you speak some of the Paleo-Indian language? Our audience would love that."

"Can we get a shot of you standing at the boundary? One foot in modern time, one foot in the Pleistocene? Super symbolic."

We refused. "We're not performers. You want to see our life? Watch us live it. Normal. Unscripted. Or leave."

They complained to their guide service. Demanded refunds. "This isn't the experience we paid for. We need content."

Tom Kowalski handled it. Escorted them to the fence. "You paid for access. We gave you access. You didn't pay for performance. We're not here for your content. You want authentic? This is authentic. People surviving. Not entertaining tourists."

They left angry. Posted negative reviews. "Correction zone survivors are hostile. Uncooperative. Don't waste your money."

Good. Maybe that would keep more like them away.

But it didn't. More kept coming.

Week three hundred one. Week three hundred seven. Week three hundred fourteen. Groups every few weeks. Sometimes overlapping. Ten tourists. Twelve. Fifteen.

We were becoming a destination. A stop on the "Correction Zone Experience Tour." Along with viewing folds from safe distance. Seeing abandoned towns. Photographing Pleistocene landscapes.

Come see the humans who stayed. The adaptation success story. The community that survived.

Most were respectful. Brought supplies. Followed rules. Contributed labor. Asked questions. Learned. Left grateful.

Some were entitled. Demanding. Treating us like attractions. Expecting us to perform. Getting angry when we didn't meet their expectations.

We expelled those. No refunds. No debate. Violation of respect clause meant immediate removal.

The tour companies learned. Started vetting clients better. Briefing them properly. "These are real people. Living real lives. Not actors. Not exhibits. Treat them with dignity or you'll be removed."

It helped. Mostly.

Week three hundred twenty, Jake returned from the Paleo-Indian village.

He'd been gone three months. Longest absence yet.

He looked more Paleo-Indian than ever. Leaner. Harder. Face weathered. Hair long. Dressed entirely in hides. Moving with that efficient grace they had.

And he was angry.

"You're allowing tourists?"

"Controlled visits. Strict rules. Resource exchange."

"You're commodifying our survival. Selling access to people who want to gawk at us."

"We're trading access for supplies we need. It's practical."

"It's degrading. We're not a zoo. We're not an exhibit. We're people trying to survive. And you're letting wealthy tourists pay to watch us struggle."

Bill stepped in. "Jake, we know it's not ideal. But it brings resources. Food. Tools. Medicine. Things that keep people alive. Is your pride worth more than that?"

"My pride? You think this is about pride? It's about dignity. About not reducing ourselves to entertainment for people who'll go home to their comfortable lives and talk about how 'brave' we are while doing absolutely nothing to help other communities facing correction."

"They bring supplies—"

"They bring guilt money. Token contributions so they can feel good about themselves. 'I helped the correction zone survivors.' Meanwhile, Detroit is evacuating. Chicago is in crisis. Milwaukee is collapsing. And these tourists spend three thousand dollars to look at us instead of using that money to help people who actually need it."

He wasn't wrong. But he wasn't completely right either.

"We can refuse them," I said. "Vote again. End the tourism. Close access."

Jake looked at the village. At the supplies stacked in storage. At the new tools tourists had brought. At the antibiotics Dr. Havelka was using to treat infections.

"No," he said finally. "Don't refuse them. But don't celebrate it either. Don't pretend this is anything other than what it is. Survival prostitution. Selling our dignity for rice and salt."

He walked away. Back toward the Paleo-Indian village. Where tourists weren't allowed. Where dignity remained intact.

Where he was becoming someone we barely knew.

Week three hundred twenty-six, a different kind of visitor arrived.

Not tourists. Journalists. Documentary filmmakers. Serious ones.

PBS. BBC. National Geographic. All working on comprehensive correction zone documentaries. All wanting to feature our community.

The settlement that survived year six. The adaptation success story. The human-Paleo-Indian partnership. The hybrid civilization being built in the ruins of modern Michigan.

They brought serious questions. Intelligent inquiry. Respectful approach.

And they brought something else: global attention.

Our story went worldwide. Again. Not as curiosity. As case study. As model. As proof.

"If Bellaire can survive, other communities can survive. Here's how they did it. Here's what they learned. Here's what worked. What failed. What killed people. What saved them."

The documentaries aired in January 2033. Simultaneous release across major networks.

Sixty million viewers. Global audience. Every continent.

And the response was overwhelming.

Messages. Thousands of them. Routed through University of Chicago, through DHS archives, through every channel they could find.

Communities facing correction. Asking for help. Asking for guidance. Asking for Jake's research. Asking for our methods. Asking how to survive.

We'd become the model. The template. The example other communities would follow or reject.

Our success—such as it was—had made us responsible. To share knowledge. To help others. To be the proof that survival was possible.

Even if that survival included tourists. Exploitation. Loss of privacy. Commodification of suffering.

Even if the price of being the model was becoming the exhibit.

One night, I sat with Karen on our porch. Watching tourists photograph the village. Watching them work in the gardens—slow, clumsy, but trying. Watching them take notes and record and document everything.

"We used to be private," Karen said. "Just us. Our community. Our struggle. Our choice. Now we're public. Watched. Documented. Analyzed."

"Did we have a choice?"

"We always have choices. We chose to allow tourists. We chose to participate in documentaries. We chose to be the model. Could've said no to all of it."

"And isolated ourselves completely. Lost the resources. Lost the platform to help other communities. Lost the ability to share what we've learned."

"Maybe that would've been better. Maybe privacy was worth more than platform."

"You think Jake's right? That we're prostituting our survival?"

She thought about it. Long time. Then: "I think we're doing what we have to do. Like we've always done. Adapting. Surviving. Making impossible choices because the alternatives are worse. Is it degrading to allow tourists? Yes. Is it worse than starving because we refused their supplies? No. So we adapt. Again. We swallow our pride. Again. We become something we never wanted to become. Again."

"Are we still human? Or have we become something else entirely?"

"I don't know. Ask me in another five years. If we're still here. If the green zones haven't disappeared. If we haven't all become Paleo-Indians like Jake or evacuated like Emma or died like Patricia. Ask me then. Maybe I'll have an answer."

Week three hundred thirty, the thousandth tourist visited.

We'd kept count. One thousand people. In eight months. Paying to see us. Bringing supplies. Taking photos. Going home with stories.

We'd accumulated: six tons of food supplies. Three hundred hand tools. Eight hundred pounds of salt. Forty bottles of antibiotics. Countless smaller items. Nails. Wire. Rope. Seeds. Things we needed.

The resources had kept us alive through year six. Through winter. Through shortages. Through crisis.

Had it been worth it?

Depends who you asked.

Bill said yes. Pragmatism over pride. Survival over dignity.

Dr. Havelka said yes. The antibiotics had saved four lives. Worth any cost.

Tom said yes. The tools had made work easier. Efficiency mattered.

Ashley said yes. The tourists learned from us. Went home changed. Spread knowledge. That mattered.

Jake said no. We'd sold ourselves. Become performers. Lost something essential.

I said... I didn't know.

Both things were true. We'd gained resources. We'd lost dignity. We'd helped other communities. We'd commodified our suffering. We'd survived. We'd changed into something we didn't recognize.

All true. Simultaneously. Contradictory but accurate.

That was year six. That was correction. That was adaptation.

Nothing was simple. Nothing was clean. Everything cost something. You chose the cost you could afford. And lived with what you became.

The last tourist group of year six arrived in December.

Week three hundred forty-eight. Three days before Christmas. Ten people. All refugees from Chicago. All facing correction in their city. All trying to learn how to survive.

They weren't tourists. They were students. Desperate students. Learning from our success. Trying to save their communities.

We taught them everything. No performance. No exhibition. Just knowledge transfer. Survival skills. Adaptation methods. Partnership protocols. Everything we'd learned in six years.

They worked hard. Absorbed everything. Asked intelligent questions. Took detailed notes.

When they left, they didn't thank us for the experience. They thanked us for the gift. The knowledge. The hope. The proof that survival was possible.

"You saved our community," one woman said. "Not directly. But by surviving. By proving it's possible. By sharing what you learned. You gave us a chance. That's everything."

That felt different. That felt worth it.

Not tourism. Not exploitation. Education. Knowledge transfer. Human beings helping human beings survive the impossible.

Maybe that was the point. Maybe the tourists were the price we paid for the privilege of helping the students. The cost of being the model. The exhibit we had to become to be the teacher.

Maybe it was worth it after all.

Or maybe I was just rationalizing. Making peace with choices I couldn't unmake. Finding meaning in degradation.

I didn't know.

But we'd survived year six. Fifty-eight people. Still here. Still adapting. Still learning. Still teaching.

Still becoming something we barely recognized.

Still human. Maybe. Mostly. Enough.

For now.

Chapter 40

CHAPTER FORTY: MORNING WALK

Year seven. Week three hundred seventy-four. May 2033.

I woke at dawn. Old habit. Seventy-one years old now. Sleep came less easily. Left more readily.

Karen was still asleep. Gray hair on the pillow. Face lined. Beautiful. Sixty-nine years old. We'd been married thirty-eight years. Survived seven years of correction together. Lost our daughter to normal life. Lost our son to the Pleistocene. Lost everything except each other.

And somehow that was enough.

I dressed quietly. Hide pants. Wool shirt—salvaged from an abandoned house six years ago, still functional. Leather boots Makwa had shown me how to make. Hybrid clothing. Modern materials with primitive techniques. Like everything else in my life now.

Outside, the village was waking. Smoke from early fires. Sounds of people stirring. Ashley and Tom's daughter—born four months ago, named Patricia after the woman we'd lost—crying softly. First baby born in the village. Hope made flesh.

The fence stood solid. Eight feet high. Reinforced twice after bear tests. Scarred from predator attempts but holding. Beyond it: woods. Yellow zone now. What had been stable green seven years ago was transitional now. Fold activity weekly. The boundaries shrinking. Always shrinking.

But not gone. Not yet. We had time. Maybe years. Maybe decades. The green zones were contracting slower now. Stabilizing at some equilibrium point we didn't fully understand.

Jake's latest paper suggested the correction wasn't total erasure. It was rebalancing. The land finding a sustainable ratio between Pleistocene and modern. Maybe seventy-thirty. Maybe sixty-forty. Still calculating. Still measuring. Still documenting.

Still my son. Even if I barely recognized him anymore.

I walked to the north gate. Nodded to the sentry—Joe Macklin, seventy-four years old, still taking shifts, still contributing.

"Morning Dave."

"Morning Joe. Quiet night?"

"Couple deer at the fence. No predators. Makwa stopped by around three. Left something for you at the meeting stone."

"He say what?"

"Didn't talk. You know him. Just left it and went back."

I knew. Makwa and I had developed our own communication. Seven years of patrols together. Of hunts. Of shared danger. We didn't need many words anymore. Understood each other through gesture. Context. History.

We'd become brothers. Not literally. But in the ways that mattered. Trust. Respect. Shared survival. The kind of bond you only built through years of watching each other's backs.

His son—Quick Hands, nineteen now—had married a woman from one of the merged bands. They had a child. Makwa was a grandfather. Teaching his grandson the same skills he'd taught Quick Hands. The same skills Quick Hands had helped teach Jake.

Knowledge passing down. Generation to generation. Unbroken chain from the Pleistocene to now. To whatever came next.

I walked north. Quarter mile to the meeting stone.

It wasn't really a stone. It was a boundary marker. Where our territory met theirs. Where modern met Paleo-Indian. Where formal met informal. Where scheduled meetings happened and casual exchanges occurred.

We'd established it in year three. Neutral ground. Both communities could access. Neither controlled. A space between spaces.

Makwa had left a bundle. Wrapped in hide. Tied with sinew.

I opened it carefully.

Inside: smoked fish. Four large ones. Preserved perfectly. High protein. High fat. Winter survival food even though it was spring. This was wealth. Calories. Life.

And a note. Not written. Carved. Simple symbols we'd developed together. Picture language. Universal enough that I could read it without translation.

For the new child. For Patricia. So she grows strong.

I felt something catch in my throat. Makwa had never met the original Patricia. She'd died before we'd established deep partnership. But he knew the story. Knew we'd named the baby after her. Knew what that meant.

And he'd given a gift. Not to us. To her. To the future. To the continuation of both our peoples.

I pulled out my own gift. Had brought it deliberately. Knowing somehow that this exchange would happen this morning.

Metal fish hooks. Twenty of them. Traded from a tourist group last month. Small. Sharp. Perfectly made. Worth more than gold here. Because they made food acquisition easier. Made survival less desperate.

I wrapped them in cloth. Left them at the meeting stone. With my own carved note.

For Quick Hands' son. For the next generation. May he always find food.

Gift for gift. Generation for generation. Partnership formalized through exchange. Through mutual care. Through looking forward instead of backward.

I kept walking. North. Into the yellow zone. Carefully. Alert. Always alert.

The woods had changed. Not entirely Pleistocene. Not entirely modern. Hybrid. Mixed species. Trees from both eras. Undergrowth from different times. Animals that shouldn't coexist but did.

I saw a mastodon in the distance. Browsing quietly. Not threatened. Not threatening. Just living. Belonging here now. As much as the white-tailed deer. As much as the squirrels. The Pleistocene and the modern sharing space. Coexisting. Finding balance.

That was correction. Not erasure. Not replacement. Integration. The land remembering what it had been. Incorporating what it had become. Creating something new from both.

We'd thought it was apocalypse. End of the world. Destruction of civilization.

We'd been wrong. It was transformation. Painful. Deadly. Costly. But transformation, not ending.

The world wasn't ending. It was changing. Becoming something that included the past instead of denying it. Something that remembered instead of forgetting.

The land remembers.

That had been our mistake. Thinking we could build on top of the past without acknowledging it. Destroy the burial mounds. Pave over the moraines. Ignore the shorelines. Pretend eleven thousand years of geological history didn't matter.

The land remembered. Even when we forgot.

And now we were remembering again. Being forced to remember. Through correction. Through folds. Through the return of what we'd tried to erase.

I found him at the overlook. Where we'd first tracked the deer together. Where we'd first hunted as partners. Where we'd become something more than modern human and Paleo-Indian. Became brothers.

Makwa was sitting on the ridge. Looking out over the valley. Over the mixed landscape. Over the world that was and the world that had been and the world that was becoming.

He didn't turn when I approached. Knew my footsteps. Knew my presence. Trusted it.

I sat beside him. Said nothing. Just sat. Shared space. Shared silence. Shared understanding.

After maybe ten minutes, he spoke. Our hybrid language. Mixed Anishinaabemowin and English and gesture and shared vocabulary built over seven years.

"Your granddaughter. She is strong?"

"Very strong. Healthy. Growing. Ashley says she has her grandfather's stubbornness."

He smiled. Rare expression. Reserved for things that mattered. "Good. Stubborn survives. Flexible adapts. Both needed."

"Your grandson?"

"Learning to track. Quick Hands teaches well. The boy will be skilled. Maybe better than his father. Maybe better than me." Pride. Quiet but real. "The knowledge continues. That matters."

"It does."

We sat in silence again. Watching the sun rise over the hybrid forest. Over the world that was both and neither. Ancient and modern. Pleistocene and present. All at once.

"Your son," Makwa said. "He is more us than you now."

"I know."

"This bothers you?"

"Sometimes. Not because he's becoming Paleo-Indian. Because he's leaving us. Becoming something his mother doesn't recognize. Something I barely understand."

"He is not leaving. He is expanding. Becoming more. Not less. He holds knowledge from your time. Learns knowledge from mine. He is bridge. That is rare. That is valuable."

"He thinks he's lost himself."

"He has not lost. He has added. Different thing." Makwa paused. "In my time, before the crossing, we had people who walked between tribes. Spoke many languages. Knew many ways. They were treasured. Honored. Not seen as lost. Seen as wealthy. Rich in knowledge. Your son is this. Rich in ways. He should be honored, not grieved."

I'd never thought of it that way. Jake as bridge. As translator. As someone who'd gained rather than lost.

But Makwa was right. Jake held knowledge from both times. Could survive in both. Could teach both. Could translate between worlds.

That wasn't loss. That was achievement. Rare. Valuable. Essential for what came next.

"Thank you," I said. "For the fish. For Patricia."

"Thank you for the hooks. For my grandson." He stood. Stretched. "We should hunt together again. Soon. Like old times. Before you are too old and I must carry you back."

I laughed. "I'm already too old. I've been too old for five years. I just haven't admitted it yet."

"Admission is the first step. Acceptance is second. You are on the path."

"What's the third step?"

"Teaching the young. Passing knowledge. Becoming elder instead of hunter. You are ready for this. I think you know this."

He was right. I was seventy-one. Still capable. Still contributing. But my hunting days were ending. My patrol days were numbered. My time was shifting from doing to teaching. From action to wisdom. From participant to elder.

That was its own kind of adaptation. Growing old in the correction. Finding role when body failed. Contributing knowledge when strength faded.

I was becoming what Patricia had been. What the elderly in our community became. Holders of memory. Teachers. Living history. Bridges between what was and what would be.

"I'll hunt with you," I said. "One more time. Before I become too old even for that."

"Good. Next week. We will take our sons. Teach them together. Show them how partnership works. How your people and my people survive together. That is important. That is legacy."

He gripped my shoulder. Brother's touch. Then turned and walked back toward his village. Toward the Pleistocene. Toward the time he belonged to but no longer lived in exclusively. Because he'd learned to move between worlds too. Just like Jake. Just like all of us who'd survived.

We'd all become bridges. Temporal. Cultural. Generational. Connecting past and present and future into something continuous. Something that remembered instead of forgetting.

I walked back slowly. No hurry. Enjoying the morning. The hybrid forest. The mixed world.

Saw deer. Saw mastodons in the distance. Saw birds I recognized and birds I didn't. Saw trees from my time and trees from Makwa's time growing side by side. Competing. Cooperating. Coexisting.

That was the future. Not one or the other. Both. Integrated. Mixed. Hybrid.

Like our village. Modern construction methods with Paleo-Indian materials. Barter economy with technological tools. Consensus governance with elder wisdom. Everything we'd been and everything we'd learned combined into something new.

Like our people. Modern humans learning ancient skills. Paleo-Indians adopting metal tools. Both groups teaching each other. Both groups changed by the contact. Both groups becoming something neither had been before.

Like me. Seventy-one years old. Born in 1962. Lived through modern America. Raised in civilization. Educated in schools. Worked with technology. And now wearing hide boots. Speaking mixed languages. Trading smoked fish for metal hooks. Calling a Paleo-Indian man my brother.

I'd changed. Fundamentally. Irreversibly. Become something my younger self wouldn't recognize.

But I'd survived. Karen and I both. Seven years. When everyone said we'd die. When the federal government tried to evacuate us. When winter came harsh. When predators hunted. When resources failed. When everything we'd known disappeared.

We'd survived. By changing. By adapting. By learning to remember what the land remembered.

I reached the village as people were starting their day.

Bill at the chicken coop. Gathering eggs. Counting his wealth.

Dr. Havelka at the medical shelter. Grinding herbs. Mixing remedies. Maintaining knowledge.

Tom and Ashley with Patricia. Teaching her to recognize plants even though she was only four months old. Never too early to start learning. Not here. Not now.

Joe Macklin finishing his sentry shift. Seventy-four years old. Still contributing. Still essential.

Jake—surprisingly—sitting at the communal fire. Visiting. Rare now. He spent most of his time with the Paleo-Indians. But he came back. Periodically. Still part of both communities. Still the bridge.

He saw me. Nodded. I sat beside him.

"Good walk?" he asked.

"Saw Makwa. He left fish for Patricia. I left hooks for Quick Hands' son."

"Gift exchange. Traditional. Important."

"He said you're rich. Rich in knowledge. Rich in ways. That you should be honored, not grieved."

Jake was quiet. Then: "Mom grieves me."

"She grieves who you were. Not who you are. She'll understand. Eventually. Give her time."

"I am who I was. Just... more. I didn't lose myself. I added to myself. Became larger. More capable. More adapted. Why is that seen as loss?"

"Because change feels like loss when you love someone. Even when the change is growth. Even when it's survival. It still feels like losing the person you knew."

"But I'm still me."

"I know that. You know that. Makwa knows that. Your mother will know it too. She just needs time."

He nodded. Accepted that. "I have a new paper coming out next month. Year seven data. The rebalancing hypothesis. Evidence that correction isn't total replacement. It's integration. The land finding equilibrium between eras. Stabilizing at a sustainable mix."

"What ratio?"

"Varies by location. But trending toward sixty-forty. Sixty percent Pleistocene, forty percent modern. Stable. Sustainable. Permanent."

"So this is it. This is what the world looks like now. Forever."

"Probably. Unless something changes the geological stress patterns. But that would take thousands of years. So yes. For our lifetimes. For our children's lifetimes. For the foreseeable future. This is the new normal. Hybrid world. Mixed time. Integrated past and present."

"Can humanity survive that?"

"We're already surviving it. You. Me. Ashley and Tom and baby Patricia. Makwa and Quick Hands and the three-month-old grandson. The fifty-eight people here. The Paleo-Indian communities. The refugees learning from us. The millions adapting in other correction zones. We're surviving. Some better than others. Some barely. Some thriving. But surviving."

"What about Emma?"

"She's surviving too. Different way. Normal way. That's valid too. Not everyone has to adapt to correction. Some people get to keep living modern lives. In places that haven't corrected. In zones that stayed stable. That's okay. That's their choice. Their path."

"Do you miss that? Normal life? Office jobs and grocery stores and electricity?"

He thought about it. Really thought. Then: "Sometimes. But mostly no. I miss the ease. The convenience. The lack of constant danger. But I don't miss the disconnect. The way modern life separated us from land, from seasons, from natural cycles. This life is harder. But it's more... real. More connected. More honest. I know where my food comes from. I know the people who helped me survive. I know the land I walk on. That matters more than convenience."

"You sound like Makwa."

"Good. He's wise. Worth sounding like."

Karen found us an hour later. Sat down. Looked at Jake. Really looked.

"You're visiting."

"I'm visiting."

"How long?"

"Two days. Then back. But I'll come again. Regularly. I'm not gone. I'm just... elsewhere most of the time."

She nodded. Processing. "You look healthy."

"I am healthy."

"Different. But healthy."

"Yes."

She reached out. Touched his face. His weathered, changed, Paleo-Indian face. Her son. Still her son. Even transformed.

"I'm trying to understand," she said. "Trying to accept. That you're still you. Even though you're so different."

"I know. Take your time. I'm not going anywhere. Well, I'm going somewhere. But I'm coming back. Always. This is still home. You're still family. That doesn't change just because I live elsewhere most of the time."

"Like Emma."

"Like Emma. Except reversed. She left here for modern world. I left modern world for... whatever this is. But we're both still your children. Both still family. Just from different places now."

Karen smiled. Sad but real. "My children. The accountant in Ann Arbor and the Paleo-Indian researcher in the Pleistocene. I used to worry about normal things. Whether you'd go to college. Whether you'd find good jobs. Whether you'd be happy."

"Are you disappointed?"

"No. Surprised. Confused. Grieving the future I thought you'd have. But not disappointed. You survived. Both of you. In your own ways. That's more than most people can say. That's everything."

That afternoon, I helped Tom with patrol.

We walked the boundary. Checking the fence. Watching for predators. Observing fold activity. Routine. Essential. Never-ending.

"Seven years," Tom said. "You ever think we'd make it this long?"

"No. Honestly. I thought we'd evacuate after the first winter. Or die in the second. Or give up in the third. But we didn't."

"Why do you think that is? What made us different?"

"Stubbornness. Like Bill said. But also flexibility. We changed. Adapted. Became something different from what we were. People who couldn't change didn't survive. We did. That's the difference."

"You going to stay? Until the end? Until the green zones are completely gone?"

"I don't know. Ask me in another seven years. If I'm still alive. If the zones still exist. If we're still here. Right now? I'm staying. Tomorrow? Probably staying. Next year? We'll see. That's all I can commit to."

"Fair enough. Same for me."

We walked in companionable silence. Two old men—he was fifty-seven, I was seventy-one—patrolling a fence against predators that had been extinct for eleven thousand years. Protecting a community that lived in multiple time periods simultaneously. Surviving in a world that had fundamentally transformed around us.

And somehow finding it normal. Finding it manageable. Finding it livable.

Because we'd changed. Adapted. Become people who could live in this hybrid world. This mixed time. This corrected landscape.

We'd remembered what the land remembered. And in remembering, we'd survived.

That night, the whole community gathered.

Communal dinner. Fifty-eight people. Plus Jake, visiting. Plus three Paleo-Indian representatives—Makwa, Quick Hands, and the elder himself. Rare. The elder almost never came to our village.

But he came tonight. Honoring something. Marking something. Recognizing something.

After we ate—venison from Tom's hunt, vegetables from the gardens, bread from the communal oven, smoked fish from Makwa's gift—the elder stood.

Spoke. Long. Formal. Ceremonial.

Sarah translated. Phrase by phrase. Moment by moment.

"Seven years ago, you came to this land. You were not prepared. Not adapted. Not suited to survive. We watched you struggle. Watched you die. Watched you suffer. Some of us thought you would fail. Completely. All of you. Within seasons."

"But you did not fail. You adapted. You learned. You changed. You asked for help. You accepted teaching. You built partnership. You honored our knowledge while keeping your own. You became something new. Something that had not existed before. Hybrid people. Bridge people. People who remember both times."

"You have survived seven cycles. Seven winters. Seven springs. This is significant. This is worthy of recognition. You are no longer visitors. No longer temporary. You are established. You are part of this land. Part of this time. Part of both times."

"My people honor this. We recognize you as neighbors. As partners. As equals. Not as students anymore. As co-survivors. As people who share this land with us. With respect. With cooperation. With mutual benefit."

"We are different peoples. From different times. With different ways. But we are one community. One territory. One shared future. This is rare. This is valuable. This is worth celebrating."

He raised a cup—pottery, made by his people—filled with water from the lake.

"To the people who stayed. To the people who learned. To the people who remembered. May your knowledge continue. May your children thrive. May the land support us all. Together."

Everyone raised cups. "Together."

We drank. Water from the lake. Shared resource. Shared land. Shared future.

And in that moment, I understood.

This was it. This was what we'd been building. Not just survival. Not just adaptation. Community. Partnership. Integration. A new way of living that included past and present. That remembered instead of forgetting. That honored instead of erasing. That built bridges instead of walls.

This was the future. Not one or the other. Both. Together. Mixed. Hybrid. Integrated.

This was what correction meant. Not punishment. Not destruction. Not ending.

Transformation. Integration. Rebalancing. The land remembering. Us learning to remember with it. Both changing to accommodate the other. Both becoming something new.

Later, after the Paleo-Indians left, after the community dispersed, after the fires banked and the sentries took positions, I walked with Karen back to our house.

"Seven years," she said.

"Seven years."

"Think we'll make seven more?"

"I don't know. Maybe. If the zones stabilize. If winter doesn't get worse. If we keep learning. If we keep adapting. Maybe."

"And if we don't?"

"Then we had seven years. Seven years of surviving the impossible. Seven years of building something new. Seven years of learning what the land remembered. That's more than most people get. That's enough."

She leaned against me. Sixty-nine years old. Gray hair. Lined face. Beautiful. Alive. Here. With me. After everything.

"I love you," she said.

"I love you too."

"Even though I'm not who I was?"

"Especially because you're not who you were. Because you changed. Adapted. Survived. Became someone who could live in this world. That's more impressive than staying the same."

"You too."

"Me too."

We walked home. To the house we'd built in year two. Log construction. Sod roof. Efficient. Warm. Functional. Not modern. Not primitive. Hybrid. Like everything else.

Like us.

And tomorrow I'd wake up. Walk the boundaries. Check the fences. Maybe hunt with Makwa. Maybe teach someone a skill. Maybe learn something new. Maybe survive another day in the hybrid world. The corrected world. The world that remembered.

The land remembers. We forgot. Now we remember again.

That was the story. The arc. The truth.

We'd forgotten what the land remembered. Built on top of it. Ignored it. Erased it. Tried to make the past irrelevant.

And the land had corrected us. Forced us to remember. Through folds. Through Pleistocene returning. Through correction.

It had been brutal. Costly. Deadly. Transformative.

But we'd survived. By learning. By adapting. By remembering.

And in remembering, we'd become something new. Something that honored both past and present. Something hybrid. Something adapted. Something that could survive the impossible.

We'd become the people who remembered.

And that was enough.

www.ingramcontent.com/pod-product-compliance
Lightning Source LLC
LaVergne TN
LVHW090545110826
845146LV00001B/29

* 9 7 9 8 9 9 3 7 6 4 4 6 7 *